In memory of the iconic Azure Window, a natural limestone rock structure in the form of an arch over the blue sea at Dwejra, Gozo. Sadly, this magnificent arch collapsed into the sea, during a storm, on the 8th of March, 2017.

ATLANTIS

AND

THE LEGENDARY BLUE QUEEN

MOIRA LESCUYER

Copyright © 2017 Moira Lescuyer
All rights reserved. This book, or parts therof, may not be reproduced in any form without the permission of the publisher, except for brief passages quoted by a reviewer in a newspaper or magazine.

First Edition: April 2017
Printed by Lightning Source

Cover design: P.M. Lescuyer
ISBN: 978-0-6480560-0-3

Website: www.moiralescuyer.com

This is a work of fiction. Names, characters, businesses, places, events and incidents are either the products of the author's imagination or used in a fictitious manner. Any resemblance to actual persons, living or dead, or actual events is purely coincidental.

Atlantis
and
The Legendary
Blue Queen

Moira Lescuyer

For my loving family who provided a continual source of encouragement, ideas and inspiration. They culminated in this book that took on a life of its own.

In loving memory of my great-grandparents, Angela and Michelangelo Inguanez, and Father Magri, whose watchful spirits connect me to our vast Over-Soul.

Table of Contents

Prologue 1

Chapter 1
The Land of the Bee 8

Chapter 2
Eve's First Spiritual Teacher 15

Chapter 3
Rekindling With Mother Earth 24

Chapter 4
The Legends of Gozo 36

Chapter 5
Buznanna's Playground 55

Chapter 6
Hollow Earth 87

Chapter 7
The Blue Queen, the Star of the Sea 114

Chapter 8
Never Letting Go 125

Chapter 9
The Spell of the Sea 136

Chapter 10
The Magical Phoenix 146

Chapter 11
Venus 162

Chapter 12
The Watery Cradle of Civilisation 172

Chapter 13
The Dogon and the Nommos 189

Chapter 14
Plato's Atlantis 201

Chapter 15
The Secret of Leptis Magna 225

Chapter 16
Athena, the Warrior Goddess 234

Chapter 17
The Omphalos Stone 258

Chapter 18
Through The Eyes of a Pleiadian 285

Select Bibliography and Sources 299

About the Author 303

THE SLEEPING LADY
The hypogeum of Ħal-Saflieni Paola, Malta.

Prologue

Syracuse, 367 BC

It has been twenty-two years since the death of Socrates and I have not stopped looking for knowledge and wisdom all this time. The love of wisdom runs through my veins. I remember when we went to Delphi and Chaerephon asked if anyone was wiser than Socrates. The Pythian priestess answered, "No one."

Those were my youthful years. My second trip to Delphi to see the high priestess was more dramatic and changed my life. I asked her, "Where is the best place to find truth, knowledge and wisdom?"

The Pythian priestess replied, "The Shrine of Atlantis."

Atlantis – that legendary story that my great uncle Critias talked about when we were young. It must exist and Socrates believed with every ounce of his being that it was a true story. After travelling for twelve years I am exhausted – I have searched tirelessly, in vain. I have looked in Egypt, in Cyrene, in Locris, in Melita and here in Syracuse.

I have learnt a lot especially in Egypt where I verified the facts in the Temple of Sais. I have learnt the ancient Egyptian language and realised the goddess that they call Athenait in Egyptian is our goddess Athena. It is written Neith but when they speak of her they refer to her as Athenait. Athens was a colony of Egypt worshipping the goddess Athena and was founded by an Atlantean king as Egypt was.

I have been taking notes of all my findings and some evidence seems to contradict itself. I have written three dialogues on the subject based on my visit to Egypt, Syracuse and Locri. I still cannot understand the clues but it seems to be next to where I am now, based on the testimony of General Hermocrates of Syracuse. The same thing applies to the writings of Timaeus of Locri – they corroborate the story of Solon that my great uncle Critias mentions.

One of my disciples, Dion, invited me here to change people's views but I am too obsessed with finding the truth. I am so close but I cannot see. The Shrine of Atlantis, which contains great records, must be close by, according to the Oracle. What if I found it? What will I do with the truth? Can the world cope with the truth? Visiting all these libraries has made me wiser and more in tune with the divine feminine. It seems the worship of the goddess as the One is the only way to balance the world. It is like the

Prologue

analogy of the cave – we can only see shadows of the truth, but the truth is more beautiful and empowering.

I have made five trips between Cyrene and Syracuse but cannot find the right place. There are many islands, volcanoes and mud shoals and many temples so close to the steles of Herakles. But where is the Temple of Poseidon? Is it beneath the Temple of Herakles? Is it in the Bay of the Cyclops? Is it next to Ogygia where Calypso the mermaid queen lived, the granddaughter of Poseidon? Or is the temple on the island of the bee, Melita, next to the Temple of Herakles?

Maybe you have to be a woman to find the secrets of the matriarchal Golden Age. All I, Plato, can do is give clues and write the truth for future generations to find where the legendary Atlantis might be and as the Pythia said to me: "You need to write about it and, in time, our Blue Queen will reveal herself."

Atlantis and The Legendary Blue Queen

Libya, Leptis Magna – AD 1907, Good Friday

The Jesuit priest Father Magri was invited to Sfax, Tunisia and travelled to Leptis Magna to preach the Lenten sermons at the ruins of the basilica for the Maltese migrant community. It was the perfect alibi for Fr. Magri. He could investigate further the leads that he had discovered in the Ħal Saflieni hypogeum in Malta that he had recently excavated and then written a complex report of his findings.

Magri was no ordinary Jesuit priest. He was an eminent archaeologist, writer and educator and spoke at many public forums. Born in Valletta in 1851 into a family steeped in the legal profession, Magri abandoned studies in law to follow his true passions. His work, research and studies took him beyond Malta to Istanbul, North Africa, Ireland, England, Italy, France and Spain. Magri was up to date with the latest reference works of the day and in contact with various scholars. He even had access to the archives in the Vatican.

He explored numerous ancient temple sites. In late 1903, Magri drew the government's attention to the site of the presumed temple in Xewkija, in Gozo. He obtained the permission of the owner when ancient sites were not protected. Magri documented the connection between the tradition of the "Golden Calf" and temple sites in Malta, but he believed only the Hospitaller Knights knew the whereabouts of the Golden Calf.

The Knights were devoted to the Virgin Mary as well as the order of Our Lady of Mount Carmel, known as the Carmelite Order, which was founded during the crusades to the Holy Land. In the bible, Mount Carmel is where Elijah was triumphant against the villainous priests of Baal in the ultimate test to see who had the real God.

Prologue

Fr. Magri wrote from the parish in Sfax to the Lt. Governor that he had an opportunity to explore Roman ruins in Thaenae, at present called Thyna, south of Sfax in this country and the yet unexplored ruins at Kasr el 'Alia, lying about twelve miles due east of El Djem. Acholla was believed to be a Maltese colony in 1000 BC. Magri was well aware that Malta had been a stronger power in the ancient past under the rule of King Battus of Libya. Magri was planning to excavate Acholla because of its links to the ancient Phoenicians, the Knights and the Golden Calf written about in Exodus.

These ruins are connected with the ancient history of Malta and Magri requested further funds to carry on with his investigations. Magri pre-explored the site of Acholla before the official excavation and what he discovered confirmed his hypothesis about the Hal Saflieni hypogeum showing interconnecting ancient links to some of the most sought-after answers to the greatest mysteries of the ancient world.

The Knights' devotion to the Virgin Mary and the Golden Calf fascinated Magri and he was desperate to research more. It would be a great pity if the French were to explore before the Maltese could examine their own sites.

Magri had an affiliation with Leptis Magna and he wanted to explore further. The Jesuit superiors acceded to all of his requests. Magri discovered many artefacts and mysteries that he could not comprehend. Why did the Knights visit the Hal Saflieni hypogeum? How did they gain access? There must have been various entry points through underground tunnels.

The Grand Master of the Knights, Jean Parisot de Valette, was a French nobleman of the Order of Malta. La Valette knew about the hypogeum and the great secrets and mysteries it held.

From the crusades, the Knights brought back holy relics from beneath the Temple of Solomon in Jerusalem that had initially been hidden in Malta, a sacred island.

Magri was aware that many civilisations and different races of people had visited the sacred hypogeum from the skeletal evidence he had discovered. Why were there so many skeletons and elongated skulls of different humans and Merfolk? These were not humans like us with congenital defects such as Spina bifida or Polydactylism. Were they a different species of Homo sapiens? Why did they worship a hermaphrodite or Virgin goddess? The evidence was intriguing and the rich evidence that pointed to a different branch of human evolution perplexed Magri.

Whilst in Tunisia and Libya, Magri carried out his intended research, preached, heard confessions and dispensed spiritual advice to those who flocked to him. His discoveries were astonishing and provided valuable links to his findings at the Ħal Saflieni hypogeum and Acholla. This knowledge was surely going to shake history and religion to its foundations, as it had occurred in the beginning of time when a pure faith existed, free of contamination that affected the system like a rampant disease.

Magri's last sermon was in one of his favourite places – the magnificent city of Leptis Magna – a place to which he felt a close affinity. The city was founded by a group of local Berbers and Phoenicians around 1000 BC. He preached his last sermon in an unorthodox manner in the outdoor ancient ruins of the Severan Basilica.

Magri felt satisfied he had completed all he had set out to do, spiritually and archaeologically, and was excited to publish his written work when he returned to Malta. He finished his sermon feeling quite exhausted by the whirlwind of activities he had experienced.

He sat on a bench to reflect quietly in the magnificent Arch of Septimus Severus, keeping his treasured notes in a

Prologue

briefcase close by him at all times. A tall, olive-skinned man with dark hair and vibrant green eyes greeted him. The man sat beside him, congratulating him on his beautiful sermon. He offered Magri a cup of water, which he kindly accepted, as he was feeling light-headed and exhausted from all the activities. Moments after his first sip, Magri clutched his throat with both hands. He felt as though a pair of invisible hands were clamping his windpipe and suffocating him, making it difficult to draw breath.

Magri turned to look at the man for help and noticed the man's pupils transform into vertical black slits contrasting with his emerald green eyes like a reptile's eyes. He revealed his stained teeth in a menacing grin and laughed hideously as he revelled in Magri's suffering. His black hair shook in disarray as laughter roared out of his foul mouth, which oozed a sulphurous smell.

"Who are you? Why?" Magri asked as he held his throat with his hands trying to look up at the man who was now towering over him.

"I am Balzor! And the entrance to my kingdom cannot be revealed. What you have discovered will remain in the cold, dense darkness forever. I promise you all your work will be destroyed as well as you and anyone else who follows in your footsteps. The human race will be forever enslaved in ignorance." He snarled like a demon.

Balzor snatched what he wanted – Magri's briefcase. Balzor knew Magri had written important documents that explained the significant discoveries that went beyond what humanity had been taught through religion and science about the truth of human origins.

In his last living moments, Magri saw Balzor disappearing among the ruins, shape-shifting into the figure of a black jackal. Magri was buried in Sfax, Tunisia, with all his secrets.

Chapter 1

The Land of the Bee

The aircraft shook, rattled and dipped sporadically, like a roller coaster. Eve secured her seat belt and grasped both armrests tightly as the small aircraft fought the turbulence. Her cup of water splattered all over the seat. She picked up her serviette and soaked up the water. She closed her eyes and prayed to the Great Mother that she would arrive safely on this small archipelago in the heart of the Mediterranean. It was Eve's fourth trip to these islands lying between North Africa and Sicily. In the past there had been much debate as to whether the islands were part of Africa or Europe, but the latter idea prevailed. This trip was important; she had a mission to fulfil, that is, if she made it to land. The turbulence became more consistent and intense. She looked out of the window at the Mediterranean Sea stretching in every direction to the horizon. The sea appeared calm from a distance and as still as a lizard basking in the midday sun. The surface shone like large flawless, iridescent multi-faceted diamonds. The rays of sunlight dispersed on the surface displaying a mosaic of brilliant colours. The sea appeared much calmer than the turbulence in the sky.

The shimmering sea was hypnotic and Eve's mind naturally wandered to her extensive studies in archaeology, ancient languages, cultures, mythology and legends. She sensed that water is the life-giving source. The powerful element of water was associated with creation, healing, regeneration and the creation of life.

In Babylonian mythology, Oannes is the water god. Babylonian depictions of Oannes show him as a complex hybrid that appeared part human and part fish, a merman, and therefore a genetic chimera. Oannes has a bearded man's head beneath the head of a fish, and the body of a fish borne upon the back of a man's body. Oannes was a therianthrope that could metamorphose into other animals by means of shape-shifting.

The Dogon people, an indigenous tribe in Mali, have legends about the Nommos, amphibious fish-like beings sent to Earth from the Sirius Star system as the saviours and spiritual guardians of the human race. After living in Libya for a time, they settled in Mali, West Africa, bringing with them their culture and religion. They have been isolated topographically and culturally from the outside world for countless centuries.

The Dogon believe that the Nommos gave them their highly advanced astronomical knowledge. Like the Nommos, Babylonian legends believe this aquatic deity, Oannes, would come on land during the day to educate humans, and would sink back at night into the Persian Gulf, where he lived in an underwater palace. Was Oannes, like Poseidon, the God of the Sea?

As the plane flew closer to the mainland, the turbulence subsided and Eve began to appreciate the spectacular aerial view of the archipelago. Eve could see the erratic zigzag patterns cut out of the circular escarpments. It appeared as though some heavenly object such as a meteor or a comet had struck the land. These distinctive massive circular bays were not just shaped by water erosion, but by the islands being pounded by electromagnetic plasma discharge. What remains are the visible scars of the plasma discharge and the fingerprint of a comet impact.

Eve could see enormous natural limestone cave formations, typical of the topography. She imagined a handsome, muscular merman, like an ancient god, draped in an azure cloak perched on a rock in a shaded cave. The sunlight dried out his skin and made him ill, so he needed to live underground and under the sea in order to be immortal. The gods possessed the secrets to immortality, renewal and the soul's resurrection as an indestructible energy. Death was merely like a snake shedding its skin, only to take on a new skin, a new life.

The sea was the first home the merman knew and were you to ask him to describe it he would not have mentioned the water or the wetness, or the waves or the water currents, just as you would not mention the air or other intangibles that may seem irrelevant if you were to describe your home. He was so accustomed to an aquatic environment that it was no more than the dull wallpaper of his existence. The merman wanted more, as he was created from the original creator and he wanted to raise the consciousness of humans. He longed to genetically modify his body to explore the world of humans on the land. The merman had compassion for humans whom he loved and cared for and wanted to see them succeed in their existence so that the truth could be preserved. He represented the twin in our unconscious minds, an archetype, which connects us to water from conception to birth. The knowledge of the existence of these water beings is stored in messages encoded in our DNA, like some hidden archive that can only be accessed by special methods. The spiritual and physical are intertwined in our DNA like written messages decoded in the centre of our brain, in our pineal gland, known as the third eye.

Although having lived in Australia since the age of two, Eve found herself feeling at home close to the sea, where her mind could instantly wander by gazing out to sea, losing herself in her own daydreaming, her own inner world. She felt a strong bond to her birthplace, which held a special place in her heart. She longed to unravel the prehistory of these islands whose hidden mystery played an important role in our existence.

She daydreamed about an island paradise, a place where humans were not falsely manipulated to live in fear, thereby releasing us from the shackles of control. It was just as well Eve had a window seat which allowed her to gaze out of the window and get lost in her thoughts and vivid imagination. As a young girl Eve could spend hours playing on her own, pretending to be Wonder Woman or some other superhero, and getting lost in her world of the imagination. It came naturally to her, as she was an active daydreamer and allowed her intuition to surface.

She knew things and sought answers, often without knowing the source; she just had an undeniable inner voice and knowing, as though she accessed answers from some invisible source. The invisible source may have been the Akashic records which are believed to be a library in a non-physical plane of existence. They contain all the information of every individual who has ever lived on

Earth. Eve remembered a series of past lives in her dreams and the people she held strong connections with. She had experienced abandonment issues in past lives, which she carried into her present life. It seemed to be a vicious cycle that was unbreakable. The more she feared these issues the more she would attract situations to help her evolve in her current life, so she was continually faced with the fear of abandonment and rejection.

As she grew into a young woman she eventually expressed her fears and dissolved them when the opportunity arose. Eve slowly realised how harmful it was to allow the fears to consume her and penetrate her belief system. She realised that believing in your fears only serves to attract similar situations so she learned to be independent from a very young age. She always felt as though there was an invisible force guiding her during times of upheaval.

The aircraft banked over the familiar megalithic temple sites, which brought a flood of fond memories of a special time in her life that she had shared with her great-grandmother, Buznanna, who was her first true spiritual teacher. It was amazing how so many temples, up to thirty-six, were scattered across such small islands. Many more temples existed but have not been clearly identified. Some were destroyed; some have been consumed by the sea or covered up by modern developments.

More temple sites are suspected to exist beneath the sea, as divers have caught occasional glimpses of them and ancient writers have documented their remains. Whatever we don't see in the physical tends to get forgotten as we are bombarded with the new. She admired the shades of red and orange picked out by the morning sun as the rays caressed the impressive limestone, imbuing the temples with mystery and intrigue. The honey-coloured megalithic temples came alive with the sun's rays, which empowered their energy, singing their stories of forbidden knowledge about the ancient past. The beauty transfixed Eve. The singing limestone had existed for an eternity and stored the ancient stories and wisdom of the past.

Eve remembered the energy she felt standing next to the temples, a kind of feeling that is re-energising and unforgettable. They were too large and heavy to be completely destroyed by cataclysmic floods and remain as some of the most intact temple sites in the world. The idea of cataclysms and flood immediately brought to mind the legend of Atlantis and the antediluvian civilisation.

Over the decades Eve had become interested in the legends of Atlantis. You could not research Atlantis without acknowledging Plato's story. The famous Greek philosopher described the watery ringed island of Atlantis as being scattered over with temples, the central one being dedicated to Cleito, a mortal woman, and Poseidon, a god with whom she had five sets of twin boys, creating the legend of Atlantis.

The thumping of the aircraft wheels being lowered interrupted her thoughts. It was followed by the sound of screeching tyres on the runaway as the plane gradually slowed. She recalled her experiences with her great-grandmother at the megalithic temple sites and goosebumps covered her arms. Buznanna was the reason for her return. Her great-grandmother had encouraged her to research and to listen with all of her senses, even the dormant ones. She had entrusted Eve with precious gifts that she would use to search for answers.

Many wonderful discoveries have been made due to clues in surviving ancient texts, in myths and on ancient maps. Myths and legends do hold truth and provide vital clues that researchers can rely on as a valuable source. Eve thought about some of the magnificent discoveries including Cleopatra's palace, Homer's Troy and the Palace of Knossos that have been discovered with the help of legends.

Oral tradition may distort some of the facts along the way, but legends and myths still hold valuable information, clues and dates. According to Plato, 9,600 BC is an important date because it is the end of the Ice Age and the time when the great civilisation of Atlantis was lost in a day and night by devastating earthquakes and floods.

Plato writes the story of Atlantis in his Dialogues of *Timaeus* and *Critias*. This ancient story of one of the greatest civilisations that ever existed had been passed down from a distant ancestor of Plato, known as Solon, a Greek lawmaker. In 600 BC, Solon visited Egypt and was told the fascinating story of Atlantis by the priest of the goddess Neith in the ancient city of Sais in the Nile Delta. Greek scholars such as Herodotus and Plato identified Neith with Athena and the traveller Herodotus claimed that the tomb of Osiris was located in Sais.

Eve was intrigued by the story of Atlantis. She could understand how such a devastating cataclysm could erase the memory of this civilisation but the survivors on high mountains or in underground caverns would remember and weave the story into oral tradition. Our beating hearts never forget. Our hearts know and feel the truth when it is presented to us, as though it is stored in the DNA of our very existence.

Eve gathered her hand luggage as she prepared to disembark in Malta. She could feel her heart pounding with excitement, as this was the start of the journey she had been longing for. She felt incredibly close to Buznanna, having arrived back to where it all started for Eve, where the seeds were sown in her mind. Buznanna had initiated her into the teachings of the mysterious ancient past and the land of the goddess. She was responsible for sparking Eve's curiosity and her obsession with ancient civilisations such as the legendary Atlantis.

Chapter 2

Eve's First Spiritual Teacher

The saga began when Eve was eight years old and lived with Buznanna on her farm in Qrendi, in Malta, for a month. Eve called her great-grandmother Buznanna, the term used in Maltese for great-grandmother.

Buznanna lived on an extensive farm where she grew her own food and created the remedies she had learnt, handed down by women through the centuries. She had her own beehive and an ancient bull, an auroch that resembled a Spanish fighting bull, plus various other animals, and she grew blue lotus in a dam. As synchronicity would have it, Eve was entrusted to Buznanna while her mum spent time with a terminally ill family member.

Now the story came full circle. Eve arrived on Buznanna's doorstep with her luggage in her hand.

"How you've grown, my little girl!" Buznanna greeted Eve at the door with a warm smile followed by a big hug. She squeezed Eve tightly and planted kisses on both her cheeks. Buznanna was happy to reunite with her firstborn great-granddaughter. "I'm so glad we can spend a month together. You were only two years old when your parents emigrated to Australia. You probably don't even remember me. I have made so many plans for us and have been counting the days to your arrival."

"No I don't remember you, but I have heard all about you. You are so blonde, I thought we would look a little alike because we are related," Eve replied in Maltese. She was happy she had learnt to speak Maltese at the same time she learnt to speak English otherwise communication would have been difficult. Buznanna was a striking lady. She was very fair with blonde hair and sky-blue almond-shaped eyes. She was tall, robust and voluptuous. Her clear complexion meant she looked quite young for her age.

"I get it from my parents who were even fairer than I am. My mum's surname was Bondin, a nickname for Blonde." Eve was the complete opposite in colouring with her auburn hair, brown eyes and olive skin. Buznanna continued, "We may not look alike, but our personalities and nature are close, my little girl," she replied. "We are more similar than you realise. We are both the firstborn females, following an unbroken line of firstborn females since ancient times, and that makes our connection very strong. We share a strong matriarchal and spiritual bond. Our reunion is pure kismet!"

"What is kismet?" Eve asked.

"It's a fortunate occurrence, due to circumstances, like being able to spend a whole month together due to circumstances bringing us together. When you encounter something by chance that seems it was meant to be, then it could be kismet, your destiny, fate or providence. Like the day I was walking down a different path to get to the piazza and I heard my future husband singing, your great-granddad. When our eyes met he sang to me from the balcony and that was pure kismet. Sometimes we take a different path that leads us to unexpected but predestined possibilities, unbeknown to us at the time."

"I like that!" said Eve excitedly. "I'm the firstborn female, so was my mum, my grandmother, you, and on it goes throughout time; it's a kind of kismet, a pre-destined event that we should come together once more."

"I like to think of it that way," said Buznanna.

She continued, "You know in ancient times, particularly in ancient Egypt, the Pharaoh would marry the firstborn female in the family in order to keep the bloodline pure. It sounds unusual but many pharaohs even married their sisters or half-sisters to maintain the bloodline. The chief responsibility of the pharaoh was to maintain Ma'at, universal harmony, in the country.

"The goddess Ma'at was thought to work her will through the pharaoh but it was up to the individual ruler to interpret the will of the goddess correctly and then to act on it. Ma'at was the goddess of the physical and moral law of Egypt, of order and truth. She is said to be the wife of Thoth and had eight children with him. The most important of her children was Amon. These eight children were the chief gods of Hermopolis and, according to the priests there, they created the Earth and all that is in it. Hermopolis, located in Middle Egypt, was referred to as the city of Hermes and was a major cult centre of Thoth, who was called Hermes by the Greeks."

"Getting back to Ma'at," continued Buznanna, "who is depicted in the form of a woman, she holds the sceptre in one hand and the ankh in the other. One of Ma'at's symbols was the ostrich feather and she is always shown wearing it in her hair. In some pictures she has a pair of wings attached to her arms. The Egyptians believed that if the pharaoh ever failed to worship Ma'at, chaos would result and Egypt and the world would be destroyed. Thereby, the pharaohs of Egypt saw it as their cosmic role to uphold the principles of Ma'at and rule the land.

"When the dead were judged, it was the feather of Ma'at that their hearts were weighed against. If the heart of the deceased was as light as a feather and thereby not burdened with sin and evil, they were granted eternal life in the Duat, the realm of supernatural beings. If the heart was heavier than the feather, Ammut, a female demon with a body that was part lion, hippopotamus and crocodile would consume the soul of the deceased. This judgement occurred in the Hall of the Two Truths or the Hall of Ma'at.

"The importance of the pharaoh marrying the firstborn female was to integrate the matriarchal intuition and left-brain qualities, keeping the bloodline pure and having a balanced leadership style of both matriarchal and patriarchal qualities. When there's an imbalance between the left- and right-brain approaches we see unstable conditions on Earth. I think our firstborn female connection holds great relevance that you will come to realise with time and patience. Trust that all will play out as it is meant to." Buznanna smiled warmly at Eve.

"That's interesting that the firstborn female was endowed with spiritual powers. What was great-granddad, Buznannu, like?" Eve inquired.

"You have the same brown eyes as your Buznannu Michelangelo Inguanez. He was a tall, dark, handsome man and very charismatic indeed. Although fiery at times, he was such a hopeless romantic. He often serenaded me with a love song when I was least expecting it. He passed away the year you were born and I lived on this enormous farm on my own."

"Mum mentioned there is a Palazzo Inguanez in the old capital city of Mdina. Is Buznannu related – because we share the same noble surname?" Eve asked.

"There is a connection because your Buznannu bore the surname of one of the noblest families in Malta and they owned a considerable area of land in Qrendi. The story starts in the 14th century when Angeraldo Inguanez and his son Antonio came to Malta from Catalogna, Spain. Angeraldo became governor of Malta for three years and then handed the governance of Malta to his friend, Francesco Gatto. Angeraldo passed away suddenly leaving young Antonio an orphan. He entrusted Francesco Gatto with the guardianship of his only son. Antonio Inguanez settled in Malta and married Baroness Imperia Gatto, Francesco Gatto's only daughter and heir.

"In 1421, Malta was ruled by the Spanish king of Aragon, King Alfonso, who gave Malta for 30,000 Aragonese gold florins to his viceroy in Sicily, Don Antonio De Cardona. The Viceroy then passed the responsibility on to Don Gonsalvo Monroy, a Castillian galley captain and trusted servant of King Alfonso.

"After a few years of chaos and hardship in Malta an insurgence broke out and Antonio Inguanez helped negotiate the freedom of Malta from Sicilian rule controlled by the viceroy of Sicily. Don Gonsalvo Monroy agreed to release Malta from his governance in return for 30,000 florins and two hostages, as long as the Maltese insurgents held his wife captive at *Castrum Maris* (Fort Saint Angelo, Valletta).

"The dispute was resolved after Antonio Inguanez offered payment and his two sons as hostages to the viceroy, until the insurgents released Monroy's wife. Thanks to Antonio Inguanez, King Alfonso of Aragon incorporated Malta in the kingdom of Aragon and agreed he would never grant Malta as a fiefdom to any third party. Impressed by the loyalty of Antonio Inguanez, the king declared Malta to be the most notable gem in his crown. The old capital city of Mdina acquired the name Città Notabile. Antonio Inguanez fathered many children linked to his noble surname and governed Malta until his death. His descendants inherited the governance of Malta.

"Casa Inguanez, located in Mdina, is the palace of this old noble Maltese family from the 14th century on. There are a number of barons and baronesses who are Inguanez descendants and married into Sicilian, Roman and Neapolitan nobility but also into French, Belgian and Austrian royalty. The Inguanez family coat of arms was placed as a plaque at the main entry gate of Mdina. King Alfonso of Aragon, as a sign of gratitude, placed the united Coat of Arms of the Inguanez and the Gatto families at the magnificent castle at Fort Saint Angelo.

"You have a rich and colourful lineage and I will tell you all about it. Overall, Buznannu and I had all we ever needed and that was love, beautiful memories and healthy children, which was more than any riches could ever buy. Our farm provided an abundance of food and resources. Once you get over your jet lag I will teach you many things. Just promise to remember them all, my sweet girl," she said with an endearing smile on her face.

"I promise, Buznanna. I'll do my best never to forget," Eve reassured her.

Buznanna directed Eve into the kitchen for the lunch she had prepared. The kitchen window was open and a fresh breeze was blowing through, as the farm was within walking distance of Wied iż-Żurrieq. She had purchased fish from the street vendor who sells freshly caught fish from a cart he wheels around, yelling at the top of his voice, as though he was in a busy market, letting people know he has fish for sale. She had cooked a fish known as Lampuka with lemons and spices and baked potatoes. She poured Eve some strange, amber-coloured drink called Kinnie and explained it's a bittersweet drink made of natural ingredients. The ingredients were bitter oranges, combined with an infusion of different aromatic herbs and spices such as anise, ginseng, vanilla, rhubarb and liquorice.

"Are you enjoying your lunch?" Buznanna inquired.

"Yes, thank you – it's so fresh and delicious."

"Most of the fruit and vegetables are from my farm, from Mother Nature, except for the Kinnie, the island's trademark drink. You will drink a lot of Kinnie here, along with ruġġata, which is made of almond and vanilla essence and includes cinnamon and cloves. Now, most importantly, if you need to drink water don't use tap water. It's undrinkable and you will be sick. I have four ancient wells on this property. The water comes from deepwater springs and is very pure and clean, unlike the water that may contain fluoride and is not great for your health. The water from deep springs has a group of three molecules called trimeres, which is easier for the body to absorb.

"The water is clean and magnetised coming from so deep down and is known to have traces of colloidal silver and gold. Use the artesian well closest to the kitchen door and I will show you how to fetch water from it. You need to be careful you don't fall in because it's very deep and there are electric eels in there to keep the water clean and magnetised. It would be hard to get you out. There is also a legend that the Kaw Kaw monster lives in the underground tunnels so be careful not to fall in! I don't want to lose you. Some children have been lost in underground chambers and couldn't be rescued," Buznanna warned.

"I understand. I won't fall in," Eve replied with wide eyes.

"That's my girl. Now eat up all your food so you grow into a strong girl, otherwise no dessert."

"Oh, but dessert is my favourite part. What's for dessert?"

Buznanna brought out a tray of assorted nut biscotti, put it on the table and went back to the kitchen to get something else.

"This carob drink is healthier than any chocolate and packed with protein, essential vitamins and minerals. I have many carob trees on my farm and the drink is great for your health, especially for coughs and colds and stomach upsets. I add carob to honey that I get from my dancing bees and it makes a potent medicine for colds, better than any medicine a doctor would prescribe," Buznanna explained.

It didn't take long to consume the nut biscotti dipped in the hot carob drink.

"Now all the essential house rules are explained. Follow me and I'll take you to your bedroom." She picked up Eve's bag.

"You have a little nap so tonight you can be fresh for our family reunion. You have so many relatives here and they are all going to want to meet and joke with you. It will make your head spin if you don't rest."

Eve stopped abruptly in the doorway when she noticed something on the wall. It was a kind of lizard with large round eyes, scaly cream skin with black spots, and stripes on its tail. Its toes had circular pads like suction cups.

"I'm not going in there," Eve declared and she stopped close to the door ready to run.

"It's a gecko. It's quite harmless. I see this one on the farm all the time. In fact, it's probably your Buznannu, Michelangelo Inguanez! He must have known you were coming and popped in to say hello and welcome. It's a noble surname which supposedly is given to one of our ancestors for exploring the Galapagos which are full of iguanas." Buznanna giggled as she gently guided the gecko out of the window, but he appeared reluctant to go through. He scurried along wagging his tail then stopped, turned around and looked at Eve, giving her a long wink, before turning back to go out of the window.

"Did you see that? The gecko winked at me! How strange. Can you please close the window?" Eve asked.

"Of course, but don't be afraid of the gecko, my girl. I'll teach you all that I know about telepathic communication so you can communicate with all things great and small. I think you'll be a natural, but you must keep it between you and me, a secret, because some people wouldn't understand. Is that a deal?" Buznanna asked.

"Yes, all right," Eve nodded, not too sure what she was getting herself into as she lay down on the bed to rest.

"Sweet dreams, my girl." Buznanna came over and kissed Eve's forehead and covered her with a light sheet. Eve's last thoughts were that it was definitely going to be an interesting month as she dozed off, letting the jet lag overcome her.

Chapter 3

Rekindling With Mother Earth

The next morning Eve woke early to the rooster's repeated "cock-a-doodle-doo" like an alarm clock that was out of control, an instant reminder that she was not in Sydney any more. The same winking gecko was basking in the morning sun on her windowsill. The gecko turned to look at her, holding his glance, as Eve rose out of bed, making sure she acknowledged his presence with a smile. He was going to be a regular visitor by the look of things.

It was a beautiful summer's morning, the temperature still bearable before the heat set in. Buznanna had prepared breakfast for them outside where they ate and caught up with each other. She was keen to show Eve around the farm and chat about their lives.

"It has been six years since your parents and older brother departed on an Italian ship, Marconi, from Malta. You were only two years old. You were such a funny girl dragging your favourite silver-framed green padded chair around with you, as though it was your throne, rather than a cute dolly, which you were never fond of but would have been far more practical. You probably remember nothing about your birthplace.

"I remember you were born on the 11th of March. Ten days after your birth, Malta was struck by an earthquake measuring five on the Richter scale. The earthquake occurred in the nearby Sicilian Channel at 11 p.m. It shook the large, solid limestone houses. Your mother ran out of her home, with you in her arms, in sheer panic as she noticed the chandelier sway back and forth. The streets were full of people fearing the worst.

"The earthquake resulted in a seismic seiche[1] and the ocean sloshed back and forth for days after. Terrified people gathered in the dark streets and didn't know whether the small islands of Malta were sinking or rising. That night we were at the mercy of Mother Nature and all the fury she unleashes from time to time. Your mother was in a panic because you had not been baptised and she thought we were all going to die," Buznanna reported.

"Wow, it must have scared everyone in the village."

"It was terrifying, having no control. Many people ran to the sanctuary of the local church and prayed to the Madonna, the Star of the Sea, the Great Mother Goddess. I believe it was our heartfelt prayers that saved us that terrible night. Prayers are very powerful and that night we put ourselves in the hands of the Madonna."

"Why do you call the Madonna the Great Mother

---

[1] Standing wave

Goddess? Is she not the Virgin Mary?" Eve asked.

"The worship of the Great Mother Goddess is an ancient story indeed. Although patriarchal powers took over religion and spirituality, the goddess was always too powerful to erase because she represented the mother, everyone's mother. It's embedded in ancient history and continues today, but given new names. For example in ancient Egypt, the goddess Isis holds the divine child on her lap just as the Virgin Mary holds Jesus on her lap. The ancient star of divine birth, Sirius, was adopted as the star of Bethlehem – ancient legends and mythical images evolve and change with the times but are likely to be the same, just adopted by the current religion. Put simply, it is common practice for the old to be adopted into the new.

"It's important to have faith in a higher good. There is more to this life than meets the eye. I want to teach you to use all of your senses, even the dormant ones. I will teach you how to awaken the dormant senses through practice because the senses are like muscles – they remain dormant until you decide to exercise them," Buznanna said.

"I see!" pondered Eve.

"There is a lot I want to teach you and a lot to be discovered. It's complex because of how materialistic and dense the world is, but I want to teach you about spirituality and an invisible force of energy you can use in your favour. We all have our invisible helpers, guides or angels as some like to call them, so we don't have to do it all alone in times of crisis or need. I want you to have faith with all your heart and to trust your instincts, as I know your instincts are strong, due to you being the firstborn female in a long unbroken matriarchal lineage of firstborn females. There will be times when you feel all alone or different and that is all right, there is nothing wrong with you, just remember who you are. When crisis arises and it will, as life is turbulent and full of hard lessons to be learnt, it's important to learn the lessons and move on rather than keep repeating them. Just trust that your answers will come from within.

"Respect your body, your temple, be careful what you consume and who you allow in because it houses your soul and the powers to unlock all the answers come from within your sanctuary. Prayer, faith and meditation have got me through some of the toughest times in my life, especially the passing of my husband, whom I miss so much. He was my soul mate and we got through all the rough times together. We are with each other in a different way now and he will always have a special place in my heart, always connected through love like an invisible thread. The farm keeps me busy managing the animals and fruit and vegetable gardens so I don't really have much time to be lonely. I have chickens and a rooster that I'm sure woke you early this morning. Can you see them in the chicken run nearby?" Buznanna pointed in their direction.

"Yes, what is the rooster doing walking up sideways to the hens, lowering his wing to the ground shuffling along by the hens trying to push them where he wants them to go?" Eve asked.

"That's my boy Zeus. He's a bossy rooster and thinks he's the leader. The funny thing is I haven't seen a hen yet who listens. Some hens run away while others look him straight in the eye as if to say, "No way, I'm not scared of you," but mostly they just ignore him. I shouldn't laugh at poor Zeus, but I think of the times when men get a little bossy and I have reacted like my hens. When the hens squabble he tries to be the peacemaker and make things right. He tries to tell them what to do, but they do it only when they're ready. Zeus is their protector whose job is never done and he has to wear many different hats throughout his day," Buznanna explained.

"That's fascinating. How do you know all of this?" Eve asked.

"I pick up on their energy and can communicate with them. All living things are made up of energy. We are able to communicate because we are all energy. Connecting with any other being is not just a matter of the mind but it's a matter of the wisdom of the heart. I communicate through a feeling of unconditional love and kinship with my plants and animals. Even though we don't speak the same language we can communicate by being still, calm, focused and by having love in our hearts. Then the thoughts and messages stream in, just like that. I love my animals and they reciprocate love and wisdom back to me. Animals sense things about humans as well and they send us messages. We just need to be quiet and in the right state to hear them. I always know what they need. It's a telepathic communication," Buznanna explained.

"What exactly is telepathy?" Eve asked.

"Telepathy is a direct communication of thoughts, a two-way sending and receiving of information. It's completely natural. Sometimes you just know what people are going to say, or what they're thinking, especially those closely connected to you. Firstly, you need to connect and tune in. You do this by remaining calm, clearing all your thoughts and remaining heart-centred. You enter into a meditative or trance-like state and this allows you to be on the same wavelength and to resonate.

"We speak an alien language to animals and plants but we can communicate and understand each other just through actions and thought. It's a powerful tool I want you to practise with me on the farm. It comes with being sensitive and it's a natural ability we all have. I bet you are like this too but haven't fully used it – but then again maybe you have? Your mum told me you had a hard time settling down before starting kindergarten.

What was that all about?" Buznanna asked.

"Oh that! I must have been nearly four years old. Both my parents worked, so I was left with a lady and an older boy, maybe her son, I don't know, in the same apartment building. My parents paid for my care but I didn't like my carer who was never around. The older boy was a strange creep. He would come over to me and insist on touching and kissing me as though I was some sort of doll he could play with. I would try to avoid him and push him away whenever he got too close. I became a fast runner to escape him. I would run away and lock myself in the bathroom for the whole day without any food. I wouldn't dare open the door because I was scared he was right behind it. I only opened it when I heard my mum had come to pick me up," Eve explained.

"I wish I had been there for you, sweetie, to protect you. You became independent at a very young age, so young, so many changes, but you were never seriously hurt?" Buznanna asked.

"Not that I can remember, so no, except once he knocked me unconscious when he pushed me off a playground slide and I bumped my head. Then I was woken from what seemed like a deep sleep. My memory was very sketchy at that age. I just remember the main things," Eve said.

"Were you there for long?" Buznanna asked.

"No, I don't think I was because I would cry, carry on and have a tantrum every morning when my mum left for work. I stressed my mum out every morning and she didn't like my behaviour. One day, the boy wasn't there and I was left to wander around the apartment by myself. I noticed a beautiful bracelet on my carer's dressing table and I threw it out of the window. That afternoon, when my mother came to collect me I could hear my carer arguing with my mother, accusing me of stealing her bracelet, as I was the only one who could have done it and that I was a horrible child and she didn't want to take care of me any longer. I remember thinking how could she possibly know what I was like when she was never around and never even made an attempt to talk or even be nice to me, let alone care for me. I didn't like her or the boy, who should have kept his hands to himself," Eve explained.

"Exactly," Buznanna agreed. "What happened after that?"

"After that incident my mum took care of me. I felt safe with my mum before starting kindergarten. I was pleased to be away from my carer and that boy. I don't recall what possessed me at the time to throw her bracelet out of the window but in the end it served its purpose," Eve smiled.

"You did the right thing, acting on your gut feelings, which is exactly what I was explaining to you previously. You are a very sensitive girl and your fear of being hurt heightened your senses further to protect yourself. Fear makes you rely on your senses more and that experience opened you up spiritually. I'm really glad we have the chance to know each other even if it's only for a short time. We will make the most of it, my girl." Buznanna let out a sigh of relief as she winked at Eve.

They finished their breakfast and walked around the farm. Buznanna showed Eve her animals, fruit and vegetable gardens and the dam where she grew blue lotus. She introduced her to the protector of the farm, her bull, Magnificent Maximus.

"He is a rare, rustic breed closely related to a prehistoric aurochs breed. He is useful for ploughing and fertilising the fields. I've trained and domesticated Maximus since he was a calf. He is a prized breed because he retains the sought-after primitive traits. Besides his intelligence and understanding, he protects our territory. He

Rekindling With Mother Earth

can be a dangerous animal if threatened by an intruder. As you can see he is fenced off towards the back of the farm, but he could break out if he wanted to. He has a beautiful soul behind those dark eyes. Come in and meet him." Buznanna invited Eve closer as she patted his head in between his giant horns and encouraged Eve to do the same.

"His name suits him. He is truly magnificent and he has such a calm presence," Eve said as she stroked his head gently.

They continued on to the dancing bees and their hives at the back of the farm. Buznanna had some amazing sunflowers in full bloom, which had several bees swarming around the heads.

"I want you to communicate with this bee," said Buznanna, pointing.

In a panic as it flew close to her face to investigate her, Eve's first thought was: "Don't sting me!"

Eve was surprised. She must have communicated to it without intending to, as she got a reaction immediately from the bee. The bee was terribly insulted by her accusing thought and responded: "Why would I sting you? I would die – I have work and better things to do." The bee flew away in annoyance.

Eve felt annoyed with herself that she had responded with fear first; hopefully the bee sensed that.

"I don't think I did very well. I seemed to have hurt the bee's feelings by warning it not to sting me," Eve reported back to Buznanna.

Buznanna giggled. "Don't worry, try again, but get rid of your fear of being hurt. I want you to place your hand on your heart, feel its pounding, quieten your mind, clear it of all thoughts, listen and feel the response. Your answers will always come from within. Can you feel your heart pounding underneath your hand?" she asked.

As Eve quietened down, she closed her eyes and started to breathe more deeply and slowly. "Yes, I can feel my heart," she responded as she allowed the calmness to engulf her.

"Now, I want you to communicate with this sunflower and ask it what it feels like to have so many bees around its head." She pointed to the sunflower.

"Remember, thought is not silent," Buznanna encouraged Eve.

With her hand still on her heart, Eve opened her eyes and focused on the rhythm of her beating heart and the sunflower and asked the question in her mind, with no fear in her heart. The response was clear and fluid.

"The bees kiss me with their knowingness and love. I am connected to the bees because they spread my pollen. We are all interconnected." As the message came through Eve broadcast it directly to Buznanna.

"Brava! You did it. Sometimes it takes a lot of failures to get something right but the key is never to give up. We humans are wired to get guidance through telepathy, dreams and synchronistic experiences. We are tuned in constantly. We just need to get into that heart-centred zone and silence the mind. When you love and have no fear, so many wonderful experiences can unfold for you, my girl." Buznanna was pleased and held her hands clasped close to her smiling mouth. Eve had passed the first of many tests that would come her way.

"Gosh, maybe we should go?" Eve asked, starting to panic again as several bees started to swarm around Buznanna's head and body.

"They won't sting me. They sometimes follow me around and as the sunflower said to you, it's like being kissed by the bee. You are safe and I want you to let go of your fearful thoughts. As soon as one enters your mind simply let it go – visualise burning the negative thought in fire. You bring the negative to you if you allow it to consume you through fear. You've done so well already. I know you can do it!" Buznanna insisted.

"Why do you call them your dancing bees?" Eve asked as the bees start to swarm around her head and body.

"Firstly, the bee is the only insect that intelligently communicates through dance. Bees communicate by doing a waggle dance forming a figure of eight. The angle and duration of the dance tells the other bees the exact distance to where the food is available. Scout bees assess the quality of a potential site for a hive. The bees report back and do a dance to describe the benefits of the site. The swarm then comes to a group decision on the best site by revisiting sites recommended by others until a consensus emerges and all the bees are performing the same dance."

"That is so intelligent!" Eve was amazed.

"It's an intelligent process of good collective decision-making that humans can learn from, rather than just thinking about the individual, which can't be sustained for our long-term survival on this planet. This collective thinking has ensured their survival. The oldest known bee fossil is 100 million years old, well exceeding the time humans have been on this planet. Did you know the ancient name of Malta is Melita? It comes from the Latin word *Mel*, meaning honey. The symbol of Malta is a bee. The hexagonal honeycomb shape was commonly depicted in artwork in many megalithic temples. The ancient Egyptian ceremonial headdress had alternating black and yellow horizontal stripes, similar to the bee. Malta was associated with the bee and the special quality of honey it produced," Buznanna explained.

"Why is there a Queen Bee?" Eve asked.

"The Queen Bee serves as the reproducer and she can control the sex of the eggs she lays according to the width of the cell. The Queen Bee is the mother, the ruler – she's strong, powerful and the mother of all bees in the hive. She develops in a pouch unlike the drone and worker bees that develop in a honeycomb cell. The Queen Bee develops faster because she is fed a royal jelly extracted from the heads of worker bees. She kills all competitors that stand in her way. The worker bees take care of her needs and fiercely protect the Queen. She is a true warrior because only the Queen Bee can repeatedly sting without dying," Buznanna explained.

"That's fascinating!"

"I have so many experiences and stories that I wish to share with you because I know you will appreciate them and you have so much ahead of you to accomplish in life. I've organised many excursions for just the two of us, as memories are the only things we take with us when we leave our bodies. If you're not too tired from your journey, we will start tomorrow from the oldest known temple, Ġgantija, in Gozo. We will take the ferry from the mainland of Malta and travel to the sister islands of Gozo and Comino," Buznanna said.

That evening Buznanna prepared a special tea. Eve sat at the kitchen table as she watched her pull apart the head of the blue lotus that she had gathered from the dam. She boiled the entire plant for thirty minutes before she drank the tea.

"It's such a beautiful coloured flower."

"It's a magnificent flower. Each afternoon the petals close and they open up each morning. The blue petals remind me of the sky and its yellow centre, the sun. No wonder in ancient Egyptian times the blue lotus had associations with afterlife, rebirth, the rising and setting of the sun and the reawakening of consciousness."

Eve spent the rest of the evening drinking Kinnie while Buznanna drank blue lotus tea, the powerful elixir she had concocted.

"What are the health benefits of drinking blue lotus tea?" Eve inquired.

"The medicinal benefits of blue lotus stem largely from the sedative properties of the plant. Blue lotus tea helps me to get a restful night's sleep because it's a natural anti-anxiety remedy and stress reliever. Blue lotus was the most important cultivated ritual plant of ancient Egypt. You could see these water lilies growing wild in ponds and it became very popular not only for its enchanting beauty but also its psychoactive effects, meaning it could change brain function and alter perception, mood or consciousness. The flower was thought to be an elite flower that produced shamanic effects, such as having powerful dreams and visions with great spiritual beings, like those I have experienced throughout my life.

"What we eat and drink, as living food, has more intense power over disease and aging than any medicine the doctor may prescribe. Always keep in mind that what you put into your temple, your body, has the power to increase your consciousness, your vibration and the understanding of your place in the universe."

The evening brought cool fresh breezes and much needed relief from the heat of the summer day. They had spent an amazing day rekindling memories like free spirits, not bound by rigid rules. Buznanna amazed Eve. She was like the Queen Bee and Eve had learnt so much interesting information from her. Eve just knew in her heart Buznanna would never cease to bee-dazzle her.

Chapter 4

The Legends of Gozo

Early next morning they boarded a ferry from Malta to Gozo. Buznanna had organised a two-day trip to the sister islands of Gozo and Comino. The name of the island of Gozo, *Għawdex*, through epigraphic inscriptions on stone or stele, comes from the Phoenician word *gaulos* meaning the round one. The Phoenicians are believed to have settled in the capital city of Victoria, as it is known today. Gozo is mountainous and known for its lush green countryside. It is believed to be an ancient dormant volcano where both hot and cold water springs once existed and rich volcanic fertile soil meant that agriculture flourished.

The island is famous for its megalithic temples – especially Ġgantija. Gozo is popularly called the Island of Calypso, Ogygia, which is a nickname originating in Homer's Odyssey. In this epic poem, the fabled island was controlled by the nymph, Calypso, who had detained the Greek hero Odysseus as a prisoner of love for seven long years. A true nymphomaniac indeed! According to Homer, Calypso's Cave is located on top of an escarpment overlooking a bay with golden sands, which matches the description of the cave at Ramla Bay, as the sands appear golden from Calypso's Cave when the sun is shining but up close the sand appears red.

Calypso is generally said to be the daughter of the Titan, Atlas. Calypso had promised Odysseus immortality if he stayed with her. The nymphs themselves were thought to be endowed with prophetic or oracular power. Odysseus attached himself to the mast of the boat to resist the alluring songs of the mermaids. Many nymphs exist in legends and represent a type of sea creature that is both human and aquatic. Similarly, sea mammals such as the dolphins and whales have a method of communication through complex sounds and perhaps even singing.

As they disembarked from the ferry the flag depicting the coat of arms of Gozo was flying in the breeze at full mast. Its distinguishing features are the three mountains in black, the centre mountain higher with a star added to its peak and it sits in front of the other two mountains. It's possible that these two mountains were the islands of Comino and Malta when the islands were all joined and formed a larger landmass as shown on an ancient map.

The mountains on a silver field appear to be rising from the sea. Below the mountains are six parallel wavy horizontal bands of silver and black, the top one silver, the bottom one black, resembling the turbulent sea divided by distinguishing bands of land like canals. The mountains and sea are enclosed in a shield. Above the shield is a gold coronet, known as a small crown, with five eschaugettes that resemble towers, worn by nobility. The coat of arms depicts an ancient landscape and an island with three mountains in the heart of the Mediterranean, which is not the landscape we see today.

Buznanna booked a taxi and a driver for the day and explained all the sites they wanted to explore starting from Ġgantija temple, Xagħra stone stone circle and its hypogeum. She planned to continue to Dwejra to see the Azure Window and legendary fungus rock and later on, Calypso's cave and Ramla Bay.

They arrived at their first destination and stood on the plateau overlooking the abundant green countryside below, beside the ancient Temple of Ġgantija, believed to be constructed by giants. The megalithic stones have withstood the test of time, still resembling a temple complex today.

"Why was the Ġgantija temple built?" Eve asked Buznanna.

"No one really knows. It's a puzzle just waiting to be put together, but in my opinion the temples were built to worship the Great Mother Goddess, to celebrate fertility and abundance. Many temples have altars with statues of voluptuous women as objects of ritual and worship. We see a lot of spiral artwork, with figures of serpents, fish, bulls, rams and many other animals carved into stone blocks. These engravings provide us with valuable information about the ancient society that helps form our opinions.

"There appears to be a pattern, a template for all subsequent Maltese temples and hypogea. In fact, curves and circles dominate the artwork of the Maltese temples. The many temples scattered above and even below ground such as the three known hypogea are all curvy shapes believed to resemble the female form, like the uterus and the breast – strong symbols of reproduction, fertility and life. All these clues point to a religion that worshipped the Mother Goddess.

"Another reason why the temples were built has to do with them being some kind of technological communication device. The temples are circular in order to transmit sound or light. As more discoveries are made there may be a pattern emerging of a worldwide pyramid temple system mounted like antennae on the key energy meridians.

"These temples could have been the abodes of a particular race of people who were attuned to sonic energies. Their circular homes promoted their energetic well-being in terms of resonance and vibration better than square or rectangular homes. The solid megalithic limestone temples provided protection. The bible and legends tell us that giants roamed the earth and giant animals like thunderbirds or pterodactyls were large predators hunting humans, especially young girls, like you!" Buznanna paused to see if Eve was still paying attention.

"I'm glad those days have passed, so you're saying the temples were used for protection from being eaten alive, some kind of dinosaur-free zone. What about the stone circles, what were they used for?"

"They kept track of time by building stone circles and monitoring astronomical events. Some are aligned to the rising sun and moon, the Pleiades and other star systems. Archaeologists use archaeo-astronomy to determine the age of a monument based on the precession of the equinox, which takes 26,000 years to complete. This is how the ancients determined the seasons and what ceremonies to conduct. The ancients were astronomers who knew about precession and they needed to watch the equinox and the stars to determine the seasons, as their lives and well-being were closely linked to nature's cycles and the environment."

"So if they lived in a different environment and were more attuned to sound, were they a different race of people?" Eve enquired, trying to make sense of it all.

"A lot of the information points towards a different race of people existing in the ancient past. It was a race that was taller than present-day humans and they had dolichocephalic skulls that appeared elongated. Their skull size is believed to be seventy-five per cent larger than humans today, and formed naturally without any forced manipulation through headboarding or wrapping.

"Having a larger brain capacity, like a dolphin for example, meant they had greater senses, perhaps sonar capacity, and could manipulate and use sound in more ways than we can today. For example, sound and echolocation is very important to killer whales and bottlenose dolphins for hunting, navigating and communicating. This long-headed race is associated with the serpent because their craniums were large with no neck to support the head and they slithered, like snakes. For this reason the long-headed race is associated with some kind of serpent-looking, aquatic race. Legend has it that the serpent race could manipulate the giant race of humans because they were more intelligent and used the docile giants as slave labour. The temples don't appear to be constructed for giants as the doorways are too low to allow entry."

"Where did this long-headed race of people go?"

"This mysterious elite race disappeared for unknown reasons," replied Buznanna. "Perhaps they fled underground in the complex network of tunnels, into the hollows of the Earth, to nearby Egypt and other parts of the world. The long-headed race set up residence around the world, once their survival was threatened, and became the teachers. They appeared to be a peaceful race and venerated the Mother Goddess. They were a race of people whose level of intelligence and senses we don't fully comprehend. Their larger skull capacity gave them additional intelligence and skills, we think, such as echo-location and dowsing skills and the ability to detect magnetism. Overall, their senses were superior and enabled them to be master sacred-geometry builders, dowsers and teachers."

As they walked around the stone temple, Eve couldn't help but feel incredibly small, like an ant, as she looked up at the giant stone slabs. Eve overheard the tour guide explaining that according to UNESCO, one of the largest and heaviest freestanding stones in the world is found in the Temple of Ġgantija and they still remain partially in form to remind us of their accomplishments and wisdom.

Eve turned to look at Buznanna and asked, "How did they manipulate such heavy blocks of stone to build the temples?"

"Humans today still have no idea how such heavy megalithic blocks were used in construction of this giant temple. The first possibility is that this ancient race possessed superior senses and skills and knew how to manipulate sound or gravity to move heavy stone. Ġgantija means belonging to the giants, as the megalithic stones are so heavy they must have been built by giants, as the name of the temple suggests. There is a legend of a giantess, the Great Sunsuna Goddess. Ġgantija is an old architectural structure predating the Egyptian pyramids and even Stonehenge.

"Oral traditions, before written history, say these islands were one. The Maltese archipelago formed mountain ranges which the people called the Sacred Mountains of the Gods. They built sanctuaries to these gods, temples and stone circles. One of the first to be completed on one of the highest plateaus was Ġgantija. Legends say that, in those ancient times, giants walked the land – just what we were talking about.

"Ġgantija, the Temple of the Giants, owes its magnificence to the strength of one in particular named Sunsuna, a woman whose strength, it is said, came from a special diet of broad beans. She carried the huge stone boulders on her head, with a baby in a cradle on her back, while she held the supporting stones in either hand and carried them up from the quarry to the temple site. The giants were benevolent and cared for and loved their young.

"However, there were also malevolent giants. Once cataclysms occurred, food was scarce and a lot of giants turned to eating humans, hence the bad reputation portrayed in the bible. Eventually the race of giants disappeared. There is a collapsed dolmen in Ix-Xagħra village dedicated to the giantess, Sunsuna. It has a stone slab propped up at an angle. A dolmen is a megalithic tomb with a large flat stone laid on upright ones," Buznanna explained.

"Maybe Sunsuna is buried next to the collapsed dolmen! The word Sunsuna sounds like the Maltese word for bee, *Zunzana*," Eve interjected.

"Always keep an open mind as anything is possible. You're absolutely correct – her name is associated with the feminine and the Maltese bee, *Apis mellifera ruttneri*, renowned for her honey. The sweet golden liquid is Maltese gold brimming with antibacterial, antifungal properties and containing all the necessary nutrients humans need to survive and develop. Besides Sunsuna I've heard that a giant eight-foot human was discovered buried in fine sand and in a standing position in the vicinity of Ġgantija temple," Buznanna said as they continued exploring Ġgantija temple.

"What is this spiral artwork engraved in stone?" said Eve, pointing to the artwork.

"They're beautiful, aren't they? The spiral symbols are an important message the ancients wanted us to know about. It's a common, repeated pattern found throughout the temple structures. If you follow the spirals from the exterior to the interior, when you reach the centre there is another spiral in the reverse direction," Buznanna explained.

"So what do you think the spirals mean?"

"When I look at the double spirals I think they denote the continuity of life – that our souls are immortal. Spirals are recognised worldwide as the symbol of eternity. The spirals represent death, regeneration and rebirth. They represent the cycle of the continual existence of the soul or the life force encased in our bodies. Perhaps they are symbols of hope, a message that more lies beyond.

"Everything works in spiral movements like rotating galaxies or the double helix of DNA. Magnetism is supposed to be two spiral waves going in opposite directions according to Edward Leedskalnin's theories on magnetism. It is believed that one or more spirals are markers to portals used in ancient times. Engraved in stones are varying series of spirals ranging from one to four spirals in different patterns depending on the power of the portals and their function. The spirals could be some form of communication giving direction or instruction about the portals and the type of electrical plasma."

"What is a portal?"

"Well, a portal is often depicted in science fiction as a doorway that connects two distant locations separated by space-time to a parallel world, past or future, or another plane of existence. Portals are similar to the concept of a wormhole in astrophysics. Put simply, a wormhole is a passage through space-time that could create shortcuts for long journeys across the universe or through time. I have experienced this type of travel in my dreams, trance and meditative states. In fact, this long-headed race might have had the ability to detect anomalies in the electromagnetic field such as portals. Some temples or abodes have been built next to portals."

They walked away from the Ġgantija temple site and to the nearby Xagħra stone circle. There was not much to see, as beneath the remnants of the stone circle is the reburied Xagħra hypogeum. They sat on a stone wall overlooking the flourishing countryside beneath the plateau as they waited for their taxi.

Some time later they arrived at the next destination, Fungus Rock, in Dwejra Bay. The ice cream van was blaring out music, attracting visitors to buy cool refreshments. Buznanna bought almond-flavoured granitas.

The view was impressive. Directly before them was Fungus Rock, some 60 metres high, believed to be the remnant of what was once an ancient sea cave whose roof collapsed into the sea, detaching it permanently from the mainland. Partially encircling the bay were the dramatic cliffs and the monumental Azure Window, a natural limestone arch, which framed the glorious deep blue sea. They looked at Fungus Rock lying out at sea in solitude.

"My grandmother told me that in the ancient past a rare plant, known as Cynomorium coccineum, grew on Fungus Rock. It is referred to as a mushroom due to its appearance, but it was a plant that secreted red fluids when broken. A profusion of beautiful yellow flowers grew on it for three months of the year. The Knights Hospitaller used it as a cure for blood-related diseases including anaemia, internal haemorrhages, dysentery and even erectile dysfunction. This miracle plant became known by its esoteric name, scarlet mushroom, which is derived from the parasite known as Fungus melitensis. It is recognised as one of the rarest endemic plant species in Malta, giving it very special status. The Knights offered the scarlet mushrooms as gifts to kings and queens worldwide. Enter the bee again, which led ancient man to those plants with hallucinogenic components, such as Dimethyltryptamine (DMT), the spiritual molecule, which transported a shaman's consciousness. DMT is produced in the human pineal gland if your pineal gland is healthy. In ancient times, they knew which parts of the plant were toxic, medicinal, healing or nourishing. The ancients practised this form of communication and it served them well."

"Can you still find the scarlet mushroom on Fungus Rock today?" Eve asked.

"It's really difficult to access but there may be some small remnants of it although it's difficult to see from where we are standing. There was a small group of Gozitian locals who knew how to access the mushroom. When I was a teenager, we use to go on trips with friends to Gozo and eat some mushrooms. The Phoenicians labelled it the treasure among medicine, followed by the Knights who were eventually forbidden to take it and were given harsh penalties if caught. In my time the nickname was *Il pasisa tal Shitan*," Buznanna explained.

"What does that mean?"

"Okay I'll tell you, but don't repeat to anyone. It means the devil's willy!"

"That's gross! Why would it be named that?" Eve asked.

"It looks like a mushroom on steroids, growing as high as 60 cm tall, shaped like a huge willy and very out of place. You know, my girl, fear is a great control mechanism. I suspect it was nicknamed like this to scare people from ingesting it. The nickname is a deterrent, that's all. The plant and parasite itself came from North Africa, not too far away," Buznanna elaborated.

"How did you use it and what did you experience?" Eve was curious.

"When I first ingested it, I had to lie down because I experienced a strong whirling sensation inside my head,

Atlantis and The Legendary Blue Queen

right in the centre of my forehead, a few inches behind the third-eye chakra. It felt as though my pineal gland, a small gland the size of a pea, was opening up. It wasn't painful, but I had an explosion of insightful visions in a violet haze. After trying to understand my experience I discovered the pineal gland contains three crystals known as apatite, calcite and magnetite. The apatite helps with psychic enhancement, while calcite is for the expansion of one's powers. Magnetite aids visionary purpose and establishing our experiences in the physical world.

"Together, all three crystals create a cosmic antenna, which helps the transfer of signals between dimensional planes, not just our own. Opening the pineal gland gave me insight into my unconscious. Premonitions and insightful dreams connected me to a powerful source, perhaps the creator, some source that made me feel that we are not alone. The pineal gland is essentially a transmitter and a receiver in our brain, an apparatus to facilitate a mediumistic experience. It was an amazing experience and what is even more amazing is the realisation that we are all interconnected with this electrical universe. Your pineal gland produces Dimethyltryptamine which enhances your psychic abilities. I think our pineal glands are well developed but you really must promise me something." Buznanna stopped and looked at Eve.

"What is it?" Eve asked, somewhat alarmed.

"Promise me to treat your body, your inner temple, well. Nourish it with good clean food and water, and keep your thoughts positive and elevated, otherwise your pineal gland may not work properly. There are many negative entities that can drag you down if you are not mentally strong enough. It is your responsibility. As the world becomes more populated, polluted and controlled, some will never activate their pineal gland because they are bombarded with too much electronic stimulation and toxins such as fluoride and aluminium. You need to be careful what you put into your body and maintain clear vision with your third eye. When the third eye is open you can achieve all that you can imagine and ultimately bring your dreams to fruition. You can tap into the collective unconscious and the supernatural and even solve the most complex of problems – anything is possible. I had dreams about you before you were even born and prophecies in the form of visions. You and I are part of the same soul family who have been entangled through many lifetimes." She kissed Eve on the forehead on her third eye.

"I was just thinking how comfortable and easy it is to get along with you. I feel as though I've known you for such a long time already. We can say everything and anything to each other. It's a connection I don't share with anyone else but you." Eve smiled at Buznanna.

"I'm glad you feel our connection too. I knew I could share all that I have discovered in confidence with you as our soul family entanglement is rich with love, respect and understanding." Buznanna smiled back at Eve, glad to know they agreed.

They reached their last destination and were having a well-earned break at Ir-Ramla l-Ħamra Bay, Gozo's largest red sandy beach. Ramla Bay is one of the most beautiful beaches in the Maltese archipelago, set in the bottom of a valley rampant with unspoilt wild and fertile nature. It has a magnificent curving bay with rocky cliffs protecting the beautiful beach. The area nearby is quite interesting and provides some rich historical treasures. Roman remains lie beneath the sand and the famous Calypso Cave overlooks the western side of the beach.

Calypso's cave is believed to be a complex labyrinth extending down to sea level but at some point, stone boulders blocked the way a few metres inside so no one can explore the labyrinth. Malta and Gozo are littered with underground labyrinths and hypogea, many left closed up and unexplored, away from prying eyes.

At Ramla Bay they sought the shade of a giant carob tree and sat underneath it eating the juicy pomegranates Buznanna had bought from a fruit and vegetable vendor on the street. Buznanna was always full of interesting facts. She was carefully slicing the top to the bottom of the pomegranate, making grooves with a knife all along the sides so she could pull apart sections of the fruit.

"Look inside, what does this ancient fruit look like?" she asked as she handed Eve the pomegranate.

"It looks like a series of hexagons, like a beehive," Eve replied.

"That's exactly what it reminds me of. When I was about your age I had a teacher who told me that the pomegranate was the forbidden fruit of the Garden of Eden, not the apple. The ancient Romans referred to the pomegranate as an apple with many seeds. The pomegranate tree, the tree of immortality, is a better representation of the forbidden fruit in the Garden of Eden than the traditional apple tree. The pomegranate, compared to an apple, is more symbolic of the regeneration process of immortality because the pomegranate is full of seeds for regeneration and so it's associated with the feminine.

"In the statue of Athena located in the Parthenon, Nike the winged goddess of victory stood in Athena's outstretched right hand on top of a pomegranate. Athena holds the spear of justice in her left hand and the pomegranate in her right hand." They finished their fruit and couldn't resist a refreshing swim in the clear blue sea to get some relief from the heat.

As they swam out Buznanna could tell Eve was a bit uneasy because she was not accustomed to swimming in the deep sea. In Australia, there are plenty of sharks and Eve knew not to venture into their territory.

"There is no need to worry, Eve – sharks are not very common here, nor are poisonous animals. In fact, in the first century A.D. Saint Paul was shipwrecked in a Maltese bay that still bears his name. Strangely, he encountered a venomous viper that bit his foot. He encountered what he claimed to be a poisonous leopard snake, Zamenis situla, but it was a non-venomous species."

"So if there were no venomous snakes on the island, St. Paul was not in any danger?"

"That's right. Perhaps the snake represents the types of humans living before Christianity. My intuition tells me the people living on Malta before Christianity were some kind of hybrid aquatic human race with elongated skulls and no feet so they slithered like snakes. The leaders of the race, the serpent priests, practised an old religion with thaumaturgy powers to work magic or miracles and so they would have posed a threat to St. Paul.

"The solution was to exterminate the serpent priest race. Any survivors would have disappeared through the network of tunnels underneath the islands. It's another possible explanation of the disappearance of a different race with a different spirituality, venerating the Great Goddess, enabling St. Paul to spread the Christian message across Europe," Buznanna concluded as she pointed to a pod of dolphins she had spotted in the distance.

"I'm going to speak to the dolphins," Eve said jokingly to Buznanna.

"How do you plan on doing that?"

"Easy, I'll show you." Eve placed her head in the water and made a series of sounds in the water.

Within minutes, Eve had a dolphin circling her body as if it were scanning her, gliding around her several times. The dolphin's skin was slippery and soft and its eyes had such knowingness and warmth about them as it turned its head to the side to look at Eve directly. It felt as though the dolphin was embracing her. There was no need for verbal communication, as the messages, concepts and feelings flowed smoothly and instantly, free of words.

"Wow! Look at this beautiful calf next to me! I've been mind-sharing with his mother, Maia. They have been named after the stars in the Pleiades. We have been communicating telepathically. Isn't it great how these beautiful dolphins have come to play with us?" Buznanna said, with awe in her voice.

Eve looked at the calf swimming playfully around Buznanna but it was no ordinary calf. He was an albino, completely white, with a few distinguishing markings beneath his eyes. Maia had named him Bozo. He was undoubtedly one of a kind. Bozo started to circle Eve closely like his mother did, allowing her hand to glide across his soft, slippery body as they frolicked in the sea.

Maia circled close to Buznanna, continuing to engage in mind-sharing communication. They were such loving dolphins and when they departed, after much communication and play, they left the women with a feeling of euphoria and curiosity.

"Why did the dolphin come to us? I was just joking around not expecting a dolphin and her calf to approach as they did," Eve asked Buznanna.

"Huh, be careful what you wish for! They sensed us and knew that it was safe for them to approach. Our sprawling aura must have grabbed their attention. I got a good glimpse of your aura on the first day you arrived. I saw your bright colours, the electromagnetic field that surrounds your body. Your colours are predominantly violet, indigo, blue, turquoise, silver and smaller patches of green and yellow. Your higher spiritual chakras are open and activated because you have exercised them like a muscle so these chakras have not atrophied. In many people they lie dormant, because they are relatively young souls.

"Your chalice chakra is located mid-aura and the pinnacle vortex chakra is at the edge of your aura. The silver in your aura represents the chalice; the gold, which is yet to be opened, is known as the pinnacle vortex. I imagine you will strive to open this vortex of energy when you are older. There is a time for everything – there's no use being impatient and going against the flow – all will happen at the time it was meant to. You will sense when that time has arrived. You exercised the chalice chakra when you were a toddler. In times of great change and upheaval, in times of fear and stress, in the dream state you can access spiritual guidance and answers. Of course the dolphins were attracted to our vibrational energy when you called out to them. Being curious mammals they had to come and give us a big hug and show their love, not through words but through the joy of genuinely connecting," Buznanna explained.

"Humans appear to be closer to dolphins in intelligence than primates. Is our human existence linked more closely to aquatic mammals than primates?" Eve asked.

"Yes I think so. Among aquatic mammals, the dolphin has a large skull and more folded cortex than humans. The more folded the cortex, the more room in the brain to house additional neurons, brain cells, with which to perform processing of information. In comparison, it is said that humans use only ten per cent of their cerebral capacity but a dolphin uses up to twenty percent and this allows it to have a natural echolocation system or sonar. Echolocation allows a dolphin to see and hear objects underwater in a detailed, holographic, magnified way and communicate these images to other dolphins that are travelling nearby.

"Self-awareness appears to exist only in large-brained primates and man. Dolphins have the ability to recognize individuals and objects, remember tasks, solve problems, adapt to change and learn complex tasks. It is more likely that humans have evolved from a watery environment like the aquatic-ape theory rather than land-dwelling apes. When you compare the two, apes can't hold their breath under water and can't swim. Humans have insulation, a layer of fat under the skin and not much hair. Humans ate the fruits of the sea full of rich omega 3 and high cholesterol, great sources of energy for brain development. These similarities provide strong evidence to support the aquatic-ape theory.

"As sea levels rose and environments changed, our human ancestors adapted to a more aquatic existence. There is a close connection between nakedness and water and that could be why humans are hairless. For aquatic mammals to keep warm in the water, a layer of fat beneath the skin is required as is the case with humans and it is more beneficial than a layer of hair on the outside. Although plenty of land animals can grow fat, they generally store their fat just around their abdomen. Another point is that humans have voluntary control over their respiratory system like aquatic mammals. We can inhale as much air as required for a dive and return to the surface again for air. Human babies can swim before they can crawl or walk. Babies have an inborn reflex that stops them from breathing water into their lungs for short periods. Sweating and tears, which occur with humans but not primates, is also the norm with aquatic mammals."

"Yes I see the strong link with humans and an aquatic existence," Eve pondered.

As the long hot day drew to an end, the defiant sky adorned itself with brilliant shades of bleeding reds and oranges sprawled across the canvas like an abstract painting. The vibrant red sands glimmered like a sea of precious rubies entwining with the liquid gold of the last rays of the golden setting sun over the vast, red sandy bay.

Eve was never keen on red and orange colours, she always preferred shades of blue and violet, but this sunset demonstrated magnificent reds, oranges and yellows that were truly breathtaking. They sat quietly on the sand admiring the sunset and feeling grateful for all the lovely synchronicities and encounters the day had brought them. Eve broke the silence as she remembered a question she wanted to ask Buznanna.

"You mentioned you saw my aura. When did you see it, what did you see and how?"

"When your pineal gland is developed enough, you will be able to see and sense an aura. I saw your aura when we first reunited. This is fairly common for me as I can usually sense and see a person's aura – it comes naturally to me. Your aura was lacking the colours of red and orange, the two lower chakras known as the root and splenic chakras. Chakras are like revolving wheels, vortexes or whirlpools of vital energy, which assist your physical body. It's important for you to ground yourself and balance your energies so all of your chakras work optimally together, otherwise you could be out of balance and lose focus on your goals."

"Hopefully I've corrected my chakra's energies after this trip to Gozo. I've definitely grown fond of red and orange after hearing about the scarlet mushrooms, the megalithic amber stones, eating fresh red pomegranates, swimming at the red sandy bay and watching this magnificent sunset. Gozo now represents in my mind the root and splenic chakras. The red and orange are the connections we have to the Earth. Where does Comino fit in?" Eve asked.

"Comino, which is the small island between Gozo and Malta, represents the green heart chakra. Comino's blue lagoon and crystal clear water is much loved by visitors. Comino represents the heart because it's a place to calm the mind and enrich the heart with all the natural unspoilt beauty. Malta, of course, represents the higher chakras of the throat, crown, mid and edge aura. These higher chakras in order represent the colours blue, indigo, violet, silver and gold," Buznanna continued.

Eve sat on the red sands quietly meditating as her mind churned over the immense amount of information and experiences they had encountered that day. She contemplated her experiences with Maia and Bozo, magnificent dolphins who possessed such wisdom beyond humans' understanding. What a truly magical end to our trip in Gozo, she thought. Eve smiled in contentment at the memories she would cherish for a lifetime.

Chapter 5

Buznanna's Playground

The mysterious ancient past encourages us to discover more. The present is a gift to seize the opportunities and the future to chase and fulfil our dreams. Their next adventure was one that Buznanna was looking forward to showing Eve. Buznanna's playground and sanctuary was within walking distance of her country home in Qrendi. Her playground consisted of a pair of freestanding megalithic temples known as Ħaġar Qim and Mnajdra.

Ħaġar Qim has openings that represent the different phases of the moon, like a moon calendar. A stone artefact representing the 27 phases of the moon had been found inside. Mnajdra, in contrast, is a sun calendar aligned to the equinoxes and the solstices. The paired temples and the artefacts discovered had astronomical significance and were used as calendars. These temples are situated on a high promontory above the cliffs on the southwestern edge of the main island of Malta.

Eve and Buznanna walked to the piazza in the neighbouring town of Żurrieq. They stopped at the pastizzerija, a place that specialised in making pastizzi. The smell of cooking pastizzi lingered in the air. It was so divine Eve felt hungry immediately. The owner of the small business was busily rolling out the fresh puff pastry dough, slicing it into the appropriate size and folding the pastry in his hands over the filling to form the traditional pastizzi shape. He sculpted the dough in his hands, like a little piece of art, to form just the right shapes and sizes. One pastizzi was diamond shaped for the filling of mushy peas known as pastizzi *tal-piżelli* and the other was an oval shape for the ricotta filling known as pastizzi *tal-irkotta*. He was placing the pastizzi on a large metal tray ready to put another batch of pastries in the wood-burning oven. Pastizzi are a popular savoury food so many more fillings have been created, now including sweet flavours. They can be enjoyed at any time of the day, for breakfast with a cup of tea or coffee, lunch with a cold drink, or as an evening snack. A family ran this pastizzerija.

The son, Sandro, cheerfully greeted them at the front counter.

"Hello Angela, what can I get for you today?" he asked politely with a warm smile.

"A dozen pastizzi please, half cheese and the other peas, and four Kinnies. My great-granddaughter is going to taste the best pastizzi ever, fresh and hot from the oven," Buznanna said.

Buznanna introduced Eve to Sandro, the teenage boy taking the order at the counter, explaining that she had

Buznanna's Playground

known their lovely family for a long time. Being a small village, it was common for everyone to know each other and they often referred to families through their surnames or nicknames. Sandro placed the pastizzi in a large brown paper bag and the bottles of Kinnie in Angela's basket on the counter top.

There were two young boys squabbling just behind them and one little boy started to cry. The elder boy said to him, "You are such a pastizz!"

"Why is that boy calling the other pastizz?" Eve asked Buznanna.

"The Maltese language, like many languages, can be very colourful. The word pastizzi has multiple meanings. It is used as a euphemism for the female sexual organ, due to its shape, and for describing someone as an idiot. The boy was calling the younger boy an idiot for crying, very insensitive indeed. Anyhow, there are lots of expressions about pastizzi. Another Maltese expression *jinbiegħu bħall-pastizzi* meaning, selling like pastizzi, is equivalent to the English "selling like hot cakes," to describe a product which seems to have unlimited demand," Buznanna explained.

"Bye and see you at the Solstice!" Sandro waved to them.

They waved back and left the pastizzerija. They approached the chapel of Qrendi where Buznanna led Eve around to the back and showed her a massive hole in the earth fifty meters in circumference and forty meters deep, known as Tal-Maqluba.

"Legend has it that the people were so bad that God punished them by opening the ground which swallowed the whole village. The ground looks as though it has been struck by some sort of heavenly body from the sky, such as a meteorite. In fact most of Malta looks as though the electrical universe has battered it." Buznanna explained.

They continued walking to the temples. The smell of the fresh pastizzi drifting out of their bag was too tempting to resist, so as soon as the pastries had cooled down enough to eat, they pulled out one of each flavour to try. The pastizzi did not disappoint. They were simply delicious, crunchy at first bite and packed with flavour. They were the best Eve had ever tasted. They walked along and continued to chat about the national language.

"Today of course, Maltese and English are the two official languages of the islands," continued Buznanna.

"What are the roots of the Maltese language?" Eve asked.

"The roots are Semitic like Arabic, Hebrew and Aramaic, but some Maltese words are pre-Semitic or Hamitic. I'll start with the oldest roots that I am aware of, from the tenth century BC. They show the Phoenician connection to Malta. The Phoenicians established a colony on the Maltese Islands around 725 BC, which was a good strategy because Malta's location was an important sea route for the Phoenicians. It was in the heart of the Mediterranean separating Europe from Africa and between Sicily and Tunisia. The Phoenician culture, religion and Semitic language became integrated with the Maltese culture.

"The Mediterranean Sea was the sea of the Phoenicians who came from the Levant, where Lebanon is today. The Phoenicians made a warehouse of this island. It made sense that they would inhabit Malta because it was an ideal halfway point on their way to fetch copper from the Iberian Peninsula. In fact Malta's pivotal location and superior ports meant it was an ideal location for the Phoenicians to set up a colony," Buznanna explained.

"Who were the Phoenicians?" Eve asked.

"The Phoenicians were brave seafarers, great navigators, astronomers, military strategists and merchants.

They explored the British Isles and African continent. They ventured great distances and navigated the open seas guided by the stars. Extensive exploration extended their commercial relationships and served as links between east and west. Along with trade and exploration, the Phoenicians brought their own alphabet and language to do business. Most importantly, they were responsible for phonetic writing."

"What cultures influenced the Maltese language?" Eve asked.

"The Maltese islands have been occupied by many different races and cultures, which have all influenced the language, religion and culture. The most important influences were Latin and Arabic. The cultural profile of the Maltese population is difficult to identify – inscriptions in Greek, Latin and Punic (Carthaginian) dialects do not rule in favour of one language over another. The Maltese language is a mixture of Latin and Semitic influences, in short, from a very convoluted story.

"I prefer the ancient history – it is a far more intriguing story. One important discovery unearthed in Malta and dated to the second century BC was two Phoenician Parian marble *cippi* or *cippus*, a term used to describe a small decorative column. They were known as the cippi of Melqart, who was the tutelary or protector god of the Phoenician city of Tyre. Ancient Tyre is in Lebanon, but the new Phoenician capital city was re-established in Carthage in Tunisia. In Phoenician, Carthage means new city.

"The Phoenicians had a colony in Ir-Rabat, Victoria in Gozo and two other colonies in Mdina and Bormla in Eastern Malta overlooking the Grand Harbour. Melqart was identified by the Greeks with Herakles and referred to as the Tyrian Herakles. These two cippi were offerings to the god Melqart, a Phoenician god and patron god of the city of

Tyre. He was also called king of the city. He was a god who protected sailors, trade and overseas colonies. During the Hellenistic and Roman periods, Melqart was assimilated as Hercules. Two inscriptions were found engraved in ancient Greek and Phoenician. They were the first Phoenician writings to be identified and published in modern times and enabled the Phoenician alphabet and language to be deciphered," Buznanna explained.

"That's fascinating. Where did they find the cippi of Melqart?" Eve asked.

"The pair of decorative columns was found in Marsaxlokk, a fishing village in south-eastern Malta. Overlooking the northern arm of Marsaxlokk Bay is the hill of Tas-Silġ, which contains remains of megalithic temples of the Tarxien phase. The hill was used as a religious site, notably as a temple dedicated to Hercules. The temples of Hercules and Hera (known as Juno to the Romans) are yet to be found, but have been strongly identified with the remains at Tas-Silġ. The columns or cippi were probably dedicated and set up inside the Temple of Hercules," Buznanna said, her blue eyes lighting up with excitement.

"Who is Hera and what is her association with Hercules?" Eve asked.

"Greek mythology is a myriad of complex stories, but I'll do my best to explain the summarised version," Buznanna replied. "Firstly, Hera is Cronus' eldest daughter, wife and brother of Zeus. She is referred to as the Queen of the Gods or the Queen of Heaven. Such titles were given to a number of ancient sky goddesses in the Mediterranean and Near East. Some of the sky goddesses were Anat, Isis, Innana and Astarte. Hera is known as the Goddess of Marriage, Women, Childbirth and Family. Cronus was the leader and youngest of the first generation of Titans.

"To answer the second part of your question, the relationship between Zeus and Hera was incredibly difficult and lasted 300 years; they even got married against their parents' wishes. The romance ended because Zeus had many affairs with other goddesses and with mortal women, so Hera was jealous and sought revenge."

"How could they marry if they were brother and sister?" Eve interjected.

"They were gods and the guardians of the laws so they were above the law and were the law due to their powers. The Romans had a saying that what is allowed for Zeus is not allowed for the mortals."

"So where does Hercules come into all of this?"

"Hercules was a product of one of Zeus' many affairs, this time with a mortal woman named Alcmene. The God of the Sky disguised himself as Alcmene's husband in order to make love to her and impregnate her. Her husband returned home later that night and Alcmene became pregnant with his son at the same time so she was pregnant with twin boys sired by different fathers. One of the boys was the legendary Hercules. Obviously Alcmene was worried that Hera would try to kill Hercules.

"Alcmene decided to expose her half-godchild, who was taken up by Athena to see Hera. Zeus' wife did not recognise baby Hercules and inadvertently nursed him out of her motherly instincts. The powerful infant suckled so excessively that he hurt Hera who pushed him away. Her milk then showered across the sky and formed the Milky Way, according to legend. Meanwhile, Hercules acquired supernatural powers from the milk.

"In defiance, Hera sent down two enormous serpents to the babies' crib so she might be rid of the twins. Unlike his brother, Hercules was not distressed and effortlessly strangled the serpent in his fist. This act confirmed Hercules' supernatural strength and his half-god status.

"Like his unfaithful father Zeus, Hercules had several wives and many affairs. Hercules tried to cross a river with his third wife. A centaur named Nessus assisted the lady but tried to take advantage of her. Hercules, the mighty warrior, was on the shore and was not pleased by the centaur's actions so he shot the centaur with a poisoned arrow.

"As Nessus lay dying, he plotted his revenge. He instructed Hercules' wife to gather up his blood and spilled semen in order to prevent her husband from being unfaithful. All she had to do was apply the centaur's poisoned fluids to Hercules' clothes. Eventually Hercules was enamoured by another and she followed through with Nessus' lethal plan of soaking his clothes in the poison. When Hercules put on his clothes he was immediately in agony as the poison burned the flesh from his bones. He then chose to die on a pyre to end his suffering. As the flames ate away at his mortal body, all that survived was an immortal and divine entity.

"Hercules then became a full god and was re-united with his father on Mount Olympus. He then married his fourth and final wife. As the legend concludes, Hercules lived on a mountain top with Hera, the goddess, whose Herculean efforts to kill him failed and in the end Hercules was killed by the trait that Hera despised so much – infidelity. Finally, what do you see as the moral of this legend?"

"That is an amazing legend. The moral of the legend is clear – that your bad choices and actions all have consequences."

"You're right! Everything that one does has repercussions. It's like the English proverb – you reap what you sow. Even when it appears they are getting away with something eventually everyone has to face up to the consequences of their harmful actions and choices, just like Hera, Zeus and Hercules. That's karma for you. What goes around comes around. We get entangled in karmic relationships where we have important life lessons to learn from each other's behaviours and choices.

"Moving on from karma, these legendary gods and goddesses left amazing temples in their honour. It was believed a diver unexpectedly saw a temple submerged in Valletta's Grand Harbour, at the foot of Fort Saint Angelo. The city was built around Fort Saint Angelo, the headquarters of the Sovereign Military Order of Malta and the military arm of the Roman Catholic Church.

"Fort Saint Angelo, like Vatican City, is a state within a city as they have their own head of state and issue passports. The power of the Knights of Malta is deeply rooted in tradition and mystery. Like Star Wars there are good and bad knights and you may have to kiss a lot of toads before you meet your knight in shining armour."

"Now I know where the headquarters of the knights is I'm not going to kiss any toads!" Eve declared.

"Fort Saint Angelo was built on top of a medieval castle known in Latin as *Castrum Maris*, Castle of the Sea. This castle was built on top of the Roman Temple of Juno, which was built on top of the Phoenician Temple of Astarte. The temple extended over a large part of the harbour, even far out into the sea and you could see that it was constructed of megalithic rectangular blocks of astonishing size, renowned in the ancient world. The temple was dismantled because it damaged ships' hulls when entering the Grand Harbour.

"The remains of the temple are under water and officially undiscovered. It has been rumoured that naval divers have caught glimpses of treasures beneath the sea. The sheer size of this megalithic temple is huge compared to Ħaġar Qim and Ġgantija temples and you can understand why every culture wanted to take over this spot. Could you imagine the telluric energy of this sacred site? It's astonishing we have barely scratched the surface as to what lies beneath," Buznanna noted.

Buznanna and Eve had been eating, walking and talking for almost half an hour. They could see the megalithic freestanding temples appearing as they approached like tiny ants. Eve only caught the beginning of Buznanna's sentence:

"Welcome to my playground! But watch where you are w..." Eve tripped over a deep grove in the ground; the basket on her shoulder and its contents went flying into the air for a brief moment before landing on the ground. Eve managed to stop the impact of the fall with the palms of her hands and her knees, which were grazed and oozing blood. She stood up slowly and although a bit shaken she could still move everything so nothing seemed to be broken.

Buznanna rushed over to help Eve. "Are you okay, darling? I was just trying to warn you about the cart ruts, but hadn't finished my sentence before you fell in," Buznanna said.

"The what? What are cart ruts?" Eve sounded a bit grumpy because she had been too preoccupied to take care of where she was walking in such rocky terrain.

Buznanna started to giggle when she realised no serious injury was caused; the fall must have looked amusing from her angle. "Let's find a big stone to sit on – that shouldn't be too hard around here! The good news is the pastizzi are still in their brown bag and the glass bottles of Kinnie are not broken so our lunch is intact. Always better to look at the bright side of every situation, my girl."

They found a large stone slab to sit on while Buznanna pulled out four Band Aids from her bag for the four grazes Eve had acquired on her palms and knees.

"I'm a bit clumsy like you. I always carry Band Aids with me. There you go, dear. All better now?" Buznanna smiled and planted a kiss on her forehead.

"Yes, all good," Eve reassured her. At this stage she

was carefully investigating what she had tripped over. She picked up her binoculars and followed the pair of cart ruts carved deep into the hard limestone bedrock all the way to the edge of the precipitous cliff where they ended abruptly.

"What are cart ruts and what were they used for?"

"Malta is home to the highest concentration of cart ruts in the world. There are as many as one hundred and fifty sites that have them, sprawling for kilometres across the islands, crossing bays – they can even be found underwater. This is evident at St. George's Bay at Birżebbuġa. The cart ruts and quarries were part of the neolithic period.

"Similar types of drilling can be seen in the unfinished sections of the hypogeum, suggesting neolithic tools and technology might have engineered the first cart ruts, well before the Phoenicians arrived. Many researchers believe the cart ruts are connected with the ancient quarries and were used for transporting materials and precious resources. The deeper these ruts are found beneath the sea, the stronger the argument becomes that they date from a much earlier period." Buznanna continued, "The presence of cart ruts near the neolithic temple of Ħaġar Qim are believed to extend from the temple sites into the sea and on the island of Filfla as well. This is evidence that Filfla was originally connected to the southwest coast of Malta when sea levels were much lower. Science confirms that during a series of apocalyptic events, the principal fault, known as the Maghlaq Fault, brutally tore Filfla away from the mainland, like some giant rock being hurled out to sea to begin its isolated existence we see today.

"Filfla is composed of upper coralline limestone but the southwest coast of Malta in the same region is made up of lower coralline and globigerina limestone. Therefore, Filfla is two hundred metres higher than the southwest coast of Malta. There are five different rock layers on the

Maltese Islands and each layer has different fossil evidence. The composition of the upper coralline limestone shows that deposition took place in a shallow and extremely agitated sea environment. The shallow deposition took place due to the uplift of the northern border of the Pantelleria Rift. This layer contains an abundance of information for researchers in the fossil remains such as the cetacean bones of whales and dolphins."

"Why were the cart ruts so extensive?" Eve asked.

"It is evidence that Malta was a larger landmass. Wherever we find the cart ruts beneath the sea, we can also expect to find the constructions they served. The cart ruts have been discovered running on the sea floor, which denotes Malta was a larger island, and the cart ruts date back to the last Ice Age. During the ice ages, the sea level dropped and then rose again as the ice caps melted. The end of the most recent Ice Age, believed to be approximately 12,000 years ago, raised sea levels leaving the islands of Malta, Comino and Gozo separated.

"The cart ruts denote that Malta was some kind of industrial complex with a sophisticated network of ruts that were used to transport valuable resources. Cart ruts, if built by these same mysterious temple builders, is further evidence of sophisticated engineering know-how and intense prehistoric activity on the islands. According to Maltese folklore, the cart ruts were used to bring sailing boats with wheels onto the land. One thing is for certain – these cart ruts have got researchers in a rut. Pun intended," Buznanna said, as she smiled at Eve.

They were at a high point on a cliff looking directly at the little island known as Filfla.

"The small rock next to Filfla is known as Filfoletta, a diminutive of Filfla."

"Has anything been constructed on Filfla?" Eve asked.

"The only known permanent structure on Filfla was a chapel built inside a cave in 1343, which served as both a place of worship and a store of food and water for sailors stranded in times of bad weather. A late medieval painting known as the Madonna ta' Filfla, showing strong Renaissance influences, was taken from the chapel probably when it was deconsecrated in 1575. The cave chapel and food depot collapsed after an earthquake in 1856 that swallowed up part of Filfla beneath the sea. The Madonna ta' Filfla painting is now in the vestry of the parish church of Żurrieq.

"One last thing found on Filfla was a freshwater spring, which provided a source of drinking water. It was feasible given that at sea level, a layer of impermeable blue clay could support a rainwater-fed, perched aquifer which recharged annually during the rainy season, eventually leaking out through a spring." Buznanna turned round to point to the temples of Ħaġar Qim and Mnajdra.

"There are a number of man-made excavations in the limestone rock surface believed to be 5,000 years old, which collect rainwater and are still used for irrigation today," Buznanna explained.

"During the last Ice Age was Malta in a good location for a civilisation to grow?" Eve asked.

"Yes I believe Malta had a temperate climate not a hot, dry Mediterranean climate. With its vast natural resources and pleasant climate Malta would have been an ideal location for a civilisation to flourish. Malta's availability of freshwater springs would have been essential for survival. Malta is fundamentally an aquifer, as the limestone rock holds usable water in interconnected fractures and cracks, which originally formed on the ocean bed some 25 million years ago. The presence of aquifers, acoustically designed neolithic temples and a complex network of cart ruts is evidence of some sort of industry that points to a sacred site where a civilisation once flourished. Limestone has shaped Malta's topography, tourism and economy and is still a valuable resource."

They turned away from the towering, whitewashed cliffs after they had exhausted their conversation and walked back up to the temples of Ħaġar Qim and Mnajdra to take another look with the sparkling azure Mediterranean Sea behind them. The refreshing sea breezes caressed their backs and dried the perspiration as they endured the arduous walk up the hill, working off the calories from the pastizzi they had eaten earlier.

"My beautiful playground and sanctuary is very close to my heart. In ancient times buildings were constructed in accordance to ley lines, sacred geometry and mirrored constellations. The intelligent temple design increased consciousness and raised human frequencies, enabling every cell to vibrate more efficiently, thus improving the ability of the body to heal itself from disease and enhancing natural holistic healing. The ancients worked in harmony with animals and the environment and used all their senses, including the magnetic sense that animals possess. The idea is that people would feel re-energised when visiting the temples. These temples of extreme significance were built on special places of energy.

"Often sacred spots would remain and new civilisations would build on top of the old because of the good energy present. These master builders understood and knew how to manipulate subtle energies and therefore you see the smaller stones being used on top of the larger megalithic stones, as they provided the right type of energy field that was uplifting. Temples and sacred places were built on telluric energy, where ley lines or dragon lines intersect. What do you think of my playground and the temples in front of us?" Buznanna asked.

"The paired temples are special beyond words. The

Buznanna's Playground

spectacular temple surroundings of whitewashed cliffs, sea, cart ruts and isolated Filfla in the distance makes your playground intriguing, mysterious and leaves me wondering. Why don't we know all the answers? How old are these temples, Buznanna?"

"I understand your frustration. It makes me feel claustrophobic and I want to break free from our current belief system. We have suppressed or destroyed the truth when it doesn't fit in with the present system. Cataclysms wiped out any prehistoric records and only those who lived on mountains survived great devastation and were able to pass on oral traditions.

"I believe the megalithic temples are much older than currently believed. A layer of virgin silt, evidence of pre-flood, has some researchers putting the date back to 10,500 BC. The silt has been found across Malta, which indicates cataclysms involving tsunamis and flooding. The megalithic structures of heavy stone blocks have crumbled to the ground and due to their size and weight remained stationary at the base of the structure.

"The artefacts from the temples would have been swallowed by the sea, just leaving the heavy stone. The stones fell in an easterly direction, meaning that a wave coming from the west of the Mediterranean destroyed the structures. There is evidence that the mortar used in construction was damaged by water and some of the mortar has joined some of the fallen blocks and petrified into hard stone. In the 1950s all the megalithic temples were rebuilt and repaired.

"The Venus of Malta statuette was found at Ħaġar Qim temple buried beneath a rectangular megalithic stone and that was a significant discovery. The Venus of Willendorf, discovered in the town of Willendorf in Austria, is a similar limestone statuette and is dated as far back as 28,000 BC, which will give you a better indication of the age of these paired temples. Three statuettes and several pieces of a much larger stone statue discovered at the temple complexes shared similar characteristics to the Venus of Malta statuette. These statuettes commonly lacked feet and sexual characteristics. The more developed types of Maltese cult-statuettes may have represented asexual or hermaphrodite beings.

"Do these statuettes that appeared throughout a wide region and over a long period of time represent an archetype of a female Supreme Creator?" Buznanna felt comfortable with this concept as the essence of the Goddess and the Divine Feminine incorporates birthing, creation and immortality because everything on Earth is born of the feminine which embraces an honourable relationship with Mother Earth, our planet.

"I agree there are a lot of legends in Malta that point towards a matriarchal society and the admiration of the Divine Feminine Goddess. There is also a strong association with the goddess, the Maltese archipelago and the Mediterranean Sea. When did the flooding take place?" Eve asked as she pondered the connections in her mind.

"Well I'm sure you've heard of the story of Noah's ark. It was believed to be during the great biblical flood that the temples were inundated; therefore, the megalithic temples were built well before the flood cataclysm struck.

"At that time the island of Malta was a larger landmass. More convincingly, extensive valleys such as Wied il-Ghasel, Wied il-Ghasri, Wied ix-Xlendi and Wied iż-Żurrieq would have needed an extensive area to support and retain the deep waters in the valleys which accrued over the millennia. The rocks are eroded deeper forming a valley known as *wied* in the Maltese language. A French geologist, Deodat de Dolomieu, observed the extensive fracture lines towards the south of the islands and concluded that Malta was an ancient mountain. Many other scholars validated his findings. I like to think of the Earth as a living organism forever expanding, contracting and changing. The Maltese islands looked different in ancient times and some of the treasures of lost knowledge still lie beneath," said Buznanna thoughtfully.

"Who do you think built Ħaġar Qim and Mnajdra?" Eve asked.

"I would say a different race of people with elongated skulls were responsible for the building of these numerous megalithic structures. These long-headed people disappeared suddenly, probably migrating to nearby Egypt when their lifestyle and existence became threatened."

"Have any elongated skulls been found in Malta?" Eve asked.

"They certainly have. Inside the hypogeum of Ħal Saflieni they discovered 7,000 elongated skulls that were buried with a small statue of a sleeping goddess, believed by archaeologists to be devoted to the Mother Goddess worship."

"That is a large number of elongated skulls!" Eve interjected.

"Scientists analysed the skulls and came to the same conclusion as in Peru, identifying two groups, some of completely natural origin, and others that had been manipulated through headboards and bandaging. The fascinating finding was that their skulls were elongated, similar to the skulls of the Egyptian pharaohs like Akhenaten and Nefertiti and provide a link between the ancient Egyptian and Maltese cultures and a race of sacerdotal men associated with the snake and goddess cult. Interestingly, they had naturally elongated skulls – and one of the skulls, out of only a handful that survived, lacked the Fossa median, the join that runs along the top of the skull. It is known that some of the skulls were on display in the Archaeological Museum in Valletta. However, all the skulls that had been found in the hypogeum, along with other elongated skulls found across multiple ancient sites in Malta, disappeared without a trace and have never been recovered. What remains to testify their existence and their abnormality are the photos and written material describing the natural abnormalities of this race with the elongated skulls.

"The National Geographic magazine wrote an article in the 1920s describing the first inhabitants of Malta as a race with elongated skulls, akin to the early people of Egypt, who spread westward along the north coast of Africa to Sicily, Sardinia and Spain and then to surrounding areas. Contrary to the official story of the Ħal Saflieni hypogeum being a burial ground, it was a more significant place than people know.

"The temple people were more than just good engineers and architects. They may well have been the custodians of great wisdom and knowledge as well. Certainly they knew how to live peacefully and lived in a Golden Age. There may be much more to discover and learn from them. The rulers of ancient Egypt, Akhenaten and Nefertiti, had natural dolichocephalic skulls like the skulls discovered in Malta. They were the popular leaders who changed Egypt's culture for the better, building a beautiful city in Amarna."

"Did Akhenaten father any children?" Eve asked.

"Yes, six girls with Nefertiti, and the most famous one was Tutankhamun possibly from another wife. The Pharaoh Akhenaten, his children and his first wife Nefertiti were all depicted with elongated skulls. These elongated skulls found in Malta and Egypt were genetic, not manipulated into shape by bound headboards. They were the ruling class often living separately and devoted to spirituality, building, art and teaching. Akhenaten constructed an entirely new capital at an uninhabited place,

Buznanna's Playground

which we now call Amarna, out in the desert. Many beautiful works of art depict Nefertiti standing equal next to her husband, honouring the feminine in balance with the masculine. Akhenaten had himself portrayed as a sphinx bathed in solar rays, sexless and with feminine features of wide hips and a narrow waistline. These beautiful works of art tell a story of equality, harmony, balance and honouring all that the feminine encompasses, which is what we are yearning for in times of unbalance, war and patriarchal dominance. As the Amun priesthood and patriarchal rule clawed back their hold on Egypt, they suppressed the matriarchal past. This switch from matriarchal to patriarchal power supported the right-brain approach to conflict we face today of power, greed, war and disagreements.

"Ancient Malta, followed by ancient Egypt, existed in matriarchal times, where the left-brain approach functioned alongside the masculine right-brain approach. Either approach dominating the other never creates an ideal environment, nor a high state of consciousness."

"I wish the Golden Age would return soon. Are you saying that the Ancient Maltese civilisation predates the Egyptian civilisation?" asked Eve.

"Yes, you may see the Golden Age in your time after much of the old world breaks down. Ġgantija temple on the island of Gozo predates the rise of Egyptian civilization officially by 2,600 years. It's difficult to be precise with the date because you can't date stone. You can only analyse associated carbon matter, like wood, and provide a general time period in history. No matter the age of the Egyptian civilisation, the Maltese civilisation is older on the basis of the weathering of the stone. It is likely that Malta contributed to the rise of the Egyptian civilisation and developments. The disappearance and decline of the temple culture in Malta corresponds directly with the development of Egyptian civilisation. The master builders of Malta may have been the same race of elongated-skulled people who at this turning point started the flourishing Egyptian civilization that occurs so close in time. An analogy is the English civilisation which started on a small island and developed a great empire from an island and colonised America."

"It makes sense that they migrated to other lands in the vicinity when their existence was threatened. Why are these temples circular when most houses today are square or rectangular?" Eve inquired.

"That's a great observation. All the temples on the islands have this common feature, described as trefoil. Circular abodes or temples that respect sacred geometry are more complex to build, but enhance acoustic properties and the body's ability to heal itself. The slabs of stone used in the temple walls are four inches thick to reverberate and echo sound. The Hal Saflieni hypogeum serves as another great example which exhibits acoustic properties due to its shape and construction."

"Why would the temples need good acoustic properties?" Eve asked.

"The only answer to that question is that this race was different from ours. They had extrasensory capacity and used sound and magnetism for many different activities in comparison to us. Sound was not just used for language and communication but for healing, for construction and the movement of large objects. They had a magnetic sense to detect ley lines, magnetic portals and manipulate the electromagnetic force to levitate objects. It is difficult to comprehend because we don't possess the same elongated skulls, but we have been left these amazing temples littered across the archipelago as evidence."

"How was the long-headed race different from us?" Eve inquired.

"The naturally elongated skulls found on Malta have also been found in Egypt and South America, where the cranium has a natural lengthened posterior part of the skullcap. Humans are born with five main sections of soft tissue in their heads to facilitate the birthing process. These sections eventually fuse as the skull grows, seen as a knitted pattern on the skull.

"A few skulls unearthed in the Hal Saflieni hypogeum remain as evidence, behind a glass enclosure today at the Archaeological Museum in Valletta. I have seen the skulls on display. One skull completely lacked the median knitting, technically named sagitta. It has been suggested by anthropologists that their heads were naturally larger and elongated, and they could slither like snakes, stand and move on land. The long-headed race appeared to be amphibious, but avoided harsh sunlight as it harmed their sensitive skin and good health. Only six skulls are on display in the Archaeological Museum of Valletta. Maybe they pose a threat to religious institutions and their current teachings," Buznanna sighed.

"Why would they pose a threat?"

"In my opinion, before the patriarchal powers took over religions, churches or places of worship, it was a matriarchal culture and one that practised greater balance between the masculine and feminine elements. It was a harmonious goddess culture that triggered the last Golden Age, a period of primordial peace, harmony, prosperity and stability. Peace and harmony prevailed and people did not have to work to feed themselves, as the Earth provided food in abundance and all the free resources they required to sustain a healthy, prosperous life. They lived to a ripe old age with a youthful appearance, eventually dying peacefully, with their spirits living on as guardians.

"The patriarchal and the fact that men are physically stronger than women enabled them to coerce their way to be the leaders of religion, locking women out. This is where the imbalance starts and we see the goddess being replaced by the god. We get the token women left, like the Virgin Mary, who couldn't be completely defamed or vilified because she represented the loving mother, with whom we can all connect in one way or another."

"What is the connection between the long-headed race and present-day humans? It seems that there is more to it than people know," Eve observed.

"Excavations at Saqqara, Egypt, by Walter Emery in the 1930s discovered a pre-dynastic group of people who had long-headed skulls, larger than the local ethnic group, with fair hair and a taller and heavier build. Scholars believe they weren't indigenous to Egypt but held important positions in government and priestly classes, avoiding the common people when possible and dealing only with the aristocratic classes. This race was connected to the priesthood known as the Shemshu Hor, or disciples of Horus.

"We get this strong connection to the long-headed serpent priests, which could only be created through a goddess. The long-headed race was different from the natives that lived in Malta first – they disappeared and then reappeared in Egypt. They were associated with the veneration of the Mother Goddess and the thaumaturgy powers of the serpent priests. Thousands of years later people venerated the Virgin Mary or the mysteries of the great Mother Goddess.

"This brings me to an important point – that the unusual acoustic properties of the Ħal Saflieni hypogeum and temples were used by the long-headed race. When I make reference to the long-headed race, the elongated skulls, the dolichocephalic skulls, the Shemshu Hor, the serpent and the Jedai priests, they are all the same hybrid humans. This long-headed race had advanced sonar capabilities like dolphins; thereby, sound had many functions, not just for moving heavy objects and communication.

"Their elongated skulls enabled sonar capabilities, increasing their intellectual and sensory capacity beyond human comprehension today. Like the dolphins, their elongated skulls gave them extrasensory abilities. The characteristic trefoil shape of the temples is reminiscent of a modern sound-transmission antenna resembling a typical 800 MHz wireless antenna pattern. All antenna patterns have similar characteristics consisting of main beam lobe, side lobes, nulls and back lobe. The temple site of Ħaġar Qim was a perfect location due to its antenna, elevation, azimuths and power settings. Ħaġar Qim has all the right characteristics to send signals, using the electromagnetic spectrum, to great distances because it is on a gentle slope.

"The ancients originally placed it there as a portal to focus the sound and energy frequencies depending on the shape and size of the temple chamber or lobe. This determined the frequencies the temple antenna transmitted. Legend has it that mermaids would lure seafarers by projecting and amplifying their singing from the high temple walls, as merfolk could live temporarily on land. This could mean that Malta was an electro-magnetic communication hub, a power grid or a transmitting station of earth energies linking all the pyramids and temples around the world. But considering it was built by a different race it could also mean an antenna pointing to the stars or something we cannot understand yet because we don't have elongated skulls and the extrasensory capacity," Buznanna explained.

"I see what you are getting at. Humans today can't relate to this long-headed race because we don't have the extra senses. You are trying to open my mind to the possibility of a different race existing."

"Exactly! When I was young there was what was known as the bell of Ħaġar Qim. This bell was a megalithic stone on the floor in ruins that we could ring by hitting it with other stones and it resonated like a bell, reaching great distances. When Ħaġar Qim was restored, the megalithic stone bell was put back where it belonged on top of the doorway, the lintel. The purpose of placing the ringing bell stone on the lintel shows advanced methods of communication and knowledge of the electronic-magnetic (EM) spectrum of frequencies.

"The long-headed serpent priests were also referred to as the Jedai priests, the enlightened, who used the language of light, sound and magnetism to tune the planet like a musical instrument."

"Wow, the Jedai priests remind me of the Jedi knights in Star Wars with their light sabres. Luke Skywalker was my favourite. Getting back to it, what was the purpose of the bell at Ħaġar Qim?" Eve asked.

"Of course, Star Wars is a great analogy. My favourite is Yoda and I know the force is strong with you, Eve. Now in regards to the bell at Ħaġar Qim, it could have been used for many things. If this long-headed race was more highly sensory and technologically advanced than we are it could have been used for inter-dimensional time travel. Another possibility is that it was used to generate anti-gravity for lifting heavy blocks of stone in building.

"This ancient race knew how to tap into free energy, employing scalar physics, like Tesla. Perhaps future discoveries will reveal the existence of a worldwide temple system in prehistory, mounted like antennae on the key energy meridians, which were used by the ancient serpent

Jedai priests."

"What would be the purpose of that?"

"Well, the long-headed race was highly evolved and able to stabilise the tectonic plates of the planet through light and sound like a musical system. For example, the Egyptian obelisks are like giant acupuncture needles, often in pairs, which can either disperse or collect positive or negative energies to benefit the populace and release tectonic pressure from the Earth. Perhaps the reason why the Great Pyramid of Giza is located at the exact centre of the Earth's landmass is not a coincidence but has some benefit in stabilising the tectonic plates. By stabilising the tectonic plates of the planet, they were able to minimise cataclysmic events, so we have cataclysmic geology at its best. When the sea levels were much lower and the Earth had a larger landmass, the centre may have shifted in the vicinity of Malta.

"I can imagine these paired temples or the abodes of the long-headed race would have been a sight to behold in all their glory with their circular gold, corbelled roofs. As the time cycle comes to an end, I feel much will be rediscovered. By understanding the ancient past we understand our present circumstances and that is an important connection. One thing I want you to remember, my girl, is don't believe everything that is told to you – use your own discernment and inner knowing," Buznanna advised.

"You mentioned the Shemsu Hor earlier. The word for sun, *xemx*, in Maltese sounds the same as Shemsu. What is the connection?" Eve inquired.

"I have also read a lot of Egyptian literature on the sons of Horus, known as the Shemsu Hor. Indeed the word for sun sounds the same as Shemsu. Note the 'x' has a 'sh' pronunciation. The sons of Horus were believed to be hybrids of the long-headed ones and Homo sapiens. Horus is the falcon-headed Sky God and the son of Osiris. Unlike humans today who have five senses, according to the wisdom keepers at that time this race had up to 365 senses.

"In the beginning, the Shesh people whose ancestors included Anubis and Osiris are believed to be descendants of Horus. The divine beings manifested more often at that time to try to halt the degradation and the loss of senses among the Shesh people. Their skulls were of abnormal size and are dolichocephalic in nature so the cranium as seen from above is oval, and is about twenty-five percent longer than it is wide. The skeletons are larger than the average population and the skeletal frame is broader and heavier. Some scholars have identified them as the followers of Horus and found that in their lifetime they filled an important priestly role. With regard to the long-headed skulls, it seems that it is not a prehistoric lineage based on evolution but rather a lineage coming from a cycle of civilization before the biblical flood. They were the masterminds behind the creation of a great civilisation during the last Golden Age."

Buznanna had a wealth of knowledge to share at her playground. They sat on a large slab of stone under the shade of a carob tree enjoying their last bottles of Kinnie. Buznanna married science and spirituality to develop her understanding of the ancient past, a kind of spiritual science that came from the intelligence of her heart as well as her mind. Buznanna was a very special woman in Eve's heart.

"Sorry to interrupt your thoughts again, my girl, but I want to give you something that is very precious to me and you must promise me to wear it all the time. You're going to need this more than I do so wear it at all times and for protection." Buznanna reached to the back of her neck with both hands and undid her necklace. She held the pendant in the palm of her hand.

"This pendant is one of a kind. It has been passed down through many generations from my great-grandmother and only to the firstborn female. This tradition is ancient and I don't know when it started. This ankh and eight-rayed star pendant is part of the strong matriarchal tradition in our family and you are the rightful owner of this pendant. Even though your parents left Malta, I am fortunate to have this opportunity to give it to you in person. I expect you to pass it on in the future."

The ankh pendant was attached to an eight-pointed star. Eve was instantly curious about the black and gold star. It was opaque looking, with an iridescent metallic sheen. The pendant looked thick and solid as it reflected the golden inclusions of mineral crystals and rock. The random streaks of gold glistened in the subdued afternoon rays of the retiring sun.

"What is the star made of?"

"It's made out of a thick piece of obsidian, an igneous rock, derived from the Latin word *ignis* meaning fire, that forms when molten rock material cools rapidly and solidifies without crystallisation. The star was handcrafted from an extremely special piece of black obsidian infused with golden streaks. It is a rare piece of obsidian known as golden obsidian, due to offsetting a golden iridescence. It would have been a sought-after specimen in the making of jewellery."

"Where did the obsidian come from?" Eve asked.

"Possibly from nearby Pantelleria, an Italian island in the Strait of Sicily or from Mount Etna, an active stratovolcano on the east coast of Sicily."

"What does the eight-pointed star represent?" Eve asked as she admired how precisely the star points had been carved.

"According to the Sumerians who were among the first astronomers, mapping the stars into sets of constellations, many of which survived in the zodiac and were recognized by the ancient Greeks, the eight-pointed star represented the goddess Inanna, the Sumerian queen of the heavens known as the Light Bringer. The number eight on its sides is the infinity symbol, the never-ending pursuit of the wealth of knowledge, destiny and justice. The eight-rayed star is linked to the themes of synchronicity and mysticism known as synchromysticism, a portmanteau word. For the Essenes the eight-pointed star represented Venus, light and mystery. The Romans use to call Venus Lucifer, meaning "light-bearer" in Latin *lux, lucis,* "light," and *ferre,* "to bear, bring." The Mayans said Venus was born in 3,119 BC when the Mayan Calendar started.

"Venus is the brightest morning and evening star depending on the season. Venus has been associated with the divine feminine goddesses throughout time. The eight-pointed star in my opinion is the symbol of infinite knowledge, abundance, mysticism and synchronicity all in one.

"I always recalled my dreams and astral travelled in my sleep and this star provided me with great insight, knowledge and protection. I never felt afraid to explore my unconscious world when I wore it. It will do the same for you. It is a matriarchal heirloom, an old piece of jewellery that has been in our family and possessed by the eldest great-granddaughters for centuries. I was around the same age as you when I received the pendant. It is my duty to explain to you everything I know. You are the eldest great-granddaughter in a long unbroken chain and this is rightfully yours now."

"It is so special, thank you. I will treasure it and promise to uphold the tradition." Eve planted a kiss on Buznanna's cheek to show her appreciation and gratitude for her inheritance that went back to a time when they worshipped the Mother Goddess.

"I have not finished. There is more to show you." Buznanna opened another device attached to the star by a spring lever.

"What is that?"

"It's an original Egyptian *ankh* made out of an unknown metal. It has a cross-like base with a circular loop handle at the top, affixed to the eight-pointed star. The loop is the perfect symbol of what has neither beginning nor end and symbolises the eternity of the soul. The loop can be attached to your finger, like a ring, with the star lying flat on the palm of your hand, while still on the chain." Buznanna placed the loop of the ankh on her finger to show Eve.

"Is this particular ankh used for anything?" Eve asked as she opened and closed the ankh in her hands.

"I don't know what the ankh is used for – I suppose that will be left for you to discover. You must know no ankh has ever been found in Egypt in tombs or in temples. This could be the one and only. Possibly it is some kind of tool that the ancients used and maybe they haven't been found because they were melted down."

"Wow, I wonder what I can use it for?"

"I'll leave that for you to discover. You will write your own future."

"What does the ankh represent?" Eve inquired.

"The ankh cross, I believe, is a powerful symbol which encompasses many difficult concepts in life. The ankh represents life, death, immortality, balance, fertility, prosperity and the symbol for a hermaphrodite and the tree of life. The ankh is the Isis knot and is also referred to as the Blood of Isis and is believed to be a stylized rendering of female genitalia symbolizing the womb of the goddess.

"Isis was the wife of Osiris, god of nature, death and resurrection whose backbone was the *djed* pillar or the tree of life. The four rungs of the djed pillar represented the four elements and dimensions of the created world. Embodying the divine masculine and the creative feminine principles, the Isis knot and the djed pillar together provided powerful protection and were two of the most popular amulets in ancient Egypt.

"The djed was considered necessary to aid in the transformation of the physical body to its spiritual form of consciousness and light. The ankh and the djed may have been tools used for spiritual enlightenment and for awakening the kundalini energy. Osiris commanded mortal humans to keep away from the tree of life until they accessed the hidden knowledge and became like him, an immortal god.

"The cross represents the state of trance or death. The immortal gods and goddesses, like Isis, are depicted holding the ankh to show that they command the powers of life and death. The dead carry it at the time their souls are weighed, as a sign that they seek this same immortality from the gods. Sometimes the ankh is placed on the forehead, between the eyes, and then it symbolizes the duty of the adept to keep the mysteries secret from the uninitiated.

"The adept is blessed by vision, endowed with clairvoyance to pierce the veil of the beyond. This loop symbolizes the inexhaustible essence of the life force identified with the goddess Isis, from her womb shaped like a chalice from which all life flows.

"These are the main representations of the ankh and I believe it's a very powerful tool. I want you to explore its possible uses in the future, as I have exhausted all my efforts. You have rightfully inherited this precious pendant, which you must pledge never to remove from around your neck. There are two specially designed safety locks on the gold chain and this is necessary because the pendant is irreplaceable. This is the perfect time for you to have it – just wear it close to your heart at all times."

Eve smiled proudly at Buznanna as she attached the necklace around Eve's neck and placed a kiss on her third eye as she touched the top posterior of her skull fumbling with a bony hump.

"What is it?" Eve asked as she could feel the small hump under Buznanna's finger.

"Your posterior parietal bone is protruding and I have exactly the same. Some would consider it a deformity of the skull, but I would say it is characteristic of a pure Mediterranean race. Malta is not a medley of various nations, but the physiological evidence suggests that the Maltese are a comparatively pure race. If we look at the 6,000-year-old skulls found in the Ħal Saflieni hypogeum they represented the oldest Maltese race, which have pure ovoid and beloid skulls, denoting the Maltese race had long-headed skulls. An analyses of skull shapes in Maltese cemeteries in the 1900s revealed that most skulls are ovoid and beloid like the Ħal Saflieni skulls.

"Another characteristic of this Mediterranean race is the blood type. Rhesus negative is considered alien or from a monkey, but in fact if you look at the concentration of people with RH-, it is concentrated in the North African coast of the Mediterranean Sea. Generally speaking this incorporates the Maltese, the Berbers, the Basques, the Welsh, the Irish, the Bretons and the Guanches. Your return to your birthplace has provided us with this valuable union and I finally get to disseminate all this information to you as it was meant to be.

"May you always be blessed and protected on your journeys. Live your life with discernment and an open heart, as love is the only way. Never listen to negativity and not being good enough, as you are a sensitive soul, so rise above it like a soaring eagle. Release your fears when they arise, have faith and patience that all will unravel at the time it was meant to. Go forward with good faith and a pure heart. Share your knowledge with love and for the greater good. The time will arrive when there will be great unrest in the world and people will be ready to really listen. It will be shifting old paradigms that no longer serve the greater good. Let the spirit of the Great Goddess who wears the blue rose in her hair with a halo of stars illuminate you and lead you to the music of truth and knowledge.

"Your boundless spiritual journey is waiting to be written. The wearer of the ankh and star pendant is destined to share these great mysteries." Buznanna held the pendant in her hands, infusing it with her loving intentions and blessings for her great-granddaughter and the adventure that would await her when she searched.

Chapter 6

Hollow Earth

They sat in a small quaint café in Paola for their scheduled private tour of the Hal-Saflieni hypogeum with one of Buznanna's friends. hypogeum means underground, as it is a subterranean structure. It is the only known prehistoric multi-storey labyrinthine complex of man-made chambers hewn out of the limestone extending at least eleven metres below street level. It is now listed as a UNESCO World Heritage Site.

They scanned the café menu to order breakfast and Eve quickly spotted her favourites – sweet ricotta cannoli and thick hot drinking chocolate. Cannoli is a fried crispy cylinder shell filled with sweet ricotta and mascarpone cream filling. The open ends are often decorated with chocolate chips or chopped cherries or pistachios. Eating cannoli was a messy experience but a delicious one. Eve picked it up and bit into the crunchy shell as it broke into pieces, the sweet ricotta cream oozing onto her fingers. She quickly licked her fingers and placed the broken pieces on her plate, as they would be easier to eat with a spoon, once broken.

"When and how was the hypogeum discovered?" Eve asked.

"It was accidently discovered in 1902, when the village of Paola was being transformed by many new housing developments. At the time, the placename for the area was Tal-Gherien meaning 'of the caves' to suggest the district was known for cave formations and underground structures. A group of workmen were demolishing a well as they were lowering the foundations of the home. Once the well was demolished the men's shovels got stuck on some large object below. They couldn't continue with their shovels so they began the slow task of revealing the object that blocked their path. After days of slowly digging around it, a large piece of gold began to shimmer in the sun. Rumour has it they found a stunning golden bull underneath the well. And beneath the well was an even bigger discovery – a multi-storey subterranean structure known as the Ħal-Saflieni hypogeum.

"Another rumour concerns a tourist who convinced a guide to allow her to investigate one of the burial chambers of the last chamber in the third sub-basement. The guide was hesitant and appeared to know something she didn't, but finally consented and told her that she could enter at her own risk. She entered with candle in hand and used her dress sash as a guide rope for her friend who followed behind. She crawled through the small passage and emerged into a larger cavern where she found herself on a ledge overlooking a seemingly bottomless chasm. Below and on the other side of the chasm was another ledge, which appeared to lead to a doorway or tunnel in the far wall.

"What happened next sounds unbelievable, but out of this lower tunnel on the far side of the chasm, she claims, emerged in single file several very large creatures of humanoid form that were completely covered with hair from head to foot, like a Sasquatch or Big Foot. The humanoid creatures noticed her and raised their arms in her direction, at which point a brisk wind began to flurry through the cavern, extinguishing her candle and leaving her in darkness. Then, something wet and slippery, apparently a creature of a different sort, brushed past her. This all happened just as the person behind her was beginning to emerge from the passage and into the cavern. The people behind could not understand her panicked attempts to get back to the hypogeum room, but they consented after she insisted.

"When they found themselves back in the hypogeum chamber, the guide saw her expression and gave her a knowing look like 'I told you so.' On her second visit she saw a new guide who denied that the other guide had ever worked there. Again she got the feeling that this new guide was hiding something," Buznanna said as she dipped her almond biscotti into her tea.

"What a strange story! Where is the golden bull now?"

"Like many things discovered in the hypogeum, the golden bull has mysteriously disappeared. Apparently even the paintings of the bull on the walls have been washed off. The bull seemed to be an important symbol in neolithic times, as it usually represented fertility and male virility. In the vicinity of the Ħal Saflieni hypogeum are the Tarxien temples where archaeologists discovered a flint knife and bull horns buried beneath the doorway at the entrance. It's not only the golden bull that went missing. They discovered over 33,000 skeletons, and among them 7,000 skulls and some were naturally elongated, but only a few have survived.

"The naturally elongated skulls of interest were analysed by archaeologist Robert Bradley, who excavated the hypogeum of Ħal Saflieni directly after Fr. Magri. Bradley found that out of eleven skulls, eight were dolichocephalic and three were sub-dolichocephalic and none of them were related to the Cro-Magnon, indicating they were a different Mediterranean race. Two of the skulls had Neanderthal characteristics, but the excessive dolichocephaly and the convexity of the forehead are not characteristic of the Neanderthals. It's a natural feature of this Mediterranean race and not the result of some congenital disease.

"Some of the skeletons were piled together in the upper chambers from an alluvial event whilst in the deeper chambers of the hypogeum they discovered the naturally long-headed skulls. Scattered amongst the bones were neolithic pottery, amulets and statuettes all jumbled into the red earth as a result of flooding. A similar discovery was made at Santa Luċija hypogeum less than a kilometre away. It was excavated and then sealed up again and covered by a modern cemetery. The Santa Luċija hypogeum is a smaller version of the hypogeum of Ħal Saflieni, with an internal architecture similar to the temples above ground and a trilithon entrance.

"The hypogeum is carved from solid rock and at least three storeys deep, a good example of architecture in the negative. It is believed to be the oldest prehistoric underground temple in the world. Archaeologists believe that the Sleeping Goddess statuette is associated with a relic with a snake symbol on it. There appears to be a strong link between the goddess and the serpent-priest race of elongated skulls. Let me remind you that eleven of the skulls found in the hypogeum were investigated and sent to Malta's National Museum of Archaeology in Valletta. Again it's highly suspicious that 7,000 skulls mysteriously disappeared. In the hypogeum they also found alabaster statues and numerous clay statues of goddesses of fertility with voluptuous figures, the most famous being the figurine of the Sleeping Lady, a real masterpiece.

"Immediately after the discovery of the hypogeum, they decided to call upon a Jesuit priest, Fr. Magri, who was a scholar of antiquities, a Maltese ethnographer, archaeologist and a writer. He was the first to go into the hypogeum and was assigned the task of supervising the excavation of the monument and writing a report on his findings. He wrote a detailed report as they excavated, and he was granted access to the entire site. As events turned out, he was called away to Sfax, in Tunisia, on missionary duties where he passed away unexpectedly. Fr. Magri's draft notes and final report were never found.

"My mother, Maria Bondin knew him personally and said he was extremely passionate about his archaeological work. The disappearance of Fr. Magri was such a loss. She mentioned that while he was researching the Ġgantija Temple in Xagħra, Gozo he discovered two walls at right angles supporting two huge monoliths. He believed it was some sort of outpost to defend the Ġgantija Temple, the nearby Xagħra stone circle and the hypogeum beneath. He referred to this place as Ix-Xagħra ta' Bondin, due to the ceremonies my mother conducted at these sites. According to my mother Fr. Magri was part of her family and they shared many interests and belonged to the same secret society."

"That is fascinating family history. Fr. Magri must have been busy, split between his priestly duties and his role as an archaeologist. It's a shame that Fr. Magri's work never got published. Do you think the dolichocephalic race lived in the hypogeum?"

"Keeping an open mind, this mysterious race may have lived in the hollows of the Earth. The underground chambers could have spanned vast distances underground thereby making this long-headed race's sudden disappearance an easy one. This is not the only hypogeum on the islands – there are many others such as the Santa Luċija hypogeum, the Xagħra hypogeum and the Xewkija hypogeum. Two other hypogea at Misraħ Għonoq and Hal Dmiegh are both in Mosta and another hypogeum is at Tal Bistra, outside of Mosta."

"That's another six hypogea." Eve was keeping count.

"There are even more hypogea, but some have been covered up, left undiscovered or have been built on top of. For example at Xewkija hypogeum in Gozo, Fr. Magri wanted to explore further, but a magnificent church, known as the Rotunda of Xewkija, dedicated to St. John the Baptist, was built over the top of the hypogeum. The Rotunda is the Spiritual Seat of the Knights of the Order of St. John. The marvellous Rotunda is the third highest dome in the world."

"It's a pity we don't know much about all the other hypogea, especially the Xewkija hypogeum that had megalithic foundations," Eve noted with disappointment.

"I agree, some places will remain a mystery, but the Ħal Saflieni hypogeum is truly an enigmatic place. Some believe there was a monumental structure built directly on top and a shrine to mark the spot, like the hypogeum in Gozo beneath the Xagħra stone circle. The monumental trilithon, a structure consisting of two large vertical stones supporting a third stone set horizontally across the top, suggests a possible passageway. This trilithon in the hypogeum has the same architecture as the afterlife door seen frequently in Egyptian monuments. This suggests the entrance to something no one knows but it could be the entrance to the underworld known as Duat by the Egyptians and Hades by the Greeks. Could it be the entrance to a portal which spirals you out into the universe, like a star gate? Or could it be the entrance to the legendary Hollow Earth, access to a gigantic subterranean world?

"According to the book *The Stranger at the Pentagon*, if you live under the crust of the planet, with other methods of lighting and supplementation with minerals and vitamins, the aging process is diminished because you are not exposed to the sun's harmful rays and one would have a higher life expectancy."

"So are you saying that if I go beneath the hypogeum it will lead me to another world, where humans live longer because they live beneath the crust?" asked Eve.

"Yes that's the idea and the hypogeum extends well beyond the limits that are accessible today. Was the underground tunnel network some sort of system of travelling to Europe in the north, and Africa in the south? There are too many unanswered questions!" Buznanna appeared annoyed and frustrated.

"Is the long-headed race linked to other cultures?"

"The long-headed skulls have been found in Siberia, China, Peru and Egypt. The numerous connections between Egypt and Malta are undeniable. It's believed that Man and mitochondrial Eve came out of Africa. The link with Malta's southern continent of Africa is strong and, most notably, Malta's neolithic population bore the natural long-headed skulls like the rulers of ancient Egypt, as I mentioned.

"Malta's links with ancient Egypt lie in the multiple prehistoric artefacts found in Malta from Egypt. Artefacts include four Egyptian stelae that confirm the link before the occupation of the Phoenicians and the statue of an Egyptian

Triad carved in local stone discovered in Gozo in 1713. The statue dated to the second millennium BC. It features a standing priest with the figure of Horus and Ma'at, the goddess of truth. The statue was believed to be part of a sepulchral monument and the hieroglyphic inscription on the triad could not be deciphered even though Champollion deciphered hieroglyphics in 1822. The conclusions reached were that the hieroglyphs were a prayer or invocation to Ma'at, the Lady of the Skies. And the dolichocephalic skulls found in the hypogeum are linked to the Shemsu Hor, the followers of Horus, according to Egyptian oral tradition."

"Are there any other strange occurrences in the hypogeum?" Eve asked.

"Oh yes, there's a dreadful story. About a week after the tourist had her encounter with humanoids, a group of schoolchildren and their teachers were trapped in the hypogeum. The schoolchildren were on a field trip in the same tunnel where the tourist had seen the humanoids. After the last child had got through the tunnel, it collapsed.

"The official version stated that the walls caved in on the students and search parties were never able to locate any trace of the teachers or the children, but the rope that they had used to fasten themselves to the lower hypogeum chamber was found to have been clean cut as if by something sharp, not by falling rock debris.

"It was asserted that for weeks afterwards the wailing and screaming of children was heard underground in different parts of the island, but no one could locate the source of the cries, making rescue impossible. As for the tunnel networks and catacombs beneath Malta itself, there are some ancient accounts which say that deep caverns beneath the island continue underground beyond the shores, and according to one source, part of this labyrinth stretches hundreds of miles northwards and intersects with catacombs beneath Rome formerly known in Latin as *Mons Vaticanus*, today St. Peter's Basilica, Vatican City, Rome."

"An underground network beneath the surface of the Earth – that's incredible! What does Mons Vaticanus mean?" Eve was shaken by the story.

"Mons Vaticanus is the hill of prophecy alluding to the oracles or prophecies which were anciently delivered in Rome. In ancient times the sacred site is associated with a giant serpent. It comes from the root *vatis*, meaning a seer who sees by omens; *vatic-anus* refers to the annual cycle the earth makes around the sun. The serpent symbolises the unbroken cycle of birth, death and reincarnation. The Moirai were the goddesses of fate who personified the inescapable destiny of man. As goddesses of fate they must know the future and were prophetic deities. Their ministers were all the soothsayers and oracles.

"In Homer's poems Moira is fate personified, which, at birth spins out the thread of a person's future life. Vaticanus was a word used for the Vatican predating Jesus the Messiah. Mons Vaticanus is the site of a sacred mound marked by a standing stone to honour Cybele, known as Magna Mater, Great Mother. The Temple of Cybele was built on Mons Vaticanus in her honour before the headquarters of the patriarchal Roman Church took up residence."

"So Cybele is known as the Great Mother – why is she important?" Eve stopped Buznanna.

"She is a goddess and the official protector of Rome. She ruled over fertility, fortresses and mountains, where sacrifices to the Mountain Mother were offered. Cybele had two sides. One side was gentle and the other was a powerful serpent. Her name is connected to the Latin word *sibilare* meaning to hiss. Again we get the connection to the serpent; its symbolic energy is revered worldwide. The symbolic serpent is associated with the renewal of life because it sheds its skin periodically.

"The life force of all important sacred sites of antiquity still resonate vitality, as the invisible electromagnetic or telluric currents criss-cross the Earth's grid trying to awaken us from our deep slumber and shed that which no longer serves us, like the great serpent.

"There are stories interwoven everywhere about the serpent race, the Great Mother Goddess and the dolichocephalic skulls discovered in the Hal Saflieni hypogeum. The ruling class associated with the serpent priests of ancient Egypt and the Shemsu Hor, relating to sun worship, are known as the followers of Horus.

"We are reminded again about our ancient sun worship in St. Peter's Basilica where there is the impressive sun wheel dome and the eight-rayed sun wheel pierced by the Heliopolis obelisk at the centre of St. Peter's Square in Vatican City. The obelisk acts as a sundial with its moving shadow crossing the white marble paving stones of the piazza, telling the time. The sun wheel and the Heliopolis obelisk are both symbols and reminders of ancient sun worship.

"Like the Maltese, the Egyptians were sun worshippers, regarding the great luminary of the sun as the creator of the universe. There you go, my girl, I hope you can begin to see how it is all interconnected – the old religion gets integrated and repackaged into the new religion. When you are older maybe you will put all the pieces of the puzzle together."

Buznanna settled the bill and they walked down the narrow Victorian-looking streets with neat rows of limestone houses on either side. The midday heat was stifling in the bustling street. They arrived in the foyer of the Hal Saflieni hypogeum, where a guide who was a good friend of Buznanna's greeted them. The gentleman greeted Buznanna as Angela.

"This must be your great-granddaughter, Eve. I've heard so much about you. It will be my pleasure to escort you around today. My name is Maurizio and I'm delighted to finally meet you." Maurizio shook Eve's hand and then planted a kiss on it, as he winked at Buznanna. Eve smiled.

"Look at that gorgeous smile and those deep dimples. She is superb! Now, Eve, you're going to get an exclusive tour, entry to all the rooms in the hypogeum, entry which is prohibited to the general public. We have the whole hypogeum to ourselves for a few hours." Maurizio smiled at Eve.

"Is there a lot to see?" Eve asked.

"This place is a labyrinth, extending great distances into the depths of the earth, so it would be impossible to see all the underground networks. What they allow visitors to see is extremely limited."

"Why would anyone want to live underground and why were so many underground chambers built?" Eve asked.

"Many possible explanations to your question – the first that comes to mind is that the earth's surface was an unbearable and uninhabitable place because of some devastating cataclysm such as a comet strike, volcanic eruptions, magnetic disharmony and flooding. The underground network would allow travel and movement to safer environments. During these times the race of people sought refuge in underground caverns. For example, the first early modern humans known as Cro-Magnon lived in caves because of the harsh environmental conditions. There are races we are unaware of – it doesn't mean they don't exist because we haven't seen them."

They continued walking from the upper to the middle level as Maurizio pointed out features.

"The hypogeum consists of a series of elliptical chambers including the main chamber, the holy of holies and the oracle room. The main chamber is roughly circular and carved out of bedrock. There are several trilithon entrances leading to other chambers. Most of the wall surface has received a red wash of ochre. It was in this room that alabaster statuettes were found and the famous sleeping lady of Ħal-Saflieni statue was found in a circular pit finished to a high standard of craftsmanship," Maurizio explained.

"The sleeping lady is an unusual figurine," Buznanna commented as they looked at a large photo of the original statue.

"These statues of the Maltese Venus and the sleeping lady are called the Goddess of Fertility or the Fat Lady. She is referred to as fat because she is oversized. Angela, what do you think is going on with the lady in the statue?" Maurizio asked.

"She is not fat but oversized for a very intriguing reason, in my opinion. Study the photo carefully. Her arm is covering her breasts, that is, if she has any. I've examined many statues found on sacred temple sites and some statues have breasts and others are flat chested. In my opinion she is not sleeping or dreaming but she is in a process of parthenogenesis where she is reproducing. For example, a queen bee is a tough warrior queen that may need to fight and kill other queens to prove her status when there are two or more queens in one nest. Once a fertile queen bee has been mated with a male drone he will die afterwards. Male bees, drones, are produced from a queen's unfertilised egg known as parthenogenesis, so that a male bee has only one parent – a mother and no father. The female worker bees have two parents – a male (drone) and a female (queen).

"The Fibonacci sequence represents reproductive patterns and can be found in art, architecture, music and nature. The Fibonacci numbers are nature's numbering system that appear everywhere from the pattern of the florets of a flower to the shell of the chambered nautilus or the cochlea of the inner ear. The reproduction of bees follows the Fibonacci sequence and forms spirals like a pinecone that represent the pineal gland. The sequence is important in nature and reproduction, and the temples depict these spirals in artwork denoting the way forward from fertility to the continuance of life as in the mathematical patterns and spirals.

"We can draw similarities between the Virgin Queen Bee and the immaculate conception of the Virgin Mary. The statue of the sleeping lady could be the real Virgin Mary of ancient times. I have seen the original statues at the National Museum of Archaeology in Valletta and this is what comes to mind when I put it all together," Buznanna said and paused.

"You are amazing, Angela! It all makes so much more sense when you put it that way. It provides valid reasons for the artwork, spirals and the message the ancients were trying to convey in the artefacts they left behind."

"The ancient race looked different from us, with their long-headed skulls," Buznanna continued. "Perhaps they reproduced more like the bees and they left spirals and other evidence in artworks and architecture that are made up of the Fibonacci sequence as clues to how they collectively sustained and regenerated precious life."

"Your Buznanna is simply bedazzling," said Maurizio. He was excited by what he just heard and smiled at Eve as he proceeded with his tour of the hypogeum as though he had some sort of an epiphany after hearing Angela's explanation.

"Now to one of the most beautiful chambers, the holy of holies characterised by its carved replica of a temple facade, characterised by a trilithon, which is in turn framed within a larger trilithon and yet another large trilithon. The sunken floor is lower than the external standing floor allowing ample standing space towards the back of the chamber or space for a table or possibly an altar. The space is characterised by a replica of a partially corbelled ceiling. The corbelled ceiling has been taken as an indication that Malta's surface temples, now roofless, could have been covered with a similar corbelled ceiling.

"There are alveoli, which are small cavities, pits or hollows scattered all over the hypogeum. One is called the snake pit. It was two metres deep and we can only speculate as to its possible uses. In fact the whole hypogeum is evident of exemplary design and artwork that leaves us baffled today about how they carved, sculpted and moved heavy megalithic stones with such precision and accuracy.

"They must have possessed superior knowledge, machinery or tools. In ancient times you could probably see the Grand Harbour from the top floor of the hypogeum and you could access the hypogeum through the Kordin Temples, a group of megalithic temples in nearby Corradino Heights. Important people may have been buried in the hypogeum and the community could pray through small window openings looking upon the deceased bones or body known as the practise of incubation. The importance of this practice was to be close to the spirit of the deceased. Only the skull and femur bones were kept in an ossuary in the familiar skull-and-crossbones position adopted by the pirates.

"It appears that each level had an important function and different corridors allow access. The main rooms are distinguished by their domed, ornamental ceilings and by the elaborate structure of false bays influenced by the doorways and windows of contemporary terrestrial constructions. The curved chambers have an effect similar to that captured by a fisheye camera lens," Maurizio rattled on as they strolled through the second level.

Eve couldn't help but think how perfectly bizarre the place was. The hypogeum was carved out of the limestone bedrock beneath the bustling streets. She had never seen anything like this before. Eve was grateful that it was a lot cooler inside as they descended further underground leaving the stifling heat outside. She was happy to escape the heat for a few hours.

"The artwork was far more spectacular than what remains today," Maurizio said. "Notice all the red ochre spirals, disks, pentagons, polygons, floral patterns and plants incorporated in the spiral design. One chamber appears to have once been painted red next to another with chequered decoration. Interestingly, the red, black, white and popular patterns of spirals and checkerboard motifs are similar to those of the Dogon tribe in Mali and their origin stories and the Berber folklore tales. This artwork can even be seen on the ceilings. It's a shame that far too much cleaning up has occurred." Maurizio pointed to a faint outline of a muscular bull that adorned the wall. He was obviously disappointed that so much had been taken away.

Finally they descended to the lower level, accessed through a flight of seven uneven steps. They walk through the holy of holies, accessible through a rock-cut trilithon, a grand entry of magnificent architecture and craftsmanship. Eve looked up to one megalithic stone block that rose to a height of two metres and wondered how they manipulated such heavy stones underground – it didn't make any sense.

"The lower, third storey contained no bones or offerings and was believed to be a storage area possibly for grain," Maurizio explained as he disappeared out of sight, taking his torch with him, leaving them in the dark chamber all alone.

Eve could feel something tugging at her ankles and legs trying to bring her down, with force. "Help me!

Something is trying to pull me down," Eve yelled to Buznanna, her voice echoing in the chamber. Eve struggled to free herself from the grip of the strong hands that were pulling at her legs. She kicked and screamed after hearing the legends of children being trapped in these underground tunnels – she feared the same fate. She managed to release one leg and used it to kick furiously, while trying to maintain her balance. She kicked blindly in all directions at whatever was tugging at her. If some kind of a Sasquatch was trying to kidnap her she wasn't going down without a fight.

"Ouch!" She heard a familiar male voice.

"You've got to be kidding! Is that you, Maurizio?" Eve cried.

"Yes, you just kicked me in the head while I was trying to prank you," Maurizio said, emerging from the lower level rubbing his red forehead.

"Let me have a look." Buznanna pointed the torch at his head.

"You're not bleeding – you will be fine. Don't worry about Maurizio. He is a free spirit and he should have known better than to try and prank us." Buznanna laughed at the fact that Maurizio's prank had backfired on him.

"Your great-granddaughter is a strong girl," said Maurizio, trying to get in her good books again.

They made their way back up to the second level to have another look. They walked through a spacious circular hall with smooth concave walls richly decorated in a geometrical pattern of red spirals. On the wall of the entrance was a petrosomatoglyph of a human hand carved into the rock. This was an important form of symbolism, used in religious and secular ceremonies, and was regarded as an artefact.

They were approaching the oracle room, which looked roughly rectangular and was one of the smaller side chambers. It has the peculiarity of producing a powerful acoustic resonance from any vocalization made inside it. The room had an elaborately painted ceiling consisting of spirals in red ochre with circular blobs.

It was at this point Eve sneezed uncontrollably several times followed by a nosebleed.

"Let's sit down on that stone slab in the oracle room, so we can get Eve's nosebleed under control," Maurizio suggested as he gave Eve his handkerchief. Buznanna sat down and laid Eve's head on her lap and her legs across the stone slab.

Maurizio started to hum a tune as he swayed around. He was an eccentric man – still a kid at heart, with his jokes and pranks. He had thick brown wavy hair that looked difficult to manage because it looked like an overgrown lion's mane with a few streaks of grey. He was tall and robust but a gentle giant at the same time and was definitely in touch with his feminine side.

"Can you hear that echo? Isn't it amazing how my humming reverberates and is heard throughout the hypogeum! This place still holds so much magic and power. It even has the researchers baffled!" Maurizio stopped his chanting to make his point.

"That's right! This chamber carved out in a particular shape from solid limestone has been called the oracle chamber for a very good reason," Buznanna added.

"And my voice and singing sound incredible in here with the amazing acoustic properties that the ancients mastered. Why are we so slow to work it out?" Maurizio couldn't help himself.

"It's believed that the hypogeum was used as a sanctuary in ancient times, possibly for an oracle to transmit her messages. I can imagine the oracle standing barefoot soaking up the good telluric energy and earth's electric current which moves through the aquifers beneath us. The oracle would receive this electrical energy as she went into trance and delivered her guidance. It would be the ideal place for an oracle, as her words would have been magnified a hundredfold throughout the structure. There was no need for a microphone in the oracle chamber. It was the perfect place to preach to your spiritual followers because all those present in the hypogeum could hear every word.

"In my opinion it's likely that the Hal Saflieni hypogeum may have been built as a sanctuary for an oracle or a goddess due to the structure of a central room with special acoustic capabilities," Buznanna responded.

"Actually researchers from around the globe came to investigate and study the acoustic properties in the hypogeum and their findings were impressive. They indicated that at 110-111 Hz the patterns of activity over the prefrontal cortex abruptly shifted, resulting in a relative deactivation of the language centre and a temporary shifting from left- to right-sided dominance related to emotional processing. This shift did not occur at other frequencies.

"They discovered that reverberating sound could affect human emotions in both positive and negative ways. Therefore the people who spent time in the hypogeum, under conditions that may have included ritual chanting or singing, were exposing themselves to vibrations that may have affected their thinking. In addition to stimulating their more creative side, it appears that an atmosphere of resonant sound in the frequency of 110-111 Hertz would have been switching on an area of the brain that scientists believe relates to mood, emotions, empathy, and social behaviour.

"The construction of the chamber was made in such a way as to affect the psyche of people, perhaps to enhance mystical experiences during rituals. The uses of fractal non-linear resonances in the acoustics of the hypogeum show that these types of frequency can alter matter and even levitate heavy building stone, which provides a more plausible explanation as to how the megalithic temples, hypogea and other grand structures were built around the world," Maurizio added.

"No doubt about that. Sound is powerful and we will slowly discover more about ancient races as greater discoveries unravel. The long-headed race had more extrasensory capacity than your average human today. This race had the brain and sensory capacity to do more tasks with sound than we can with our five senses. Some ancient text I've read said that the ancients possessed and used all of their three hundred and sixty-five senses," Buznanna explained.

"Utterly amazing! I think we need to keep an open mind in order to understand the mysteries of the past. It's hard to believe that these perfect elliptical chambers cut into the solid bedrock were accomplished with only flint, stone tools and their bare hands. On a much lighter note, High Priestess, do you remember this song from last solstice?" he asked Angela as he swayed to his own singing.

"Sshhh! Maurizo, I told you not to call me that in front of anyone," Buznanna frowned.

"Why did Maurizo call you High Priestess, Buznanna?" Eve inquired.

"Briefly, our bloodlines bestow on us special responsibilities related to the Great Mother Goddess, where I chant to herald in the solstices and equinoxes and I act as an oracle to deliver messages from the Great Mother Goddess. I am an oracle, a shamaness to many active sacred sites including the Ħal Saflieni hypogeum where I led the ceremonies," Buznanna concluded and started to sing along with Maurizio.

By this stage Eve had managed to get her nosebleed

under control. She was engulfed in their singing, as though she was inside a giant bell, surrounded by the beautiful, angelic music they sang in harmony together. The sound was so absorbing that Eve felt transfixed as it vibrated through her bones and tissue, not just her ears. The singing came alive, as the hairs on Eve's arms rose and the sounds bounced around the limestone walls. The walls were like the bones of the earth as they vibrated, awakened and transferred sound. The sound echoed through the whole hypogeum. Buznanna was stroking Eve's hair as she sang with Maurizio and before Eve knew it she was completely relaxed, hypnotised and deeply asleep, dreaming as though she had been heavily sedated.

Eve dreamt she was being embraced, completely enveloped in an indigo haze, just like the singing resonating in the far distance. Eve twirled in the arms of a charismatic gentle Blue Queen wearing an azure-coloured coat with a distinguishing halo of stars. The spinning formed a vortex of spiralling indigo lights pulsing hues of a dark purplish blue. Eve was light-travelling with the Blue Queen. There was no need for verbal communication because they could telepathically communicate and the Blue Queen was answering her questions. She was holding her by both arms as they faced each other in this spiralling indigo vortex of energy. She was at least six feet tall. Blue roses were pinned to the side of her thick auburn hair that cascaded to her waist. She was stunning, breathtaking and truly divine, with her large eyes, high cheekbones and full lips. She was wearing a low-necked white cotton robe gathered at the waist and a cloak over the top that was held together by a twin-spiral brooch.

Eve stared at her in disbelief. She radiated a visible blue wavelength aura. She referred to herself as the Blue Queen, a great cosmic Mother Goddess from another star system. She was a sky goddess in the ancient

Mediterranean and Near East, like Mother Mary, Isis, Inanna and Astarte. She called Eve an indigo hybrid. She light-travelled with Eve to another dimension and it was definitely not earth. The scent of jasmine filled the air as they travelled across the blue sky. Eve saw a fertile plain rich with colourful flowers, fruit and vegetables of all kinds. There were vast herds of animals grazing. The air, land and sea were clean. It was an abundant environment that used free energy. It was so abundant there were two suns shining in the sky.

"Holy Mother! Really? As if one sun wasn't enough!" Eve gasped because she disliked the heat and was already beginning to feel incredibly hot, uncomfortable and thirsty. She noticed a magnificent waterfall cascading down some rocks. She ran to it, the grass soft and bouncy under her bare feet. She placed her hand under the flowing water and cupped the water into her mouth – it tasted so fresh.

She was relieved to have a drink otherwise she would have collapsed in this heat, when she noticed something small touch her toes and pass comments as if it were reading her feet, analysing the size of her toes in relation to the others, like a palm reader. It was a small disgusting beast that was a cross between a cockroach with the black venomous fangs of a deadly funnel web spider on the top half and a small kangaroo, with a strong flapping tail on the bottom half. A Roo-Roach! Eve moved away in disgust, but it clambered over her feet, with its black hairy legs, black beady eyes, long tentacles, and foul-smelling mouth that oozed venom from two large black fangs. She was overcome by the stench of sulphur as it came closer. Eve covered her nose with her hands to try and stop the smell. The creature continued to chat away.

"I found the one! The toes don't lie! Balzor will be pleased! You will not escape me and I must take you to my master." The Roo-Roach's aggression increased.

"What are you talking about? You're not taking me anywhere. I don't want to go with you!" Eve shouted.

"How dare you disobey me!" he roared at Eve.

The creature was getting annoyed by her resistance to cooperate and in protest it reared up on its hind legs and displayed two black razor-sharp fangs. When it became obvious there was no talking her way out of this situation, the only thing left to do was run for her life. Unfortunately, the chase was over quickly as its kangaroo hopping was so fast she could not compete. It caught up with her and swiped her to the ground with one blow of its strong tail. It clambered over her foot again and pierced her flesh with its fangs so hard it drew a fountain of blood.

"Ahh!" she gasped in agony. Eve's blood was splattered all over the creature's body and before her very eyes her blood was being absorbed by this creature into its skin – it was feeding from her blood. The Roo-Roach was extremely excited by the blood, as it appeared to nourish it; it must have had no digestive system.

It telepathically communicated to Eve that it was going to take all of her blood for its consumption. The Roo-Roach attempted to bite her for a second time, but as it was manoeuvring for the second bite, rearing up on its hind legs, with pure adrenaline Eve managed to shake it off her foot and picked herself up off the ground. Her foot felt hot and painful and it was bruised. She ran for her life, ignoring the pain. She knew that a bite from a funnel web spider would be a fatal one and she would have only fifteen to twenty minutes at the most to live.

"Blue Queen, help me, I'm dying," Eve yelled with the last of her energy as she felt her nervous system slowly shutting down.

The Roo-Roach was hopping behind her, making a threatening whizzing sound with its cockroach wings flapping wildly, just waiting for her to collapse from the poison and then it would finish her off. She didn't know how much further she could run with this horrific injury. Her heart was pounding wildly in her chest in sheer panic. She was doomed. She started to pray in her head. Then when she thought the situation couldn't get any worse, a large bird zoomed past her like a high-speed missile, missing her face by just millimetres.

"What on earth!" Eve thought as she turned to look at the powerful bird. It looked like a peregrine falcon, a bird of prey, with a black head, piercing eyes, blue-black upper parts and creamy white chin, throat and underparts, a hooked beak, long tapered wings and a short tail.

She watched in relief as the falcon swooped down on the Roo-Roach and caught it with its powerful hooked talons. The bird bit off its menacing head, killing the creature in an instant.

Then before her eyes, the falcon shape-shifted into a black-cloaked man with the head of a falcon but the body of a man. By this stage Eve had collapsed into his arms. She awoke disorientated to find herself on a round, laser-cut crystal quartz table in a cool cave. She could hear gushing water. Beneath the table were zigzag tunnels of running water, occupied by chanting creatures that resembled Merpeople, with the upper torsos of humans and lower halves consisting of the tail of a great fish. They referred to themselves as the Nommos. An aquatic and intelligent race, they lived mainly underground in caves or tunnels because their skin could not tolerate the harshness of the sun and needed to be kept moist. They communicated with Eve telepathically and told her not be afraid, they were healing all her injuries and trauma. She was being regenerated and healed in this cave, through sound and water on a round crystal quartz table. "There is no disease or injury that we can't heal," they said.

"Where is the falcon-headed man dressed in the black

cloak that saved my life?" Eve thought. As Eve asked where he was, he manifested before her without verbal communication, just telepathy. Eve received the answers to her questions.

"I am Horus, the falcon-headed sky god – the son of Isis and Osiris. I am a high initiate. I existed thousands of years before history even began. I can shape-shift to a powerful bird of prey and soar to great heights. With my powerful eyes I can see everything. You, Eve, are a hybrid, whose distant ancestors are from the bloodlines of the Shemsu Hor race and the Blue Queen. Your bloodlines are ancient. I am one of your spiritual guides. It is my duty to protect you and to be of service to you and humanity."

"Why are you my spiritual guide? Why me?" Eve asked.

"You have a strong will and we can see you will be a powerful, influential woman who can achieve great things in this lifetime that will benefit humanity. A strong woman needs a strong protector. In your case, because of your hereditary connection to the Shemsu Hor bloodlines, you have more than a man – you have a falcon sky god. You possess the link to the Shemsu Hor. You are the eldest-born female in a successive line of firstborn females.

"You are only at the start of your journey and it will be turbulent. The Shemsu Hor race was the intellect behind the megalithic structures around the world that leave humans today in awe as to how they were constructed because humans have forgotten. These monuments are a reminder of the Shemsu Hor's intellectual and sensory capabilities beyond what humans possess." He continued, "The Shemsu Hor race honoured the Great Mother Goddess and her child, my mother Isis, whom Christians perceive as the prototype of the Virgin Mary and her child. The race with the elongated skulls erected gigantic temples for their all-loving Mother Goddess. This ancient sacerdotal or priestly caste built the megalithic temples and avoided mixing with the local population. This elite class continued reproducing through the millennia, producing hybrids like you. They were more than just good engineers and architects. They are the custodians of great wisdom and knowledge and they are immortals. They lived peacefully in a matriarchal society honouring the Great Mother Goddess or the Blue Queen as she is also known. Humanity has a lot to rediscover, Eve, and you will play an important role in that."

He went on, "The ancients aligned their temples to the solstices to mirror constellations in the sky, such as the Pleiades, as if to capture the celestial energy from above and connect it to the earth. This alignment helped them to keep track of the seasons and to work in a natural flow with Mother Nature, never abusing the free and bountiful resources that sustained a long life.

"The Shemsu Hor are the descendants of an antediluvian race, that is, before the biblical Great Flood. The destruction caused by the flood was horrific. The earth was covered in hundreds of feet of sediment. It was such a long time ago that the remaining evidence is scanty. The scientific community is quick to dismiss any artefacts that contradict their interpretation of the time sequence. Nevertheless, their advanced civilization left traces of temple and pyramid constructions that withstood the test of time and show evidence of their existence.

"I know you are frightened of me especially in my black cloak because I look like some kind of Darth Vader, but don't be afraid! All you need to do is think of me and I will be there to protect you. The great thing about being telepathic is that I can read your thoughts and feelings. I can feel everything running through your mind so I'm just going to keep explaining to you until you gain understanding and shed your fear.

"The battle of good versus evil is an ancient story indeed and one that keeps raging. When we reach rock bottom and fall to our knees, we can soar to new heights and levels of advancement. Things are ruined only to be built again and reach a new level of development and understanding, so the cycle of life continues. The gods had to manifest on earth at one time to educate and help humanity rebuild. Yes, the gods walked among humanity to protect you, to preserve life and help you battle against evil.

"I have guided my bloodline group, teaching the arts of astronomy, mathematics, agriculture and especially architecture to ensure that the ancient knowledge would continue. The divine ones – the gods and goddesses if you like – needed to appear among humans to raise their consciousness. Rest assured the gods still walk among humans, disguised as whatever they wish to aid the hybrids who come from their bloodlines. You humans don't walk alone, so have no fear in your heart because evil feeds off fear. The gods are still guiding and watching."

At that, Horus closed his vibrant eyes as he bowed to Eve, bidding her farewell. A whoosh of wind nearly toppled Eve over as Horus spread his magnificent iridescent wings. Eve bowed her head in gratitude to thank him for saving her life. She felt his wings wrap around her, embracing her with his love before he took flight. She watched as Horus flew around in circles four times before he disappeared into the clouds.

As Horus departed, the Blue Queen reappeared, embracing Eve in the whirling indigo vortex that had the same distinctive haze, as if they were in some protective bubble. A giant white anaconda appeared, hissing at the Blue Queen. It didn't appear threatening but quite friendly. It had a sparkling oval ruby on its third eye.

"Don't be afraid!" Eve could hear the Blue Queen telepathically communicating as the giant snake opened its massive mouth wide and swallowed them both up. They slid down the inside of the anaconda in their protective indigo vortex, twirling along in their bubble, as though they were in a game of Snakes and Ladders. Eve bounced off the tip of the snake's tail when she reached her destination and slowly awakened from her deep dream. She found she was still lying on Buznanna's lap in the Hal Saflieni hypogeum.

Chapter 7

The Blue Queen, the Star of the Sea

Blue is a colour with no dimensions, like the vast sea and limitless sky. Blue encompasses us all, as we have the potential to be limitless. Eve's last week coincided with the village feast of the Blue Madonna of Mount Carmel in Żurrieq celebrated on the 16th July, coinciding with World Snake Day. The strict dress code permitted only blue to be worn, which Eve didn't mind, as she loved blue.

Żurrieq is one of the oldest continuous settlements in Malta. It is approximately seven kilometres south of the capital Valletta, where Eve was born. Many tourists visit the village because it has a spectacular, picturesque coastline with deep fjords cut into a rugged valleys known as wied, which are popular swimming and diving spots.

The Blue Queen, the Star of the Sea

From the wied, a short boat trip to a series of natural sea-level caves can be viewed including the well-known Blue Grotto. Far from the whitewashed cliffs of Wied iż-Żurrieq lies the isolated islet of Filfla, cut off from the bustling mainland. Żurrieq town's motto is *Sic a cyaneo aequore vocor*, which translates to "*From the blue sea I took my name.*" There is no doubt that the town of Żurrieq got its name from the colour blue, known in Maltese as *zoroq*. There is disagreement among authors as to whether its name refers to the blue sea of the Blue Grotto or to the colour of their blue eyes, a characteristic of the town's inhabitants.

Buznanna was helping Eve prepare for the festa. She took delight in braiding Eve's long thick auburn hair, carefully weaving and threading through it small turquoise beads. As she braided she sang the Madonna's anthem, Reġina tal-Karmelu, to familiarise Eve with the song.

Madonna tal-Karmnu
int fjur l-aktar sabiħ,
bħall-vjola u l-ġilju
b'kuruna rand ġo fih.

Int l-Omm ta' min ħalaqna
meqjuma kullimkien;
tal-Martri Int Reġina,
Sultana tal-ħolqien.

She painted Eve's nails blue. She had a special festa T-shirt with the Blue Queen of Heaven on it. Eve inspected the detail on the T-shirt carefully. The Madonna held baby Jesus in one arm and the other arm was reaching out in front of her. She wore a magnificent star-spangled crown with twelve prominent stars and she was dressed in a gold and blue embroidered robe with a cloak held together by a brooch.

Eve's shorts and sandals were blue so she was wearing her team's colour from head to toe ready for her first festa. Blue is a colour associated with royalty, peace and nature where sea and sky meet, consolidating the universal principle of "as above so below." As Buznanna was helping Eve get ready she rattled off some history as she often loved to do.

"The festa of the Madonna of the Karmelitani order is linked to the Queen of Heaven who was originally associated with pagan goddesses and then later applied by Christians to the Blessed Virgin Mary. Mount Carmel is located in the city of Haifa, north of Israel and was significant in ancient times as a barrier to traffic along the coastal plain. The 1500-foot-high limestone mountain impeded armies and merchants travelling to the Jezreel Valley. A Carmelite monastery was founded at the site shortly after the Order itself was created. High places such as Mount Carmel were frequently considered to be sacred. The Karmelitani Order was dedicated to the Virgin Mary under the title of Star of the Sea, in Latin, *Stella Maris*. The Order grew to be one of the major Catholic religious orders worldwide."

"Why is she called the Star of the Sea?"

"It's a reference in the Old Testament to the prophet Elijah. On Mount Carmel he saw an apparition of a holy woman, a Madonna, a Goddess who rose out of the sea and hence the title, Star of the Sea. That holy woman is associated with the Virgin Mary 850 years before Christ's birth. Mount Carmel means Garden of God in Hebrew and is located 20 miles from Nazareth and near Tyre, the ancient Phoenician capital. The Star of the Sea appeared as an apparition, like Fatima or Lourdes, and is the mother of all people. The Carmelite Order was created when a chapel was erected in AD 83 on Mount Carmel to venerate this apparition of our blessed lady."

They walked to the village piazza hand in hand. As they approached they could hear the church bells ringing and the wind instruments and drums beating as the band played. The energy was electrifying when they arrived in the piazza filled with religious statues, large fringed embroidered umbrellas and brightly coloured banners, flags and street decorations. The piazza was a sea of blue as people jammed in like sardines. The bars were open, colourful lights hung around and stalls sold nougat, cakes and biscotti; a sweet smell wafted in the air. The church bells were ringing rhythmically in the steeples and colourful banners were blowing in the welcome breeze. There were several ornately decorated blue and white umbrellas with gold embroidery and long golden fringes.

Preparations had begun weeks in advance for the fireworks, stalls and decorations of the piazza and churches. The village piazza was bustling with preparations as each year they planned to be bigger and better. There were two feasts celebrated in the village of Żurrieq, one for the Madonna of Mount Carmel and the other for Saint Catherine, who were both viewed as goddesses by the locals. Each year the competition was fierce, like two football teams competing against each other as to who was going to have the best festa, the best fireworks display, food stalls and the weeklong picnic afterwards.

The other village festa was celebrated in early September for Saint Catherine and was associated with the colour red. The site of Saint Catherine's Monastery is in the city of Saint Catherine in Egypt's South Sinai Governorate. The villagers were just as passionate about the festa honouring their saint every year.

Eve started to contemplate the meaning of the vibrations of the colours red and blue. She knew from Buznanna's teachings that there were seven primary energy centres inside the body known as chakras that are anchored in place. *Chakra* is a Sanskrit word, meaning wheel. The human chakras are "wheel-like" vortices that exist in the etheric human body. Each of the seven chakras has a corresponding colour that follows the colours of the rainbow: from bottom to top red, orange, yellow, green, blue, indigo, and violet. Each chakra relates to a different aspect of life. The first chakra is red and is associated with the root chakra that is located at the base of the spine in the tailbone area known as the coccyx. The root chakra relates to issues dealing with financial security, stability, abundance trust and fear. It is associated with the adrenal glands and survival instincts. Red is associated with our foundation and with grounding to Mother Earth's centred energy.

Buznanna had made Eve aware of her imbalance as many changes had occurred in her early years till the age of seven. Eve felt much more confident and aware of so many things after spending a month with Buznanna, who was the best teacher. She finally understood why she had had such a hard time fitting in to her adoptive environment, which had made her feel abandoned, scared and anxious. The feeling of not fitting in and having to be independent from a young age affected Eve in ways she hadn't understood until meeting Buznanna, who made sense of it all.

Eve was a natural daydreamer who escaped her environment by fantasizing about her life as she dreamed it should be. Her root chakra may have been off-kilter, but what she was lacking in one area she was well endowed with in another. The throat chakra is represented by the colour blue, the third eye chakra is represented by indigo and the crown chakra is represented by violet. Eve discovered more about herself through Buznanna's teachings about colour, sound and healing by balancing all the chakras so they worked optimally, as they are interlinked and affect health and well-being.

Eve had been amazed by Buznanna's ability to detect her dominant energies by the colour of her aura and individual chakras upon their first reunion through her third eye and natural clairvoyance. The aura shows an individual's dominant colour, but it's the individual chakras that tell the detailed story. She had instantly assessed information about Eve's current physical, mental, emotional and spiritual state. Buznanna explained that the colours were fluid and changed as emotions change. The colours can be muddy, faded or bright. Colour is a wave travelling through space.

There are seven basic frequencies of visible light which correspond to the wavelengths of the electromagnetic spectrum. Light is sound in the form of audio-frequency bands. Sound is vibration, so the electromagnetic spectrum that permeates the universe is vibrating and moving at a different speed. The highest vibrating frequency in the spectrum is gamma. Gamma corresponds with alpha brainwaves which are connected with being awake and self-aware. Alpha waves are often created when you're daydreaming or meditating.

As Buznanna had explained to Eve, our eyes register different colours, depending on the wavelength, the space between the peaks measured in nanometres (nm). Each chakra vibrates at a particular frequency and responds to different vibrations or wavelengths of light. Sound and colour can be used as therapy and many scientific tests have shown that unpleasant sounds actually increase our blood pressure, change our pulse and turn respiratory rates and moods from calm to aggressive.

Buznanna had done her best to get Eve's chakras aligned and functioning properly through listening to music of a certain frequency beneficial for each chakra and exposing her to colour therapy. Buznanna used the information she gained from Eve to help her heal and balance her chakras. The goal was to have all her chakras open from the crown to the root, continually receiving the energies from the universe and earth in constant flow and union, so that all channels are open, vibrant and flowing.

By healing Eve's chakras she naturally activated Eve's kundalini energy. The Sanskrit word *kundalini* means coiled, like a snake. Eve's reunion with Buznanna was a happy event and she felt a great love and soul connection to her. Not only was Buznanna her first spiritual teacher, but she healed Eve's childhood trauma. Eve hoped she would be as good a spiritual teacher as Buznanna, who taught her that colour and sound are universal languages that appear simple but are important functions.

"You've been very pensive, my girl. Let's make our way into the church to see the magnificent statue of the Lady of Mount Carmel. They have taken her out of her glass enclosure, as she will be paraded outside the church in front of all her devoted worshippers. The Lady of Mount Carmel is associated with the Virgin Mary, also called the Queen of Heaven, Queen Mother because her son, Jesus Christ, is the heavenly king of the universe," Buznanna explained as she took Eve's hand to lead her through the crowd of people.

The Queen Victoria band was elevated on their designated platform playing all their special songs dedicated to their Madonna. The band was so loud it was impossible to speak without yelling. As Eve left the church she was handed a blue banner to hold as she was whisked off her feet from behind and hoisted upon her uncle's shoulders, who was chuckling as he caught her by surprise. Eve's uncle was tall so she had a bird's eye view of all the festivities.

As soon as the band started to play, the crowd recognised it as one of their favourite tunes and broke into singing and clapping. Eve recognised the song the band was playing as the Madonna's anthem, *Regina tal-Karmelu*, the song Buznanna had sung to her whilst getting ready. The crowd exploded in singing, cheering and clapping as the lifelike statue of Mount Carmel, the Star of the Sea, was carried on the shoulders of village men out into the centre of the piazza. Eve started to wave her blue banner like everyone else. She felt a surge of excitement and emotion flow through her, as the medley of trombones, clarinets, violins, drums, cymbals and trumpets sounded rhythmically to the anthem.

She observed the crowds of people; some were cheering, praising, singing, laughing and others had tears in their eyes. A cocktail of emotions ran through Eve as she came face to face with the Queen. The crowd cheered and clapped as though they were at a rock concert. As the band and orchestra picked up the tempo, so did the crowd of people.

The music and vibrant colours had them in some kind of trance as they expressed their devotion to the all-loving and compassionate Queen. As the music filled the piazza the crowd continued to sing joyfully and as the band reached the climax of the chorus the people jumped and shouted. The banners were dancing wildly in the air and tiny pieces of blue streamers were pouring down from the flat rooftops, showering the masses in a sea of blue. Colour tells a story to the eyes as music does to the ears. Many people, young and old, male and female, had their arms outstretched with their palms facing upwards towards the sky and the Madonna, their Queen.

The crowd seemed to have forgotten about their human existence for a while as the music and the sea of blue enveloped them. Outstretching their arms in surrender, giving up their worries and concerns to her, the Madonna of compassion, mercy and understanding, Eve couldn't help but be reminded of the Blue Queen in her dream at the hypogeum. The crowd stood in awe as they stared at the Madonna as if to acknowledge there is a greater plan to life that we have little control over. We are interconnected in this human experience, here to seek out knowledge and truth, through times of prosperity and tribulation. There is great comfort in knowing that at the end of the human existence, our spirit will be in the hands of this all-loving, kind and merciful Queen Mother.

The numerous outstretched hands were a symbol of surrender, an epiphany or an awakening for many, where intuition and intellect blend and become one to show the way forward. The grand lesson is that we are all spiritual beings first, learning through our own life experiences to be human.

As Eve watched the Madonna being carried back into the church to be placed in her glass enclosure for another year, it felt that everything was coming to an abrupt end, including her time with Buznanna. Eve felt sad inside and at the same time overwhelmed with emotions of love and gratitude.

Her reunion with family and her birthplace took her back to her roots and it was exactly what Eve needed. She would treasure the memories in her heart forever. She looked down at Buznanna, from her uncle's shoulders and Buznanna looked up to smile at Eve with luminous eyes filled with tears. Eve reached to hold Buznanna's hand as she savoured their last moments together.

Eve's bags were packed. The month had come to an end. Buznanna came over to embrace Eve and she whispered in her ear an endearing proverb in Maltese – *qalb ta qalbi* – heart of my heart. Eve was the only great-grandchild in a very large family to have met and really got to know Buznanna.

"Hopefully we will reunite again. You are the heart of

my heart too and I love you. Even though we live so far away from each other, I will keep in touch and always treasure our memories. How lucky I am to have a Buznanna like you!" Eve murmured as emotion engulfed her, making it difficult to speak.

"It has been a real blessing having you around. It has made me feel like a young girl again rediscovering a new reserve of energy," Buznanna replied. "It has been a delight to get to know my eldest great-granddaughter and a highlight for me in my old age. I got the opportunity to transmit my knowledge and spiritual teachings to you, as it should be. We have a special matriarchal lineage and bloodline, Eve. You are a special girl and never forget that! You don't even realise how special you are. You have a special mission and calling. This calling and passion is in your bloodline.

"I know it's difficult to comprehend the scope of what I'm saying, but with time it will all come to fruition. You will learn to trust your instincts and you will be led in the right direction at the right time. Timing is everything – don't be impatient – follow the flow. Everything happens when it is supposed to and for a reason. I wanted to be completely open and share everything with you during your visit and I feel we have accomplished a lot."

"We live oceans and continents apart. It's not as though I can just drop in to see you whenever I want. What if I never see you again?" Eve asked, expressing her worst fears.

"But you will. Death is never the end. Death is the end of our physical body, like a snake sheds its skin. Our spiritual essence can't be destroyed. That energy is immortal if you like. Humans are made of stardust – just look up to my favourite star, Venus, and I will be with you. I will be your gatekeeper when I leave this world. I promise you it will be that easy. Our connection to our soul family is eternal and not even death can steal that from us. Be courageous and be on your way now, qalb ta qalbi. All will be well, have no fear in your heart, trust that you will be guided well." Buznanna opened her arms to embrace Eve for the last time.

Chapter 8
Never Letting Go

There is no stopping time and no retrieving time once it has passed. Time metamorphoses into memories, just as caterpillars transform into butterflies. The greatest gifts Buznanna gave Eve were her time, patience, her spiritual wisdom and unconditional love and for that she would never be forgotten. Eve had spent her life completing all the urgent things and not enough time on the important things. Engrossed in her studies and work, years seem to have flown by in the wink of an eye. Eve had always believed she would have time to see Buznanna. She kept in regular communication with her.

Eve planned to visit Buznanna again after she had graduated from university. She earned a degree and worked to save the funds for the long trip she was planning to Europe and the Middle East. Buznanna had influenced her so greatly at a young age that she had chosen to study archaeology and ancient languages. Eve knew Buznanna was not well and one day she passed away in her sleep before Eve's planned visit. Eve distinctly heard Buznanna call her name at the time of her actual passing. That same year Eve's grandmother came to visit her family in Sydney and bought her a special gift from Buznanna that she wanted to pass on.

Eve was devastated and extremely saddened by the news. She had cried so much that in the end she had no more tears to shed. One thing she knew for certain was she would never let go of the love and gratitude she had in her heart for Buznanna. Shortly after Buznanna's passing, Eve had a vivid dream about meeting Buznanna and it helped with the overwhelming grief that engulfed her, healing the sorrow she felt in her heart. It shifted the grieving to a more bearable stage where she didn't feel so sad.

In her dream she met Buznanna in a vast field of red poppies. She appeared just as Eve remembered her, when she was eight years of age. She was her usual self. She embraced Eve as she always did and Eve could feel the love and mystical bond they shared. She told Eve she was in a good place, free of suffering or pain and very happy to be reunited with loved ones. She told Eve she was busy taking on different roles of teaching and helping others. The dream was so real she could feel Buznanna squeeze her hand and talk to her in her familiar, loving voice.

Buznanna kissed her hand and said, "No more tears need to be shed *qalb ta qalbi,* heart of my heart, all is well. I want you to know that when you are sad, I feel even sadder. I don't want you to be sad and hurt. I'll always be around you – don't think you're getting rid of me that easily. I'll be with you in a different way, in spirit energy, which never dies. I will be by your side in times of need and I will be your gatekeeper as promised. Being the firstborn female in a long line of firstborn females it was my duty to impart to you all I knew about spirituality and ancient wisdom and at least we got the opportunity to do it. Know that we have a bond of love like an invisible golden thread that binds us to our soul family and not even death can take that away. All our beautiful memories are ours to keep. Do you understand that not even death can separate us? Our mystical bond and our love binds us forever."

Eve could feel Buznanna's warm hand wiping away her tears as she heard her words. She kissed Eve on both her cheeks and told her to be strong and have courage and that she expected this from her.

"Can you do that for me?" Buznanna wanted confirmation.

"Yes, I will try. The circumstances are as they are and there is no other choice."

"You always have choices; you have the choice to move forward knowing that our love and our souls are immortal. Even though we never want our adventures to end, ultimately they have to for something new to be created. I want you to look for the opportunities – don't dwell on what is lost – for something new will be found."

"It's like the proverb – when one door closes, another one opens," Eve answered.

"That's right. I don't want you to be overwhelmed by my death, otherwise you will miss the doors of opportunity that will open for you and you have so many adventures ahead of you, my girl. We must all face death, it's inevitable, but I promise you it's not the end. You remember my dancing bees? I communicated to them about death and they told me that they were not afraid of death. They would sting and die to protect the Queen Bee, the great warrior mother, as they knew their reincarnation would follow. Just as the infinity symbol is a never-ending loop, so our souls have never-ending possibilities. Our souls, our spirit, our essence, however you want to put it, are infinite. You have always had a sensitive, good heart, my girl, and I wanted to communicate with you because I knew you would take the news harshly. Rest assured, I'm doing well, I'm happy, and I'm in a wonderful place doing meaningful work. Look ahead to your bright future." Buznanna smiled at Eve, kissed and squeezed her in one big hug as they slowly faded away from the field of red poppies.

Eve woke from the dream feeling extremely happy to have communicated with Buznanna on the other side. She had experienced intense heartache for several days after she had heard the news of Buznanna's passing and wondered if it was ever going to stop. After the dream, her heartache eased. The dream was therapeutic and she felt a heavy weight had been lifted from her. The dream was real, her experiences and feelings were real. It was amazing to interact with Buznanna and have meaningful conversations as they used to. Eve didn't want the dream to end, but everything must come to an end. The dream ultimately helped her with the grieving process and moving on to the next stage.

From that moment onwards Eve decided to put everything Buznanna had taught her into practice and to access her ocean of gnosis, her inner knowing, in dealing with life's challenges and obstacles. This is what Buznanna expected of her – nothing less – and she wouldn't let her down. Although Eve missed her she would still communicate with her.

Eve was convinced that dreams are powerful and provide messages from the subconscious world that unlock our past lives and make us face our fears and traumas, but also provide messages about our current circumstances and

Never Letting Go

the future. Dreams can unlock our past, present and future, where time is not an issue as if the past, present and future are intertwined as one and there is no linear time as we know it.

Eve's grandmother gave her a gift from Buznanna. It was a snakeskin handbag that had belonged to Buznanna.

"This handbag has been in the family for a very long time and Buznanna wanted you to have it. I promised her I would give it to you. She loved you so very much and spoke about you till her very last days," Grandma said.

"Thank you, I will treasure this bag. She has given me so much already," Eve said, excited, accepting this special gift with open hands.

Eve took the handbag to her bedroom so she could have some privacy and take a careful look. When she looked inside there were some photos of their special time together. She had wanted Eve to keep these photos which brought her so much comfort. There was something strange about one side of the bag. It appeared bulky as though something was hidden inside. She ran her hand along the side and it seemed to be packed with something. She noticed the large side pocket was carefully hand-stitched tightly closed in black cotton, the same colour as the lining of the bag to camouflage its opening. What was behind it? Eve thought to herself. There was only one way to find out. She found scissors and carefully cut the stitching, ensuring she didn't damage the bag.

Inside the lining was an object. She could see a rectangular black leather pouch and pulled it out of the lining. The pouch was made of soft black leather with a diagram of a large colourful bird with wings outspread flying out of flames of fire. The bird was brilliantly coloured in reds, purples, and yellows and appeared illuminated in the sky. Its eyes were a vibrant blue. Underneath the picture was the inscription PA-HANOK.

Eve researched the meaning. The inscription was the Greek word for Phoenix, which derived from the Egyptian word meaning the House of Enoch. How interesting! Eve thought to herself. She would investigate these two subjects further.

Inside the ornate leather pouch were a letter and a map from Buznanna. The map was well preserved and looked as though it had been handmade, showing a high standard of artistic ability and workmanship. Eve opened the papers and looked at them. She put the map down and started to read the letter first. Buznanna started with her signature greeting:

"Hello *qalb ta qalbi*,

By now you know and I want you to accept that I have passed on. Do not be sad, my girl. We are immortal through the reincarnation process and I'm certain we shall meet again, but there is no rush – you have so much life still to live so make the most of it. Our memories are our treasures to keep and they are never taken away from us because they are embedded in our DNA so we can remember.

"Speaking of treasures, I have a special treasure for you. The enclosed map was given to me by my Buznanna, who was the firstborn female. This map was given to her by her Buznanna and so on. This map is very ancient. It now belongs to you. I hope it will end with you and you solve the mystery. I spent most of my life searching for knowledge and truth. I had some success and I passed on what I knew to you. This was my matriarchal duty and it was my absolute pleasure.

"My heart was broken when you left. Believe me you will not be alone because you have a large soul family, even though life will be really challenging and hard at times. I will be there when you need me – all you have to do is think of me, that's it. Our bond is eternal.

"You have even more resources than I did and you have the acumen, drive, sensitivity and clairvoyance to discover what treasure this map may reveal. I have faith in you. Have no fear. You are never alone. Have the fire of courage in your heart, qalb ta qalbi."

Eve put the letter down and unfolded the old map. She took out her magnifying glass to examine the fine print. She didn't want to miss any details so she scrutinized every written detail and symbol on the map. On the left corner there was a strange seal with a lavender flower and a bee. She looked again at the ancient papyrus map. It was well preserved considering it was probably very old.

It portrayed the Mediterranean with Sicily to the north, Sardinia to the northwest and the African coast to the south. The writing was in Latin. To the south of Sicily there were many fragments of small islands, some that don't exist today because they have sunk beneath the sea. One island was clearly marked with a vortex, perhaps a symbol of some sort of energy centre. Eve investigated other ancient maps to draw comparisons. After sifting through several maps she finally found a close match – an ancient map called *Tabula Europa VII*. She superimposed the map on Buznanna's map and saw that the vortex was directly over an island labelled *Herculum templum* (Latin for the Temple of Hercules).

Eve knew from her research that the Temple of Hercules was an ancient wonder for the Romans. She could see other islands labelled Melita, Glauconis, *Junoni Templum* (Latin for the Temple of Juno), Cape Hermes and *Mare Africum* (Latin for African sea). The original map is located in the Hermitage museum in St. Petersburg, Russia.

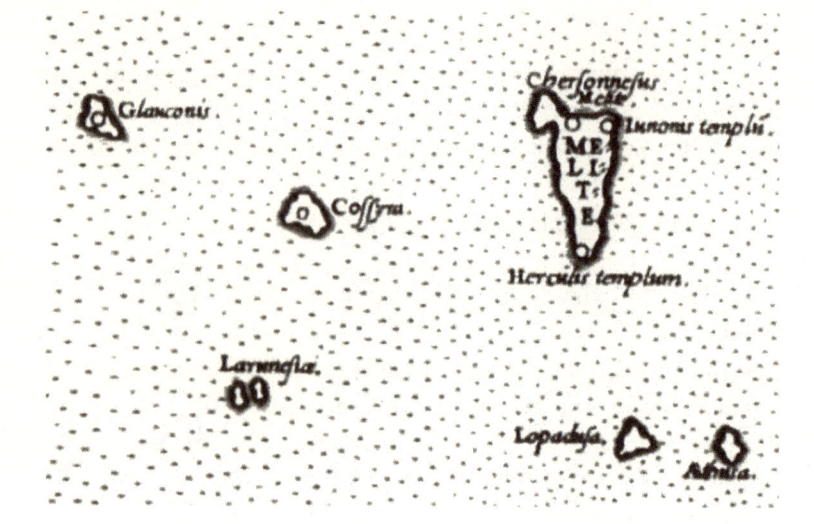

Her eyes kept wandering back to the vortex where the Temple of Hercules was positioned. Was this what Buznanna had been in search of? The symbol of the Queen Bee was nearby. Why the symbol of a vortex? Was it some sort of energy centre in the heart of the Mediterranean? Why have the Pillars of Hercules been located in Gibraltar, while there's reference that the Pillars of Hercules and the temple of Hercules are near Tunisia? It made sense that the temple of Hercules would be near the Pillars of Hercules. Ancient Greek writers located the Pillars of Hercules on the Strait of Sicily but this changed with Alexander the Great's eastward expansion; Eratosthenes, another ancient Greek scholar, moved the Pillars to Gibraltar.

This forced Eve to think outside the box and draw upon her intuition and discernment as Buznanna had taught her. She realized she was not to accept everything that is written in books or broadcast in the media, which is often manipulated by those in control.

Eve found other ancient maps to compare. The general topography has remained but the area between Sicily and Tunisia has drastically changed. Her impression was that it was a highly volatile area surrounded by active and dormant volcanoes, experiencing tectonic movement, so the geography today is very different.

When she looked at Google Earth, she could not help but notice the vast amount of silt between Sicily and Tunisia, which corresponded to her maps. The silt is evidence of cataclysms and earth-shaking events pounding the earth, changing its appearance and raising sea levels. This was a feasible explanation for why this ancient map looked different.

The temple of Ħaġar Qim was situated on a high promontory near the edge of the Mediterranean Sea on the southwestern edge of the main island of Malta. It shows evidence of an enormous wave, possibly a tsunami, coming directly from the west and throwing the huge megalithic stones towards the east. A careful examination of the stone ruins reveals how the huge stone blocks were lifted up and thrown against the tops of other stones in the building. Three feet of silt landed on Malta, six feet in France and eight feet in Mesopotamia. This distribution of silt indicates that Malta was more elevated or in the direct path of the tsunami and experienced the greatest impact resulting in the least amount of silt being deposited on Malta whereas the majority of the silt accumulated in Mesopotamia. The cause of this tsunami is unknown, but the most common hypothesis is a comet strike. The amount of accumulated silt and the direction in which the megalithic stones fell give some clues about pre-flood civilisations.

Eve was aware that Melita is the ancient name for Malta, believed to be a sacred mount. It seems that something special was going on, as there are some 36 megalithic structures scattered around these small islands, not to mention those that have been found on the surrounding seabed. Many of these structures have been deconstructed to use for new buildings such as Fort Saint

Angelo and Fort Mosta.

She referred to the second map of *Tabula Europa VII* based on information from Claudius Ptolemy, the armchair geographer in Alexandria. Eve believed Ptolemy's ancient maps were accurate, as he had access to a vast number of maps in the famous Library of Alexandria, which stored a wealth of knowledge before it suffered fires or acts of destruction over many years.

Claudius Ptolemy demonstrated that the Maltese island was much larger and extended south towards Africa. Eve could see exactly what Ptolemy described in regard to a larger landmass as shown on Buznanna's map, instead of the fragments of small islands that exist today. On her inherited map this larger island is referred to as *Cherfonefus Melite*, which is Malta connected to Comino, Gozo and Filfla, when sea levels were much lower and revealed a much larger island than is seen today. Looking at the larger island, the two famous temples of Hercules and Juno are marked on the coast. The temple of Juno is located in the northeast and the temple of Hercules in the southwest. These maps are drawn from Ptolemy's reference point in Egypt.

The maps made Eve wonder about so many things. On one map the temple of Hercules is on a separate island and on the other it's on the southeast coast of Melita. This goes to show that there were cataclysms in the past and the geography changed, considering Malta is at the intersection of two tectonic plates. The temples could have been submerged by the rising sea levels and fragmented megalithic blocks remain as partial skeletons on the islands.

There was a symbol in purple that looked like a spiralling energy vortex, like two intertwined snakes. Today it is a common symbol for medicine; in the ancient past it symbolised Hermes' sceptre. This place was in the centre of the map so it must have been important enough to take centre stage. Eve decided that the place marked with the vortex would be one of the places she would search for.

Eve referred to Buznanna's map which showed the vortex island surrounded by three soaring mountains that do not appear on the Leningrad maps. The three mountains reminded Eve of the ancient coat of arms of Gozo. It reminded Eve also of the legend of Atlantis, a large island surrounded by three mountains that disappeared in a single day and night. Ancient legends describe the Atlantis territory as being fenced by a belt of mountain ranges – could this be a link to Atlantis and one of the sister islands of Malta, known as Gozo or *Għawdex* today?

As her mind raced through the possibilities, Eve started to fidget with the ankh and star necklace around her neck. She needed to rely on her intuition as well as her intellect to find answers. After much contemplation and research Eve decided she would search for the central vortex point, the temples of Hercules and possibly Juno. All the sources including the ancient maps led Eve to believe that Malta was the target location. This would be her starting point. Buznanna could not find any relevance in this map but thanks to modern technology Eve knew the starting point.

She owed it to Buznanna who taught her to have an inquiring mind, to seek her own knowledge and answers which came from within. She taught Eve not to believe everything that was told to her and most importantly to have discernment. She showed Eve how to listen not only with her ears, but with her heart and use all of her senses as Buznanna had done.

Chapter 9

The Spell of the Sea

Eve was ready to pursue her investigations. She knew success was not guaranteed, but she felt stronger and more courageous after overcoming immense grief and loss. With great pain comes great change and she was prepared for anything that the future would bring. She recalled Buznanna saying that with the courage, tenacity and intuition to follow your heart, your dreams would come true. Buznanna had always had faith in Eve and she wanted to make her proud. Dreams don't have an expiry date. It's never too late. Eve was incredibly excited that her pursuit was finally taking place.

Eve's first stop was in Malta, which she would use as a base to pursue further travels. Being an orderly and organised person, she had meticulously planned all the places of interest for her research. She needed to accumulate as much information as possible so she could put the pieces of the puzzle together based on the old map that had been entrusted to her by Buznanna. She wanted to put this mystery to rest once and for all. She would need to learn how to scuba dive, as some of the answers lay hidden beneath the sea, inaccessible and hopefully not plundered by humans.

Before she knew it, she was in Malta ready to begin her journey. Eve's first mission would be to find a suitable scuba diving school at the Tourist Information Office in Valletta. The capital city of Valletta was named after its founder, the Grand Master of the Knights Hospitaller of Malta, from the Order of St. John, Jean Parisot de la Valette. As Eve approached Valletta she saw that it still held its dignity and charm as she remembered it.

Valletta is a magnificent fortress city which rises steeply from two deep harbours, Marsamxett and the Grand Harbour. She caught sight of the impressive bastions, forts and cathedral of Valletta and recalled how they were completed in as little as fifteen years, considering the fact that tools were basic by our standards. The whole city was built by hand. The City of Valletta, the megalithic temples and the Ħal Saflieni hypogeum are the three places in Malta that are on UNESCO's list of World Heritage Sites.

As Eve made her way to the main entry to Valletta, she could hear the familiar sound of gushing water from the oversized classical Triton fountain designed by local sculptor Vincent Apap in 1959. Eve liked the statue and stood there admiring the artwork. It consisted of three muscular god-like mermen, holding a large disk above their heads with one upright arm. Copious amounts of water flowed down the three mermen who strongly resembled Poseidon, a god portrayed as having the head and trunk of a man and the tail of a fish. Three rings of water cascaded from the circular disk encircling the god-like mermen.

The entire city plan of Valletta matches a depiction of the headless Maltese goddess. The position of the symbolic Triton fountain in the city plan was the womb of the goddess. Eve appreciated the Triton Fountain even more now, looking at it with the eyes of a young adult. Was there a secret code in the planning of Valletta? The Knights of Malta protected their beloved goddess from their headquarters, the Castle of the Sea at Fort Saint Angelo. Is Poseidon linked to the headless goddess? Her appearance remains a mystery.

Valletta had its own code. She passed through the Gates of Valletta, acknowledging the many times this entry and city had been reconstructed, as the islands had been subject to severe bombardment during the Second World War. The islands' strategic location once again made it centre stage in the theatre of war in the Mediterranean. Malta holds the record for the heaviest sustained bombing attack over some 154 days and nights with 6,700 tons of bombs devastating many buildings. Eve remembered the resilience shown by the populace at that time.

The main street was bustling with activity and was now lined with multi-national branded shops selling fashion, jewellery, food and much more. As she looked around, she saw that the fortresses remained the same and she was glad the capital still held its particular charm and character.

Eve veered off the main street to a café for her morning fix of coffee and pastry. She fondly recalled walking through the grid of narrow streets full of small, specialised shops and cafés, ornate churches and palaces and some of Europe's finest artworks including the paintings of Caravaggio, who made Malta his refuge from 1571. He produced several paintings for the Order and was eventually inducted into its ranks as a Knight of Grace. Eve could quite easily have spent a whole day just walking through the narrow streets, getting lost in the city or visiting one of the peaceful gardens overlooking the magnificent harbour. She reminded herself to remain on task for she hated not completing what she had started. She finished her coffee and headed straight to the Tourist Information Office where she was given a list of diving schools across the islands. There were quite a few to choose from, as Malta is a great destination for scuba divers. As Eve scanned the list, one school stood out, based on the great location and the name – it was the obvious choice. She made arrangements to attend the Atlantis Diving School on the island of Gozo in Marsalforn; the Atlantis lodge accommodation was right next to the diving centre and within walking distance of Marsalforn sea front. Tomorrow morning she would cross by ferry from Malta to Gozo, the tranquil sister island, and would get started on her plans.

Eve sat on the warm wooden bench on the ferry. The tranquil sun rose steadily, warming her with its magnificent rose-gold rays. She looked over the vast aquamarine sea as spears of light danced over the glistening surface. The short twenty-minute trip was over before she knew it and she prepared to disembark with her luggage and important maps stashed away in her backpack. She had always loved Gozo since her childhood experiences with Buznanna. The surroundings had the same natural beauty she had seen when she was younger, sparking a flood of happy memories.

The cab pulled up at the front office of the Atlantis Diving School. She recognised it by the artwork and logo she had seen on the brochure in the Tourist Information Office. She paid the driver and got out to look at the beautiful hand-painted artwork on the wall outside the office. The logo was the Greek god Poseidon, known as

Atlantis and The Legendary Blue Queen

Neptune to the Romans. His muscular semi-naked body showed his strong arms and legs and powerful physique. He was holding a trident, a three-pronged spear, the weapon he is often depicted with. He is known as the God of the Sea, as well as the Earth-shaker because when he struck the earth in anger he caused mighty earthquakes. He used his trident to stir up tidal waves, tsunamis and sea storms. Eve loved art and she got so engrossed at looking at the mural she was startled when she sensed someone was standing beside her.

"Hello, you must be Eve," the man said with a distinctly French accent.

"Yes that's me." Eve turned around and was pleasantly surprised by the incredibly handsome man in front of her. He was about six foot three, in his late twenties, bronzed, with an athletic muscular build, brown hair, dark blue eyes, a square jaw and well-defined lips. She decided he was more than movie-star handsome. She must have blushed at her own thoughts, while smiling at the same time. She often smiled when she felt awkward or didn't know what to say.

"Welcome to the Atlantis Diving School, I'm Etienne. Have we met before? You look very familiar."

"No, I'm sure I have not met you before," Eve replied. She was certain that if they had met she would not have forgotten him.

"You haven't been to my diving school before?" he probed.

"No. Maybe we met in another lifetime." Eve continued to smile, but she would have to sleep on that idea to know for certain, she thought to herself.

They walked into the front office and he stood behind the counter to retrieve Eve's booking details.

"What is your role here?" Eve asked.

"I'm the owner and director of the company and one

The Spell of the Sea

of the head diving instructors. Lucky you – I will be your teacher and diving instructor for your stay," Etienne smiled, revealing a cute dimple on each cheek. Eve couldn't help but be distracted by his good looks, with his wild wavy thick brown hair, olive skin and piercing blue eyes. He had one visible tattoo on his upper arm just below the hem of his T-shirt sleeve of two intertwined snakes around a staff. Eve scanned him while he was busy putting together the paperwork and thought he seemed intriguing.

"So what do you want to achieve?" Etienne asked as he finished up with her booking.

"I want to learn how to scuba dive at an advanced level so I can explore ancient remains out at sea. I have little experience, in fact I'm a bit afraid of scuba diving, but I need to try," Eve replied.

"What are you scared of? Scuba diving is such an amazing experience," he said.

"It's a long story, but I've had a few dreams when I have died at sea. One was out at sea looking for some sort of a treasure, wearing old diving gear, with the round helmet, like a scaphandre, and my oxygen was cut off and I died at sea. I have a love and a fear of the sea's power and unpredictability," Eve explained.

"That sounds strange. I like to keep an open mind – anything is possible. Don't worry, you will be safe and I hope you will put your fears of the sea to rest. We will start off with the basics and work towards the more complex stuff."

"You are French, right?"

"Yes, my strong accent gives it away all the time. I grew up in Paris but fell in love with the diving experience and life in Malta and live here most of the time. Why did you pick this school?" he asked. "There are so many great diving centres around the islands because Malta is one of the best diving locations in the world."

"Those dreams I mentioned are just the tip of the iceberg – there's more but I'll try not to scare you away. I just liked the name of your business and I once visited Gozo with my great-grandmother, Buznanna. I have many fond memories here and that's why I chose this diving school. Why did you name your business Atlantis?" Eve asked.

"Firstly, I loved the seaside and diving from a very young age so I established my dream business here in Malta. When I was young I watched all of Jacques-Yves Cousteau's underwater diving expeditions. I was his biggest fan. Cousteau was asked by a reporter where he thought Atlantis was because he was an experienced diver worldwide with his boat *La Calypso*. Cousteau reported that Malta is the best candidate for Atlantis even though his son believes it is Bimini.

"I should explain that Napoleon took all the Vatican archives and brought them back to Paris when he invaded Europe. He did not return all the archives to the Vatican and some pieces disappeared. French intelligence has kept many a secret to protect the existing system. Jacques Cousteau was connected to the French intelligence services so he knew more than he would tell, unlike his son. I'm intrigued by the legendary Atlantis, hence the name of my company," Etienne explained.

"I'm definitely at the right school, with the right teacher," Eve thought. Now all she would have to do is not get distracted by his good looks as she had hit the jackpot of eye candy with her teacher.

"Take your luggage to your room in the building next door," said Etienne handing Eve the room number and key. "We can take a boat ride around the islands and get started with our lessons. Meet you at the front of the office in 40 minutes. And, don't laugh – I even named my boat *The Calypso*."

Eve could see Etienne waiting for her by the quay a few minutes later, smoking a cigarette. He extinguished it immediately when she approached him. She couldn't miss that he wasn't wearing much except a red budgie smuggler and a red cap. And that was all! She knew she would need to stop getting distracted by him if she was going to learn anything.

"Well hello, Jacques Cousteau," Eve said, looking at his outfit.

"Very funny! I'll have you know I served in the military service wing of the French army, the French Foreign Legion. I'm tougher than I look and the training I underwent was not only physically challenging but also very stressful psychologically," he replied.

"Well I'm just learning to scuba dive, so I hope no military style of teaching is required. I'll try to be a good student," Eve replied.

They walked to the small marina, where they boarded the Calypso. Eve could see it was full of diving gear and equipment. Her first lesson was learning about the gear. Etienne went through and explained thoroughly every single device and how it is used.

"We will do a lot of practice as well as theory especially because you want to dive beyond the limits of recreational diving, so we will use more technical diving scuba equipment for this. Please don't hesitate to ask me questions if you don't understand how to use your equipment. Going beyond recreational diving areas the sea can be unpredictable but, trust me, I have loads of experience. You will be in safe hands. So tell me about your Buznanna – she sounds as though she was important to you."

"She was the most influential person in my life and shaped my future direction. She planted the seed of curiosity in my mind about ancient mysteries and spirituality and she influenced the direction of my studies. I have just completed my degree in archaeology and ancient languages. Buznanna was my first spiritual teacher. I'm eternally grateful for the esoteric knowledge she shared with me and she will always be in my heart and thoughts. This ancient map, ankh and star pendant were gifts from her, passed down to the eldest great-granddaughter consecutively for many generations. She gave me all the tools I need. She is the reason I am here and learning how to scuba dive. I just wish I had one last opportunity to spend more time with her before her recent passing, but it was not meant to be."

"I'm sorry to hear of your loss. She sounds like a remarkable woman. I always love an adventure with a beautiful woman. You're fortunate to find a military man on your side for this mission and I'm happy to be of assistance," Etienne reassured her with an adorable smile, revealing his deep dimples. He anchored the Calypso at a semi-circular bay Ir-Ramla l-Ḥamra – the Red Sandy Beach. Eve knew this beach well as she had visited it with Buznanna and had their dolphin encounter here. The wide sandy beach is located at the bottom of a rich and fertile valley on the northern side of the island of Gozo.

The golden-reddish sand makes this beach different from all others in Gozo and Malta. The area around the beach is quite interesting and provides some rich historical treasures. Roman remains lie beneath the sand and the famous Calypso Cave overlooks the western side of the beach.

Etienne was very thorough as he outlined safety strategies and provided different scenarios and examples. He had every safety issue covered. They prepared for their first dive at Ramla Bay. Etienne helped her get organised as she put on her wetsuit and he attached her gear going over the main points again to reinforce his instructions.

"In all dives I will be your buddy, meaning I will remain close to you at all times should an emergency arise."

"I'm a bit nervous about doing this, but it feels easier having you by my side," Eve said.

"I have been a professional diver for the best army in the world. Don't worry – I won't let go of your hand until you signal. You will be great once you are in the sea. It's another world down there. Trust me, you will love it!"

They were fully equipped in wetsuits, standing at the back of the Calypso getting ready to jump in feet first.

Etienne grabbed Eve's hand and held it tightly in his.

With that last encouragement they plunged into the sea hand in hand. She was submerged and the oxygen was flowing freely. It was an amazing watery world. That first scuba dive was the beginning of Eve's love affair with diving. She discovered a whole new colourful world down there, a world she couldn't get enough of. After this experience, they dived every day until Eve was ready for their planned deep-sea diving expedition.

Chapter 10

The Magical Phoenix

Dawn's scintillating rays over the tranquil sea lavished a silver path that looked to be encrusted with diamonds from the shore all the way to the distant horizon. Eve stared at the glistening path that brought her a day she had never been promised, yet she planned meticulously to make this adventure a reality. She let the moment sink in as the sun touched her skin and soothed away her nervousness. Her first deep-sea exploration could result in an amazing discovery and this brought with it a renewed sense of hope and possibilities.

They left Marsalforn at dawn with the first glimmers of light reflecting across the sky and illuminating their path. The conditions out at sea appeared calm as they motored to their destination at Marsaxlokk Bay. Eve watched the sun rise nonchalantly, a giant revolving orb of fire entwined in shades of red and gold rays over the horizon, transforming the opaque sea surface to one of diamonds as the vibrant rays danced on the surface.

Eve stretched her arms out in front of her with her palms up to the sky. She saluted the sun and gave thanks for all the synchronicities that had come her way to lead her to this day. She placed her hands in prayer position with both palms pressed against the other over her third eye as she lowered her head and eyes, the sun's warm amber rays pouring through her fingers, down her face and into her grateful heart. Eve had an open mind and was ready for anything.

Under the same sun that had shone for the ancients, the cosmic connections between the ancient and modern worlds collided and consciousness continued to transform to new heights and new horizons. We are all on our own personal journey discovering our place here on earth she thought, as she soaked in the sun's rays. The past grief was a memory that seemed to disappear, simply washed away with the waves like a softly sung lullaby in perfect unison with the fiery sun illuminating the porcelain sky.

Etienne had organised a small crew to be on board. Eve was seated on the boat holding the ornate leather pouch while Etienne had her inherited map spread out on a small table trying to pinpoint the exact co-ordinates to search for their target, the temple of Hercules.

Eve sat on her own, holding the pouch in her lap, enjoying the solitude. Her fingers glided slowly over the large colourful engraving of the Phoenix, a highly mystical bird, which she had researched thoroughly when the beautiful pouch came into her possession. She knew that a lot of powerful symbolism was attached to the legendary and majestic bird. The Phoenix on her pouch was portrayed like so many others she had seen in her research, coloured in reds, purples and yellows, with a nimbus, some kind of a luminous cloud or halo surrounding it, illuminating it. Its iridescent eyes were vibrant, shining like bright blue gems.

It builds its own funeral pyre when its end is approaching – a nest with the finest aromatic woods, cinnamon and myrrh in preparation for its fiery death. From the ashes, a rejuvenated and more powerful Phoenix arises. The Greek historian Herodotus described the bird as living for 500 years before building and lighting its own funeral pyre. The Phoenix collects the predecessor's ashes and it is believed that it deposits them at the altar of the Sun God at Heliopolis, known by the Greeks as the City of the Sun. It then shows its immortality by gloriously rising after death from the ashes, renewed, powerful and wiser. It takes flight immediately, demonstrating its renewed and powerful state. This symbolises among other things regeneration, resurrection, immortality, royalty, the sun, metempsychosis and consecration.

Commonly named firebird, the Phoenix was a symbol of the sun rising and setting. The fire and the sun symbolise the Phoenix's resurrection, as the sun sets and rises again as a new sun, resembling a ball of fire. Perhaps in the earliest instance of the legend the Egyptians told of the Bennu, a heron that is part of their creation myth. The Bennu is an ancient deity linked with the sun, creation and rebirth, periodically renewing itself. It lived atop ben-ben stones or obelisks and was worshipped alongside Osiris and Ra. Bennu was seen as an avatar of Osiris, a living symbol of the deity. The solar bird appears on ancient amulets as a symbol of rebirth and immortality, and it was associated with the flooding of the Nile, bringing new wealth and fertility.

Other cultures have associated the Phoenix with their own birds, such as the native American Thunderbird, the

Chinese Fèng Huáng and the Russian Firebird. In Asia the Phoenix is the symbol of the matriarchal and the sun. It is a good sign that a wise leader has ascended and a new era waits. Ceramic protective beasts, led by the Phoenix, guard the temples. The Phoenix has been incorporated into many religions, signifying eternal life, destruction, creation and fresh beginnings.

The Phoenix has also become an important Christian symbol and symbolizes the death of Christ and his resurrection from the dead, which is celebrated each year at Easter. It is also symbolic of a cosmic fire some believe created the world and which will consume it. So unforgettable is the symbolism of the Phoenix that its motif and image is still used in popular culture and is reborn across cultures, resurrecting throughout time. Eve's research always came back to how interconnected we all are. Even in our religions there appears to be a common root with different branches and different names for the same concepts hijacked and renamed over time.

Eve was contemplative as she enjoyed her meditative time before the dive. She was excited but a little apprehensive as they headed to their diving destination at Tas-Silġ, a rounded hilltop overlooking Marsaxlokk Bay. They had planned their first deep-sea diving expedition in southeastern Malta.

They chose this site based on Buznanna's ancient map and discoveries of ancient remains. In the past, remains of a pair of carved marble columns known as cippi, were discovered in this location and were believed to belong to the temple of Hercules and dedicated to Melqart who was the tutelary god of the Phoenicians. Melqart was patron god of the city of Tyre. He was called king of the city. He protected sailors, trade and overseas colonization. During the Hellenistic and Roman periods, Melqart was identified with Hercules and always depicted with

Hercules' iconography and attributes, such as the lion skin draped over his shoulders. Melqart is referred to as the Tyrian Herakles.

In ancient times, Carthage was the capital city of the ancient Carthaginian civilization, situated on the east coast of Tunisia in North Africa. The city developed from a Phoenician colony into the centre of an empire dominating the Mediterranean. With the Phoenician colonization along the Mediterranean Sea, people founded Melqart temples in the new settlements, thus creating famous temples for Melqart in Leptis Magna on the Libyan coastline that formed a natural harbour. Founded by the Phoenicians as early as the 7th century BC, it was empty until almost a millennium later when, under the rule of Septimius Severus during the Roman Empire, Leptis enjoyed its Golden Age.

The emperor Septimius Severus was born in Leptis Magna in the Roman province of Africa. Rome appointed him ruler of this city because he had good relationships with all the tribes of the region, and therefore could secure trade routes for the Roman Empire across Africa.

Eve's map showed the temple of Hercules situated between Tunisia and the periphery of the ancient Maltese archipelago, now underwater. One of the maps shows the temple to be on a separate island and the other shows it on the island of Malta.

Many great Roman writers and scholars, such as Cicero, one of Rome's greatest orators, writers and philosophers, mention the existence of the temples of Hercules and Juno on the ancient island of Melita, being Malta. Juno is the Roman goddess, the Greek equivalent of Hera. Cicero speaks of a celebrated temple of Juno situated close to the sea, near the Castle of Saint Angelo, in Valletta. In fact the Castle of Saint Angelo was part of the original temple of Juno. There is an Egyptian temple column made of pink granite and large ashlar blocks on top of Fort Saint

Angelo. This is one reason why Valletta is special and listed as a UNESCO World Heritage Site. The evidence points to these two temples being in Malta. Based on all the evidence and maps they chose to search for temple of Hercules at Marsaxlokk, first.

Eve pulled her attention back to the Phoenix artwork on the pouch, as she didn't want to think about the dive yet. Drawing analogies to life, the Phoenix is all about rising from the ashes after inducing its own death by fire. Life is often a series of major challenges and changes, a bit like a death. How often our lives reach rock bottom, through misadventure, illness, grief, heartache, loss and separation but somehow if the human spirit is willing, it can rise above the hardship and adversity to renew, resurrect, find a new approach, a new understanding or lease on life. Just as the sun rises every morning, so does the Phoenix and so does the courageous human spirit. When the human spirit is willing and strong, consciousness can soar and rise from the ashes just like the powerful firebird.

The Phoenicians were a maritime trading culture that spread across the Mediterranean, setting up a colony in Malta due to its central location and usefulness for trade. It is believed that the Greeks called the Canaanites the Phoenikes or Phoenicians, which may derive from the Greek word Phoenix, meaning crimson or purple. In fact, the symbology of the Phoenix is closely tied with the Phoenicians and was an important link to the temple of Hercules. The ancient past is a complex puzzle and Eve knew that putting the pieces together was never going to be an easy task.

One of the most astonishing discoveries Eve made was from the engraving of the Egyptian word *pa-hanok* in vibrant gold. The Greek word for Phoenix comes from the Egyptian word, which means the House of Enoch. Eve knew from her extensive research that Enoch was no

Atlantis and The Legendary Blue Queen

ordinary man and is in fact one of the great gods. The prediluvian patriarch appeared for the first time to humans from the labyrinth in Hollow Earth, after a devastating deluge and floods. These gods who appeared for the first time among human survivors have been termed *Zep Tepi* by the Egyptians. Zep Tepi means "the first times." These mysterious gods appeared among the human survivors after great cataclysms. They helped them through their scientific and spiritual teachings in the rudiments of civilisation.

Enoch is the teacher fusing spirituality and science, a kind of priest-scientist. Enoch is the great-grandfather of Noah and is credited in the bible as the architect of the city of Yahweh and inventor of the alphabet and calendar. He is shown the secrets of heaven and earth and returns to earth to be one of the great godly teachers.

The Egyptians know Enoch as Thoth, the Greeks know him as Hermes, and the Celts know him as Merlin the wizard. Enoch, this godly hero, holds the secrets between heaven and earth and immortality and vows to return when humans need to start all over from the beginning like children.

Enoch was also an astronomer and the legend is that he saw the Vela star exploding into a supernova and he was aware that the debris would cause havoc on earth when it arrived, so the pyramids were built to store treasures. The bible is based on the Book of Enoch so all religions stem from the same root.

According to Ancient Egyptians, Enoch is Thoth, the Atlantean; all religion stems from the old religion of Enoch. Eve ran this summary through her head as she stared at the image of the Phoenix on her pouch. The Phoenix is the House of Enoch, the root of many great civilisations and cultures. The Phoenix represents earth's major renewal that occurs every 25,900 years. The Enochian knowledge proposes that regular cataclysmic occurrences act as a transformative experience to quicken all life forms to the next evolutionary phase. As our cosmic connections between ancient worlds and modern times collide, human evolution is likely to proceed more rapidly than we realise.

Unexplained mysteries are starting to be explained because the present system that has been taught to us is breaking down. The old adage "as above so below" is coming to the forefront of human awareness and we see our roots are embedded in the stars. Our inner radar is being activated as evidence appears of other inhabitable planets and records of civilizations before us who mastered the physical continuum and progressed beyond this world. As with everything, those who approached it with the greater good for the collective in mind to enhance beauty and consciousness made progress but others who were negative, individualistic and greedy, ultimately failed.

They approached the dive site far out at sea, with glimmers of the Maltese islands in the distance. Eve was feeling anxious because she had never attempted anything like this before, but it was part of her plan and she had promised Buznanna to do her best. She couldn't back out now. Etienne would be right by her side on the dive and a sturdy rope connected to a belt around their waists, called a buddy line, would connect them. The rope connected them and prevented them from being separated in poor visibility and for communication by line signals. In her training Eve had been taught to pull on the rope twice if she was in danger. This rope would be connected to a surface marker buoy and when it descended it was a signal to the support crew to assist the divers out of the sea.

She calmed herself knowing she was in good hands because Etienne always put safety first with every dive, meticulously checking all diving equipment. And there was plan B, should plan A fail.

Eve was fully kitted up and Etienne was checking she had all her gear on properly and that it was functioning. Visibility would be an issue as they descended into the deep sea. Eve and Etienne each had two diving torches attached to their suits. They also had two dive beacons, small lights attached to their tank valve, that would help them locate the other diving partner.

Once the crew that remained on board had checked their equipment for the third time, they descended together to investigate underwater with torches beaming. It was amazing down there, with a vast array of aquatic life. Eve noticed some giant megalithic slabs of limestone lying semi-buried on the sea floor in a disorderly pile like a stack of giant Lego pieces in disarray. She investigated the limestone slabs carefully with her lights on high beam. She could see distinctive cart ruts, deep man-made grooves in the blocks running as far as her vision permitted. The cart ruts were overgrown with sea grasses but they had the same appearance as those on the land. She saw decorative carved megalithic blocks which lay scattered and broken. They looked like the remains of some important temple complex. Eve took some pictures of the artwork carved on the slabs and standing stones, which might help her later to identify the civilisation that created such temples. Etienne found some bronze and metal statuettes and placed some gold coins he had discovered in a bag to investigate later.

Without any warning, they were suddenly interrupted by what felt like a strong current that made the sea swirl back and forth as though they were in a tumble dryer. Eve was pulled away from Etienne for a few metres by the forceful current but was still connected by the heavy-duty rope. She panicked at the sudden change in conditions and tugged at the rope several times as hard as she could to signal she was in danger. Some type of commotion was occurring in the sea. The strong current continued to push her back and forth relentlessly and she lost control of her ability to move freely. The current continued to strengthen, pushing her in one direction and then the opposite way. Something was wrong with her breathing apparatus and she was struggling to get enough air. Eve frantically tried to reattach it, but she couldn't see anymore with the amount of silt that now clouded the water. The last thing she remembered was being overcome by complete darkness.

Eve drifted off into oblivion, into another space, another dimension, where no time existed. She woke to see her lifeless body completely wasted, an empty shell, retrieved from the sea and lying limp on a bench on the Calypso. Something had gone terribly wrong. What had just happened?

She could see Etienne was distressed and leaning over her body desperately trying to resuscitate her. She saw him frantically zipping down the top half of her wetsuit, turning her on her side to clear her passageways and start blowing air down her throat. He pumped with both hands on her chest to restart her heart. He checked for a pulse and pleaded with her to come back. She could see his continued frantic efforts and the fear on his face when he got no response. He paused for a few moments, never taking his eyes off her. Eve could feel his immense sadness and distress. She came alongside him and placed her hand on his shoulder.

"But I'm still here," Eve said in his ear as she caressed his face. "I want to come back!" This time she yelled but it was no use, no one could hear or see her. She was invisible.

Etienne continued trying to resuscitate her. He was not giving up.

She looked around the Calypso and could hear the crew talking about a freak earthquake that no one saw coming.

"There were no warning signs – it just happened. We were at the worst place at the wrong time. Marsaxlokk Bay is one of the few sectors of cliff in Malta that coincide with the Maghlak Fault, bordered by cliffs in Marsaxlokk Bay. It is one of the unexpected dangers of diving in this region with an active fault in the seabed making it a very dangerous site. An undersea earthquake can be as deadly as the ones on land, causing all types of havoc in the sea. Our only saving grace was that it appeared to be a relatively small earthquake, otherwise it could have triggered a tsunami and we would all have perished in an instant, not just Eve," one of the crew explained.

"Fuck! She can't pass away like this." Etienne cursed the sky as he stood up and punched a wooden post with his fist, causing his knuckles to bleed.

Eve's soul was floating over her body. She was looking down at the commotion. She could see and hear everything that was going on as though she were watching some drama on television. It was a strange sensation. She didn't feel any pain, she had no idea of how much time had passed and her soul was gliding through the air, not knowing how to get back inside her body.

"You have done all you can, Etienne! I'm sorry, buddy, but she's dead. Just let her be." The crewmember hugged Etienne, trying to calm him down. He sat Etienne down to bandage up his bleeding fist.

Eve found it hard to comprehend. This is not what she had expected, as she had such high hopes. Dying was not part of her plan. It was a strange feeling seeing her lifeless body. It was like she was there but not there, like she was in a room next door or a different dimension, stuck in-between realms of the living and the dead.

She placed both hands on her face – it was still there – and she looked down at herself. She was still in the same body.

"Where am I?" Eve asked out aloud.

She looked up and could see the silhouettes of a large group of people approaching her. She didn't feel afraid or threatened but incredibly light and calm. As they came closer she instantly recognised some, like her much-loved Buznanna, who embraced her immediately. This time Eve didn't want to let go and she held tightly onto her. "I've missed you so much," Eve said, so emotional she could hardly speak. There was no need for words here anyway.

Eve could feel the connections and emotional ties she had with everyone in her soul family. Others in her soul family joined in, embracing her. Her grandmother, grandfathers, daughters, husbands and others gathered until they all connected in a giant group hug forming a revolving circle, much like a spiral, where she received telepathic messages to the numerous questions racing through her mind. She was being shown her soul group, people that were closest to her and that she was connected to in this lifetime and others. It included the villains, not just the people she got along with. She would continue to reincarnate with this soul group and sort out issues from lifetime to lifetime, like an informational matrix as our DNA brings information from life to life, until we learn our lessons and sort it all out.

It was a huge telepathic reunion with her soul family. Eve could feel the connections she had with people in this group and all her thoughts were being answered. The last voice to come streaming through her mind was of Buznanna wishing her good fortune and courage, *qalb ta qalbi* – heart of my heart – till we meet again. As the souls faded, she was left alone digesting the experience. There was no urgency in this realm, no clocks, no deadlines to meet, no time. The past, present and future were intertwined as one and Eve had just got a glimpse of that.

Eve felt a gust of air and a tall presence standing beside her. She looked up to see who it was. She looked so familiar with blue roses in her auburn hair, large almond-shaped eyes, high cheekbones and fine clothes. She was even wearing the same azure coat with the distinguishing halo of stars. It finally dawned on Eve who she was. How could she ever forget her? It was the Blue Queen, the Great Mother Goddess who had appeared to her when she was younger.

"I understand you have unfinished business and I'm here to help you, but only if you want to go back inside your earthly body," she said telepathically to Eve.

"I want to return but I don't know how. I don't want to leave yet – I have many goals and dreams to fulfil before I leave this life."

"Indeed you do, Eve. I know you better than anyone else. You have a lot to accomplish. You are going to need the help of Bozo and the ankh and star pendant to find the knowledge you are after – that is the only way," the Blue Queen hinted as they travelled in a vortex of spiralling blue light back onto the Calypso.

Eve could see that Etienne had restarted his resuscitation efforts. It appeared he was not giving up. She could hear him stubbornly pleading with her to come back. Eve couldn't bear to see Etienne distraught. He had been incredibly good to her.

"That is your last cue to re-enter your body and I will help you, so focus all your energy on returning. Set your intentions to go back inside!" the Blue Queen demanded as she radiated a visible wavelength aura that covered Eve in a thick violet haze. She encouraged Eve to be determined and visualise the process.

Eve lingered and aligned herself from head to toe over her lifeless body. She focused all her energy on reuniting her soul to her body and felt a force start to pull on her aerial body which grew stronger and more intense. For an instant it was like free falling when you've bungy jumped off a cliff, plunging with speed and with no control until WHOOMF! With the sudden hair-raising plunge of the bungy jump, Eve drew an enormous gasping breath, bouncing back into her body like the rebounding rope that prevents you from the fall. She opened her eyes to see the stark blue sky above her. She'd done it, she thought to herself with immense relief.

She immediately looked at Etienne who looked as though he had just seen a ghost. It quickly changed to a look of sheer relief and delight. Etienne squeezed her shoulders as he drew her up flush against his chest and just held her. Eve could hear his heart beating wildly. He held the back of her neck with his hands as he moved in closer to firmly kiss her lips.

"Thank god you're back! You really scared me. I thought I'd lost you forever." Etienne could not help but be excited by her return.

Even though it was nice to be kissed by Etienne, she could feel all the aches and pains that plagued her body. She felt nausea as she pulled away from him and violently coughed up bucket loads of seawater from her lungs. Her throat was burning as she held her head in her palms trying to recuperate. She felt much better after dispelling the liquids from her body. She was reborn again, just like the magical Phoenix.

"I hope you're not going to have that response every time I kiss you," Etienne joked as he helped Eve settle down.

Etienne instructed the captain to head back to the island of Gozo as he held Eve in his arms.

As they approached Gozo at the end of a traumatic day out at sea, a pod of dolphins were frolicking close to the Calypso. One in particular was torpedoing itself high into the air, showing off its strength, agility and speed, as if it wanted to be noticed. It looked different from the other dolphins in the pod. As the crewmembers secured the Calypso in the Marina the albino dolphin came close to the boat and peered into it.

Eve noticed the dolphin looking. Could it be Bozo? Eve wondered. Surely she would recognise him from his unique markings underneath those brilliant eyes. She remembered marvelling over Bozo when she had first encountered him as a calf on Gozo. His mother Maia had introduced him to Buznanna and Eve. Now he would be all grown up, with his own family. Eve would never forget Bozo's eyes so she kneeled against the side of the boat as the dolphin came face to face with her.

"It *is* you, Bozo!" Eve smiled as she stroked the side of his face. He had the same dark brown eyes with the distinctive blue edging around both eyeballs.

Bozo instantly acknowledged that she was correct by telepathically communicating with her and nodding. It was like meeting a long-lost friend. Bozo was incredibly happy and loyal and he made it clear he would help her find what she was looking for when she was ready to recommence her search. He was certain they would need his help and sonar skills to be successful. Bozo reassured Eve that he would be around for her next expedition. His home is this vast sea and he will be waiting for her.

"It's Bozo!" Eve introduced Etienne as he knelt beside her. Bozo in sheer excitement splashed Etienne right in the face, as his tail pounded the water.

"What a gorgeous, playful dolphin – he has followed the boat all the way home."

"What a day!" Eve sighed. "And what a pleasant surprise to reunite with the magnificent and intelligent Bozo. He will be our guide next time."

This day out at sea unravelled the unexpected. They had planned things to go one way and got a totally different outcome they never saw coming. Looking on the bright side she was still alive and her will to carry on was not broken. She would only be broken if she gave up after this accident.

Eve's near-death experience made her even more determined to go after her dreams and goals as she realised how finite our time is on earth from one life to the next. Her experience showed Eve she was not alone in her mission and that she had powerful spiritual guides to help her find the right path. Her resurrection from the dead had given her a deeper spiritual knowing that thinned the veil between reality, divine connectedness and the eternity of souls.

Chapter 11

Venus

The brightest evening and morning star, the beautiful planet of Venus, has captured the hearts of many as she shines in all her glory. Venus is often recognized as the evening and morning star because it is the brightest star in our sky after the moon and the sun. Eve loved to look up at the stars and always searched for Venus first. Besides feeling close to Buznanna when she looked at Venus, she felt re-energised looking at this planet, a powerhouse of brilliant energy. Eve had been even more reflective after her near-death experience. The experience had made her lose her fear of death and gain a deeper understanding that we are never truly alone.

Eve and Etienne were both emotionally exhausted from their terrifying experience out at sea. They agreed that, for the moment, there would be no more deep-sea diving expeditions. They both needed a break so they boarded the *Calypso* for a relaxing afternoon trip to Comino, a small island between Malta and Gozo.

"What you are searching for is very challenging. We will need to have a better strategy the next time round. It will be safe to snorkel around Comino and explore the caves of the Blue and Crystal Lagoons – the crystal clear water and fine white sand is incredibly beautiful and relaxing. It's just what we need."

"I agree, the undersea earthquake nearly claimed my life, but I'm back thanks to your efforts. I don't like not finishing something I have started and invested so much time researching. I don't want to quit now, but I agree we need a break."

"You are a courageous woman! Your tenacity will get you far in life," Etienne said as he steered the boat. He picked up her hand and gently planted a kiss on it revealing a cheeky smile as he looked into her eyes showing his admiration for her. Eve blushed as her experiences with Etienne had drawn her closer to him in ways she hadn't expected.

"I'm the lucky one to have a strong army man as my diving partner," Eve said, to pay back the compliment.

As the Calypso approached the Blue Lagoon it was exactly how Eve remembered it as a girl – an unspoilt and tranquil paradise.

"I recall associating the Blue Lagoon with the heart chakra when I visited with Buznanna all those years ago, due to it being in between Malta and Gozo. It's a kind of paradise that one falls in love with at first sight. The shimmering aquamarine water over the white sandy sea floor reminds me of a giant, cyan-hued swimming pool, so clean and inviting. The lagoon is hugged by limestone cliffs and hidden caves. It would have served the pirates well as a hideout." Eve recounted her childhood memories of Comino to Etienne as he anchored his boat at the Blue Lagoon.

"That's right," Etienne agreed. Comino is the perfect place for us to unwind and snorkel without having to face the dangers out at sea so far from land."

It was late afternoon and Comino was as stunning and tranquil as Eve remembered it. Most of the tourists had disappeared or were making their way home on the main passenger ferry.

"This tiny island measures only three and a half square kilometres. There is just a family of four living here. In the past the population reached its maximum at approximately 100 people. I know the caretaker of the island – he is accustomed to me bringing scuba diving students here for diving expeditions. He is a creative man who makes boats and hovercrafts from scratch and takes good care of the island, along with the parish priest that has visited every Saturday for the past fifty years and is his link to the outside world, bringing the family all that they require," Etienne explained as he passed Eve some flippers. He grabbed Eve's hands to help her up as they jumped into the warm inviting crystal clear waters from the back of the boat.

It was a colourful world beneath the clear waters of the Blue and Crystal lagoons. The underwater topography was stunning and included a network of tunnels, caves, massive blocks of coralline limestone covered in red and green algae, seagrasses, colourful sponges, corals and strange rock formations one can swim through, forming a rich and diverse aquatic ecosystem. As they explored the lagoons and tunnels with their torches when there was not enough natural light, a myriad of fishes and aquatic animals crossed their path from crabs, lobsters, sea urchins, morays, octopus, large groupers, amberjacks, barracuda, tuna and multi-coloured cuckoo wrasses. As they slowly ventured around they were fortunate to see several flying gurnard fish picking their way across the sand, with their large, prominent eyes. These fish didn't notice their presence otherwise they would have closed their wings and taken flight. They displayed their iridescent blue wings, spread out like a fan. The wings were tipped with a beautiful phosphorescent bright blue probably to scare away predators. There was such a vast array of different aquatic creatures it left Eve in awe of the beauty that lay beneath the surface.

Etienne signalled to Eve that he was returning to the boat. She acknowledged him and continued exploring the shallow waters in a large open cave, which reached approximately twenty metres in either direction. There were two openings to the cave. From one opening she could see the Blue Lagoon and on the other side the vast Mediterranean Sea. She sat on a rocky ledge to watch the amazing sunset and felt such a strong sense of gratitude for getting a second chance at life, and for Etienne.

She watched the mirage of reds, oranges and yellows intertwining and dancing on the water as the sun shed the last rays of its colourful light show upon the sparkling blue sea. Eve sat back and admired the opaque moon hanging full beside Venus and a burst of blazing stars above her.

These were the same stars that had greeted the ancients. The Romans named the bright star Venus after the goddess of love because of its beauty. Ancient Egyptians connected Venus to the House of Horus and Hathor. There is a connection to the goddess Isis, who was the mother of Horus, the child whose father was the god Osiris. Ancient Egyptians associated the mysterious planet of Nibiru to Venus in the past. Venus was identified with the goddess that could also be a powerful planet of destruction, destroying the old to bring forth the new.

Eve was waist deep in water, looking up at the stars, when Etienne swam back into the shallow cave with a bottle and two wine glasses in his hands.

"Be careful what you wish for!" Etienne said. He had obviously seen her admiring Venus as he was approaching.

"You don't miss a thing. What is this you've brought?" Eve asked.

"I bring you the best bottle of rosé wine for us to celebrate," Etienne replied.

"Celebrate what?"

"How precious life is and how important the people are that we meet on our journey. Cheers to you, Eve, for pursuing your quest with incredible bravery." Etienne passed her a glass of wine and lifted his glass to salute her.

"Cheers, I will drink to that." Their glasses gently clinked before they drank. The tranquillity of the lagoon, the constant rush of water and clink of the glasses were a refreshing and relaxing change, perhaps a promise of better things to come.

Etienne was right – the rosé wine was one of the best she had tasted and they managed to slowly finish the bottle.

"You were looking at Venus. She is as beautiful as you, on the inside and out."

Etienne moved in closer until his face was only centimetres away. Eve was reluctant to get too close at first. Etienne smiled at her reaction as his hands pulled her legs directly towards him so she was straddling him while still sitting on the ledge. Eve placed her palm against his firm chest to resist him, but was mesmerised by his approaching mouth as he lowered his lips to gently kiss her. Her whole being was focused on the feel of his body and lips against hers and a tingling sense of euphoria rushed through her body like an unstoppable wave. As they kissed, he tugged at the bow tie releasing one side of her bikini, leaving her exposed.

Eve could feel her excitement soar as she kissed him back passionately this time. His hands cupped and squeezed her bottom as he gently rocked Eve, pulling her sex close to his erection. He purposefully waited for her orgasm to start soaring. She pulled him by the waist towards her when she could no longer wait. He entered her at the right time and pulsated repeatedly inside of her, triggering a multiple orgasm. Eve felt a wave of uncontrollable pleasure rush through her body. She could feel him throbbing and pulsating inside her when she was in her most excited state.

The orgasm was so intense and exhilarating it felt as though her soul had floated out of her body and into the fresh night air, high into the star-studded sky, gradually getting pulled back into her body like a rebounding elastic band. She felt she had left her body again, like an out of body experience where her soul ventured out into the sky. When Eve was back inside her body they slowly released their tight grip on each other as their muscles relaxed. The intensity of the orgasm slowly subsided.

Eve looked at Etienne in amazement, his face reflecting the intensity of his climax simultaneously with her. As they held their embrace afterwards Eve's hands caressed his strong muscular arms and back as his body was still flush against hers. She knew he cared deeply for her.

He had retrieved her body from the sea and not given up on her and for that Eve loved him and wanted to give him everything. Etienne's actions spoke louder than any words. Eve's mind drifted off to daydream land as she came off such a high, like some potent drug, drifting into a state of calmness.

Eventually, they dissolved their embrace as Etienne searched for his swimmers to put them back on. Eve thought she would take advantage and couldn't help herself but scan every inch of his muscular body. She was feasting on some serious eye candy. He reminded her of the famous Renaissance sculpture of David by Michelangelo.

Eve had always been a bit of a nerd, preferring to have her nose in books, and wasn't very experienced when it came to men. Etienne pulled on his swimmers in front of her revealing his manly parts; she smiled as she thought to herself that he could have done some serious damage with that thing if he had wanted to, but he was a gentleman the whole way, and she couldn't imagine a better person to have such a memorable experience with in such a beautiful secluded paradise.

"What are you smiling at?" Etienne asked. It was a rhetorical question and one that Eve didn't need to answer. He moved in to kiss her passionately again. This time he knew she would not resist him. His blue eyes were still filled with desire and passion as he smiled back at Eve and embraced her once again. They swam together out of the cave through the shallow waters and back to the Calypso anchored nearby.

On board Etienne had snacks and drinks prepared so they could chill out by the sea. Eve was impressed by his organisation and timing as she was famished and wanted to talk.

"When are we going diving again?" Eve asked.

"Is that a joke? The only thing I want to do with you in the sea is make mad passionate love to you, ma chérie!"

Eve laughed at his response. "You just reminded me of the French skunk, *Pepé Le Pew*. Did you ever watch that cartoon?"

"Yes and you are so odour-able and hot in your bikini, my ravishing beauty."

"I'm going to slip into something more comfortable." Eve searched for her clothes.

"But where are you going, chérie? My new hobby is

chasing you." Etienne came up close to Eve. He slowly kissed the base of her neck all the way to her lips, as his touch sparked another shiver all the way up her spine.

"Okay, you obviously picked up a few good lines from Pepé Le Pew. I'm sure you have more tricks up your sleeve."

"Yes, I sure do, but on a more serious note, how did you ever manage to get back? Your heart had stopped beating for five minutes and the crew were convinced you were dead. I think in a few more minutes you would have been clinically dead." He picked up her hand and slowly kissed it, looking deep into her eyes.

"I didn't want to die. It's not my time to go and I still have so much unfinished business. I would be devastated if I didn't finish what I have planned. More importantly, I have a great team of spiritual guides that helped me come back to you." Eve winked at Etienne.

"What is all this unfinished business on your plate?"

"I have completed my studies and received my degree in archaeology and I never took the time out, with work and study, to visit the places I've researched and have been fascinated with. These places include the villages of the Dogon tribe in Mali, the Valley of Whales known in Arabic as Wadi Al-Hitan, the Cave of Swimmers in the mountainous Gilf Kebir plateau of the Libyan Desert and Leptis Magna, a prominent city of the Roman Empire in Libya," Eve explained.

"So you want to visit all these places as part of your research?" Etienne asked.

"Exactly, and it is the perfect time to have a break from searching for the temple of Hercules. Sometimes it's better to look at things with a fresh perspective. My research has always come to one conclusion – that civilisations stem from water. The Valley of the Whales was once an ocean and now it's a desert containing skeletons of whales with arms and feet. The rock art at the Cave of Swimmers depicts a battle between mermen that dominated the oceans and the humans on the land. This rock art painting may have been created approximately 10,000 years ago, during the most recent Ice Age. I would like to visit Mali because the Dogon religion is about aquatic god-like beings who lived in North Africa. All these places and sites are connected to understanding our aquatic past. Most importantly, their proximity to the Maltese archipelago can give me clues to the answers about our ancient past and the relevance it holds for us today."

"That sounds like a good plan, but what makes you so sure that our aquatic existence is the missing link in human evolution?"

"I've done loads of research and reading of ancient texts. Ancient Sumerian legends first point to the existence of an aquatic and amphibious being known as Oannes, a bit like the legend of Poseidon, perhaps even the same being. He was half-man, half-fish. Legend has it that he was the teacher of civilisation and interbred with earthly women. These aquatic mammals have been labelled the Nommos, and in order to discover more about the Nommos I must visit the Dogon tribal elders in Mali.

"The symbolism in the temples always points to these aquatic beings as though they needed to be remembered. The Dogon originally came from Libya but migrated to isolated Mali and preserved their religion from outside influences. The Dogon religion is based on these gods of the water. Enter the ancient legend of Atlantis which was founded by Poseidon, the God of the Sea, a merman, like Oannes. So many interconnections pointing to our aquatic existence are not all coincidences."

"Okay, I'm not sure what I'm getting myself into with you, but you're convincing and not only because you are a ravishing archaeologist on a mission. It sounds as though it's time for an adventure in the desert. I am definitely coming with you to Africa. I don't think it's wise for you to travel alone and besides, you will need my protection and someone who can speak fluent French to the native Mali elders. *Je connais le desert comme le fond de ma poche!"*

"That sounds very romantic, but what did you just say?"

"I know the desert like the bottom of my pocket."

"You mean like the back of your hand!" Eve was relieved that Etienne wanted to accompany her.

Chapter 12

The Watery Cradle of Civilisation

The aircraft descended from the blanket of clouds that looked like giant pieces of cotton wool teased apart. The first appearance of dawn's bleeding shades of oranges and reds were strewn across the sky as in a Monet masterpiece. The crack of dawn gave promise of an exciting adventure, a new beginning. Eve couldn't help but feel excited about visiting places she had only read about. The aircraft steadily descended towards the well-lit landing strip as the plane made a smooth landing at Cairo International Airport.

Etienne had pre-booked a four-wheel drive equipped with camping gear and all the supplies they needed for their two-day adventure in the desert. Before they drove out into the desert they visited the marvellous building feats of the

The Watery Cradle of Civilisation

Giza pyramids and the Sphinx. Eve suggested they take a camel ride around the area. Eve spotted an Egyptian man wearing a traditional Egyptian garment known as a jellabiya, a long shirt, and holding the reins of a camel.

"Hello, can we both ride?" Eve asked.

"Yes, he is very strong." The camel knelt down so they could climb up. The man passed the flimsy reins to Eve sitting in the front and instructed them to hold on tightly. He clapped his hands and the camel lurched to his feet, making grunting, roaring, grumbling, bellowing camel noises and ambled off. As its hooves sank into the sand, it flew up and scattered all over the place. Etienne had his arms wrapped tightly around Eve from behind and they were both holding on for dear life.

"Wow this camel is bumpy! We are like jockeys!" Etienne spoke loudly in Eve's ear.

All Eve could manage to do was laugh as they bounced around from side to side. The unruly camel zoomed past the Great Pyramid of Giza, the oldest remaining monuments of the Seven Ancient Wonders of the World and around the Sphinx at record speed as if he were on some imaginary racetrack, striving for first place.

It felt like watching a fast-paced documentary getting a spectacular view of the pyramids and the Sphinx, a limestone monument with the face of a man and the body of a lion. The camel raced back to his owner when he saw him clapping his hands in the air directing him back in. It came to an abrupt halt and knelt back down so they could disembark.

"He's in training to be a racing camel," the man declared.

"No kidding! I would never have guessed that!" Etienne retorted as he tucked his shirt back into his pants.

"The grand prize is $1 million dollars. You know the average speed of racing camels has increased by 30%," the man continued.

"You've got yourself a winner here!" Eve smiled at the man as she re-tied her hair. The camel still had a crazed look in its eyes.

They were both relieved to be off the camel and in one piece as they drove southwest through the desert to the Valley of the Whales, known as Wadi Al-Hitan. One hour into the drive they had a break at the Faiyum Oasis, next to Lake Moeris. As they stared out into the abyss of the desert they could see the silhouette of a man approaching them from out of nowhere. As he came closer they could see he was wearing a white turban and a jellabiya, a long blue shirt with wide sleeves and slits on either side with trousers underneath. As he came closer they could see his short grey beard, his bronzed skin contrasting with his hazel eyes. The gentlemen introduced himself as Ismael and welcomed them to the oasis in Egyptian.

"Kifinti," Eve greeted the man in Maltese. Eve soon discovered she could communicate in Maltese as well as in English with the Egyptian man.

"Are you here to seek the Labyrinth?" Ismael asked.

"No, what is the Labyrinth?" Etienne asked.

"It's believed to be somewhere around here buried beneath the sand. It's a marvel that was greater than the pyramids. The lost labyrinth of ancient Egypt is a colossal temple said to contain 3,000 beautifully adorned rooms connected by a confusing array of passages, chambers and stairs. The lower level of the labyrinth contains tombs of kings and the sacred crocodiles."

"What are the sacred crocodiles?" Eve asked.

"Sobek was the crocodile god. He was the god of the Nile River, who brought fertility and prosperity to the land. Tame crocodiles were often kept in temples in pairs and fed choice cuts of meat. They were considered sacred. Sobek was the god of the Army, but his mother Neith was the goddess of War. She has a temple in Sais dedicated to her."

"That's right! Neith is the patron goddess of Sais and is identified with Athena, and that's why Solon visited the temple of Sais, to pay tribute to the goddess. It was at this stage he heard the legends of Atlantis from the high priest. Are there any legends associated with the Valley of the Whales?" Eve asked.

"There are many legends, but let me tell you my favourites. There is a legend that the Valley of the Whales was an inland sea connected to the great ocean and this inland sea was where dying whales would finish their life. The whales knew the way to their cemetery by following magnetic lines using their sonar capabilities. This place is the aquatic mammals' safe haven."

"What type of aquatic mammals are we talking about?" Eve asked.

"Dolphins, orcas, dugong, leviathans, plesiosaurs, basilosaurs, megalodon and even the legendary mermaid."

"Are you for real? The plesiosaur aka the Loch Ness monster came to die here during the last Ice Age?" Eve was astonished.

"These are the legends, and it's your choice what to believe, but remember there is truth in legends. You should speak with my brother, Hakeem, who is an archeologist and a scholar in ancient Egyptian pre-history. He lives next to the Gilf Kebir plateau, next to the Cave of Swimmers. Are you going in that direction?"

"In fact, yes, we were planning on seeing the Cave of Swimmers, so I'll contact him today. Thanks for your help." Eve was pleased to have made such connections.

"*Saħħa, Sliem għalik.*" Eve bowed her head in gratitude bidding him farewell and peace in Maltese.

"*Salam alaikum,*" Ismael replied, wishing them both peace and good travels.

They continued their journey through the impressive

desert landscape. The Valley of Whales, also known as Wadi Hitan, lies in the middle of a distinctive desert landscape of wind-eroded rock platforms surrounded by sand dunes and hills. Etienne drove as far as allowable with their four-wheel drive to respect the rules and not damage any fossil remains. They walked the remaining distance to the site.

They were greeted by blazing heat and a cloudless sky that offered no protection from the sunshine. The lizards took shelter in the shadow of the huge petrified rock formations where the sand was not so hot it would fry them alive. Eve and Etienne did the same as they stopped for regular drinks of water, seeking shelter from the harsh rays. At that moment, drinking ice-cold water in this desert heat felt like the greatest luxury on earth.

Walking to the valley they captured the beautiful sight of the pristine desert, the rippled sand dunes that appeared like a vast undulating sea. Their sneakers sank into the searing sands with every step as they walked towards the basin of Wadi Hitan. It was hard to believe with so much clean fine sand everywhere that this place was once submerged in water, as an ocean, some forty or fifty million years ago

Their eyes feasted on the serenity and peacefulness of the desert that holds evidence of what was so long ago. The scorched sand shimmered in the intense white rays of the sun as they approached an outdoor and indoor museum. Their hats cocooned their heads in warm sweat but the heat wasn't going to stop them from exploring this ancient treasure trove. They discovered numerous excavation sites of various aquatic mammals and fish including whales and sharks. Organic matter had petrified – such things as mangrove bushes, corals, shark teeth and fossil remains were scattered all over the valley. Discoveries of buried fossil skeletons had been continually made by archaeologists as wind exposure unearthed new fossil remains. The site contains over 390 known whale skeletons of five different varieties, showing the major evolutions in Earth's aquatic life.

The earliest ancient whale is known as the Basilosaurus, which has been trapped for millennia in sandstone formations in this ancient sea. The ancient collection of whale fossils in Wadi Hitan provides evidence of the evolution of the whales from land to a marine existence.

The first skeletons of Basilosaurus (meaning King Lizard) were originally thought to be of a huge marine reptile. It was only later on that the species were identified as whales that moved easily between land and sea. The whale site and fossils at Wadi Hitan clearly show the transitional phase of the mammals' evolution. Research teams discovered that whales were land-based animals before becoming ocean going. Fossils were found showing the whales retained useless legs, feet, and toes, representing rear legs that were lost in the evolution cycle.

This evidence is reliable, as many of the whale skeletons are in excellent condition, preserved in the rock formations. Other well-preserved skeletons of a Basilosaurus evolution resemble a giant sea snake. These evolving skeletons provide valuable information about how the whale swam and made the transitional phase from land to ocean. The excavated skeletons show evidence of the last stages of evolution from land animals to a marine existence involving the loss of the rear limbs and an alteration to the typical body form of modern whales while retaining certain primitive aspects of skull and tooth structure.

Etienne was ecstatic to see the remains of his favourites, the oversized teeth of a Megalodon, an extinct mega-sized shark that could consume two full-grown whales in one bite. His other favourite was a Basilosaurus whale skeleton with limbs for walking and the face of a crocodile. Eve thought she would share some of her favourite research with Etienne and some interesting sexual trivia about aquatic mammals.

"Do you know that many scientific researchers have argued that the pelvic bone in whales and dolphins will atrophy, as it is no longer used? This assumption has been reversed as scientists argue that the muscles that control a cetacean's penis are attached to the creature's pelvic bones and that species in promiscuous, competitive mating environments, where females mate with multiple males, develop larger testes, relative to their body mass, in order to outdo the competition. The pelvic bone, an inherited throwback to ancestors that once walked on land has in fact a very useful function for reproduction and continuation of the species for aquatic mammals."

"No I didn't know that about the male's pelvic bone, but that's amazing! You have researched all the strangest things you could get your hands on. Like a sea nymph!" Etienne was amused by her sexual trivia stories about aquatic reproduction.

"It's no laughing matter! Reproduction is one of the main roles of our existence. I even had a dream likely to be a past-life memory that I swam among giant-sized killer whales with their distinctive black and white markings. My role was to collect their seed, in a vessel, for genetic engineering purposes. I could breathe underwater for long periods and the whales were cooperative and domesticated. There was no danger. My legs were longer with larger feet, which enabled me to be a strong swimmer. My skull was elongated. I was human, but a different-looking human that could swim in the water for a long time. It's possible that before the last great flood there were many species of humans, some with a strong aquatic link and some were giants as stated in the bible, in Genesis."

"When you look at this amazing place and how it was the sea floor 40-50 million years ago and now it's a desert, I begin to think anything could have been possible."

They headed to their next destination, Gilf Kebir, the famous Cave of Swimmers, one of the driest deserts in the world. Eve contacted Hakeem and organised to meet him in the foyer of the International Hot Springs Hotel in Bahariya. Hakeem turned up right on time. He resembled his younger brother Ismael and had the same hazel eyes and bronzed skin. Hakeem pointed out that the foyer has a reproduction of the Cave of Swimmers which is actually better than the cave of swimmers itself, as the paintings have unfortunately been vandalised and damaged. Hakeem spoke fluent English and he suggested they go hiking to see all the caves and remaining artwork.

They ordered some fruit-flavoured shisha to smoke and some mint tea. Hakeem was curious about Eve's pendant. He showed them a portrait of the goddess Neith who was wearing a similar pendant, carrying an ankh in one hand and a spear in the other. Neith wore a helmet like Athena, the warrior goddess. Hakeem told Eve she must be a descendant of an ancient royal lineage to carry this pendant. The Egyptian pharaoh had to marry his eldest sister first before taking on other wives. To access the underworld and to be a complete spiritual leader the pharaoh had to possess his firstborn sister's inherited intuitive and spiritual powers through their union and close bloodlines. It was a necessary union in marriage and procreation to carry on the genetic lineage of the firstborn female through the generations. By doing so the pharaoh ensured his next incarnation would be in a family closely related to him so that he had a better chance to be pharaoh again in another lifetime.

"I was born in Bahariya, but travelled and lived abroad to complete my university studies in archaeology and became a senior lecturer in the Faculty of Archaeology Department of Egyptian Antiquities at Cairo University.

"As kids we had so much fun playing in these ancient caves whose precious art told the stories of the ancient past, stories that give us insight into our true origins. I still have a good recollection of the artwork and have even redrawn many images I did as a child, fortunately before they were vandalised.

"There are numerous caves here such as the Cave of the Archers and the Cave of the Beast. All present fascinating artwork and stories. My interest in archaeology first started here. Of course, now I am retired, and enjoy meeting foreigners who are interested in researching my special hometown."

"We are both extremely grateful for your assistance at such short notice. Do these coins mean anything to you?" Etienne pulled the coins from his pouch that he had retrieved from their diving expedition in Marsaxlokk. Etienne placed the gold coins in his hands. Hakeem appeared to be intrigued as he analysed the coins carefully.

"These are absolutely amazing – they are rare and I believe they are ancient Sumerian or Akkadian. One looks like Oannes, and the other looks like a Sumerian sage known as Abgallu who assisted the gods like Oannes for the Babylonians or Thoth for the Egyptians. In one of the caves, one of the Abgallu is watching a battle. He's a Watcher. In the teachings of many cultures they are called many names like angels or the shining ones, or the Elohim. To the Egyptians, the Watchers are known as Ptah, Anubis, Osiris and Horus.

"The Cave of Swimmers depicts a battle between the humans on land versus the humans of the sea. Different species of humans existed 12,000 years ago. There were giants, dwarfs, mermen and other chimeras. The most authentic experience would be for us to go camping to nearby caves that I know and no one else knows about and I'll show you my childhood sketches of the famous caves before they were damaged and share my opinions with you both regarding my interpretation of the rock art."

"Wow, you would do that for us? That sounds amazing. We are well equipped with camping gear, food, drinks and water in our four-wheel drive." Eve was extremely grateful for such a generous offer to share his knowledge and insight.

"You're both very welcome! Eve, you possess the ankh and star pendant and you should be a guardian of the truth."

They left the International Hot Springs Hotel in Bahariya and took a two-hour drive south onto Farafra Road which leads to the Farafra Oasis in the White Desert. During the time of the ancient Egyptians, Farafra was named "Tahet," meaning the land of the cow, in reference to its agriculture. They camped next to Wadi el-Obeiyd near the rock formations well before dark. After they had set up camp they went to a special cave that only a few locals like Hakeem knew.

"What's so special about this cave?" Eve asked.

"This cave has not been tampered with and it depicts many scenes of an ultimate battle. It is a battle between the mammals on the land versus the mammals in the sea, and there is an intervention by our legendary ancestors. One ancestor is depicted in red ochre and is half woman, with breasts and wings and the body of a lioness. Her name is Lebe. She is depicted five times the size of a standard lioness. She is leading the battle, protecting her troops behind her in the sea. She's the symbol of the protective mother. Her armies are aquatic mammals consisting of mermen, dolphins and whales.

"The giant humans are trying to restrain the beast that resembles a Sphinx by tying her up with thick golden-coloured ropes, held by numerous men circling her, trying to entrap her. The men outnumber her and at one stage Lebe is lying motionless and lifeless on the floor. The men roar, lifting their spears to the sky, claiming their victory.

"Despite their premature claim to victory, Lebe opens her eyes and raises herself on her hind legs, roaring back with all her might, breaking her bondage. She devours the assailant men one at a time and spits out their bloodied limbs, leaving their body parts strewn all over the battlefield.

"The other legendary ancestor is a giant, dark-skinned, muscular man with the head of a jackal. He is leading an army of archers from behind, manipulating the archers' minds. A battle is raging between all the hybrid human species. The archers were releasing their arrows against the aquatic beings, while Lebe steamrolled the remaining archers into the sea. Some archers and men with spears were on boats where the aquatic mammals could fight back in their territory. The land beings stood no chance because the aquatic beings were stronger and possessed a superior intelligence and communication system. Some aquatic mammals were depicted in the artwork with elongated skulls. They had more evolved skills and senses than the modern-day human.

"Lebe and the aquatic mammals possessed greater wisdom and spirituality and they only went to war to defend their home and their territory. The Jackal was a master manipulator and forced their hand to fight and go to war. Lebe and the aquatic mammals were peaceful beings and the majority chose to retreat to sacred places in the ocean and to large cavities under the earth's surface, known as Hollow Earth.

"They knew the Jackal would be a constant annoyance on the land. The most powerful remained and that was Lebe, as she was a shape shifter and could change herself into any creature from a merman to a soaring falcon in the sky. She retreated to an island but kept her eye on the Jackal, as she knew he was the bad seed and could not be trusted. Someone needed to fight the Jackal and the evil he would constantly create. Lastly, there's a depiction above the battlefield of a cluster of six stars – the formation represents the Pleiades."

"Aren't there nine stars in the Pleiades? What's the relevance of the Pleiades in the scene?" Eve butted in.

"In fact you are correct. With a telescope you can see nine stars forming the cluster but to the naked eye you can only see six bright stars and one faint star. They provided a heavenly marker for the beginning of the autumn and spring equinox around 15,000 BC. Most likely this indicates the timing of the battle.

"The ancient Greeks could see seven stars in the sky and in ancient mythology associated the clusters of seven stars with the seven daughters of the Titan named Atlas. The Greek word for the seven daughters of Atlas is *Atlantis*. In this location, we are not far from the Atlas Mountains in Morocco, so this battle could be associated with the legend of Atlantis. Atlas was believed to be one of the sons of Poseidon and he was the first king of Atlantis.

"Greek literature implies that Atlantis literally means daughter of Atlas, and this is where it gets interesting. In 30 BC, the famous Greek historian Diodorus Siculus recorded the legends of the Near East and the Mediterranean area. Unfortunately, only fifteen of his forty books have survived. In his third book, Siculus described a wild female tribe known as the Amazons. He said they lived on the farthest outskirts of Western Libya.

"Siculus is strongly implying there was a battle between the Amazon and the *Atlantioi*, ancient Greek for Atlanteans. The word *Amazon* is derived from the Old Persian word *hama-zan* meaning all women. The homeland of the Amazons was a huge fertile island called Hespera, famously known for the garden of the Hesperides, and was located in the Tritonis marsh. Nowadays, Lake Tritonis is a large body of freshwater in northern Africa that was described in many ancient texts. Siculus concluded that the Tritonis marsh disappeared when an earthquake separated the coastal areas."

"The world of the Amazons was ruled by warrior women and correlates to the fictional story published by DC Comics of Wonder Woman, based on ancient Greek mythology," said Eve. She couldn't help but make comparisons.

"That's right. The Libyan Amazons were matriarchal warriors. They had suppressed all the neighbouring nations, including the most civilized people of that area, believed to be Atlantis. The Amazons defeated Atlantis with a force of 30,000 infantry and 3,000 cavalry. The Atlanteans submitted to the Amazons and reluctantly agreed to do whatever the queen of the Amazons, known as Myrina, demanded of them. Myrina was a true warrior but also a queen of hearts who showed compassion. A new city on the remnants of Cerne was named Myrina, in her honour. There is no doubt that the Athena of Herodotus, whom the Amazon worshipped around Lake Tritonis, was none other than the Libyan goddess Tannit, also known as the goddess Neith or Nit by the ancient Egyptians, long before the Phoenicians returned to venerate her as Tanit. The patriarchal powers have discredited the whole existence of the Amazons and it has been dismissed as a myth. Diodorus Siculus pointed out that Atlantis was in fact in the vicinity of Tunisia," said Hakeem.

They walked back to their campsite through the sandstone-coloured desert, threading their way downhill. The pale golden sand appeared rippled from the wind, like an expansive ocean with no end in sight. They admired the occasional flower stone made of silica glass by an ancient meteorite strike, still glowing like green and gold translucent jewels, all etched by sand and wind on the desert sands. The sky grew deep ultramarine as the sun's rays and heat slowly subsided. They relaxed at their campsite enjoying a cold drink and admiring the desert sunset.

Hakeem commented how the sunset appeared like a giant lotus growing in the waters of the Nile, closing its petals and dimming its lights. The Nile Delta is shaped like a lotus flower, a symbol of regeneration and rebirth. The flower of the lotus is connected by its placenta-like attachment with the womb of Isis through the water of the River Nile, by means of the long cord-like stalk, the umbilicus. Sometimes a child is represented as seated in or issuing from the flower.

The Egyptians associated the lotus flower with the sun and creation. Each of her blazing rays represents large lotus petals held together by the stems. The layered petals took it in turn to retreat and slowly close as if they were being consumed by the horizon, only to regenerate when the sun woke at dawn. Eve and Etienne enjoyed the tranquillity of the desert and listening to Hakeem's analogy of the lotus and life's continual regeneration.

Etienne set up a campfire as they continued to talk about Hakeem's sketches from the Cave of Swimmers where *The English Patient* was filmed. He had other intriguing sketches from the Cave of the Beast, the Cave of the Archers and the Cave of the Negative Hands. He showed them other cave drawings and pictures of the Lascaux Cave in France and the Cave of the Spider in Spain, which has early depictions of a man collecting honey from a tall tree, showing that there was a skill in collecting honey. Around the campfire they continued to discuss art and symbolism. Hakeem had a great appreciation of the role of the bee and the warrior goddess, the matriarch.

"Throughout history there have always been battles between good and evil and the cave paintings are telling an important story to help us understand the missing links of the ancient past and the relevance they hold for us today. There is much unbalance between the matriarchal and patriarchal powers and, as a result, life and relationships are deteriorating. We need to re-establish some balance between the two approaches to life otherwise our civilisation faces real upheaval and war," Hakeem pondered.

"Agreed," said Eve. "We need to work not only on balancing the power between the sexes and re-establishing mutual respect but we must not forget Mother Earth, which provides us with abundant resources to sustain life. We need to replenish, regenerate and respect our beautiful planet. We pollute our waters, disturb natural ecosystems and endanger the lives of different species of animals. The bee population is diminishing with the use of Round Up and pesticides.

"By continuing in this way our food supply is threatened. As Einstein said, when the bees die, humans have only four years to live. Bees help the formation of fruit by being the catalyst of the fecundation of flowers. Harmful frequencies and magnetism that are not controlled can disrupt magnetic fields in the earth, sea and in human cells, leading to destructive diseases and mental instability. If it is not controlled, the earth will be affected and major cataclysms will increase. Humanity needs to be aware before Mother Earth retaliates," Eve vented.

"Society can learn from the ancient ways and be observant about the increasing warning signs of natural disasters and erratic climate changes before it's too late. This requires shifting our focus from the materialistic, individual approach to a collective concern about the well-being of our planet and all life on it. It's difficult for a society to maintain an individualistic approach for long-term sustainability.

"Collective societies such as the ants and bees have been on this earth for a hundred million years, working for the collective and working with Mother Earth. These animals must be doing something right to survive that long. We need to reach a happy medium. We need to love our planet and all life on it to sustain it for future generations. What do you see as the way forward for civilisation?" Hakeem asked Eve.

"The way forward is the matriarchal way – a more left-brain approach in balance with the right brain, one that works with respect and in union with all living things – that is the only way to create a new prosperity and harmony.

"In the ancient past there was a cataclysmic epoch that lasted from 10,800 BC to 9,600 BC, that is 1,200 years when the earth changed completely after massive flooding and increasing temperatures that melted the ice caps. Plato gives 9,600 BC as the date of the destruction of Atlantis.

"Scientists believe a giant comet on the outer edges of the solar system caused these two spikes in cataclysms. Sometimes these comets cross earth's orbit and break off into lethal fragments. Two fragments 12,800 and 11,600 years ago hit the earth, resulting in the extinction of the last species of dinosaurs and a global civilisation that was strongly maritime in nature. The earth and our solar system have gone through many cataclysms.

"Edgar Cayce, the American prophet, said that Atlantis was destroyed three times. The Native American Indians say that the human race has been through five great destructions involving water and fire alternatively. The entire solar system goes through a constant cycle of destruction and renewal, like the concept of the Phoenix but we can delay the process if we are open to change. What are your opinions on our way forward?" Eve was interested to hear what Hakeem had to say.

"Agreed. It seems as if culture and religion have got out of control and war is not the solution. I believe respect is. Science is well advanced and the great minds out there need to think of ways to reduce our risk of being wiped out by lethal comet fragments that have crossed earth's orbit in the ancient past. It's the past that holds the answers to our future success but threatens those individuals who hold the reins of power. A collective approach is not very appealing to them," Hakeem concluded.

Eve could smell their dinner being warmed up by the campfire.

"Dinner is ready!" Etienne hollered.

"It smells so good! What's for dinner?" Eve asked.

"We have kushari in this pot, a delicious Egyptian vegetarian recipe consisting of green lentils, macaroni and rice mixed with caramelised onions and a herb-based tomato sauce. We have falafel in this pot, a deep-fried patty made from ground chickpeas and fava beans and various dips such as babaganoush made from pureed aubergine, fava beans, lemon and herbs. For dessert there's a tray of pastries filled with figs, dates and nuts, drenched in honey of course. For beverages there is karkaday, a bright red drink made from hibiscus flowers and kahwa, thick, strong coffee for our long conversations into the night by the campfire."

They dined around the campfire underneath a glistening star-studded sky, more beautiful than any fine restaurant. They admired the light show of a series of shooting stars, streaks of light falling into the earth's atmosphere as dust and rock burning up. The meteor shower was spectacular and completely unexpected, just like their chance encounters. Everything was synchronistic as though they were following some grander plan.

Chapter 13

The Dogon and the Nommos

Bang, clank, thud! The plane's wheels were released for landing, absorbing the shock on the asphalt concrete landing strip in Bamako, the capital and largest city of Mali. The first sliver of sun peeked over the skyline. Radiant gold and orange rays bled like rain over the clear, silt-free waters of the Niger River, the third longest river in Africa after the Nile and Congo rivers. The scene was luminous and mesmerising; it invited Eve to stare deep into the horizon, entranced by the beauty of the liquid gold and silver reflected over the river. The lush green surroundings kissed by dewdrops seemed to glow with their own golden radiance. As the sun revealed itself, it gently warmed her face and her pupils contracted, a gentle reminder in the breeze as it blew strands of hair to caress her face and tell her that things were changing. An uplifting feeling engulfed her that her dream of finding answers and honouring her promise was not far away now.

The plan was to speak with a Dogon elder, perhaps show the ancient map if they met the right person and get information or clues to continue their search. The Dogon are an ethnic group living in the central plateau of the country of Mali, in Western Africa, south of the Niger bend, near the city of Bandiagara, in the Mopti region. Eve and Etienne took another flight from Bamako to Bandiagara, as the Bandiagara Escarpment is known as the Dogon country of Mali, and they booked accommodation in this central location.

As soon as they had sorted out their belongings they ventured around Dogon country. They found it was enigmatic and had an otherworldly quality about it. Dogon cosmology and the spiritual obligations it entails rank among the most intricate of all African stories, layered with symbolism, meaning and mystery.

The escarpment is set against the steep sandstone cliffs and shows off the beauty of Dogon's earthen architecture. The cliffs rise approximately 500 meters above the lower sandy flats and run for approximately 150 kilometres.

Traditional Dogon villages were located high above the plains and were well positioned in case of attack, as advancing enemies could be seen from a distance. Steep gorges and loose rock made it hard to get to the villages at the top of the plateau. Caves in the cliffs provided additional shelter. Dogon architecture seems to spring from a child's fertile imagination with ancient cocoon-like cemeteries attached to the cliff face from centuries past. A series of thatched granaries with elaborately carved wooden doors were scattered all over the place. The nine-pillared togunas or palaver huts were open-sided shelters, served as important meeting places, perched on the escarpment below the plains.

As they explored the village, they could hear beating drums in the distance and followed the sound. Eve loved music and even more she loved to dance. She hadn't realised until she heard the band how much she missed it. The music was unfamiliar, but the beating drums were hypnotic and very powerful. The increased crescendo of drumming made her sway to the rhythm, longing to dance as she could see some local women dressed in bright indigo-dyed robes dancing. Intoxicated with the music Eve started swaying to the tune and was pulled into the circle by a smiling lady from the Dogon village of Ogol-Du-Haut. She introduced herself as Sara before she was drowned out by the drums.

Nearby was a circle of Dogon men in masquerade, some dressed as women on stilts, wearing the great plank masks called *sirige* that seem to reach for the heavens as their tall superstructures, like giants, bridge the earth and sky. The dancers swung the mask in a figure of eight, touching the tip of the mask to the earth in the four cardinal directions. The masks were elaborately made of wood, fibre, cowry shells, plastic beads, metal and cloth, a tradition learned from their ancient ancestors. The masks represented animals and humans. When the noise subsided, Sara stopped to converse with Eve in her limited French. At that moment she felt a familiar touch around her waist and knew it was Etienne without even looking.

"You arrived just in time to talk French with this lovely lady, Sara. Please ask her to recommend an elder we could interview about the Dogon myths."

Etienne and Sara talked and Etienne made a few notes on his phone. She referred him to an elder by the name of Mamadou from her village. They thanked Sara and the music returned.

"Now where were we?" Etienne took her waist again, pulling her flush against him. Eve knew her Latin dancing very well. She had taken her fair share of dancing lessons in the past and recognised the dance instantly. He was doing the merengue with his knees slightly bent and there was a marching action to it and a lot of close hip motion. Their hips seem to meet at the right location following the rhythm in unison to the pounding drums. Their movements were compatible with the exotic music being played.

"You are a surprisingly good dancer for someone in the French Foreign Legion," Eve commented in his ear as she followed his lead. She enjoyed the close dancing contact as he held Eve firmly against his strong body and they moved as one to the rapid pounding of the drums. The exotic music had a Latin feel to it.

"I am a man of many talents," Etienne commented in her ear as he twirled her around and enjoyed pulling her hips back to his.

The crowd separated around them, clapping and dancing, until they were encircled, becoming the centre of attention for a moment but they felt as though they were the only ones there dancing, engrossed in their own little world.

She snuggled gratefully against him. She would have not gotten this far without him. He filled her senses. The warmth of his skin seeping into hers, the hardness of his muscles and his scent were all very reassuring; she felt safe and cherished in his arms. She felt his smiling lips brush her shoulder. His lips worked their way up to her neck gently kissing until he reached her lips, where Eve kissed him back, opening her mouth to him as she felt his tongue touch her lips and plunge into her mouth.

He had a way of marauding all of her senses that she had never experienced with anyone else before. His hand moved from the back of her neck slowly down her back, until he squeezed her backside firmly in his hand, drawing her even closer.

Etienne was truly her knight in shining armour, rescuing her from the ocean and bringing her back to life. When she saw him plead and wait for her to return into her body, she knew there was no other choice. She had to find her way back to him.

She recalled their first meeting. Etienne was convinced he knew Eve and he asked her several times about the possibility. Eve had a dream of their intimate soul connection as a married couple in a past life that still lingered with Etienne on some deep level, but he couldn't quite put his finger on it.

Eve had lost her beloved Buznanna in Malta only to find Etienne's beautiful soul waiting for her. Eve smiled as she remembered the proverb, *when one door closes another one opens*. Like Buznanna's message in her vivid dream, it's always important to stay positive and have faith that after much heartache, better days will be ahead. She held Etienne tightly in her arms and whispered "thank you" in his ear.

She was finally doing what she had only daydreamed about. She couldn't believe she was here in one of the poorest countries on earth but rich with intrigue, mystery, art and music. She was in paradise.

The next morning they walked along the escarpment to visit the Dogon elder by the name of Mamadou. Sara had told Etienne that he would be at the toguna and that he was one of the superior elders, extremely knowledgeable, and he would be able to answer all their questions.

Information was passed on via oral traditions and stories learnt from their families. Apparently, Mamadou was the eldest grandson of the blind Dogon elder, Ogotemmêli, who had taught the main symbols of the Dogon religion, known as the Gods of the Water, to the

French anthropologist Marcel Griaule in 1946. Eve planned to record the conversation so she could go over it as many times as she liked.

The toguna was located in the centre of the village. Eve studied the building carefully before entering. Each hand-carved wooden pillar was fascinating and told a different story in its artwork. There were numerous carvings of twin babies – twin souls – portraying a hermaphrodite concept. There were other carvings of single entities with arms raised to the sky. There were carvings with bearded figures, horsemen, women bearing vessels on their heads, snakes, lizards and numerous black and white checkerboards again pointing to the concept of the twin soul, twin flame. In fact twin births were viewed as a sign of prosperity in the Dogon religion.

They walked past the carved wooden pillars at the entry and were instructed to bend down and lower their heads to enter the toguna. The roof was low and covered with several layers of millet stalks; it didn't allow anyone to stand upright, which avoided violence when discussions got heated.

Eve and Etienne bent down as they entered to find a seat on the floor. They were instructed to sit on the woven straw mat. Soon afterwards a tall, dark, lanky man with dark brown eyes and a grey beard wearing loose white clothing and a white cap sat directly in front of them and they shook hands. He introduced himself in French as Mamadou.

Eve had written a list of questions to ask and suggested to Etienne that they ask Mamadou's permission to record the conversation on her mobile phone. Mamadou seemed to have no issue with Eve's requests, including entering the toguna with Etienne, which was usually a male-dominated environment. Mamadou appeared to be an easygoing person. He simply responded by saying *sewa*, which means that everything is fine, actually meaning the same in the Maltese language. Etienne and Mamadou start talking in French.

"Mamadou wants to know where you got your ankh and star pendant from," said Etienne.

"Tell Mamadou that my great-grandmother entrusted it to me, being the eldest great-granddaughter. Why does he ask?"

"Legend has it that when the female wearer of the ankh and star pendant comes, the elders will show you the way," replied Mamadou.

"The way to what?" Etienne asked.

"Before I tell you what I know, you need to know where the Dogon came from. The Dogon tribe originated from Northern Libya, when it was a tropical paradise. Caucasian people came to live with the Dogon and taught us their religion and the story of the world. This was the time when the Nommos lived on the earth among men."

"Who were the Nommos and where did they come from?"

"The Nommos were amphibians, serpent-like beings. They moved slowly on land. They had a shapeless neck and some were described as having a cow's nose and horns. They spent more time in the water and avoided direct sunlight. The Nommos communicated like dolphins through sonar. The pressure and vibrations of their teeth sent messages to their brains. Unlike humans, dolphins see their environment through sound rather than visual analogues. They came from the stars because their world was dying."

"What did they do when they came here?"

"They needed to survive on this earth so they needed to re-combine their DNA with the local gene pool. There was no intelligent life on earth so they combined their DNA with the animals. When they first combined their DNA they were successful and created self-fertilising androgynous beings that were immortal, like the Nommos."

"Who were the Caucasian people?" Etienne asked, straying from Eve's list of questions. He would check the list at the end to ensure she got all her answers.

Mamadou answered, "They were the teachers, the offspring of the Nommos who fled from their island paradise due to cataclysmic events. They had elongated skulls inherited from the Nommos who bred with earthly women to create a hybrid Nommos female race. Interestingly, the word *Elohim* in Hebrew does not only mean gods but is the feminine plural for goddesses. The Elohim referred to in the Bible could be the Nommos hybrid race.

"The Nommos are self-fertilising females and reproduce by parthenogenesis, a mode of asexual reproduction in which offspring are produced by females without the genetic contribution of a male. In many insects such as honeybees, ants and wasps, female eggs are produced sexually, using sperm from a drone father, while the production of further male drones depends on the queen.

"This means that female workers and queens are always diploid, while male drones are always haploid. There are several differences between diploid and haploid cells, the main one being the number of chromosome sets found in the nucleus so two sets for diploid and one set for haploid. Parthenogenetically, all female virgins produce a male offspring to create gene bio-diversity. I know it's complicated, but do you follow me?"

"Yes, it's like the immaculate conception of Jesus from the Virgin Mary and Horus from Isis or like the Greek goddess Athena who was born fully grown and with horns that look like a helmet, in armour. Athena sprang out of Zeus' skull. Her appearance at birth associated her with a warrior goddess of justice and wisdom," Etienne clarified.

"That's right! Zeus was a Nommos – not a self-fertilising female but a single-sexed male, the necessary genetic error. Through the generations the sexes eventually separated into male and female. Naturally the males were physically stronger than females and the patriarchal ways took control and rewrote the history. Strength is a control mechanism and the matriarchal ways were buried and lost. In fact, Metis, Zeus first wife, was a self-fertilising female who gave birth to Athena, as Zeus fits the description of the Jackal and wanted to be venerated more highly than the great female goddesses."

Etienne sighed. "We can see the results of a patriarchal society today with wars, religion, and unnecessary violence between the sexes. Just as every religion uprooted the previous religion by destroying the temples, the people, the relics, books and sacred sites and then rebuilt their own temple on the previous sacred site. Only the victors write the history, which is not necessarily the full truth, but they spread their own propaganda through their strength."

"You've got it! The Nommos and their offspring had the sonar capacity and the ability to manipulate sound and objects beyond normal human capacity. They communicated telepathically through sounds and could emit whatever frequencies they wanted. They could sense the earth's magnetic ley lines."

"What do you mean by emitting frequencies? How did they use frequencies?" Etienne interjected.

Mamadou continued, "The dolphins' teeth vibrate and emit a sound wave that has the capacity to make matter resonate no matter what its weight. You could explode the matter, move it or even levitate objects. The ankh pendant around Eve's neck was commonly used to amplify frequencies. An ankh like Eve's has never been found in history.

"Let me continue the story of the Nommos. A disorder, an error, appeared at the beginning of time, when a single-sexed male was born. He was referred to in Latin as *Thos Aureus* or the Jackal. He was the first son of God and God's error for forcing his union with the pure earth female. The Jackal was not permitted to reproduce and like a bad boy he broke all the rules.

"He created imbalance due to his single sex versus the normal androgynous offspring who were balanced between the masculine and feminine hormones and qualities. The Jackal was alone from birth and forcefully procreated with his mother, which was forbidden. He procreated with his mother because he wanted to acquire the DNA to enable communication and speech. The symbol of DNA is represented by weaving in the Dogon religion."

"The Jackal was a terror, a failed biological experiment that could not find any spiritual fulfilment. This error could not be undone?" Etienne asked.

"That's right. The Jackal is the outcome of God's initial decision to rape Mother Earth at the wrong time, without consent. Even the white ants tried to defend Mother Earth and God crushed them. At the right time, God created other offspring and had androgynous female twins with Mother Earth. The birth of twins is viewed as a good omen in Dogon religion, as it represents the masculine and feminine, the twin soul mate connection.

"The Jackal just wanted to procreate with anything, eternally struggling and searching for his twin soul, his soul mate. The Jackal's incest was the original sin. The union of the Jackal with related androgynous females, including his mother and sister, created single-sexed twins, in other words masculine and feminine, thereby separating the sexes for the first time for the Nommos. Thereby, the Nommos appear to be the offspring of God.

"The Jackal was cast out for his sins. The ability to speak allowed the Jackal to communicate and reveal God's plan to all the shamans and mystics of the world. The central problem was that the other half was always searching for their soul mate to reunite as one androgynous being as it had been in the very beginning. It is very complex I know, but this is the story of the Nommos which is the basis of our Dogon religion," finished Mamadou.

"Are you saying that males are an accident of nature, an error?" Etienne asked.

"It looks like an error, but it created a new dynamic in the world, for better and worse! Think about it, Etienne, and digest all I have said for a moment." Mamadou paused as he could see Etienne's head was spinning with all the information he had just presented.

"Without good and evil, there is no struggle; there is no dynamic, no destruction, no renewal, to make way for the new creation – no change, no competition. You become stagnant. There are problems with perfection. It's boring, there's no emotion," said Etienne, pouring out his thoughts.

"That is why the bad Jackal is so important because from a wrong something good eventually develops. We need a big soup of DNA to create biodiversity in order to perfect what we are creating. It was a necessary evil. You need to go through the suffering to appreciate what you have. The main problem with the Jackal is that he was born without a twin soul, and to avoid this ever occurring again all humans had to be converted into single-sexed beings with one soul, continually seeking the other half, the second or twin soul," Mamadou continued.

"Most of us are seeking our soul mate, our other half, to complete ourselves. When you meet your soul mate you will just know!" Etienne exclaimed, winking at Eve, who was intrigued and curious by the lengthy French conversation and occasional glances her way, but oblivious to the content of their conversation.

"What was the role of the Jackal in all this?" Etienne continued.

"The Jackal was the so-called bad seed, bad boy, which was combined in a second and third experiment with the good seed of the Nommos called the Master Orator who was the perfect combination of human and Nommos. Like many women she must have been intrigued by the bad boy. The Nommos did selective breeding and five generations later there were no more androgynous, immortal offspring. We see the creation of the first single-sex beings, male and female, who were mortal. It's a lot to digest, my dear friends, but that is the oral story I inherited from my blind grandfather, Ogotemmêli, who was a well-respected elder. *Sewa* – in other words, are you good with it all?"

"Not yet. You mentioned the legend that the female with the ankh and star will return. When she returns you will show her the way. The way to what? You still have not explained," probed Etienne.

"As you know from our history, Lebe led us from Northern Libya to Mali. At that time the Blue Queen from the great island visited us and was wearing the same ankh and star pendant. She said she would return and we will have to show her the way. The way to the island is north of where the Dogon started. North of Libya lies the legendary Blue Queen's Island, the Great Mother Goddess and the navel of all civilisations. That's all I know about the way. Finding the way is a reward, but the journey itself and what you learn along the way is the true reward. Remember the eyes are blind and one must look within the heart to find the way."

"Sewa and merci beaucoup," said Etienne and Eve, thanking Mamadou for his generosity in sharing his knowledge and inherited oral traditions.

Chapter 14

Plato's Atlantis

The synchronicities that had eventuated on this trip were signs to Eve that they were on the right path. This occurred every time she listened to her instincts. They were fortunate to have met the right people at just the right time. All the information presented itself as though some divine hand was guiding them. They boarded their flight from Bamako airport in Mali to Tripoli in Libya for the last stopover of their trip to visit the UNESCO World Heritage Site of Leptis Magna. They had a lot to talk about on the four-hour plane trip to Tripoli. They boarded with heads full of fresh knowledge and insights.

Etienne wanted to know how much Eve knew about Atlantis. "You've implied that Malta could be the location for Atlantis several times. Malta is a minute island on the world map, so insignificant!" Etienne was clearly playing devil's advocate with her. He was teasing her and fishing for a reaction to see how passionate she was.

"What have you read or know about Atlantis?" Eve asked Etienne.

"I've read comic books about Atlantis and watched the television series *Man from Atlantis* and followed all of Jacques Cousteau's diving expeditions. What is so special about Malta?"

"I'm going to get really nerdy with you here. Are you up for the challenge?" Eve warned him.

"Yes I am. I find it really sexy when you get nerdy with me," Etienne smiled.

"Even though comics are great I have read extensively on the topic of Atlantis. As you remember from what I've already told you, from the age of eight when I reunited with Buznanna she sparked my interest, shaped my future studies and planted the seeds of curiosity in my head. I chose an archaeology degree and specialised in ancient languages and linguistics to decipher ancient texts in my research.

"The more I delved into the subject the more I couldn't disprove it, which is what I originally tried to do. In fact I would go as far as saying that the more I dug out information the more Malta appeared to be the best fit for Atlantis or one of its outposts, according to Plato's descriptions."

"Why is Plato so highly regarded in terms of the story of Atlantis?" asked Etienne.

"Plato is the key because he provided the first written record of Atlantis, and it can't be all fictional because he's a serious scholar. You can't investigate Atlantis without examining the written works of Plato, an ancient Greek philosopher, who founded the Academy. He is the author of philosophical works of unparalleled influence in Western thought. The fact remains that Plato's influence is based on the study of Egyptian texts and is adapted to Modern Greek philosophy. Based on my personal experience of decoding Plato's work in ancient Greek and understanding that the Atlantis story was originally told by Sonchis, an Egyptian priest, it's possible to discover the legendary Island of Atlantis.

"Plato investigated the truth of the story in Egypt and travelled around the Middle East and Mediterranean in search of evidence. Plato heard about the story of Atlantis from his friend Critias. They were debating the importance of women in Athenian society and somehow they got on to the subject of an incredible society that was on an island they called Atlantis. It may have been known by other names, such as the legendary island of Ka and the magical island in the Tale of the Shipwrecked Sailor."

"What's the Tale of the Shipwrecked Sailor? I've never heard of it," Etienne asked.

"It's a legend of a sailor just going about his business when a storm sinks his vessel and casts him up on the shores of an island of great riches and magic. The sailor encounters a great wise talking serpent that calls itself the Lord of Punt and helps him find his way back home. The sailor was not on some grand adventure and is not tempted to stay on the magical island because his home back in Egypt holds all of the earthly treasures he is interested in.

"So intertwined throughout legends we hear of a mysterious, magical island with serpent-like intelligent beings. Could these references be to Atlantis? It's easy to get sidetracked by the Atlantis story because there are so many tales and legends.

"I was telling you about Critias and Plato. Critias

heard the story from his grandfather who heard it from a great man known as Solon. Plato was born around 428 BC and Solon was born 200 years earlier. Solon is one of the council of seven wise rulers known as Archons or sages of Athens. He was a man involved in law, politics and business trades.

"Around 600 BC Solon travelled to Sais in Egypt and while he was there he paid his respects at the temple of the goddess Neith. Interestingly the goddess Neith looks exactly like Athena, the patron goddess of Athens, wearing the same armour with the distinguishing helmet. Solon started promoting the glory of the Greek civilisation and cosmology in an arrogant manner to all the high priests in the temple. He was interrupted and put in his place by Sonchis, a respected high priest of Sais. Sonchis' Egyptian name is "Se Ankh" meaning "The invigorating."

"The Temple of Sais was the main school of knowledge where all the important statesmen were initiated into the knowledge of the time. By the way, after this unpleasant first encounter Sonchis initiated Solon and Plato who went to study the ancient wisdom of Egypt in Heliopolis and Sais.

"Back to our story – Sonchis was obviously insulted and criticised Solon for telling mythological stories and scorned his lack of knowledge of the true history of the Athenian ancestors. Sonchis pointed out to Solon that some of the Greek myths are astronomical events and lectured him on astronomy. Sonchis then explained to Solon that the Egyptians still retained their ancient records and the Greeks do not have a record of how their civilisation started, only myths. Sonchis adamantly assured Solon that the events he was revealing were absolutely true.

"The key points to remember were that Sonchis revealed the story of Atlantis from an Egyptian perspective and Solon began translating the story into the Greek language, deciphering the names of the characters in this ancient epic saga. Solon thought the proper names recorded in the Egyptian records were too unfamiliar to Greek citizens, so he changed all the names to Greek names.

"Unfortunately, he did not record the original Atlantean names or the Egyptian names. Solon invented the name Atlantis. He named the adversaries of his Greek ancestors' empire Atlantis in honour of the ancient Greek Titan, Atlas, who fought against the Greek god Zeus in a war between the Titans and the Greek gods. To this day, the mysterious island is known as Atlantis.

"Solon basically adjusted the story to fit Greek mythology. When decoding Plato's written work you need to be aware that the Atlantis story was told in ancient Egyptian and converted to ancient Greek and there are obvious errors in translation that occur when this takes place," Eve explained.

"What are the errors in translation? It seems as though Plato's work is like a treasure map full of clues," Etienne observed.

"Firstly, all Plato's texts are in ancient Greek. It was translated into Latin, then Modern Greek and then into English, so understandably some words can be interpreted in different ways. There are errors in translation and even Plato couldn't work out where Atlantis was so he had to travel and search for it.

"Secondly, I went to the Vatican archives in Rome straight to the source and examined the ancient Greek texts of *Timaeus* and *Critias*. First there is the word *meson* that has two meanings – one is 'as great as' and the other is 'between.' Many researchers look for an empire as great as Asia being present-day Europe and Asia combined. Libya in present-day North Africa could be interpreted as an empire between Asia and Libya. According to Plato's original description the location is between Europe/Asia and North Africa.

"Another ancient Greek word is *pelagos*, which means 'the sea', not ocean, so Plato talks about the sea of Atlas not the ocean of Atlas. The location of Atlantis is in the sea of Atlas not the Atlantic Ocean. The sea of Atlas is located north of Mount Atlas in Morocco. Herodotus, who mentioned the Atlantic sea not ocean, corroborated that.

"There is another issue with translation. Some researchers say Atlantis is before and others say beyond the Pillars of Hercules. In the original text the word used is *pro*, which means 'before' and not *meta*, which means 'beyond' in ancient Greek. Atlantis had to be before the Pillars of Hercules, which points strongly to a Mediterranean location.

"Finally, Plato never even mentioned the Pillars of Hercules. He described the Steles of Hercules, which according to the great poet Pindar are situated in the centre of the Mediterranean. Other ancient historians mention the Straits of Messina, between Italy and Sicily, as being the Pillars of Hercules.

"Now what's interesting is that the Straits of Sicily did not exist in 9600 BC because it was above water and one of many land bridges. This would have made Atlantis easy to access by an army.

"Diodorus Siculus, the Greek historian described a trip from the Pillars of Herakles to the island of Ibiza next to Spain and said it takes three days to voyage by boat from the Pillars of Herakles to Ibiza. If the Pillars of Herakles were in Gibraltar, south of Spain, Diodorus calculated it would take only twelve hours. This shows that the Pillars of Herakles were not in Gibraltar, but in the vicinity of Sicily. It was only when Alexander the Great conquered Europe and North Africa that the Pillars of Herakles were identified as being in Gibraltar because the Pillars of Herakles represented the limit of the known Greek world."

"Based on your research the Pillars of Herakles must be in the vicinity of Sicily, which makes Malta a prime candidate for Atlantis." Etienne pondered the prospects. "Oh, that reminds me!" Etienne's face lit up. "When I was researching the twelve labours of Hercules before our trip to Leptis Magna I found some interesting facts about the Pillars of Hercules. Aristotle believed the earlier name for the Pillars of Hercules to be the Pillars of Briareus which are located near Ogygia, according to Plutarch. It's reasonable to suggest the Pillars are next to Ogygia which is identified as Gozo, the sister island of Malta.

"As Hercules' eleventh labour he had to retrieve the golden apples, a wedding gift from Hera to Zeus, from the garden of the Hesperides. The Hesperides are the daughters of Atlas. Calypso, the sea nymph, is one of the daughters of Atlas and the granddaughter of Poseidon.

"The Hesperides are associated with the Amazon women in Libya. All of Hercules' labours were performed in the eastern side of the Mediterranean Sea with the boundary being in the vicinity of Gozo-Malta and it's another pertinent clue to the true location of Atlantis.

"Even today there is still a lot of controversy as to where Atlantis could be located because there are errors in translation from the original source. What was the brief story of Atlantis and its demise?" Etienne asked.

"The story of Atlantis describes a mighty power situated in front of the Pillars of Hercules. In a single day and night the island sank into the sea. The island was larger than Libya and Asia put together."

"What do you mean by Libya and Asia together?" Etienne interrupted.

"Remember an Egyptian high priest is telling the story from an Egyptian perspective. To the north of Egypt is Asia which incorporates present day Asia and Europe, and to the west is Libya which incorporates all of North

Africa at that time in ancient history where the geography was identified differently.

"Continuing with Plato's story, the Atlanteans went to war with the Athenians in about 9,600 BC. According to the Egyptian high priest, the war took place against those who dwelt outside the Pillars of Hercules, the Atlanteans, and all who dwelt within them, the Athenians. Plato's description of the war implies proximity to Athens.

"There is no description of a naval battle, but a battle fought on land. The sea levels around 9,600 BC were much lower and the geography would have been completely different from the landscape we see today. At this time there were land bridges that would have allowed an army equipped with horses and chariots to march onto Atlantean territory.

"To the Athenians, beyond the Pillars of Hercules was the end of the known world. They believed the island of Atlantis was a fertile place where the people harvested the fruits of the earth. They had both domesticated and wild animals on the island including elephants. There were hot and cold springs. The city of Atlantis was a series of concentric rings with canals of water encircling the city. Next to the city was a level plain surrounded by mountains that descended to the sea.

"Atlantis is described as an advanced society that had mastered the use of crystal technology. It was an island city with a temple at the centre dedicated to Poseidon, the king. The legend is that Poseidon fell in love with a beautiful mortal woman called Cleito, who lived in the mountains. She bore him five sets of twin boys, an effort great enough to be honoured as a goddess, in my eyes! The ten sons ruled as kings, clothed in azure cloaks, of all surrounding lands. The eldest son, Atlas, ruled Atlantis.

"When the Athenians arrived to fight the Atlanteans, a cataclysm struck and Atlantis sank, resulting in its demise with heavy losses on both sides. The battle appeared to be fought on land because no boats were mentioned in Plato's description. The island sank before the battle took place in forty-eight hours; the area was characterised by low-lying mud shoals, making it hard to navigate a vessel in 600 BC according to Sonchis, the Egyptian high priest," finished Eve.

"Why are you so sure that Plato's story is not just a fiction?" asked Etienne.

Eve continued, "Crantor, a student of Xenocrates, who was one of Plato's students, went to Egypt and viewed the columns that depicted the story of Atlantis and wrote a book about it which has disappeared from history. Luckily, another Greek writer, Proclus, wrote commentaries about Plato and mentioned Crantor's book and his visit to Egypt, so it's not just a fiction.

"The Atlantis story takes place 9,000 years or more ago and therefore you need to consider a different climate and geography at the end of the last Ice Age. Nine or ten thousand years ago the geology and climate of the Mediterranean landscape was tropical. There is evidence of pigmy elephant and hippopotamus on Malta and even Sardinia. The climate was tropical in Egypt and Malta and habitable, whereas Northern Europe and America were still covered with ice. There is evidence that the Sphinx was surrounded by water at some stage.

"For an island to sink as Plato described, Atlantis must have been situated on the edge of two tectonic plates, that being the Eurasian and African plates in the argument for the Malta location. And indeed, Malta is in a high-risk seismic zone surrounded by fault lines and active volcanoes such as Etna, Stromboli and Mount Vesuvius.

"Besides what exists on the surface, Italian scientists have discovered a huge underwater volcano off the southern coast of Sicily. It's shaped like a horseshoe and with a peak more than 500 metres high – higher than the Eiffel Tower in Paris – with another peak just seven metres below the surface.

"It was just like Graham Island, located halfway between Sicily and Pantelleria, which appeared as an island in July 1831 and disappeared beneath the waves in January 1832 after it erupted. As crazy as it may sound, islands do rise up and sink.

"Let me tell you, Graham Island is not the only one – there are also the volcanic islands of Pantelleria, Linosa and Lampedusa on the west coast of Malta and they are located above a drowned continental rift in the Strait of Sicily. These volcanic islands have been the focus of intensive volcanic and tectonic activity in the vicinity of the Maltese islands." Eve concluded.

"How would Atlantis just sink so quickly?" Etienne asked.

"We can only go on Plato's description so something must have triggered the sinking. One can assume it must have been in a susceptible location with extremely high seismic activity. In addition, scientists have proven that heavenly objects such as comets have struck the earth and this contributed to the sinking of Atlantis."

"I'll give you credit – it all tends to mesh together and it can't all be coincidence. Are there any other reasons you think Malta is the location of Atlantis?" Etienne continued.

"Yes, there are other reasons. The second largest of the Maltese islands, Gozo, known as *Gaulus* in Latin and *Għawdex* in Maltese, is believed to be an extinct volcano. Gozo is also known as the Island of the Three Mountains and the numerous conical and pyramid-shaped knolls resemble extinct volcanoes. Plato's name for one of the ten kings of Atlantis is Gadeiros, which sounds more similar to *Għawdex* or *Gaulus* than to Cadiz, Spain.

"The coat of arms of Gozo depicts three mountains

that descend towards the sea, similar to Plato's description of the landscape of Atlantis. Plato described mountains descending to the sea that surrounded the plain of Atlantis. Interestingly, ancient authors, including Herodotus, Diodorus Siculus and French historian, Marquis de Fortia d'Urban, have clearly identified Ogygia with the ancient name of the island of Gozo. Ogyges was the last king of Atlantis, who ruled an island that existed between Libya and Sicily, and which is now semi-submerged. The summit of Mount Atlas retained the name of Ogygia, that of its last king."

"Are the Maltese islands really the remaining mountain top of Atlantis?" Etienne queried.

Eve continued, "Ancient authors believe this to be the case. Plato described Atlantis as a place where impressive temples were built to their gods and goddesses. The Maltese islands have a high concentration of the most sophisticated and freestanding megalithic temple sites. They present as the most intact temples in the world and are a thousand years older than the pyramids of Egypt. The numbers vary, but approximately 36 known places in Malta and Gozo have megalithic temples and several underground complexes known as hypogea.

"Besides what is visible, there are also legitimate claims of temples submerged in the silt of the ocean, based on Ptolemy's maps. He obtained his data from the ancient legendary library at Alexandria, once the largest and most prosperous city in the world. Ptolemy's maps and calibrated coordinates locate three significant temple sites. Ptolemy identifies the temple of Hercules as equating to the Phoenician god Melqart and the temple of Juno for the Phoenician goddess Astarte in his map *Tabula Europa VII*.

"This map places both temples on Malta, even extending to the surrounding sea because the island's land mass was far greater in the ancient past when sea levels were lower. Ptolemy's maps lead us to the massive temple complex identified as belonging to the renowned goddess Astarte. Her temple has been located in the Grand Harbour of the capital city of Malta, Valletta.

"Jean Quintin, a French writer, known by his Latin name *Quintinus*, who lived in Malta between 1530 and 1536 when he served in the Order of the Knights of St. John wrote in Latin about the ancient history of Malta with particular interest in the temples of Hercules and Juno. Juno's temple ruins lie scattered across many acres of land and the foundations cover a large part of the Grand Harbour. Quintinus, among others, believed that it was considered to be one of the greatest temples of antiquity. Even at the proposed site of Tas-Slig, for the temple of Hercules, there are dedications to the Phoenician goddess Astarte, rather than Hercules or the Phoenician god Melqart. The temple of Hercules is believed to be to the south of the islands, whereas the temple of Juno is towards the Grand Harbour in the east."

"You certainly have done your homework on Atlantis. Why is Juno's temple one of the greatest temples in antiquity?" Etienne asked.

"Before the Romans constructed the temple of Juno it was the temple of the Phoenician goddess Astarte who was associated with many great goddesses. Her symbols were the lion, the horse, the sphinx, the dove and a star within a circle, indicating the planet Venus. Astarte appears to be the most important goddess worshipped by the Phoenicians. The Sumerians knew her as Inanna and the Babylonians knew her as Ishtar.

"In Egypt, Astarte was identified with the lioness warrior goddess Sekhmet but fused with Isis to judge from the many images found of Astarte suckling a small child, portraying Isis with her child Horus on her knee. Astarte is the Semitic goddess of fertility, love, beauty, fertility, medicine, war and vitality. Her worship was widespread, covering much of the Middle East, including the Phoenicians and Canaanites. She was the great goddess who created, preserved and destroyed. She represented Mother Nature and the Virgin Goddess, like the Virgin Mary.

"Astarte was a solar and lunar deity or goddess. She is depicted with a moon crescent above her head, representing the Divine Feminine. Other images depict her holding the Sacred Lotus in one hand, while in her other hand she holds two entwined serpents. Many believe that Astarte was a Great Mother Goddess of the many temples, artwork and artefacts that litter the Maltese archipelago. The central faith centre of the goddess culture appears to be prevalent on the Maltese islands because the magnificent temple of Astarte, renowned through the ancient world, is believed to be located in Malta by ancient scholars.

"Like the Dogon twin-soul concept, most temples appear to be in pairs, representing the masculine and feminine, as is the case in the temples of Hercules and Juno.

"The third temple site identified by Ptolemy is the temple of Proserpine. It's a Roman temple discovered in Mtarfa bordering the old capital city of Mdina. The large stone and marble temple was dedicated to Proserpine, goddess of the Underworld and Renewal. A chapel dedicated to Saint Nicholas was eventually built near the site with a statue of St. Nicholas situated directly on top of the temple site."

"I also saw a documentary that located Atlantis in Santorini. Is this possible?" Etienne probed.

Eve replied, "Atlantis can't be the location of Santorini, Greece because the Atlantis destruction occurred at least 9,000 years before Plato's time and not when Thera on Santorini erupted, which archaeologists have placed at approximately 1,500 BC.

"Solon was told the story from the Egyptian priest Sonchis in 600 BC. Researchers supporting the Thera case specify 900 years prior to Solon's time. Again there are errors in transation, from Egyptian into Greek, which resulted in an interpretation of 'hundreds' instead of 'thousands.' This is incorrect because in Plato's book, *The Republic*, written in 380 BC, Plato clearly states that Egyptian art hadn't evolved for 10,000 years so there is no confusion about the timing. Plato was a diligent scholar and meant 9,600 BC for the Atlantis destruction not 1500 BC when Thera erupted."

"You've covered so much and I don't mind listening to you all day long. I'm going to confess I'm a sapiosexual and I find your intelligence and insights are incredibly sexy and exciting. Are there any other reasons you think Malta is Atlantis?" Etienne focused on her face as she continued to talk.

"Huh, is that right! Just as well because I'm not finished yet – there is so much more. Another reason is that Malta was a much larger island than what we see today, extending in all directions. Ptolemy's maps that resided in the ancient library of Alexandria are a reliable source and strongly confirm a larger southward expansion of the Maltese islands to the North African coast, directly north of Tunisia and Libya. To the southwest there is an uninhabited islet known as Filfla, which is believed to be the remnants of a great expanse of hill and valley which once extended unbroken towards what was to be Carthage, modern-day Tunisia, the Atlas and the great lakes of the Sahara.

"When Plato described Atlantis in his dialogues, they had lost their advanced technology millennia before. By this stage they used more primitive modes of transport such as wooden boats to sail the sea, whereas previously they used anti-gravity flying machines that could submerge like a submarine.

"Plato described an important bull culture in Atlantis probably for religious and recreational activities. Every ancient culture was connected to the worship of the bull and cow. They were symbols of strength, power and fertility. There have been numerous bas-relief carvings of bulls and cow paintings discovered at prehistoric temples such as Tarxien. On the walls of the hypogeum of Ħal-Saflieni a discernable shape of a bull carved and painted in black has been washed off to remove all traces of paint. Astonishingly, a solid gold calf was discovered in a field when excavation commenced around the Tarxien temples, but no one knows its whereabouts.

"Moreover, some of the animal drawings near the Maltese temples closely resemble the prehistoric cows and bulls known as aurochs that existed on the island until relatively recently. Wenzu was one of the last aurochs living on Malta and was 96% pure genetically because he was a first-generation hybrid. His mother was the last pure 100% Maltese auroch. Marvelous Wenzu was the last surviving prehistoric bull and provided historical and biological interest, like other flora and fauna on the island.

"Talking about animals on Atlantis, there were elephants, which narrowed down the search. In a cave, known as Għar Dalam meaning Cave of Darkness on the outskirts of Birżebbuġa is a prehistoric cul-de-sac, containing the bones of humans and animals that were stranded and washed in at the end of the Ice Age. Dwarf elephants and their tusks were found and thousands of molars and other skeletal parts have been discovered including the skull of a neolithic child. Hippopotamus, deer and bear bone deposits of different ages were also found.

"What made all these animals special was the fact that while some became smaller than normal, others turned into giants and others became extinct as they adapted to the environment. Malta is one of the candidates that have both elephants and a strong bull culture.

"On the subject of genetics, Atlanteans must have had knowledge of genetic manipulation and probably created all the domesticated animals which appeared in ancient times. An interesting fact is that the cheetah's genetic traits are made for speed and racing as they were in ancient times. Today the cheetah population is dwindling because of poor genetic diversity. Atlanteans domesticated marine mammals such as dolphins and orcas that still retain the memory of working with man.

"Plato described Atlantis as an advanced industrial civilisation and on Malta we find the highest concentration of cart ruts in the world. These cart ruts are man-made and carved into the limestone forming an intricate network of channels over rocky terrain. One location near Dingli Cliffs possesses so many cart ruts it has been nicknamed Clapham Junction like the busy railway station in London. This network of mysterious cart ruts shows evidence of some form of industry, whatever it may be." Eve paused as she emptied her brain of years of research on the topic of Atlantis.

"Besides the network of cart ruts, you'll be interested to know that Quintinus was not the only Frenchman interested in Malta," Etienne added. "Napoleon Bonaparte occupied Malta from 1798 to 1800. The French rapidly dismantled the institution of the Knights of St. John, including the Roman Catholic Church. Napoleon was Corsican and had a hidden interest in his origins and the occult, much as Hitler did. He had stolen most of the archives and precious books in the Vatican and he would have done the same in Malta in his thirst for knowledge and power.

"Don't you think it is strange there are so many churches built in Malta? It's not just another coincidence!"

Etienne remarked.

"No, I don't believe in coincidences. It's quite crazy how many churches, chapels and even cave chapels exist on the islands. I've wondered the same thing myself and have taken count. Many town and village cores feature two or more churches and chapels. On the islands of Malta and Gozo, which are two separate dioceses, there are 359 churches, excluding the cave chapels, so that means 313 churches on Malta and 46 churches on Gozo. That is an astonishing number of churches on a small archipelago. Usually, new religious sites are built over the older sites or temples and deeper is older in archaeology. My conclusion is that the island must have been littered with sacred temples for so many churches to be built on top. So many sacred sites must mean there is more to it than meets the eye. But let's not get sidetracked and get back to the evidence.

"In Plato's description of Atlantis, he mentions red, white and black stone. At the seaside in Sliema you can see a strange circular or hexagonal mound with a large mixture of minerals and rocks from whites, reds, blacks, oranges and quartz in a variety of colours, thickness and forms. The locals call it Krystal Rock. The transmuted limestone conglomerate has a cemented matrix of red, black and white stone pieces of limestone burnt by electromagnetic forces.

"Quartz is a replacement mineral, especially on an island of limestone and sandstone like Malta. Maybe it is a replacement mineral but the host rock has been converted into quartz by the application and forces of heat, energy and pressure. The quartz plating in the fissures is the missing limestone material itself, transformed into quartz. How the host material was transformed into quartz is unknown. Any process that can apply energy and pressure could be the cause. If these fissures were involved in electrical activity it could create a magnetic field that applies pressure and energy to a localised area.

"The red, white and black stone can be found all over the islands and is one of the distinguishing features of Atlantis and a sign that these islands have been battered by the electrical universe."

"What is the electrical universe and what does it have to do with Atlantis?" Etienne asked.

"The electrical universe is a theory that shows the importance of electricity and the role of ionized gases known as plasma throughout the universe. Plasma reacts strongly to electro-magnetic fields and explains the phenomenon of gravity. Based on this theory, a comet or an asteroid apparently striking the earth will not actually hit the earth but will exchange plasma discharge. The earth, being stronger, means the comet, the asteroid or the celestial object will disintegrate and form impact craters, unusual circular bays and giant fulgurites found all over the Maltese archipelago.

"Fulgurites are electrical discharge patterns that look like a lightning strike that has raised the limestone mineral from the ground. These are the thunderbolt scars that have battered the Maltese islands and are obvious from the air. Our ancestors tell of legends of gods hurling thunderbolts at each other and great celestial wars. Catastrophes have struck the earth on a regular basis. You would expect that the remnants of Atlantis would bear heavy scars of massive electrical discharges as evident on Malta.

"In addition, the dugout valleys or wieds are too deep to have developed on the small island we see today. This indicates that Malta was a larger landmass with huge mountains and flowing rivers. After Atlantis was submerged, Plato describes large deposits of mud shoals making it impossible to navigate a vessel."

"Where are the mud shoals found?" Etienne is curious.

"There are mud shoals between the Straits of Sicily and Malta as you can see from satellite images. Considering the sea levels were lower in approximately 9,600 BC it was impenetrable back then and Sonchis, the Egyptian priest, believed it was still difficult to navigate a vessel through.

"Geographically, it was believed that the Maltese islands were connected via a land bridge to Sicily and nearby North Africa in the ancient past, resulting in a larger land mass. When you examine Ptolemy's map, the whole area appears volatile because of the rise in sea levels over time and the geological changes.

"The Maltese islands are surrounded by a number of active or dormant volcanoes. To the north we have Mt. Etna, Sicily; the volcanic islands of Stromboli and the Lipari Islands; Mt. Epomeo (Ischia, Bay of Naples); and Mt. Vesuvius, Mt. Albani and the Phlegraean Camps (Italian mainland). To the northwest lie the submarine Graham volcano and the young volcanic island of Pantelleria.

"To the southwest are the volcanic islands of Linosa and Lampione. Further away to the east is the Santorini volcano, Greece. The islands of the archipelago lie on the Maltese plateau, a shallow shelf formed from the high points of a land bridge between Sicily and North Africa that became isolated as sea levels rose after the last Ice Age. The archipelago therefore sits in the zone between the Eurasian and African tectonic plates. Malta is considered a high-risk zone in terms of earthquake risk.

"Another clue that Malta is Atlantis is the presence of hot and cold water springs. The central island city of Atlantis had two springs of water from beneath the earth, one of warm water and the other of cold, which encouraged crops to spring up abundantly from the mineral rich fertile volcanic soil. The entire archipelago of Malta is made up of limestone, making it an ideal aquifer for hot and cold springs and it's in a region of intense volcanic activity. Based on Plato's dialogues about Atlantis, Malta satisfies them all.

"Even Edgar Cayce, the American prophet, mentioned Atlantis in his readings. Cayce prophesied that Atlantis would rise in 1968. This didn't occur literally but it could mean that many more people born after this year have an unusual reawakening, fascination and rise in human consciousness about Atlantis. The sleeping prophet Cayce believed there are three halls of records buried by the Atlanteans. One is under the right paw of the Sphinx in Giza, another is in the Yucatan peninsula, and the last was completely destroyed in Bimini. In his trance Cayce stated that Atlantis had been destroyed three times. This is what creates confusion as to the whereabouts of Atlantis because many societies rebuild after destruction. The Atlanteans would have built on fertile volcanic soil for the benefit of crops and the minerals needed to sustain life. They located close to hot and cold springs so they had a freshwater source and in a place with a warm climate. An island location was ideal because it provided isolation and protection from enemies and large beasts that roamed the earth.

"The first Atlantis is believed to be in the Caribbean, the second in the Azores islands, and the last in the heart of the Mediterranean. According to Cayce, the surviving refugees fled to Egypt and the Pyrenees Mountains, the natural border between France and Spain, which was a colony of Atlantis. When there is destruction, the survivors flee in all directions; therefore, it's likely that Atlantis was in the heart of the Mediterranean and that is why there is evidence of Atlantean survivors founding Athens, Egypt, Spain, Morocco, the south of France, Italy, Bosnia and

Libya.

"During the first destruction some fled as far as the Yucatan peninsula and founded Central American cultures; others merged with the existing American cultures. Atlantis fascinates many people and there have been thousands of books written on Atlantis. Not only has the island of Atlantis been written about but there have been television shows, films, comics and other creative works of popular culture. Atlantis still resonates strongly with people and for all these reasons I have become secretly obsessed with finding Atlantis.

"To tackle the subject you need to understand many fields of science including, archaeology, astronomy, Egyptology, geography, geology, linguistics, mathematics, metaphysics, mythology, oceanography and religion just to mention a few, so I never thought it would be easy. For example, you need to understand biology and anthropology to study the spread of Rhesus negative in the Mediterranean. The earliest concentration of Rhesus negative is found mainly on islands in the vicinity of North Africa and is associated with the long-headed skulls and possibly a connection to the Atlantis race."

"Do you think Atlanteans were everywhere on the planet?" Etienne interrupted.

"No I don't believe so. According to esoteric and channelled sources, they co-existed with other civilisations such as the Lemurians or the people from the land of Og, which started the South American civilisation. It is suggested that the ancient ruins discovered in Indonesia are prediluvian remains of the Lemurian civilisation.

"Actually, Atlantis sprang out of Lemuria. The submarine ruins off the coast of Yonaguni in Japan are also linked to the Pacific civilisation associated with Lemuria. Similarly, the underwater city discovered in the Gulf of Cambay on the west coast of India, which is linked to the

Indus Valley civilisation, is also a remnant of the Pacific civilisation after the destruction of the land of Mu or Lemuria.

"During the Atlantis period there were other civilisations flourishing, which doesn't mean that every underwater city discovered is Atlantis. Before Atlantis there were other civilisations like the Lemurian in the Pacific, the Hyperborean in the Atlantic, and the Polarian in Antarctica, that rose from the destruction of the previous civilisation.

"Each civilisation incorporated different human species and each root race buried the memories and achievements of the previous race. The Atlanteans had elongated skulls and some were giants compared to us. They were master manipulators of sound which is an incredibly powerful tool employed in many areas such as communication, protection, medicine and healing, building, geology and so on.

"Understandably, the past and present are one, and those in control have no interest in revealing our true origins as though it's forbidden knowledge which is capable of turning religion on its head. Atlantis resonates truth with many people across the world. The fact is that so many places existed in the ancient past and we have a soup of confusion which suits many because they can dismiss Atlantis as just a myth. That's why the search for Atlantis is so complex. Which Atlantis? Which civilisation are we actually talking about?" Eve stopped to take a drink of water as her throat felt dry from all the talking.

"I'm with you on the complexity of the whole legend. That was amazing how Hakeem noted that Siculus wrote about the all-female Amazon warriors being located in Libya and they defeated the Atlanteans in battle. Libya is very close to Malta, another pertinent clue to Atlantis' true location." Etienne winked at Eve.

"Wonder Woman – that was one of my favourite shows growing up."

"Well that explains a lot about your behaviour at times!" Etienne smiled.

"If you're not nice I will have to tie you up with my magical lasso," Eve responded.

"Why is your lasso so magical?"

"It was originally named the Magical Lasso of Aphrodite, golden in colour, and it forces anyone it captures to obey and tell the truth. The lasso would be my kind of weapon!" Eve chuckled.

"You have a way of making me listen and obey you already, Wonder Woman! Do you think your Buznanna had past-life memories of an ancient culture?" Etienne asked.

"I would say so. Many people have dreams of past-life memories or have been regressed in hypnotherapy in order to deal with present-day issues and realise that it was due to a past-life trauma. It's possible that our soul memories come with us from one lifetime to another as we evolve through the reincarnation process.

"Some of our ancestors survived the cataclysms and have a residual memory. During great cataclysmic events of floods and fire, the people who survived lived in the high mountains and passed down information from oral tradition. Just let me know when you feel convinced and you want me to stop!" Eve smiled.

"I'm thoroughly convinced! I'm on Team Wonder Woman and as long as you take charge and promise to restrain me with your lasso all will be well. On a more serious note, your research points to the fact that Malta is the best location for Atlantis. Even Jacques Cousteau agrees with you." Etienne reassured Eve that he believed they were on the right track.

The stewardess instructed the passengers to secure their seatbelts for landing. Eve accidently knocked her glass of ice-cold water down Etienne's crutch, saturating his trousers.

"I'm so sorry, but that's going to cool you down," Eve giggled.

"You will never cool me down, girl. You're too ravishing." Etienne soaked up the excess water with his serviettes.

They disembarked at Tripoli International Airport in Libya with newfound knowledge and a confident stride. They were the perfect partners in crime, even though Etienne looked as though he had wet his pants. Eve held onto his arm enjoying every adventure they embarked on together as they made their way to the Severus Hotel for their overnight stay.

Chapter 15

The Secret of Leptis Magna

If we trust our inner knowing, we can still hear the voices of our loved ones, a valuable link to our past to build bridges to a better future. The past speaks to us in many ways because our progress depends on knowing the truth to free us from the shackles of deceit. Eve had only read about the archaeological site of Leptis Magna but was particularly drawn to it and included it on her must-see list. Along the Libyan coast are the three cities of Oea, Sabratha and Leptis Magna, UNESCO World Heritage Sites, known as the three cities forming the African Tripolis or Tripolitania.

Occupying a rocky promontory overlooking the Mediterranean Sea and located due south of Sicily, Oea (Tripoli) was founded by the Phoenicians and later controlled by the Romans. During the invasions, the walls of the cities of Sabratha and Leptis Magna were destroyed and this resulted in the growth of Tripoli, which had previously been the least important of the cities.

Rome appointed Septimius Severus as ruler of Leptis Magna because he had come from this region and had good relationships with the tribes of the region. Importantly, he could secure trade routes for the Roman Empire across Africa. Founded on a natural harbour, Leptis Magna grew to become the capital of the Roman Empire in Africa.

As Eve walked into Leptis Magna she had an overwhelming sense of déjà vu. The landscape and buildings felt as though this were her home in a past life. Instant flashbacks plagued Eve's memory, overpowering her amnesia. They wandered around the ancient city with its lavish artwork and grand buildings made out of the finest stone and marble. Carved gorgons and griffins, a legendary creature part-lion and part-eagle, were a remarkable addition to a typical column, placed above between the capital and the architrave. The head of Medusa was carved on a stone arch in the ruins of the forum, perfectly preserved. Eve pinched herself as she slowly walked through the site and day-dreamed about how lavish life would have been as her archaeologist's eyes feasted on the marvellous ancient Roman ruins in this seaside paradise.

Eve gazed at the scintillating reflections in the water that filled the pools in the Hadrianic Baths and created enchanting reflections of the towering decorative marble columns reaching to the clear blue sky. The baths consisted of hot and cold chambers and pools because this place was all about luxury. They passed the triple-stacked grandeur of the Nymphaeum, a monument dedicated to the nymphs, a mythological spirit of nature imagined as a beautiful maiden inhabiting waterways. The monuments were originally natural grottoes, assigned as habitations to the local nymphs; eventually artificial grottoes took the place of natural ones. Eve couldn't help herself as she allowed her imagination to drift off to the sound of the cascading water of this enormous public fountain, surely impressing any visitors and Berber traders riding in from the Sahara. The Berbers came from Ancient Libya and she could start to see a connection between the Phoenicians, Maltese, Egyptians and the Dogon.

Her thoughts drifted to the cave art of the Acacus Mountains in the desert of the Ghat District in western Libya, still part of the Sahara. The area has a rich array of prehistoric rock art. The images depicted battles between archers and Merfolk or Merpeople. Large elephants and bulls were similar to the rock art in the Cave of Swimmers in the mountainous Gilf Kebir plateau in southwest Egypt where they had been with Hakeem. The similarities were astonishing and made valuable connections.

Eve's first impressions of the Severan forum was mesmerising, made even more powerful by the ambience, processional avenues and the epic scale of the buildings embellished by the founder of this extraordinary dynasty, Septimius Severus. His family was proud of their Phoenician ancestry and their Libyan identity. It was one of the most beautiful cities of the Roman Empire, with its imposing public monuments, a basilica of grand proportions, harbour, marketplace, storehouses, shops and residential districts. Leptis weathered the Roman conquest of North Africa and emerged as one of the leading cities of the region.

The extraordinary site contained remnants of white marble triumphal arches that are still embedded with past intrigue. The Arch of Trajan now looks modest because only one limestone arch is standing, but it used to have four, known as a *quadrifrons* or a *tetrapylon*, meaning four gates or four fronts. These monuments were built as landmarks at major crossroads or geographical focal points, or simply as aesthetically pleasing ornamental architecture. The four-faced design is similar to the Arch of Septimius Severus, which was built almost a century later. It is within sight of the Arch of Trajan and may have been inspired by the older monument. The arch is covered with marble panels that show the emperor, his wife the Syrian princess, Julia Domna, and their two sons participating in imperial duties.

"Every carved work of art in stone tells us a myriad of stories and songs from the past. Have you noticed anything amusing in the artwork?" Eve broke her silent reflections as she turned to Etienne.

"Now let me see. Oh yes there are huge erect phalluses in the elegant frame of a classical Roman scroll scattered all over the place."

"So you noticed!" Eve laughed.

"How can these monstrous phalluses be missed – they are placed right at eye level. I've seen double-headed phalluses next to an eye being attacked by a scorpion. Other huge and hideous phalluses can be detected entangled with crabs, serpents and scorpions, again attacking an eye. Why were so many phalluses depicted in art? I'm sure you've researched this!"

"Of course! The phalluses were carved and painted to help deflect the power of the evil and envious eye that could bring harm to the noblest and greatest households. They were a protection and good luck symbol in one."

"Who would have thought envy would be such a problem," Etienne laughed.

"Unfortunately, the phalluses failed to protect the

great Leptis from the Evil Eye. By the end of the fifth century Leptis was demolished by an earthquake and civil war. Tripoli, ancient Oea, survived the storms of history and its Castle Museum is a treasure trove of antiquity from Leptis Magna."

Etienne was keen to examine the twelve labours of Hercules depicted on two large columns flanking the apses of the Severus Basilica. They separated while Etienne explored Hercules' feats and Eve wandered into the Arch of Septimius Severus, which had attracted her attention.

All living energy in the universe is always speaking to us, causing coincidences and serendipities. Eve had learned to stop and listen with all her senses to the messages, as they presented a path to move forward and achieve what at first we only dream about.

As Eve stood alone in the magnificent arch, she felt overwhelmed by a deep sadness. She knew something terrible had occurred here. She couldn't shake off the feelings and they engulfed her. She had some sort of spiritual connection to a soul that had passed away here. The feeling persisted and she asked in her mind's eye what had happened here. In her mind's eye a revolving white orb appeared. She knew she could communicate with this orb of energy and Buznanna, her gatekeeper, facilitated the correspondence because it was important for Eve to know.

Eve felt comfortable and asked the orb to identify itself. She could feel the spirit had passed away in most unfortunate circumstances, a long time before his natural time of death. He was poisoned and suffered from what felt to Eve like suffocation. Eve could feel the pain of the soul's passing on so many levels. His soul's essence still lingered because of the trauma connected to this arch where he was murdered.

"I have been waiting for you to come here. I'm one of your spirit guides. I preached my last sermon in this basilica and died tragically here alone."

"You must be the priest I've been told about by a clairvoyant. She said you've been holding a secret," said Eve quietly.

"Yes I am the one! I knew your Buznanna as a young child and her mother. Her matriarchal bloodlines are linked to the Great Mother Goddess and the eldest females in your family have an important role to play in the Great Mother Goddess hierarchy. I made the connection with your Buznanna's matriarchal family, associated with the ankh and eight-pointed star, after my discoveries in the Hal Saflieni hypogeum pointed to the bloodlines of her family.

"Even though I was not related by blood I felt I was an integral part of the family and I worked closely with the firstborn females as previous priests have in our secret society dedicated to the preservation of the Great Mother Goddess whose home was on a sacred island. It's imperative you listen to what I have to say, as you are the next eldest female descendant. While excavating the Hal Saflieni hypogeum in Malta, I found many civilisations have used the hypogeum and, remarkably, found that the High Priestess has always preserved the teachings of the great Mother Goddess and been a watchful guardian of her sacred sites."

"I have been told by a skilled clairvoyant that I have a high priestess on my left side with an eight-pointed star on her third eye, representing the sacred feminine, the symbol of the Goddess," said Eve. "On my right side was an ancient priest wearing a black beret to cover his elongated skull, but distinctly dressed as an ancient priest. The clairvoyant could not get the secret out of the priest or any clue as to what the secret was about. She told me the old priest's lips were tightly sealed as he pretended to sleep. The only thing she could tell me was that the priest holds deep family secrets and he was part of your family, but not a blood relative. I was repeatedly told that the ancient priest could only reveal the secrets to me and I would have to go and search for the answers. I couldn't work out the connections," Eve said, sharing with the spirit energy.

It suddenly dawned on Eve like a thunderbolt! "You are Fr. Magri! You were murdered here!" Clear images, details and feelings of his death flowed into her third eye. She was receiving information like a movie being replayed of the terrible events that took place in Leptis Magna. At the end she caught sight of the black Jackal with his distinctive large pointed ears, part-dog, part-man, running away with Fr. Magri's briefcase and she knew an evil force was behind his premature death and the destruction of his research and knowledge.

"I was on the brink of revealing major discoveries regarding the Hal Saflieni hypogeum before it was all taken away from me, so easily, so quickly. My discoveries, my knowledge, my hypothesis were taken to the dark side, never to see the light of day. You know about my work. Beware the evil force known as Balzor." The sound of his name sent shivers through Eve as she knew this evil force would not stop at anything to get what it wanted. She would never forget, as she too had experienced this evil as a young child and it still stained her memories.

"He is an evil force that will destroy all your attempts to seek answers and enlightenment. Be very aware and prepared, my girl. You are the last hope, the last link to the Great Goddess and the Blue Queen. Don't let this knowledge be lost to the forces of evil forever." Fr. Magri was giving Eve a chilling, stern warning. He didn't want Eve to share his fate.

"You are wearing a sacred holy relic, the ankh and the eight-rayed star, around your neck. Hundreds of Knights Hospitallers' blood has been shed to bring these powerful relics from Jerusalem to Malta. The ankh and star pendant is one of them. Whilst conducting my excavations of the hypogeum, I encountered Maria Bondin, the High Priestess Oracle at the time, your Buznanna's mother. She revealed there were several entry points to the hypogeum and that the eldest matriarchal oracle regularly visited before it was officially discovered. Maria called the hypogeum the entrance to a complex labyrinth of enormous proportions that leads to all the sacred sites associated with the Great Mother Goddess. The Knights Hospitaller were devoted to the order of Our Lady of Mount Carmel, known as the Carmelite Order, and to the Virgin Mary. The Knights Hospitaller worked with the secret society associated with the High Priestess Oracle and used the hypogeum temporarily as a storehouse for the tomb of Mary Magdalene and other ancient holy relics such as the golden calf. The Grandmaster of the Order, La Valette, directed the relics to be moved to their final resting places." As he communicated his messages she felt the final release of his grief and sadness at his untimely death.

"I was so close, but the world was not ready. I discovered another secret in the Ħal Saflieni hypogeum, a map that showed the underground network of tunnels passing through many ancient sites. Some I have recognised and they include Mdina, Valletta, Fort Saint Angelo, Calypso's cave in Gozo and even the islet of Filfla. Some of the sites on the map I have not heard of, other sites appear to be under the sea. The underground tunnels lead to other mysterious sites that have not been uncovered because it would be a shock to the human race. Can you imagine that! Balzor has it all. You must get it back!" Fr. Magri insisted.

Eve was shocked to hear the extent of knowledge and power that had been stolen by the dark side but all she could do was console and reassure Fr. Magri that she would do her very best to retrieve the knowledge.

"I understand your frustration, grief and why you are trapped in this location. You have released the truth, which no longer burdens your soul. You can rest in peace now. I will be alert and aware." Eve closed the communication and thanked Fr. Magri's spirit.

The intensity of sadness gradually lifted once the messages had been relayed and understood. The revolving orb appearing in her third eye slowly disintegrated until it disappeared and she lost her connection. So he was murdered after all. His revelations must have been a tremendous threat. Eve knew that the mind will play tricks but the way you feel in your body and in your heart is the truth. She knew she had connected with the spirit of Fr. Magri. The brilliant revelations were a timely warning to be aware of evil, as it lurks and feeds on fear. Eve knew she could always rely on the truth of her inner voice.

North Africa was completely enchanting with its surviving oral traditions, artwork and monuments telling an interconnected story of our incredible ancient past. Information and clues were scattered all over the place, like small pieces in a gigantic jigsaw puzzle, just waiting to be pieced together. They arrived back in Malta after a short fifty-five minute flight. Her last thoughts were that Malta would be the last piece of the puzzle.

Chapter 16

Athena, the Warrior Goddess

Eve walked down a series of winding, dusty gravel roads in the small rural village of Żurrieq, being careful she did not trip on the uneven surface. She was overtaken by a herd of goats and asked the Maltese herder if he could direct her to the cemetery on San Leone Street. This village was like a maze. The farmer was going past the cemetery and suggested she follow him, so she did, avoiding stepping on any goat droppings along the way. She stopped to purchase her favourite flowers, orchids, at a local market. She bought a few bunches of a variety endemic to the Maltese islands, known as the Maltese spider. Buznanna would have loved the bee appearance of the orchids. The lip of the Ophrys melitensis resembles the abdomen of a bee, the sepals look like the wings, and the inner parts of the flower resemble the head and eyes. She had bought enough to put on all her beloved family members' graves. As she approached the large white gates she felt her heart pound harder than normal as goosebumps covered her arms and legs. The only regret that weighed heavily on her was that she had not reunited with Buznanna before she passed away but that had been out of her control; circumstances and distance had got the better of them. She walked down the central pathway and towards the big white marble statue of the Pietà, which was her family's gravesite. She stared at the beautiful headstone sculpture for a while and then laid the orchids on the family graves.

"I'm sorry it took me so long to return. I hope you know my love for you in life is immeasurable. In death, I love you still. You took a piece of me with you in your passing and your return home to the stars." She leaned over to kiss Buznanna's photo and other beloved family members she recognised. She missed not seeing them on this return visit but they would be forever in her heart, just a memory away. She reached for some tissues in her bag to wipe away her tears and looked down at her mobile phone. The time was 11:11 – she often noticed this moment in time. She noticed a bee flying around the orchids. There were so many places and occurrences that reminded her of Buznanna. With time you just have to come to terms with the loss and find peace. Eve always liked to look on the bright side of every situation and even though she lived abroad, she was the only great-grandchild that had met Buznanna and spent quality time with her. For that opportunity she was immensely grateful.

Eve felt relieved to pay her respects at the cemetery. She renewed her promises to Buznanna that she would never forget her teachings and that tomorrow they were going on another deep-sea diving expedition. As she walked out of the cemetery, the realisation of how limited our time is on earth dawned on her. She thought, "We need to make the most of our time because it is a present, a gift, and we all get an opportunity to leave our own loving signature on earth."

The ferry trip back to the sister island of Gozo went by quickly as she ate half a dozen pastizzi, washed down with a bottle of Kinnie, her favourite beverage. Eve collected her car at the port and drove straight to Red Sandy Beach, Ir-Ramla l-Ħamra, the unspoilt haven she had first discovered with Buznanna. It was at this beach they had met the dolphins Bozo and Maia, but this time she swam out alone. Eve swam far out until she could see dolphins in the distance. She put her head underwater and made some noises as she had done with Buznanna when she jokingly said she would speak to the dolphins. Bozo heard her and came in closer to greet her. She told him they were planning another dive tomorrow morning. He was adamant that he would be there to help them and would follow the Calypso. Eve wasn't surprised at his willingness to help, as dolphins are intelligent mammals that have helped humans in the past. They would have been an invaluable resource in an aquatic environment.

Etienne had business errands to attend to and prepare for their diving expedition the next morning but she looked forward to meeting him for dinner. Eve decided to spend her spare time revisiting some of the places she had seen with Buznanna and reminiscing about the happy days of her youth.

Her next stop was Ġgantija temple and Xagħra stone circle, located in a field about four hundred metres to the west of Ġgantija. The stone circle is believed to be an underground cemetery inside a system of natural caves and tunnels, just below the surface of the hilltop overlooking the temple.

Eve stood on the hilltop by the temple enjoying the refreshing breeze as she admired the expansive view of Gozo's fertile countryside. Then she walked through the magnificent ancient temple of Ġgantija. She got an instant flash of what the temple had looked like in all its glory as she touched the giant stone wall with her palms. She got glimpses of a magnificent gold corbelled roof, internally decorated with precious metals and stones, a black granite floor and numerous large pink granite columns. She felt energised and uplifted as she approached the central altar that overlooked the countryside below.

Later Eve left the temple and walked down the hill to Xagħra stone circle. She knew that this stone circle was not just a burial site as so many had claimed. She had discovered the artwork of Jean Houel, who had been an artist for the king of France. In the 1770s, Houel had travelled to Sicily, Lipari and Malta. He drew many illustrations of the magnificent sites he discovered on his travels that were later published in Paris in four volumes called *Voyage Pittoresque des Isles de Sicile, Lipari, et de Malte*. He had sketched the Xagħra stone circle when many of the outer circle stones, including the huge entrance megaliths, were still in situ. The sketch of the stone circle shows evidence that it was more than a burial site. They had discovered statues that would have been considered masterpieces. One statute shows two figures seated on a bed, and an intriguing group of nine strange almost triangular-looking figures. These delightful human statues closely resemble Urfa man statues discovered at Göbekli Tepe, an archaeological site at the top of a mountain ridge in southeastern Anatolia.

Aerial views taken of Ħaġar Qim and Göbekli Tepe show uncanny resemblances, both having the trefoil shape resembling a wireless antenna. Were they in fact built at a similar time by similar people or cultures? How can archaeologists compare the age when Göbekli Tepe was buried intact, whereas the Maltese temples were destroyed by the sea in some form of cataclysm? The megalithic stones are similar in appearance and size in both Anatolia and Malta. The Ħaġar Qim facade contains the largest stone used in Maltese megalithic architecture, weighing 57 tons, whereas the largest at Göbekli Tepe weighs 50 tons, the same weight of a stone at Ġgantija temple on the island of Gozo. Eve knew it was not a competition as to which temple had the largest megalithic stone, but she often got annoyed at how certain conclusions were reached without proper comparisons being drawn. Ħaġar Qim and Mnajdra are paired temples. Mnajdra is aligned to the summer solstice, but Ħaġar Qim was aligned 52,000 years ago to the summer solstice, based on data in archeo-astronomy. In Eve's mind Ħaġar Qim existed pre-flood (at the end of the last Ice Age) and was more eroded than Göbekli Tepe, which had been preserved in the ground with all its valuable artefacts and art.

Numerous megalithic temples have been discovered in the vicinity of the Maltese Archipelago in the Mediterranean Sea. One example is the megalithic temple structure discovered underwater near Sliema in 1999, known as *Gebel Gol-Bahar*. The other is the huge megalithic temple complex, renowned in the ancient world, as it was believed to be dedicated to the Mother Goddess, starting at the foot of Fort Saint Angelo, in the Grand Harbour of Valletta. In addition, the mysterious network of cart ruts leading into the Mediterranean Sea point to the fact that the megalithic civilisation on Malta was flourishing when sea levels were much lower and the land mass was greater, determining the age of the megalithic temples to be pre-flood when the last Ice Age ended in approximately 10,500 BC. Eve made comparisons based on her discernment and realised that modern humans have barely scratched the surface of ancient history. Humans don't know as much as they think they do and information is often controlled by institutions. One of Europe's smallest capital cities, the city of Valletta, measures 900 metres by 630 metres and there are over 25 churches probably occupying a sacred site. Eve felt agitated and yearned for the day when great truths will be revealed so we can understand our human origins and the true nature of our existence.

Eve arrived at the high, wired gate, hoping it would be open but she was locked out. She could barely make out the stone circle but she had a visual image of the artwork produced by Houel in her mind. The area was like a ghost town. Overgrown flora and megalithic stones lay on the surface unable to be moved because they were joined to what lay beneath and because of their sheer weight. The stone circle was in a rugged place, quiet and secluded, which she didn't mind. She rolled out her towel on a patch of green grass and enjoyed the solitude of this forgotten ancient treasure. She began to meditate in this unspoilt natural environment.

Before she had realised it, Eve drifted off to sleep with many unanswered questions still lingering in her mind. She dreamt that a person in a long black hooded cloak was opening the gate for her. The person had their head down and was hiding their face, but she caught a glimpse of a prominent bird beak. Eve followed the cloaked person down a path to the entry of the stone circle. She climbed a few stairs up to the front entrance which was made of huge megalithic stones. At the entry was a tall lady dressed in a flowing red gown that covered her feet. She was waiting for Eve. The lady was incredibly beautiful with wavy auburn hair, walnut-coloured eyes, full lips and fine features. Despite her beauty she looked stern. She identified herself as the Goddess Gaia and the Maltese archipelago as her home and as the Land of the Goddess.

"The islands of Malta are the spiralling vortex of the divine feminine energy. Although the islands are deceptively small to the eye, the vortex is the powerful navel of the earth," she said. "Legends were born on these islands. I have birthed many types of human species with my first husband, Uranus, including the Titans and one of my sons Briareus, who had one hundred hands and fifty heads. Briareus guarded the entry to Atlantis because he was stronger than any Titan or Giant and later the Pillars were named in his honour, the Pillars of Briareus. Later on they were referred to as the Pillars of Hercules.

"All the female Oracles were brought to the Xagħra stones for initiation. The Blue Queen's bloodline was renowned on this sacred island. She was renowned for having an extremely well developed pineal gland and for this reason the Oracles of Malta were much sought after for divination around the world. The famous Oracle at Delphi was initially created in my honour. Like a typical patriarch, Zeus wanted to possess more power so he wanted to find the navel of the world known as the Omphalos Stone. He sent two eagles from opposite ends of the earth to search for the centre of the world where he believed the Omphalos would be found. The eagles united at Delphi and this became the famous site of the Oracle of Delphi.

"When Zeus discovered that the centre of the world was a sacred site in my honour he decided to build a temple on top of it in honour of Apollo. He slew one of my serpent dragons and forced me out of Delphi, but my dragons took the Omphalos Stone with me, unbeknown to Apollo. The temple of Delphi became the temple of Apollo, identified with the patriarchal and no longer Mother Earth.

"The powerful serpent-like dragons of the earth have protected me for thousands of years, but now you come to my doorstep and seek answers. I summon you to enter my sacred stone circle." She drew Eve in with her crystal pinecone. Gaia was holding her staff in one hand, directing the pinecone at the apex towards the temple area of Eve's head.

It was the powerful staff that drew Eve to the goddess. Eve knew the pinecone was associated with the pineal gland, immortality and knowledge. The pineal gland is activated by light and it controls the various biorhythms of the body. It works in harmony with the hypothalamus gland, which directs the body's thirst, hunger, sexual desire and the biological clock that determines our aging process. The crystal pinecone was a powerful tool. Gaia must have been thousands of years old but showed no signs of age. Being a goddess she had mastered immortality and longevity.

The goddess paused to show Eve the pinecone she was pointing at her forehead. The apex of the pinecone was transmitting some energy frequencies through her third eye into her pineal gland and it felt wonderful and empowering.

"Your DNA is being upgraded as you have already activated some of your junk DNA, the ninety percent unused part of your DNA that has been suppressed in most humans, and for this reason I can communicate with you," she said.

When Gaia held out her hand and pointed the crystal pinecone at her third eye, Eve felt every chakra in her body come alive, merge and align like a giant snake climbing up her spinal cord. Gaia was awakening and strengthening Eve's kundalini energy, a spiritual energy in the body depicted as a coiled serpent at the base of the spine rising up to the third eye and pineal gland. In the moment of enlightenment, Eve's crown chakra opened up as never before and she received information and divine wisdom through Gaia in preparation for her second dive.

"You will merge our humanity with the lost divinity and spirituality of the divine matriarchal goddess that was known in ancient times – a spiritual science that existed in all the great Golden Ages as the Great Goddess knew it when she was held in great reverence and respect. The old will crumble. This cycle will return and the matriarchal will take its rightful place!"

The goddess continued, "Like the gods and goddesses, the human race evolved and came from the stars. We are all divine and eternal spiritual beings. Our journey is to make known the unknown and keep on living, as we are immortal beings of light. We are not here on earth to be tormented, to suffer, to punish, but rather to gain wisdom through our experiences. As we grow older we can build new paradigms of thought and reality based upon that wisdom. The only thing that matters in this world is love, unconditional love. The material world is an illusion. The only true religion is about love. Humans have deeply buried memories of the eternal plan of our soul's origin but you will remember, as I, Gaia, have commanded this of you, Eve!"

At her loud command Gaia thrust her staff with great force into the ground. She meant business and Eve was listening attentively. There was no way she would disobey this tough goddess. Eve stared at her intriguing staff carved with two entwined winged serpents like a DNA Helix. Within moments, the stone beneath Eve's feet started cracking and breaking as the floor beneath gave way. Eve fell to the base of the staircase, surrounded by stone rubble and covered in dust. She was woken by the sound of her ringing mobile phone.

Eve searched for her phone. Etienne asked, "Hello ma chérie, what are you up to? I'm waiting for you in the courtyard of Ta' Frenc restaurant for dinner, remember?"

"Oh yes, I will be right there." As Eve stood up she noticed she was covered in dust. She dusted herself off, collected her belongings and went directly to the restaurant.

"Looks as though you had a busy day," Etienne commented as Eve hurried into the restaurant.

"Sorry, I didn't have time to change, had a full-on day, but you look impeccable." Eve embraced Etienne. They sat in the courtyard overlooking the countryside enjoying champagne.

"We have done so much in the last few days. What have been the highlights for you?" Eve asked.

"Firstly meeting you has been the biggest highlight of all. This trip has shown that there appears to be strong connections stemming from our aquatic existence through to the hermaphrodite Nommos and to the long-headed dolichocephalic skulls, to the serpents and the goddess culture." Etienne was suave and receptive as always. She admired him for always being a good sport and being open to her suggestions, even though he didn't always agree with her.

"And you?"

"Comino was a climax for me." She blushed at her own pun. "On another subject, the highlight was to realise the important role the matriarchal played in the ancient past. The worship of the Great Mother Goddess is a very ancient story ingrained in us all. Even though patriarchal powers took hold of religion, dismissing the matriarchal, people loved the goddess too much to destroy her because she represented the all-loving mother, the giver of life. For example in ancient Egypt, the goddess Isis holds the divine child on her lap, like the Virgin Mary with Jesus on her lap. The ancient star of divine birth, Sirius, was adopted as the Star of Bethlehem. Ancient legends and mythical images evolve and change with the times but are likely to be the same, just adopted by the current religion. The new buildings cover up the old temple remains. This appears to be the cycle.

"My feeling is that the tide will change again and the matriarchal forces will rise from the ashes to regain their rightful position alongside the patriarchal. I think of the yin and yang symbol, the perfect union, both different, but doing the best work when they work together and focus their energies in the same direction, rather than struggle against each other separately. Only when we have this paradigm shift will we see more peace, balance and harmony in our existence through a more give-and-take, cooperative mentality. War and violence are not the solutions to everything." Eve voiced her opinion with much passion as she finished off her aperitif before dinner.

"I get your point of view," replied Etienne. "I have some interesting trivia for you about the goddess culture, which is still interwoven in our present-day society. For example, the name of the capital city Paris means for Isis, *Par Isis*. Napoleon issued a drawing and written instructions that the Egyptian goddess and her star, Sirius, must be included on the coat-of-arms of the French capital city. As I recall, a wreath of wheat in red, gold and silver surrounded the coat of arms. A golden crown is placed on top of the coat of arms, on which perches an imperial eagle with its wings outspread. The Hermetic Caduceus staff pierces the crown horizontally with two winged snakes wrapped around it, like my tattoo. There is an image of a silver boat floating on the sea and on its prow is the goddess Isis seated on a throne and guided by a star hovering in front of the boat. Three golden Queen Bees are above the boat and are symbols of divine solar matriarchal rule. Even the Arc de Triomphe was a symbol of Isis and her star, Sirius.

"Those in the know, like Napoleon Bonaparte, left powerful names and symbols in place for those who have eyes to see the big picture, beyond the surface. Carry on, ma chérie; I just thought I'd share some interesting trivia with you."

"Like you," said Eve, "I must be sapiosexual because your interesting French trivia knowledge and Foreign Legion stories really excite my brain. The feminine approach relies on the right-brain functions, and the masculine on the left-brain approach. Some of the right-brain functions include intuition, imagination and empathy. When they are out of balance and one is more dominant in society we get greater imbalance; as more men are in top leadership positions we tend to get greater violence and wars. Unfortunately, as humans suppress or deny their feminine side they also suppress their inner knowing; their intuition and experience unbalance emotions and relationships with each other. The external happenings are a result of what is happening within us. Your observations show that you're reawakening and getting in touch with your suppressed emotions," Eve observed.

"Thanks to you, I'm seeing so many things differently," smiled Etienne. "Malta is a mysterious island. Does its name mean anything?"

"The name Malta has a few meanings. Spelt backwards we get Atlam, perhaps a reference to a mountain in Atlantis. Ancient Malta was known as Melitē to the ancient Greeks and Melita to the ancient Egyptians and Romans meaning sweet honey due to Malta's production of honey and an endemic species of bees that lived on the island, giving it the popular nickname of the land of honey. The ancient symbol of Malta is a honeycomb with a bee at the centre. In conjunction, one of the symbols of the pharaoh in Egypt is the bee. Another theory suggests that the word Malta comes from the Phoenician word *maleth*, meaning a haven in reference to Malta's many bays, coves and caves or perhaps a safe haven after great cataclysmic events. The climate, location and land were habitable so they could start anew after much destruction or severe weather conditions."

"Changing the subject," said Eve, "I've been thinking about the best location for our dive tomorrow. I have gathered various ancient maps but there are bound to be some distortions in the mapping. Based on Malta being in a geological hot spot there would have been a lot of movement and the topography of the archipelago would have dramatically changed since the last Ice Age. Taking all this into account we have two options for our next diving expedition. According to ancient writers and travellers such as Quintinus and Jean Houel, the temple of Hercules was located in the most western part of Malta, which narrows it down to two locations.

"The first location of the temple of Melqart associated with Hercules could be Ras ir-Raħeb, which lies in the north-western corner of the Rabat-Dingli-Mdina plateau. The second location is to return to Marsaxlokk, in southeastern Malta, beneath the promontory of Tas-Silġ, as the Phoenicians established a sanctuary to Astarte there. Are we in agreement?" Eve asked.

"No! I don't like either of those locations you have in mind." Etienne raised his voice to show Eve he was serious about his decision. "We have already attempted a dive at Marsaxlokk, in the southeastern region. I have given this much thought and research and I think we should search elsewhere. I don't want to return to that area!" Etienne was adamant.

"But the site of Ras ir-Raħeb is where archaeologists suspect the temple of Hercules is located. In fact some valuable artefacts have already been retrieved from the sea. These include a group of terracotta figurines, an ivory plaque depicting a crouching boar, some coins and potsherds of jugs, plates and vases. The Phoenicians occupied this area and worshipped Melqart who was the equivalent of Herakles which translates to the Glory of Hera. Tas-Silġ is another possible site for the temple of Hercules and the Phoenicians established a sanctuary to Astarte as well," Eve explained.

"No! I think you are wrong. The temple of Astarte is located in Valletta's Grand Harbour. You are not an experienced diver like me and I think I should dive alone with Bozo. It's too dangerous for you," Etienne repeated, raising his voice and pounding his fist on the table.

"Do you think you are Hercules? Why are you raising your voice and being so aggressive? We need to decide together!" This was an aggressive and dominant side to Etienne she had never seen before and she didn't like it. Eve never responded well to aggression, dominance and judgments. She always steered away from anyone who possessed such traits.

"We are not deciding – you are! It's too dangerous! You only listen to me when I raise my voice. You're a dreamer, Eve! It's impossible to find what you are searching for, especially in a dangerous, unpredictable environment like the sea, so close to the edges of tectonic plates. You're dreaming to think you will discover some renowned ancient temple or ancient mystery that will change the world for the better. The world is already filled with too many Jackals."

"Please don't hold back Hercules – or should I call you the Jackal! And by the way, Mr. Cousteau, you look ridiculous in your red budgie smuggler!" Eve snapped.

"What's the red budgie smuggler? I haven't killed any bird. I don't understand! Always dreaming about Atlantis – it's gone already – destroyed by fire and water." Etienne had clearly had enough.

Eve was stunned and felt briefly paralysed. Her eyes were wide open in sheer disbelief about what she had heard coming out of Etienne's mouth. Even though it felt he had stabbed her with a dagger in her heart, she would not cry in front of him, nor would she respond in greater anger and possibly say something she would regret later. She shook her head in disbelief and snatched her backpack, storming out of the restaurant to get as far away from Etienne as possible. She ran out into the countryside and kept running until she was out of breath, dispelling her anger by the vigorous run.

Eve looked over her shoulder and felt relieved that Etienne had not followed her and she was well out of his sight as she sat on the ground alone with nature. She should have never allowed herself to get too intimate with a Frenchman who wore an absurd red budgie smuggler. She would not allow Etienne to distract her from her path, her goals and her promise to Buznanna. She was not going to sit there and hear Etienne ramble on and dictate how to carry out the next diving expedition.

Eve gazed out over the verdant countryside that extended to the rocky cliffs and the Mediterranean Sea and slowly switched off her tumultuous feelings, retreating to her inner sanctuary, her safe world where no one could hurt her. Her eyes fixed on the intriguing countryside of Gozo. What is the real story of Gozo, known as the Island of the Three Hills and the island of Ogygia? Why is the sea nymph, Calypso, one of the daughters of the Titan Atlas also named Atlantis? Does Atlantis[2] mean the island of Atlas or the daughter of Atlas? Why did her research always point to the direction of the Maltese archipelago? Eve pondered, deeply engrossed in her thoughts. She desperately sought answers but no one really understood, except Buznanna.

---

[2] "Atlantis" means the daughter of Atlas.
See entry Ἀτλαντίς in Liddell & Scott.

Had Etienne just been pretending to be interested in her endeavours all this time? Her eyes scanned numerous conical knolls resembling extinct volcanoes, which popped out of the ground calling for her attention. Gozo was always considered to be more fertile, agricultural, hillier and greener than Malta and the extinct volcanoes were responsible for this. She admired the flourishing countryside which was green and segmented into ploughed fields and occasionally separated by stone walls. The thriving prickly pear cactus sprawled over the countryside with its yellow, red and white fruits.

She fixed her vision on the backdrop, the dark blue Mediterranean Sea. What secrets are held beneath the sea? At this moment so many things were uncertain but one thing Eve knew for certain was that she would not stop until she found answers with or without Etienne's help. With that last thought she felt a hand on her shoulder. She turned around to see Etienne standing behind her. He sat by her side.

"Why are you here? I'm not interested in hearing your excuses." Eve had experienced aggression, dominance and judgements before and she would not tolerate such behaviour from any person, even Etienne. But she didn't want to be abandoned by Etienne, of all people. As thoughts raced through her mind, her head felt hot again and she fought back the tears from her eyes as she reminded herself to be strong. She took a deep breath and calmed her inner turmoil.

"You're too much of a dreamer! Let's just put it in the too-hard basket and let things be," Etienne suggested gently.

"I can't believe you found me to say this to me. I can do this on my own with Bozo by my side. There are dozens of great diving schools on the archipelago that probably provide a better service than your business. Mother Earth, the world, needs more dreamers! Without dreamers the world would be stagnant, there would be no progress or scientific and medical breakthroughs. No man would have ever ventured out into space or onto the moon if no one had dreamed to do it first, or dreamt of a solution to make the dream a reality. There is nothing wrong with being a dreamer. I'm proud of being a dreamer. You should try it!" Eve retorted.

Etienne paused for a while and reached for her hands so she could face him.

She repeated, "I can do this on my own! And you don't need to raise your voice for me to listen to you." Eve turned to look at Etienne sternly.

"You're absolutely right. I'm truly sorry, ma chérie! I'm not perfect and sometimes my anger gets the better of me, which I need to learn how to control, especially with you. I suppose spending years in the French Foreign Legion going off to special missions in wars has caused my sensitive side to be replaced by insensitivity, causing me to close down sometimes. It's not always easy for me to navigate through my feelings and I prefer to find a man-cave in the ocean. Going to wars makes you insensitive.

"From a man's perspective it's difficult to talk like women do and express sensitivity and feelings. I know we are all the sons or daughters of a patriarch, BUT…" Etienne paused, "being around you, my precious Eve, has taught me to be more introspective and I think I've become a better person who has discovered a new sense of wholeness in your company." Etienne smiled warmly at Eve but saw she needed more convincing from the stern look on her face, so he continued.

"I realise I need to be responsible for my responses and actions rather than take on values that have been handed down to me through the patriarchal approach. I have learnt so much from being around you. Sharing our travels has opened me up to the feminine approach. I've learnt that it's better to play outside the lines that have been drawn for me, as it has opened me up more than I ever realised possible. My other half, my better half, is my sensitive side which you, Eve, bring out in me and that is no easy task. You are absolutely right, as always! I should learn to be more of a dreamer.

"I learnt so much from our visit to Mali about humanity's possible evolution and how we all possess masculine and feminine qualities like the hermaphrodite Nommos. That was a turning point for me and it's all due to you and this driving passion you have running in your blood. There is no stopping you! Every morning, as soon as your feet hit the ground you are on your mission. You are by far the most extraordinary woman I have ever met. And hopefully if you can forgive me, there's no stopping us?" Etienne held on so tightly to Eve's hands she could feel the perspiration start to build up and she sensed he was stressed and probably still traumatised from the previous diving experience at Marsaxlokk.

Etienne gazed into her eyes that appeared green after one tear drop escaped her eye and he knew she had forgiven him. Their feelings, reactions and responses showed one important element, that their undeniable love would conquer all obstacles and disagreements. Etienne wiped the tear away and embraced Eve. The embrace melted the anger between them. Eve realised relationships were not meant to be perfect or easy but at least they were building a better understanding of each other and how to keep their relationship alive and well.

"I can be patriarchal too at times," Eve pointed out.

"You don't say, never!" Etienne acted surprised.

"Sometimes to survive in a male-dominated environment, you have to be. In a more balanced world both men and women need a more heart-centred approach to rediscover the feminine aspects. At least we are aware and trying to unite the masculine and feminine qualities to build a more balanced relationship. It's a difficult process, as men and women are very different, but if men and women can come together, ultimately a better world will result."

"Certainly there are differences between men and women and in France we say, *Vive la différence!* And the best part of it all is we can make up again." Etienne winked at Eve.

"Is that right?" she retorted. "You capitalise on every opportunity Pepé Le Pew, who always has love and romance on the brain. You are also a man of great heart and that's essentially what I need," Eve admitted. "It's important we recognise and respect our essential differences and respond from a place of love so we can unite and flourish in our wholeness. Even though conditioning is rooted in the aspect of self, slowly a new world will emerge from ways that no longer serve us as a society.

"We are being drawn to address the imbalances and global crises threatening our survival on the planet during the Age of Aquarius, which is regarded as a spiritual turning point for society. We either make it through the issues or break it all down, but something new will emerge either way." Etienne was listening intently, but got distracted by something protruding from Eve's hair. He carefully removed a twig deeply entangled in her thick auburn hair.

"It's been an interesting day! A lot of pent-up emotions have been released today." Eve smiled at the twig in Etienne's hand.

"There is never a dull moment when you're around, ma chérie. You are always diligently on task. Now, I have some surprises for you. I have been doing a lot of research as your endeavours have truly interested and consumed me. I think our next diving location should be at Filfla, as it's at the approximate half-way mark between your two suggested sites of Tas-Silġ and Ras ir-Raħeb. We need to take into account that Filfla was much bigger than it is today and would be the most western point of the Maltese Archipelago on the route from Africa. I have plotted Ptolemy's co-ordinates for the temple of Hercules and the temple appears to be situated in the vicinity of the Islet of Filfla."

"What evidence do you have that Filfla was a larger landmass?" Eve asked.

"Like I said, chérie, I've been doing a lot of research and discovered a map found in Germany from 1798, made by Napoleon Bonaparte. Look at this map – you can see that Filfla was a much bigger island that had a fort, a lighthouse, some idle megalithic slabs and a monastery with a chapel.

"The map shows what Filfla looked like 200 years ago. Examining the coordinates of Ptolemy with the coordinates of Filfla in the present day there is only a three-kilometre difference, which is minute. The most striking thing that comes to my attention is that the temple of Hercules is marked by Ptolemy as being in the vicinity of Filfla. This is something of great significance. I understand that Ptolemy links both Tas-Silġ and Ras ir-Raħeb as possible sites of the temple of Hercules and the sanctuary of Juno. Your inherited map from Buznanna has a vortex at the centre of the map and the temple of Hercules is marked probably on an island that fragmented and sank, whereas the other maps have the temple on the mainland of Malta. All three locations could reveal something of significance.

"I think by discovering the temple of Hercules, we may find the relevance of the purple vortex symbol and the links to the ancient great goddesses. The remains at Ras ir-

Raħeb and Tas-Silġ megaliths have already been explored and show evidence of a prehistoric structure. Sure there is always more to explore but I'm more inclined to explore Filfla even though it may not be the safest diving site, for two reasons. Firstly, it's located next to a fault line and it's perilous because any undersea earthquake can see us trapped or endangered again. Secondly, there are rumours of undetonated bombs from the days when Filfla was used by the British as target practice during the war. My mind is made up, but what do you think?" Etienne put his strong views forward.

"Filfla! Of course! Maybe the megalithic blocks used to build the fort, lighthouse and monastery were taken from the nearby temple of Hercules when Filfla was a larger landmass. All your research correlates with Buznanna's map. A monastery, a cave chapel and even the dedication of the Madonna Tal Filfla all created on a tiny, uninhabited islet. Was this to mark the relevance of another sacred site? The secret society of the sacred feminine must have been guarding this site.

"You've convinced me. Filfla should be our next diving target and having Bozo accompany us will make the experience safer this time round. I like the location of Filfla and your perspective because essentially we are trying to discover the role of the Great Goddess, but also the purpose of the vortex. Does the vortex have anything to do with the manipulation of light and sound? How did the matriarchal and patriarchal co-exist in the ancient past, or were they hermaphrodite?" Eve wondered.

"Ptolemy's maps link the ancient island of Filfla to the temple of Hercules and the sanctuary of Juno in Valletta's Grand Harbour, but what is the connection again between Juno and Hera?" Etienne asked.

"Hera is the oldest goddess in Greek mythology and predates the worship of Zeus. The Romans referred to her as Juno. She was the wife of Zeus and queen of the Olympians. Hera hated Herakles (Hercules) because he was the son of her husband, Zeus, and a mortal woman so she commanded two snakes to kill him at birth. Hera was not only the wife of Zeus but she was one of his three sisters and their brother was Poseidon. Hera was jealous of Zeus giving birth to Athena without her involvement. Cronus and Rhea were the parents of Hera, Zeus and Poseidon. Cronus swallowed all their children and his brothers who were Titans, because he believed an oracle that one of his sons would dethrone him, as he dethroned his own father Uranus.

"Cronus was unable to swallow Zeus because Rhea and Gaia, Mother Earth, threw an egg-shaped stone covered in clothes into his mouth to trick him. Zeus became a legend because he defeated his father Cronus by forcing him to disgorge first the egg stone and then his Titan brothers and sisters. This special stone is known as the Omphalos. I've mentioned it before. It represents regeneration and was kept in the Adyton where the Pythia, the high priestess delivered her oracles in Delphi. Zeus broke Cronus' destructive cycle, but this created another evil of the patriarchal rule."

"It sounds as though Zeus and Hera were hermaphrodites, like the Nommos. When you hear of these virgin births and how the gods and goddesses were brought to life there is so much interconnection with the hermaphrodite Nommos, described by the Dogon. Didn't you say Athena was born out of the head of Zeus?" Etienne asked.

"Yes, but the truth can get distorted by the victors, who were men and dominant due to their physical strength over women. Another point is that the victors control and write the history. Patriarchal powers have written history and changed it to foster their agenda. In this day and age, with more civilised thinking and knowledge of culture, men are still using their physical strength to dominate women and impose their will. Like all cycles in time, we may see the tide slowly turning as the matriarchal slowly emerges from the ashes like the Phoenix. There is a great sense of renewal of the matriarchal in the Age of Aquarius.

"The birth of Athena re-established the importance of the warrior goddess and the role the divine feminine plays in the creation myths. One cannot exist without the other; in other words, we need the seed and the egg for creation. We need both contributions – one is not greater than the other. The patriarchal strength is a way to spread the seed in search of a vessel. Actually, there are accounts that Zeus didn't father any of his children but Hera did it all by herself. Zeus had intercourse with his cousin Metis, whom he swallowed because it was professed that she would have powerful children and one that would overthrow Zeus. When Zeus swallowed Metis, it was too late because Metis was already pregnant. Athena leapt out of Zeus' head when it was cut open with an axe," she smiled.

"All this mythology is confusing. Is there any truth to Athena sprouting out of the head of Zeus, all grown up and armoured?" Etienne asked, scratching his head.

"It's confusing so humanity can forget its origins. Legend does have truth embedded in it – it's just finding the evidence to prove it that's difficult. Athena's helmet is like the horns of a cow and her armour is like scales. Was Athena in fact a Nommos? Everyone is trying to search for answers in their religion, but the true answers are only held within us individually. It's our own personal quest to go in search of those answers.

"Athena is a symbol to remind us and awaken us to what we have forgotten. We've forgotten our origins because fear and confusion have been installed in us as a control mechanism. We've forgotten the value in fusing the matriarchal with the patriarchal, not for one to overpower the other.

"Athena is holding a long spear with a crystal shield, and a large snake accompanying her or beneath her feet, as the Virgin Mary is often depicted, reminding us of the Nommos. Nike the Winged Goddess of Victory is thought to have stood in the outstretched hand of the statue of Athena that stood in the Parthenon. Athena's popularity reminds us of the matriarchal role; it can't be overshadowed or mistreated otherwise she will rise against injustice. I can relate to that."

"Did Athena have a magical lasso too, Wonder Woman?"

"She had more powers than you can even imagine." She pulled him closer by grabbing the front of his shirt as she pressed her lips against his.

Chapter 17

The Omphalos Stone

Take time to deliberate, but when the time for action has arrived, stop thinking and go in.
Napoleon Bonaparte

The captain anchored the boat on the western side of Filfla, facing North Africa. He manoeuvred the Calypso to get as close as possible to the island. Etienne and Eve sat on the ledge at the back of the Calypso semi-dressed and equipped in their diving gear. They stared directly in front of them at their proposed diving spot. The conditions appeared peaceful and calm. They looked at the isolated, uninhabited island of Filfla – a gigantic mountain separated from the mainland.

The Omphalos Stone

Etienne and Eve were confident about the choice of location based on the ancient maps they had scrutinised thoroughly before they planned this major dive. Bozo was swimming and frolicking around the Calypso. He looked over to them several times as he somersaulted in the air, making his presence known. Bozo seemed excited about the dive and Eve certainly felt safer having him nearby. Bozo's wisdom always exceeded her expectations. He was a highly evolved species that had superior senses to humans. He would be an invaluable resource on this dive.

Etienne looked worried. He was having flashbacks from their last diving experience and understandably he was still traumatised. "Are you sure you want to do this? We are diving into this vast unpredictable sea that is susceptible to any seismic activity. Mother Earth sneezes and we get crushed like mincemeat. Since I've met you I've definitely got more grey hair." Etienne was getting anxious.

"Sometimes not getting what you want, Mr. Cousteau, is a magnificent stroke of luck," replied Eve. "Since our last dive experience we have become stronger and charted a new direction, a new approach better than the first plan. The three of us, as a team, have tenacity, knowledge, strength, courage, acumen, planning and diligence – the ingredients of good fortune. We have the perfect combination this time around. I understand it's daunting venturing out into the unknown, but if you never open your heart to life's possibilities you never discover the blessings hidden in every trial. If you never search, ask questions or use your intuition how will you find the answers? My heart is telling me to go forward – how about you?" Eve squeezed Etienne's hand.

"You are a tenacious woman and that's why I love you so much. I'm coming with you whether you like it or not and I'm wearing my red budgie smuggler. I'm not sure if Bozo will be able to handle you. We will go down as a team like The Three Musketeers watching each other's backs." Etienne squeezed Eve's hand even harder.

"I loved you from the moment I laid eyes on you again. It's not something I've said before." Eve planted a big kiss on his lips.

"What do you mean – again?"

"I'll explain some other time. And we love you too Bozo!" Eve yelled across the sea, quickly changing the subject.

Bozo was getting incredibly excited. Even though he was grown up, an adult with his own family, he still acted like a playful calf. Eve couldn't help but smile when she saw him. Eve knew she needed his help and skills and that he would do all that was necessary in the ocean. He would give unconditional love.

Etienne dived into the sea to have a brief swim with Bozo, while Eve watched them from the boat. She pulled out the ankh and star pendant she had worn since the age of eight when Buznanna had given it to her in the nearby paired temple complexes. She recalled all the times she had looked out to Filfla from the high promontory, which has the best views of the islet and wondered what Filfla's story was.

Goosebumps covered Eve's body – a sign that her soul family was with her. She kissed her ankh and star pendant as she prayed with an open heart to invite the divine goddess, the Blue Queen, in because Eve knew that when she entered the scene, miracles happened. She expressed her gratitude for all her blessings and for a safe journey; she believed in the Blue Queen's guidance with all her heart. She slipped the necklace down into her wetsuit next to her heart. Etienne and Bozo had bonded very quickly, which was essential for the dive.

Etienne swam back to the boat and he appeared calmer about the dive. He signalled to the crew to assist with putting on the last pieces of diving gear and equipment. The crew performed the last safety checks and instructions for the dive. They had several pieces of advanced diving equipment and tools, including a torpedo, a propulsion vehicle, to help them swim down the side of Filfla more efficiently, covering as much range as was needed.

Etienne and Eve hugged each other and plunged into the sea. Bozo was right by their side ready to go. Eve and Bozo had some mind talk – she hadn't forgotten how to communicate telepathically with animals and Bozo instinctively knew what to do. Eve allowed Bozo to take the lead and they followed right behind him, each holding onto a torpedo with a bright light beaming so they could scale down the side of Filfla at a good speed.

Filfla appeared to be an enormous submerged mountain. Bozo took a slight turn into a cove, a small sheltered bay cut into the side of Filfla. The astonishingly beautiful cove reflected an array of turquoise shades on the walls from the ivory sands only metres below. It was not as deep as they had anticipated because there was a massive build-up of silt and sand.

Bozo was communicating to Eve that this was their entry point. He was staring at the enormous rock face that was overgrown with sea grass as if he were expecting something to come out. As Bozo went in closer, a large menacing moray eel peered from behind the rock, opening its mouth to reveal razor-sharp serrated teeth. They had obviously disturbed its home because it exited on the defensive. The moray eel and Bozo stared at each other for a few minutes as they communicated. Etienne and Eve remained motionless a couple of metres behind Bozo. The eel still appeared extremely agitated when it zoomed out from behind the sheltered rock cove. Without notice, the eel charged at Etienne who could see the large two-metre snake-like creature coming in his direction with its mouth wide open, on the attack. Etienne instantly pulled out his knife to defend himself. With great speed and agility, Bozo swiftly intercepted the eel and captured him firmly in his mouth, immobilising him in one bite.

By this stage a swarm of about twenty large moray eels had gathered. Bozo swiftly turned to face the supporting troops. He had the leader of the pack firmly in his mouth and had a standoff with the rest of the eels. Bozo demanded they either let them pass or the leader gets crushed to death. The decision was made clear when Bozo released the eel as the whole swarm scurried past them, letting them gain access to this heavily guarded entry point, their home, which they protected and barricaded. Bozo followed the swarm closely, should they happen to change their minds and attack. Within moments, the eels had shot off into the distance and out of sight.

Etienne approached the cavity the moray eels had been protecting so fiercely, with Eve following closely behind. They explored the cove but could sense some commotion outside. They peered out of the cove and saw a giant serpent emerge from the depths of the sea. The strange-looking sea monster resembled a dragon-like sea creature, with a long pointed V-shaped crocodile snout. Its mouth was slightly parted, revealing a huge set of teeth. The monster was about five metres in length. It had slit pupils, typical reptilian-looking eyes. The dorsal surface was armoured with large osteoderms, bony plates embedded in the skin. It had two front and rear fins which propelled it through the water.

They were astonished at the sight of this creature – they had seen nothing like it. Could it be a Leviathan? They are believed to guard Atlantis and are mentioned in the bible, Eve thought as they both hid in the cove, hoping the monster would pass them by.

The Omphalos Stone

Bozo was metres away when he returned after escorting the eels away. Eve telepathically communicated to Bozo to keep his distance because it appeared some predator was approaching and they should allow it to pass. Bozo agreed as he confirmed her request but remained in the vicinity, closely monitoring the situation.

The creature slowly approached the cavity and started snapping with its pointed snout at the rock crevice, knowing they were inside. It was communicating telepathically with Eve. The sound of its deep voice was disturbing. The deep, rugged voice echoed clearly through Eve's mind.

"The great evil master, Balzor, has sent me to destroy you and you cannot proceed. Turn back or you will perish! You are not permitted to access the truth. I am the gatekeeper, the Leviathan." Its message was stern and its chilling voice echoed in her head.

"Don't tell me what to do!" Spontaneously, she triggered her harpoon from behind Etienne, aiming straight for the head of the beast.

The arrow missed his head but lodged in his armoured skin, causing him little grief but great rage as he pounded his snout into the rock crevice where Etienne and Eve cowered. Eve panicked and wished for the great sky god Horus to be there to protect them.

The beast persistently bit into the rock crevice and broke off a large piece of rock, partially exposing Etienne. As soon as he caught sight of Etienne he swiftly bit down on his shoulder, ripping into his thick wetsuit and flesh, holding Etienne in place. Armed with knives they fought back by stabbing him in the head and neck. Blood clouded the water and the beast released Etienne, as they both zoomed out of the rock crevice before they were eaten alive.

Etienne was holding his wound to control the bleeding. Bozo had come by Eve's side as she held on tightly to her long knife. Bozo and Eve would need to counterattack any further advances because she knew the Leviathan would not give in without a fight. Etienne stayed behind them holding his shoulder.

"It's me you want. I'm not afraid of you or Balzor, you cowards!" Eve was angry. She held the knife in front of her, ready for the beast's next advance as she watched it closely. She didn't take her eyes off it. She was like an assassin, knowing her next move, but keeping it out of her thoughts, as she knew the beast could read them. Bozo was alert, agitated and ready to defend them as he began rapidly circling Eve and Etienne.

The Leviathan was paddling around them carefully calculating its next move. In an instant, it whipped Eve with its strong tail, belting her backbone, jolting Eve's entire body. She recovered quickly and manoeuvred around to stab it in its unarmoured side, where the skin is smoother and easier to pierce. She pushed the knife in as deep as possible, twisting it around before she pulled it out again.

Bozo swiftly moved in, fiercely pushing the beast metres away from Eve and Etienne with his rostrum before biting into its side and belly with his sharp teeth. The Leviathan was still thrusting its crocodile head around and snapping. It took a bite out of Bozo's dorsal fin, hurting him. Eve was beginning to panic, when she noticed another creature emerge out of the deep blue sea. This time it was an eight-metre killer whale. It was obviously assessing the scene. It stared directly at Eve and telepathically communicated: "Stay back! Let me take care of him."

Eve instantly knew it was Horus. "Horus, you're here!" Eve was relieved he had answered her call.

The Leviathan was thrusting its strong tail and head around trying to capture Bozo in its jaws, but Bozo was quicker and more agile in the water. With one quick motion Bozo and the killer whale flipped the beast upside down with its heavily wounded belly facing up, completely immobilising it like a shark. The large killer whale ripped into the beast's throat in one large bite, pulling the creature's head from its neck. Blood oozed out, colouring the water a deep red. They watched its mangled body gradually sink to the sea floor.

Bozo and the killer whale went in closer to Etienne and Eve who were immensely grateful and relieved that they had come to their rescue. Eve recognised Horus' vibrant eyes and placed her hands in prayer position as a gesture of thanks and gratitude and bowed her head to the great protector who had come to her rescue, before he swam gracefully away.

Bozo instructed Eve to go to the entry of the crevice and started pulling away at the grasses with his teeth. Eve cut the long grass with her knife until she could see a shining black wall. The wall appeared thick, solid and glass-like, as though it was constructed from a slab of obsidian. She shone her torch over the wall as they took a closer look. She saw a white marble plaque on the door with a keyhole shaped like her eight-pointed star. Eve immediately placed her ankh pendant ring on her finger, as Buznanna had shown her all those years ago. The ankh was used as the ring and the star lay flush on Eve's palm. Eve placed her palm with the star into the matching keyhole. It was a perfect fit. She waited for something to happen but nothing did. Bewildered, she turned to Bozo for help. Before any dialogue began, Bozo was one step ahead of her. She could see he was clicking and vibrating his teeth to emit a sound frequency she had never heard before.

She could feel her hand and the star start to vibrate. The sound must have reached a peak of resonance, activating a trigger to unlock the door because they heard a loud, distinct click. Eve removed her star key and before their eyes, the black slab slid open. Now that's security, Eve thought in amazement.

The entry tunnel was only large enough for Etienne and Eve to swim through. Eve hugged Bozo to thank him for all his efforts in defending them and leading them to the entry point. Bozo sustained terrible injuries and was still bleeding, but was happy to be of assistance. He sent them on their way wishing them fruitful discoveries.

Eve and Etienne swam through the tunnel toward the light they could see ahead of them. They arrived in a large circular air-filled cavern, which allowed them to take off their diving gear and disconnect their oxygen. They heard a loud thud. Click! The thick heavy door had closed behind them and they realised they were locked into whatever place Bozo had directed them to. They were at the base of a giant cavern.

"What the hell was that creature that was trying to kill us?" That was the first sentence out of Etienne's mouth.

"It looked like a Leviathan which used to guard the entrance of Atlantis. That was the last thing I was expecting to see," said Eve.

Etienne shook his head. He had a hard time comprehending what had just occurred.

"First thing, let me apply a constrictive bandage to your shoulder," said Eve as she helped him out of his wetsuit. She got a tourniquet out of her bag and applied it firmly around the puncture wounds on his shoulder to stop the bleeding. "Luckily your wetsuit was thick and that creator's teeth did not penetrate too deep to cause any serious injury. You will survive, darling!" Eve could see the bleeding had stopped. "Just try to relax – no sudden movement to your shoulder – we don't want the bleeding to start again. How are you feeling?" Eve was extremely relieved that he had sustained no serious injury.

"Maybe you should kiss me to make it better because I'm still feeling stressed about that ferocious beast trying to eat me alive."

Eve's diving mask was still on her forehead and she accidently head-butted Etienne as he moved in closer, eagerly awaiting his kiss. They both laughed at the collision and Eve knew he would be okay.

"Nothing worth having comes easily. That was one ferocious creature trying to destroy us. You, Bozo and the killer whale were a force to be reckoned with out there. Bozo was amazing, hopefully he will recover. You were like an Amazon warrior, Wonder Woman." Etienne was constantly surprised at how tough Eve could be.

Looking from the ground up it seemed they were in an enormous egg, in the navel or centre of a sacred place. The curved stone walls were covered with intricate carvings reminding her of the hypogeum and temple structures but on a much grander scale. Eve knew from her archaeological studies of the ancient world that the egg structure they were in, known as the Omphalos stone, was a powerful spiritual symbol.

She scanned the magnificent oval structure and wondered how it could be so perfectly shaped and on such a large scale inside the islet of Filfla. The construction was more skilful than in any ancient monument she had seen. Eve followed the exquisite black marble spiral staircase along the outer edges of the egg, which seemed to be a complex helical structure, like a corkscrew roller coaster at an amusement park. They approached a tall glistening gold trilithon, with two vertical stones supporting a third stone across the top.

"It looks and feels like solid gold," murmured Eve as she examined the posts.

Underneath the trilithon was an ornate throne covered in precious coloured stones and inscriptions. Eve went in closer to observe the throne and found on the armrest another keypad requiring the star key. Eve was curious so she sat on the throne and put her key in. As she looked forward she felt a fine crystal beam, less than a millimetre wide, implanted in her eyes. This was not the first time this had happened to her – she had experienced the same sensation in her dreams, but now it was occurring in her waking state. The crystal beam triggered her third eye all the way to the back of her head. It gave her extraordinary vision and insight as though she was being upgraded to be able to absorb much more information and knowledge.

She had suffered from terrible migraines growing up and when she had her head scanned, the results showed a slight deformity of the parietal bone to the rear of her skull. The whole experience was not foreign to her so she didn't feel alarmed, frightened or any discomfort in the process. On the contrary, it felt empowering just as it had been in her dreams.

Etienne could see the flashes spark over and into her.

"Are you okay there?"

"Yes I'm fine. This egg structure is spectacular. There are intricate carvings, gold statues, furniture, precious metals and precious stones everywhere you look," Eve said as she got up off the throne feeling more revived than ever.

"What have we found? Is it the temple of Hercules?" Etienne was bewildered.

"No it's much better. We have found the Omphalos stone. The temple of Hercules must be preserved in another layer of sediment above this enormous egg. The Omphalos stone is believed to be just a legend, but this legendary egg which symbolises the navel, the heart of all creation, is real!" Eve was excited; this discovery was spectacular and she was keen to investigate it at all levels.

"I imagine the way out would be through the top level closer to the surface because that is the last thing Bozo communicated to me," Eve reassured Etienne.

They began walking up the helical staircase. Eve couldn't believe her eyes when they entered the next level and were greeted by another golden monument – a colossal statue of Poseidon holding his signature trident, with six large winged seahorses harnessed to his chariot.

"When I see the trident symbol it reminds me of a powerful Maserati, which uses the symbol of the trident as their logo," Etienne observed.

"Amazing! You're thinking of your dream car right now! Many large companies use ancient names and symbols in their branding and logos. Neptune was the god of freshwater and the sea in the Roman religion. He is the counterpart of the Greek god Poseidon. Besides that, Neptune is a lovely blue outer planet in the solar system and bears its closest association with Pisces, the most watery of all the signs. In astrology, dreams, illusion and Neptune govern all abstract thought and the mysterious. Our spirituality is important not only to ourselves for our personal betterment, but to this planet. Neptune symbolises the insights of truth and heightened awareness, not only a Maserati."

Their eyes feasted on the intricate detail of the solid gold monument as they walked past it to a red granite door, but this was no ordinary door. Eve recognised it as the door to the Afterlife, found in most ancient Egyptian tombs. It was built to take the spirits of the dead to and from the Afterworld. The door was covered in religious texts in hieroglyphics. Eve thought this door to the Afterlife could be a porthole of some kind. The door was encased in three trilithons, leading them to a solid emerald stone altar. The face of the altar was engraved with a picture of a cloaked man with large feet and the head of an ibis. Eve's first thoughts were they had discovered the legendary emerald tablets of Thoth, the king priest of Atlantis, who had supposedly founded the Egyptian colony and orchestrated the building of the pyramids.

Thoth played a part in many of the myths of pharaonic Egypt. In the creation myth, he was the scribe of the gods, and he was the principal pleader for the soul at the Judgment of the Dead. It was he who invented writing. He wrote all the ancient texts, including the most esoteric ones such as The Book of Breathings, which taught humans how to become gods. He was connected with the moon and thus was considered ruler of the night. Thoth was also the teacher and helper of the ancient Egyptian trinity of Isis, Osiris and Horus; it was under his instruction that Isis worked her sacred magic love spell whereby she brought the slain Osiris back to life.

Eve noticed another keyhole matching her star so she placed the ankh over her finger and pressed the star into the keyhole with the palm of her hand. The altar started to glow and vibrate, producing a soundwave. Eve stared at the ancient characters which reverberated the meaning of the ancient characters in her brain. She was instantly zapped with a download of information. The ancient characters embedded with gold and red alloy changed before her eyes, telling an ancient story:

"Here lies the last temple of the City of Khor on the Atlantean island of Undal, after the great destruction.

"I, Thoth, have moved to the land of Khem. This temple must be protected as a sacred place as our heart spirals are heavy in sorrow. This is the shrine in memory of Atlantis. This was all that remains of my race before the denser hybrid race was established in Khem. Children of the Law of One should protect and worship their place of creation. My people had the all-seeing eyes of a falcon, elongated skulls like the dolphin and originally we were hermaphrodite. The sons of Belial misused the sound technology and hurt Mother Earth. After three destructions this is all that is left of our sacred land. We fled in every direction.

"The descendants of the Pleiadian Blue Queen, and only them, will come secretly on pilgrimage to this sacred place. This place is worthy of worship because it was a safe haven, a refuge for the people that lost all to the destruction. The memory of the Great Mother Goddess and the Golden Age lingers in our minds and hearts and the longing to recreate such greatness burns deep within us. This sacred place holds sacred artefacts and records, a vast library of the Golden Age for those who seek knowledge and who have pure hearts that are spiralling out love energetically. This sacred place is for the teachers, the masters of light, who will go forward and teach the way.

"Our appearance is different from the human race, but we are human as well. Our twin souls are both masculine and feminine; the duality resides in our body.

"We are masters of sound and water, and from water we are all created. We are children of the Mother Goddess. Humans will come who gradually awaken their consciousness and remember every great cosmic year. It can't be lost, as it is entangled like the twin souls into the fabric of existence, the Tree of Life.

"The Golden Age was harmonious and everyone worked for the greater collective good, like the Queen Bee. The human Queen Bee is the conductor of the symphony ensuring harmony, balance and prosperity. Society flourished like an abundant beehive overflowing with sweet golden nectar, the juices of life. There are many ancient tablets stored in this haven, but only for the eyes of those who are of pure heart and enlightened mind.

"Let me talk about my master teacher, Osiris. He was born in Atlantis 25,000 years ago. As a young man he went to the motherland to become a priest and learnt the sacred Lemurian teachings. When he came back to Atlantis he purified the Atlantean religion, which was becoming decadent. He established the glory of our Mother Goddess based on love and simplicity. When he passed on, it became the Osirion religion and I, Thoth, have carried the torch to make it the khemet or Shemsu Hor religion."

Eve was intrigued because so much information was coming together.

"The technology is incredible. I have seen nothing like it," said Eve.

"What is it?" Etienne asked.

"Our persistence has paid off. Inside this giant Omphalos Egg we have found the last remnant shrine of Atlantis," Eve exclaimed, her eyes shining.

Eve noticed more altars and gold, stone and clay tablets studded with precious gemstones. She rubbed her eyes in disbelief at the magnificence. They looked at all the tablets. One papyrus scroll caught Eve's eyes – it looked more recent as it was written in ancient Greek. Eve started to read.

"What does it say?" asked Etienne, as he could not read ancient Greek.

"This scroll is written by Plato. He came here with an Oracle who was required to show him the shrine!" said Eve as she read.

"What does he say?"

"Plato discloses a lot. He provides a lengthy description of what he has discovered, but firmly believes that the world was not ready to revert to matriarchal ways. That's why he kept the story of Atlantis a cryptic legend that only the tenacious seeker of truth would understand

and discover one day. He didn't want this discovery to fall into the wrong hands, risking that such a sacred site could be destroyed and used for one's own personal gain. The Athenians would never have understood that their beloved Athena is a descendant of the Pleiadian Blue Queen, an Atlantean high priestess, and the carrier of the Mother Goddess lineage passed to the eldest daughter.

"Plato knew Atlantis could only be in front of the old pillars of Herakles and in between Libya and Asia. The great Oracle in Delphi, who came from this archipelago, told Plato that a female who possesses the ankh and star pendant and who is strongly associated with Athena would search and find this haven. In fact she is believed to be a reincarnation of Athena and is of the lineage of the Mother Goddess. Through much persistence she will discover this Atlantean site. She will be worthy and will understand and respect the sacredness of the site. She is one of the firstborns through a long line of firstborns, so it is her birthright. She will decide how and when to bring the information forth.

"The Oracle told Plato that many special people will come before the female that possesses the ankh and star pendant but their role is solely to protect this place and not to reveal it. They had to wait for the Great Year to end. Much destruction and heartache would occur before a new era that is ready for a matriarchal awakening to emerge from the rubble, like a phoenix rising from the ashes to herald a new beginning. Trust that everything will occur when the time is right, when the cycles of time come to their imminent closure and a wave of inaugurations commence. This is why this place was guarded," Eve proclaimed.

"Ding dong! It sounds like the female is you! You are the only one that possesses the ankh and star pendant and the description matches your story. How was this haven guarded?" Etienne asked.

It dawned on Eve that he was right. "Plato discloses that it was guarded by the high priestess of the Mother Goddess who settled in the nearby village of Żurrieq whose name refers to the colour blue as the people in the village have blue and violet auras and came from the Blue Spirit race.

"The high priestesses are Oracles hence they have divination powers. The high priestess was identified with the serpent, and identified with nymph-like mermaids, the most famous ones being Calypso and Pythia (Python) from the House of Snakes. Pythia proclaimed the prophecy sitting on a sacred tripod set at the mouth of a natural crack in the stone from which vapours believed to be ethylene were inhaled by the Oracle. It enhanced Pythia's natural ability to enter the trance state.

"The gorge in Delphi is at the intersection of two fault lines and when a major earthquake occurred around 300 BC the vapours ceased because the fault lines got distorted, as Pythia had predicted in her last prophecy. Apollo built his temple on top of the site and slew Gaia's dragon and banished her from Delphi. Gaia took all her treasures to their true origin, Malta.

"Pythia had been taken from Malta to Delphi to become the Oracle as ordered by the goddess Themis. Themis was the founder of the Oracle of Delphi. Every Oracle after Pythia's death had to renounce their name and take on the title of Pythia. Each Pythia was sought after because of her elongated or dolichocephalic skull and of course her ancient bloodlines connected to Cecrops and Calypso. The House of the Snake is the ancient religion of the Mother Goddess. Even the word pyramid in Egyptian hieroglyphs means the House of the Serpents or *the nakkash* in Hebrew.

"I know all of this from studying the Leningrad

Papyrus, a hieratic scroll dated to 1,115 BC conserved at the Hermitage museum, in Saint Petersburg, Russia. The papyrus describes a serpent populace that was destroyed by a celestial object that fell from the heavens. Only one person survived and became known as a Serpent Priest, King or God on an island destined to be completely submerged," Eve explained.

"I know that Calypso is the fabled mermaid in the Odyssey, but who is Cecrops?" Etienne asked.

"Cecrops was the mythical founder and first king of Athens. According to legend he was half-human and half-serpent. He came to Attica from Egypt and constructed the Acropolis, spreading the cult of Athena."

"Cecrops – sounds as though he's a Nommos!" Etienne sounded like an expert now.

Eve replied, "The Nommos kind of look like snakes and the two are interchangeable. Remember Lebe, the famous shape-shifting Nommos? The Dogon told us when they dug her grave they discovered a large snake which was alive and they followed her underground until they reached the escarpment in Mali where they finally settled. Saint Paul and Saint Patrick both went on missions to chase the snakes off Malta and Ireland, islands not known for having poisonous snakes. This being the case, what were those snakes discovered on these islands? In my opinion it's a symbolic representation of the changeover of religions and spiritual beliefs. Why did the saints target the two islands? Maybe Jesus knew about the Mother Goddess and the House of Snakes.

"So many temples and churches have been directly built on top of these sacred sites to hide, guard or bury the truth. For example, St Paul's Cathedral, where Lady Diana was married, was constructed directly on top of the Roman Temple of Diana, which was probably built on top of other temples or sacred sites. Diana's ancient Greek equivalent was Artemis who was Athena's half-sister. These temples were constructed on good energy where dragon or ley lines intersect. Before the ancient Romans this site was sacred to the Druids."

"Look at this egg-shaped stone! Why is this name, Mariamenou-Mara, etched in the metal?" Etienne pointed out the one-metre-tall egg to Eve.

As Eve got closer to the egg her ankh star pendant got stuck to the metallic-looking stone surface. She removed her pendant from the surface and scanned with the palm of her hand. It had distinctive markings and holes through it. A thin shiny silver rind covered the surface. The egg looked like an ancient meteorite.

Eve looked at the scroll next to the meteorite and said, "Here are the answers we are seeking and why Saint Paul targeted Malta. Jesus and Mary Magdalene knew about this sacred island."

"What do you mean?" Etienne asked.

"This egg is a meteorite. It's the Holy Grail and can only be protected by the Blue Queen who possesses the royal ancient Pleiadian bloodlines and lineage. The Blue Queen's race, the great matriarchs, were one of the first civilisations that walked the earth and created life, peace and harmony.

"Mary Magdalene is the Holy Grail, the holy bloodline and the co-messiah with Jesus. Union with the first female sibling gives the power of foresight to the ruling patriarch as in the ancient Nazarene and Egyptian tradition. The Holy Grail and the secret to immortality can only be accessed by the ancient Pleiadian bloodlines. Mary Magdalene left the Holy Grail here in the safety of the Omphalos stone.

"So are you saying Mariamenou-Mara is Mary Magdalene and the Holy Grail and it's only through the female that the secrets to immortality can be revealed?"

asked Etienne.

"Yes, mara means 'from the sea' and according to this scroll, a descendant from the Blue Queen of Atlantis. It's a clue that civilisations started from the water, like the Nommos, like the Carmelite order, and refer to our Lady as the Star of the Sea."

"So Mary Magdalene left the Holy Grail here, the secret tool to immortality, and went to live in the south of France at Saint Mary's of the Sea to be able to die and reunite with Jesus, like Romeo and Juliet?" Etienne suggested.

"How romantic! But Mary Magdalene was the wife and also the sister of Jesus and they came to this shrine to embody the truth of their royal bloodlines. Mary Magdalene is from the House of Snakes and represented the Mother Goddess.

"The patriarchs tried to delete Mary Magdalene's story from the Roman records because they wanted the new religion to be predominantly about the male, the patriarchal, and discarded the ancient matriarchal religion, associated with the snakes and the power of women. It makes sense that the apostles Saint Paul and Saint Patrick needed to exterminate the snakes associated with the Mother Goddess, as it was a threat to their religion.

"Jesus' teaching balanced the masculine and feminine energies, but the two saints dismissed the matriarchal because it hindered the spreading of propaganda about the emerging religion.

"Mary Magdalene and Jesus were direct descendants of Akhenaten through their grandmother Cleopatra. Their mother, Julia Ourania was the daughter of Caesar and Cleopatra and, being an Egyptian female, Julia could never be emperor of Rome.

"Mary Magdalene had to marry her brother, Jesus or Issa by tradition, and she had a colossal dowry. The two of them became king and queen of many renowned kingdoms from Persia to Jerusalem. The Roman elite married into the best Egyptian royal bloodlines, incorporating the matriarchal powers. The point of the scroll is so that the role of the matriarchal would never be forgotten.

"Mary Magdalene wrote this scroll and her name was etched on the meteorite stone to ensure the truth would always prevail. The scroll is signed in remembrance of the Star of the Sea, one of the many Great Mother goddesses, Mariamenou-Mara."

"That's some revelation!" Etienne was amazed. "It reinforces the importance of balancing the duality of the masculine and feminine qualities. Without Mary Magdalene, Jesus could not be the great Magi or Magician."

"Like Jesus, the three wise men were the Magi, the architects, the high priests of ancient Persia. Jesus was not a poor carpenter but a king who ruled beside his queen. We have rediscovered Mariamenou-Mara and all that it encompasses," Eve clarified. "If you want to be a powerful magician like Jesus, you must always listen to me!" Eve winked at Etienne.

Eve looked at another tablet. It was a teaching from MU, LA-MU-RA, as she recognised the Blue Lotus symbol of MU. The teaching was about soul integration. At the bottom of the tablet were a few hieroglyphs meaning Shemsu Hor, the followers of Horus. It was an adaptation of an ancient text made by the followers of Horus. Eve began to translate the text to Etienne.

"In Atlantis, the Atlantean root race had the whole soul in the body and great capabilities enabling them to communicate telepathically with each other and with all living things. After the destruction of Atlantis, the new root race lost the ancient psychic capabilities and so, at least partially, did the followers of Horus from the Atlantean root race. Only a quarter of the soul could fit in the body of this new root race. Since then humans have tried to reunite the higher self with the physical body.

"The earth has an energy frequency which connects the soul with the body. The first chakra, the root chakra, resonates at the frequency of the earth. It roots the soul to the earth. In many respects gravity does not exist – it is just an effect created by electromagnetic forces. What keeps humans on the earth is the root chakra because it roots everything to the earth and it needs to be raised to maintain the whole soul within the body.

"There have been different races before us with different capabilities due to their elongated skulls with larger brains. The human bodies are highly compact forms of energy. The soul origin (the Pleiades) is human in appearance but they have been integrated by the souls from the Sirius star system, which are taller but more water-based mammals in origin and serpent-like in appearance.

"One thing is for certain, regardless of our exact origins and the physical characteristics of our star families, that we are all children of the universe and members of a galactic family, whose home is among the stars once our journey on earth has reached its natural conclusion. We will proceed to make our transition back to the essence and return to what our souls will know as home. It is signed: Shemsu Hor."

"Who are the Shemsu Hor?" Etienne asked.

"Shemsu Hor is a loose term which describes several concepts such as the followers of Horus, the sun worshippers and when the gods manifested as humans for the first time. Sun worship was prevalent in the ancient Egyptian religion. The sun was worshipped and portrayed as a falcon-headed god surmounted by the solar disk and surrounded by a serpent. The earliest deities associated with the sun are all goddesses. Hathor is one of the most famous goddesses of ancient Egypt. She is depicted as the cow-headed goddess, with a sun disk between her horns, and as the great one with many names such as Isis. She was important in every area of life and death. She occasionally took the form of the Seven Hathors who were associated with fate and oracles. The Seven Hathors were linked to the Pleiades constellation.

"The stone tablet explains Zep Tepi as referring to a time when the divine appeared among humans to recreate civilisations and raise consciousness. These gods, aliens or watchers monitored and ruled on earth after great floods. Once the waters of the abyss receded, the primordial darkness vanished and the human biogenetic experiment emerged from the break of dawn. They lived on earth with humans in the beginning. The gods were part of the elite or shining ones with elongated skulls and believed to be the Atlantean root race.

"The first root race were the Polarian, the second the Hyperborean, the third Lemurian, the fourth Atlantean, the fifth Aryan, the sixth has commenced life and will replace the present root race – the Aryans."

Eve moved to a solid gold tablet on which was engraved "The Conference of the Five Nations." This tablet required her ankh key and activated a visual download into her brain as though she was watching a movie.

Eve explains, "The conference was on the large wild animals, which were presented as dangerous pests. It describes the conference taking place between five great nations and delegates, including the Atlanteans, the Lemurians, the Sudanese from East Africa, the Siberians and the Gobians from Mongolia.

"The delegates were from Peru, known as the land of Og, and from India. The gigantic animals that looked like pterodactyls, mastodons and Tyrannosaurus rex, elephants, mammoths, wild cats and wolves roamed the earth. These gigantic animals created havoc by destroying plantations and preying on humans as their source of food. They fought savagely among themselves for their primary food source, humans, so the conference was gathered to find a solution to exterminate the killers.

"The Atlanteans were appointed to use chemical weapons to destroy these large beasts and as a result the development of technology increased immensely. Their daily lives changed drastically and they were free to carry on their daily activities with less fear. Children were better educated, mining could continue freely and societies around the globe flourished, especially in Atlantis where they mastered technological solutions to solve worldwide problems.

"Atlantis presented as the most technologically advanced civilisation," Eve continued, "however, we see the emergence of two groups in Atlantis each trying to gain power and this was divisive. One group was known as the Sons of Belial, which is associated with the god Baal, symbolised by the bull. They were concerned with material possessions to make their life easier, more comfortable and pleasurable. The other group was known as the Children of the Law of One and they were concerned with love and spreading divine knowledge and wisdom. They practised collective prayer and meditation. They were named the Law of One because they preferred the collective approach, rather than looking after individual material needs. The Law of One means one religion, one state, one home and one god.

"The Belial left-brain approach took over the right-brain approach, which was more feminine and matriarchal and dealt with creativity and the arts. The Belial was the more dominant patriarchal group by nature and they continued to develop chemical, explosive and crystal weapons that severely hurt Mother Earth. Eventually, after enough battering, a major polar shift occurred with complete devastation around the globe.

"The Law of One built temples, altars and shrines on higher ground such as huge mountaintops; some moved away to other nations. The Law of One collectively spread their love to honour the Great Mother Goddess, our earth. They intuitively knew that the Mother Goddess would eventually retaliate and punish the sons of Belial for their decadence, immorality and abuse of earthly powers. This was the first destruction of Atlantis. The perpetual cycle continued, but with different problems emerging. In brief, the second and third destruction of Atlantis resulted from more wars and abuse including horrific crimes of murder and human sacrifice. There was no balance between the masculine and feminine hemispheres of the brain. Ultimately an imbalance between science and religion, and overindulgence in one rather than the other, resulted in the decline of civilisation."

Eve came across another tablet about the Birth of Planets. A large comet, which she identified as Venus, passed next to a large red planet, Mars. Gravity appeared to be sucking away all the water and life, channelling it to another planet. Eve wanted to see where all these resources were going and as soon as the thought entered her mind she could see another water planet between Mars and Jupiter. She couldn't recognise it or provide a name. This mysterious water planet, Tiamat, looked to be an earth-like planet that could sustain life. In a massive explosion, Venus collided with the earth-like planet and all the resources were trapped.

The planet fragmented into millions of pieces; however, one large piece that contained all the resources was ejected out of orbit and located close to the sun next to a satellite that keeps the earth in place. She recognised this satellite as the moon. The large piece that is broken off she recognised as earth and in an orbit closer to the sun. The amazing images were breathtaking and captured the enormity of what she was being shown – the creation of our wondrous Planet Earth as we know it. It seemed a star-like being, maybe a type-three civilisation, terra-formed Earth so souls could move from their star system to earth.

Type-three civilisations were responsible for preparing the habitat to be liveable. It was no easy task to integrate a soul into a body but through experimentation, they created life on earth by using the resources of the galaxy.

Eve got a visual snippet of some large creatures that looked like the extinct dinosaurs but they were not on earth. They lived on another planet with much lower gravity that could sustain their massive weight and ultimately their survival. This made sense to Eve, as catastrophic events are not included in archaeological dating, which is distorted due to events we have no record or understanding of.

Eve managed to get through all the tablets that took her attention. This level in the Omphalous Egg was indeed a great Hall of Records, piled with ancient tablets, papyrus and visual records. At the exit of the Hall of Records were a large pair of sphinxes, one black and one white.

The symbolism was powerful, capturing our yearning to understand creation, our existence and to learn the lessons about unity, love, compassion and kindness. The sphinxes were a reminder that humans need to find balance between the masculine and feminine. The sphinxes represented a union of opposites like the yin and yang. Opposite or contrary forces are actually complementary, interconnected and interdependent. Many tangible dualities, such as light and dark, fire and water, expanding and contracting are thought of as physical manifestations of the duality symbolised by the yin and yang. They may pull apart in opposite directions, accomplishing little, but when made to work together in one direction towards the same goal there will be no stopping them.

The sphinxes symbolise that we can achieve more with a collective approach rather than as an individual. We are more powerful when we unite rather than trying to struggle and fight against each other's beliefs and religions, which becomes a never-ending battle.

They left the library to walk up the stairs to what appeared to be the top floor of this enormous egg-shaped structure. The floor was made of predominantly feminine elements, earth being the limestone and water. On top of the limestone was water. There were stepping-stones one could walk on to move around the level. On some of the stepping-stones were statues of goddess fertility figures. Some were completely naked with large breasts, others were flat-chested. Some goddesses were dressed in exquisite gowns; some just had pleated skirts and braided hair. The feminine energy in the room of earth and water made Eve feel very introverted, drawing her energy back in.

"How are you feeling?" Eve asked Etienne as she turned to look at him.

"I feel as though I'm getting in touch with my feminine qualities," Etienne said tranquilly as his voice echoed round the room.

Eve couldn't help but giggle at his response because everywhere you looked there was the female form revealed in a beautiful statue. Eve noticed an amazing structure emerging from the calm shimmering waters; somehow she felt the best was still to come.

Chapter 18

Through The Eyes of a Pleiadian

The apex of a tetrahedron rose slowly out of the shimmering water. Etienne and Eve watched the shiny pearl-like pyramid emerge and spin on the surface of the water. It looked like some kind of advanced, high-tech machine and produced a low humming as it spun and then stopped revolving.

Eve walked closer to the pyramid because she was extremely curious. She wanted to go inside but wasn't sure how. She carefully stepped on each stepping-stone circling the pyramid. It was not very large – about four metres by four metres she estimated. The sides were made of a shimmering metal she didn't recognise. She scanned the surface carefully with her hand. One panel looked as though it could be a sliding door. She touched the surface and before her eyes an eight-pointed star started to glow. "That's the cue," she thought, so she put on her ankh ring and placed the star over the glowing surface. Sure enough, the door opened.

"What are you doing?" Etienne yelled across to her.

"I'm going inside."

"Are you sure you want to do that? Are you going to be safe?"

"Yes, I've got the ankh and star pendant. I'm going in. You stay here and wait for me, darling." She ran back and planted a kiss firmly on his lips.

"I won't be very long." She wanted to reassure Etienne. He had become her knight in shining armour always protecting and looking out for her.

"Don't be long, my Maltese dreamer," Etienne said as he blew her a kiss. He knew it was not worth arguing with her as her dreams were set in stone a long time ago.

Eve entered the pyramid and the door closed automatically behind her. She explored the small sterile, clean and orderly environment. The pyramid structure was filled with gadgets and devices, most of which she didn't recognise or understand their use. Instantly Eve could see a tall blue shape in the centre of the pyramid manifesting before her. It was the Blue Queen appearing to her in all her beautiful glory. She was making herself visible to Eve once more.

"You've arrived!" The Blue Queen greeted her with a warm smile and embrace. Eve was engulfed by her loving presence as the Queen towered over her.

"What is this place?" Eve asked her.

"It is what you know as an Omphalos Egg, carved inside an enormous mountain that survived great cataclysms. It is a remnant mountain of the legendary Atlantis dominion. It is my haven, a place where I can meditate and communicate with the earth. You humans are not alone – we are watching you and we come to your aid in times of dire need when you must rebuild and be educated. We are the gods and goddesses, the kings and queens if you like. We have unconditional love and compassion for our descendants and come forth as the great teachers from ancient times to the present.

The Blue Queen continued, "This sacred haven has many uses. It is a storage house of our great treasures, artefacts and monuments and it's one of the Halls of Records and a place we can travel from. It's a place of great spiritual significance to mark the first place we inhabited when we came from our star system. We keep it all stored in a giant Omphalos stone egg. The egg is a symbol of the heart or centre and the origin of the divine goddess here on Earth.

"When you inherited the ankh and star pendant from your Buznanna, you inherited great responsibility along with it. You showed me time and time again that you have the inner strength to be of great assistance to your spiritual helpers from the stars. We watched to see if you would persist in finding this haven. You have proved yourself through your unflinching and tenacious efforts. These sacred islands are our chosen land and the first home of the great goddesses. What human would ever think to find such a discovery here? You will need to be careful about how to bring this information forth as societies struggle to evolve in times of great unrest and world change."

"What star system are you from?" asked Eve.

"I am from the Pleiades star system. Do you want me to take you there?"

"How can you do that?" Eve probed.

"My dear child, we are in an advanced pyramid machine, equipped with many gadgets and machines that humans haven't yet invented. I'd love to show you my other home."

"Yes please!"

At that, the Blue Queen started to activate various machines. She said, "I will need to dematerialise you into a blue light form, as I first appeared to you, in order for us to travel into space at the speed of consciousness, a kind of blink drive. By changing into a light form our physical bodies will not be hurt in our travels to view the vast galaxies. We will still have all our senses intact as we travel with our ethereal bodies and we will rematerialise in our earthly bodies upon our return. We will only be absent for a few minutes, as the concept of time is irrelevant, so Etienne won't even have time to miss you," the Blue Queen explained to Eve in preparation for their travels.

The Blue Queen directed Eve into the centre of the craft, right under the apex of the pyramid, where she zapped Eve with a crystal laser beam through her crown chakra penetrating through her head to dematerialise her body to a vertical blue light form.

Eve could see her physical body lying on the floor of the craft, reminding her of the near-death experience when her soul had detached from her physical body. There was some kind of device on the floor that looked like an ancient sarcophagus. Inside it was Eve's body cocooned in cotton straps, from her head down to her toes, leaving her airways open. A perfectly shaped glass lid automatically slid over to shut the sarcophagus as oxygen flowed in. This device held Eve's body securely in place and she could hear the slow hiss of oxygen.

They were both vertical blue light forms and Eve could see, hear, sense and feel just as if she were in her human body. The Blue Queen took Eve's phantom hand as their light bodies zoomed off through the roof of the Omphalos Egg. They shot out into the spiralling Milky Way Galaxy heading straight for the galactic centre, which looked like the most extravagant light show Eve had ever seen. She didn't know where to look first, as the galaxy was filled with dazzling coloured lights forming spirals and geometric shapes like a collection of exotic objects. They moved into a wormhole, which shortcuts space-time. In an instant they were in another galaxy and Eve could see dense stellar super clusters hosting mysterious and massive stars. A family of gas streamers and dust appeared, spiralling toward a dark centre. Numerous comets, asteroids and dwarf planets were in frenetic orbit around binary stars.

The sight of a twenty-mile-wide comet made Eve feel worried as she remembered a time when a giant comet wreaked great destruction on earth and could very well threaten the earth in present times. She hoped that such a giant comet never made a return strike and that scientists keep a careful watch on it and intercept its lethal and devastating blow. The return of this comet could very well occur in our time. The thought scared Eve and reinforced how fragile and small humans are in this vast solar system.

They moved from wormhole to wormhole as though they were switching from one high-speed train to another to go in another direction. She saw the birth of a planet before her very eyes, as the planet's consciousness and colour beamed vibrantly like an aura, possessing a living consciousness and soul. It was just like the strange births of the gods and goddesses born of virgins in the legends. Their birth is cosmic and occurs above before they come below to earth. We understand the sky-earth match – *as above so below*, as Thoth known as Hermes Trismegistus taught in ancient times. The Blue Queen came from the Pleiades to earth and ignited life and consciousness.

They finally arrived in a galaxy that Eve recognised by the two beaming suns from her dream in the hypogeum. The Pleiades! The Seven Sisters, the seven brightest stars! The seven stars symbolise an empowering archetype related to the seven goddesses and principles. The seven goddesses include Isis, Kali, Hathor, Artemis, Inanna, Persephone and Kwan Yin.

To a certain degree the venerated goddess has been pushed aside as patriarchal monotheistic religions displaced her. In every ancient spiritual culture it is the goddess who gives birth to the world. The feminine always emerges first – even a human fetus is female in the beginning, although it is already male or female at the DNA level. Like all cycles in life we wait for the return of the seven great goddesses and honour their archetypes.

Eve was in the constellation of Taurus in the cluster of the Pleiades, which comprised of at least five hundred stars. She was so far from earth. It was surreal to be among these open star clusters at least four hundred light years away. They went straight to the star Atlas and off towards the Blue Queen's home planet, Atlam, Malta spelt backwards.

"Why did you pick Malta?" Eve asked.

"I came from the Pleiades to be of service to all my children who were created here. It's where the great regeneration of the Pleiadians' souls occurred. Just as seven stars in the heavens form the Pleiades, the seven sisters are known as Sterope, Alcyone, Merope, Maia, Electra, Celaeno and Taygete. The seven stars above directly match what is below on earth, that being the seven islands of Malta. A long time ago, the Pleiadians chose Malta and made their first contact because of the direct match with the seven stars above and seven islands below. It was a sign from the heavens that this was the place to begin civilisation. Those seven islands still exist beneath the sea after a series of great cataclysms struck earth. What remains today is Maia, known as Malta. Today as a fractal memory there are still seven small islands including Malta and Gozo, Comino, Cominetto, Filfla, Manoel Island and Saint Paul's Island."

The Blue Queen continued, "The seven ancient Maltese islands presented as markers from space and directly mirrored the location of the seven Pleiadian stars. When we explored the planet we likened those seven islands to our home in space and it was a tropical haven that could sustain the advancement of all life.

"The familiar seven ancient islands made it easier to transition. We guarded all our ancient treasures and information in this storehouse known as the Omphalous Egg, the egg of creation. It was the best location to transfer souls from the Pleiades because the seven islands of Malta faced the Pleiades most of the year. Malta is the first home of the Great Mother Goddess. This was before any other race or star people came here."

They swept through this beautiful, watery blue planet that showed evidence of an unbelievable advanced civilisation. Eve felt the planet's energy of love and harmony and she felt she was at home and that this was her heavenly origin. Eve observed the Blue Queen as a massive supernova of blue energy as she communicated with her home planet's consciousness.

The Pleiades is a powerful archetype in the human subconscious, as we have a great soul connection. The mother stars are the creators of our soul origins and the reason for our existence. Many cultures used the rising of the Pleiades at the autumn equinox as the starting point of the Remembrance of the Dead festival and they have built temple calendars to keep track of their movements.

A cluster of stars appeared in the outline of a huge praying mantis; there appeared to be a gold energy field around her body. The Blue Queen looked in her direction as if to be guided by her grace.

"Who is that? She is the size of a star!" Eve was beyond amazed.

"She is a higher and loving energetic being. She is

unconditional love and has our interest at heart. She is the gatekeeper for the mother source." The giant praying mantis opened her arms to them.

"She is not going to rip our heads off, is she?" Eve looked at the Blue Queen with a sense of urgency.

"No, we are females and not her mating partners whom she needs to consume."

They entered into her arms and immediately accessed a golden wormhole heading towards another planet. In an instant they were at the glowing red planet of Mars. She noticed one impact crater that revealed dark traces of sediment possibly cemented together by water from an ancient groundwater reservoir before being carved away by wind, making life on Mars a real possibility in the ancient past. The surface of Mars looked like a pimply face, with over six hundred thousand crater impacts on the planet.

As Eve started to connect and get close to Mars, she could hear her heartbeat and she started to feel the consciousness of the planet. Mars relayed the sad story of being beaten and battered as violent impacts pounded its surface over billions of years, leaving hundreds of thousands of craters of a kilometre or more in diameter.

Eve got a flashback of how beautiful Mars had once looked when it possessed a stronger atmosphere and oceans before a rogue planet ravaged it. When the rogue planet passed Mars it left scars of plasma discharge. Mount Olympus looks like a volcano on Mars and is three times taller than Mount Everest. The mountain looks like a blister created by a massive lightning bolt. Another scar is *Valles Marineris*. It is four times deeper than the Grand Canyon and is almost five thousand kilometres long, created by plasma discharge and not water, like many valleys.

Electrical discharge has been sculpting the surface of many planets like Mars and Earth. Mars gets its red colour because the planet's soil is rich in iron. In ancient times, the

Babylonians, Greeks and Romans associated Mars with their gods of war, since its red colour reminded them of blood.

We could hear Venus beckoning like a mermaid luring us with her singing as we travelled in her direction.

"I'm sorry, Mars, for hurting and scarring you. The people who live under my crust wanted to come to this solar system and when we passed you we created destruction and havoc as we pushed our way through to our destination."

Venus is a comet planet with a magnetic tail. As we approached, Venus revealed to us that she had partially destroyed a planet that was between Mars and Jupiter. The asteroid belt is left over from that destruction. The leftovers of that planet went rogue and destroyed Mars, taking its water and atmosphere; it settled in third position around the Sun. This is your home planet, Earth. Venus kept on going and settled five thousand years ago in its present position. Her cosmic tail still lashes out at Earth and influences our magnetism.

The Blue Queen explained to Eve, "The Mayans start their calendar with the birth of Venus and that year was set at 3114 BC. Even though Venus is millions of years old, she's a travelling rogue planet that acts like a comet; her resting position is relatively young in the solar system."

Venus had a lot to say and when she wasn't talking she was singing and luring us towards her. She was intriguing, as we couldn't really see her. She was covered in a thick blanket of opaque cloud and twirling in the opposite direction of most planets. She was the second brightest object in the sky, after the moon. The Romans knew her as Lucifer, the fiery light. Finally, she was referred to as the goddess of love and beauty. Venus asked us if we wanted to see the planet's surface and the inhabitants who have close ties to Planet Earth's development.

"Of course," we signalled.

Venus removed the opaque shield of clouds as though she was shifting a curtain with an invisible hand. The veil of mystery was removed. Eve couldn't believe what she was seeing. It was truly amazing if only humans knew. Perhaps these revelations about Venus will release humanity from the shackles of the present, she thought. Eve stared in complete disbelief and amazement until the thick cloud returned to block her view of Venus once more.

"Farewell, Venus!" Eve called as she felt the strong pull to return to the Omphalos stone. In an instant they were back inside the pyramid, where Eve and the Blue Queen had materialised in their bodies.

"Every individual, Eve," said the Blue Queen, "is eternally connected with every living thing in the universe for we have our own unique over-soul which shares similar DNA or the same gene pool. This omnipotent over-soul can live in many different bodies, which possess varied egos. Together we are a powerful force and can achieve great goals. It is only with a collective, united approach that the human race will accomplish great feats. A person's individual feelings will never make a difference in the world, but with a collective approach great transformations and metamorphosis can occur to create a better world and a return to a Golden Age.

"This over-soul connection to our soul group or soul family is like an invisible unbreakable thread that eternally links us to our soul group. Each person is not completely separate because they are part of the over-soul, a stronger everlasting bond. This bond is what brings people and the nature of the universe together as one. It comes to speak to our senses when someone in our soul group needs to communicate an urgent message."

"That is exactly what I experienced at the moment of Buznanna's passing. I heard Buznanna call my name as if she were in the same room and only inches from my ear. At that moment I instinctively knew something had happened to her. She called out to me as she passed away. It's like an instant wireless Internet connection to those people whom you love and share a special bond with. Distance is no barrier when it comes to the love of your over-soul connection."

"Buznanna is part of your over-soul as I am and this is imprinted in your so-called junk DNA. You are connected to the divine feminine, a Blue Queen, and even though my soul is completely inside of me because I'm immortal, I still have my over-soul's essence to share with my soul family," said the Blue Queen.

Eve could see all the chakra colours running through her body like a rainbow, but with extra colours ending in silver and gold.

"How do we create a better world and advance as a human species?"

"You have a brain that is so powerful it is capable of anything you can think of. There are at least one hundred trillion neural connections, which means there are more neural connections in the brain than stars in the universe. These neural connections process and transmit information, so the brain is a powerful device. On a bigger scale, many brains coming together for the collective good of all living things on this planet can accomplish the unimaginable. Imagine what could be accomplished if we focus on the common good for our planet's advancement and longevity. We can achieve great things with our collective brains learning universal truths.

"We need to transform to a collective approach and love our earth and all that exists on it by renewing and protecting our resources and environment. The ants have been marching on this earth for millions of years and just like the dancing bees they have specialised roles to play in a collective approach to surviving, where they share and cooperate. A good union is one that connects the mind and heart.

"The union of masculine and feminine approaches is necessary for greater harmony. With emotional maturity, enlightenment and thinking beyond the individual to encompass the whole picture, the big goals can be achieved. Once humans learn the universal truths, their entire soul will integrate into their body at a time when the energy patterns will increase to allow us to bring the soul back into the body. Then humans will be immortal and in perpetual unity with all things in this world. Within us is the soul of the whole, the internal wise silence that possesses the answers. We all have little pieces of an eternal loving heart and a great big soul.

"You were born on the island of the divine goddess and have the spirit of a warrior goddess," continued the Blue Queen. "You will follow your birthright as a long succession of firstborns has done before you. Buznanna instilled in you that burning desire to discover what lies beyond. The struggle between good and evil is an arduous battle and one that has existed since the dawn of creation. In the end, goodness of heart and love will always prevail over the darkness that constantly looms and preys on the souls of the weak and fearsome. Great knowledge has been revealed to you – follow your heart on how to reveal it. Those in control are ignorant of this truth. Be wise, cautious and go forth with courage, teaching others in times of great hardship and upheaval!

"You are aware of our dual mortal and immortal existence because you have ventured extensively in the world of spirit. You are aware of the eternal and inseparable connection of mortality and immortality, of the biological and the spiritual. Your unconscious mind has fused with the conscious mind and you are rediscovering the immortality of your soul as you were originally created. You have become fearless, Eve, and you must continue on your path knowing a Blue Queen stands by you. Challenges are opportunities to elevate the innate wisdom of your soul. Cultivate and cherish the knowledge that has been revealed and given to you. Always work from a place of love for the collective good during fearful and uncertain times as one of Mother Earth's allies," the Blue Queen advised.

"How shall I reveal my discoveries?"

"How you reveal the Shrine of Atlantis is up to you, but be aware of the dark forces who are ready to do anything to stop you. You have discovered one part of the puzzle in Filfla and that is only the tip of the iceberg. Wherever there are sacred sites built directly on top of ley lines, the knights have built something to watch over it. The tentacles of the Knights of Malta are widespread and they are not all devoted to the Mother Goddess. Be cautious and discerning!"

"I shall be," Eve reassured the Blue Queen. "I have encountered the duality of good and evil. When will this conflict of duality end?"

"That will be in the hands of the existing human race. There will always be many endings, my dear one, but with endings come so many new beginnings. Don't be afraid of the unknown, as we are all in a state of constant transition and knowledge about the unknown which is truly liberating. You've just started on your journey to help rebalance and transform the world to a more matriarchal society. There are greater mysteries and secrets to reveal to expose our true origins and the power of the goddess. It is your destiny to be the carrier of hope for humanity to reconnect with the Mother Goddess."

The Blue Queen was aware of the confusion of emotions running through Eve. She held Eve tightly in her arms, calming her thoughts with immense unconditional love and acceptance for who she was.

From a very young age Eve knew she had an important role to play but she was not always understood, or labelled as a dreamer. With the Blue Queen she knew she was accepted and understood and was part of some grander plan that would change the world for the better and that is what Eve deeply yearned for.

"What do I say to someone who believes in nothing?"

"Everybody believes in something, even nothing is a belief. Tell them to believe in unconditional love, to have a courageous, hopeful spirit and have faith in the miracle of life. Where there is love, light and truth there is eternal life – immortality – *qalb ta qalbi*."

Select Bibliography and Sources

Adams, M. (2015). *Meet Me in Atlantis.*
   Melbourne: The Text.

Aloisio, F. X. (2014). *An Alternative Handbook to the Maltese Temples.*
   Malta: Culture3sixty.

Aloisio, F. X. (2015). *The New Temple Dreamers.*
   Malta: Malta-Temple-Journeys.

Andrews, S. (1997). Atlantis: Insights from a Lost Civilization.
   USA: Llewellyn.

Bauval, R., & Gilbert, A. (1994). *The Orion Mystery.*
   New York: Three Rivers Press.

Bonanno, A. (1986). Archaeology and Fertility Cult in the Ancient Mediterranean. Amsterdam: Gruner.

Boulter, C (2011). *Matriarchal Societies in Prehistory.*
   Youtube.com: Megalithomania.

Bradley, R. N. (1912). *Malta and the Mediterranean Race.*
   London: Unwin.

Churchward, J. (1931). *The Lost Continent of Mu.*
   New York: Washburn.

Cotterell, M., & Gilbert, A. (1996). *The Mayan Prophecies.*
   New York: HarperCollins.

Coppens, Philipp. (2011). *The Ancient Alien Question.*
   NJ: New Page Books.

Dona, K. (2011). *Giants, Elongated Skulls & Ooparts.*
   Youtube.com: Megalithomania.

Dorey, S. (2011). *The Day of the Fish.*
   Victoria, BC: Trafford.

Dorey, S. (2004). *The Nummo.*
   Victoria, BC: Trafford.

Dorey, S. (2002). *The Master of Speech.*
Victoria, BC: Trafford.

Gimbutas, M. (1989). *The Language of the Goddess.*
San Francisco: Harper and Row.

Gimbutas, M. (1991). *The Civilisation of the Goddess.*
San Francisco: Harper and Row.

Gough, A. (2008) *The Bee: Beegotten, Beedazzled and Beewildered.*
http://andrewgough.co.uk.

Griaule, M. (1948). *Dieu d'Eau.*
Paris: Fayard.

Hancock, G. (1995). *Fingerprints of the Gods.*
New York: Crown.

Hancock, G. (2002). *Underworld.*
New York: Crown.

Hancock, G. (2015). *Magicians of the Gods.*
UK: Thomas Dunne Books.

Hatcher Childress, D. (1996). Lost Cities of Atlantis, Ancient Europe & the Mediterranean.USA, IL: Adventures Unlimited Press.

Hebert, J. (2004). *Atlantide, la solution oubliee.*
France: Carnot.

Kirkpatrick, S. (2001). *Edgar Cayce: An American Prophet.*
USA: Riverhead.

Leedskalnin, E. (1936). *A Book in Every Home.* 2012 Reprint.
USA: Martino Fine Books.

Magri. Fr. E. (1901). *Maltese Folk Tales and Lore.*
Malta: Government Printing Office.

Mifsud, A., et al. (2001). *Malta, Echoes of Plato's island.*
Malta: The Prehistoric Society of Malta.

Morgan, E. (1972). *The Descent of Women.*
London: Souvenir Press.

Morgan, E. (1999). *The Aquatic Ape Hypothesis.*
London: Souvenir Press.

Select Bibliography and Sources

Nikas, A. (2008). *Why Atlantis was Never Found!*
  Greece: Atlantis Conference 2008.

Sitchin, Z. (2004). *The Lost Book of Enki.*
  USA, VT: Bear.

Stranges, F. E. (1967). *The Stranger at the pentagon.*
  USA, CA: Van Nuys.

Velikosky, E. (1950). *Worlds in Collision.*
  New York: Macmillan.

Tellinger, M. (2009). *Adam's Calendar.*
  South Africa: Zulu Planet.

Tsoukalos, G. (2014). In Search of Aliens: The Mystery of the Cyclops.
  USA: History Channel.

Tucker, C. (2011). *The Maltese Dreamer.*
  USA: Verita Holma Press.

Tsarion, M. (2004). *Atlantis, Alien Visitation and Genetic Manipulatio*n.New York: Angels at Work Publishing.

Vella. N. (2002). The Lie of the Land: Ptolemy's Temple of Hercules in Malta. Belgium: Peeters.

Von Daniken, E. (1968). *The Chariots of the Gods.*
  New York: G. P. Putnam's Sons.

About the Author

Moira Lescuyer is a senior secondary Economics and Business Studies teacher. A series of synchronistic events led her to delve into her passion for writing. Her interest in Plato's legendary Atlantis, Maltese prehistory and her own spiritual quest have led to the writing of *Atlantis and the Legendary Blue Queen*.

Even though the story is fiction, it incorporates many archaeological and geological facts in her proposition about the location of Atlantis. Moira hopes to contribute to the mysterious puzzle and identify our possible human origins.

She is the published author of a children's book, *Little Life Reminders*. In 2011, she was interviewed on One T-V in Malta about *Little Life Reminders* and her closing comment was that the next book would be about the sacred Maltese archipelago.

The impetus was provided when she was eight years old and met her great-grandmother in Malta who became one of her first spiritual teachers and a driving force.

Moira enjoys teaching, counselling and writing as a therapeutic outlet for her independent research and active imagination.

www.moiralescuyer.com

Printed in April 2023
by Rotomail Italia S.p.A., Vignate (MI) - Italy